OF CHAOS AND HASTE

OF CHAOS AND HASTE

ANOTHER BEAST'S SKIN
BOOK III

JESSIKA
GREWE GLOVER

Copyright © 2023 by Jessika Grewe Glover All rights reserved.

No part of this book may be reproduced in any form or by any electronic or mechanical means, including information storage and retrieval systems, without written permission from the author, except for the use of brief quotations in a book review.

Published by: Pip & Plum Creative LLC

Editor: Anna Corbeaux

Front Cover Design by: Miblart

Map by: Demi Hargreaves

Kintsugi-inspired Art by: Mitch Green

ISBN: 979-8-9875838-6-9 (e-book)

ISBN: 979-8-9875838-7-6 (paperback)

For the ones who never fit in, the misunderstood hatchlings, the chaotic ones.
And for Damian, who didn't let me give up.

A NOTE REGARDING CONTENT IN OF CHAOS AND HASTE

Of Chaos and Haste has some themes which may be sensitive. These include, sex (consensual), violence and death, loss, mental health struggles/PTSD, and miscarriage.

Aoifsing
Characters by Province:

Saarlaiche
Cadeyrn
Silas
Magnus
Lina
Baetríz
Rhia
Turuín
Stea Ledermaín
Belleza Ledermaín

Maesarra
Ewan, King
Corraidhín (originally of Saarlaiche)
Pim, Crown Prince
Efa, Princess
Neysa, Princess
Cyrranus, Representative
Reynard
Dean
Arneau
Alan
Etienne
Francois
Solange (deceased)
Cook

Laorinaghe
Yva Sonnos, Representative
Arturus, Representative

Farus, Representative
Xaograos
Ylysses Sonnos
Cathe Sídhe

Veruni
Elíann
Lord Dockman

Prinaer
Ainsley Mads
Thurnton, Ainsley's second
Sleípnyr

Heilig
Characters by Land:

Kutja
Saski, Queen
Arik, Prince, Hand to the Crown
Ludek, Prince, Hand to the Crown, Intelligencer
Basz, Captain of the Guard, mate to Ludek
Marja (originally of Sot), Dowager
Pavla, Ludek's twin (deceased)
Jens Umvelt, Captain of the Heiligan Royal Guard, Gepard race
Gunther Umvelt, Soldier
Sig and Glyn, Schloss Specialty Guard
Dorn, Squire to Eamon

Sot
Varno, Governor

Annos
Terin, Governor

Ech
Eamon Sr., Governor
Eamon Jr.

Manu
Cassia, Governor
Patricius, Cassia's brother

Biancos
Perla, Governor

Gods
Rán, Goddess of Sea, Wind, and Water
Hermód, God of Speed
Heícate, Goddess of Darkness and Magic
Eos, Goddess of Air
Twin Gods:
    Aíne, Goddess of Love and Family
    Eír, God of Protection
Kaeres, Goddess of War and Death
Kalíma: The Mother, a "lesser goddess" though extremely powerful

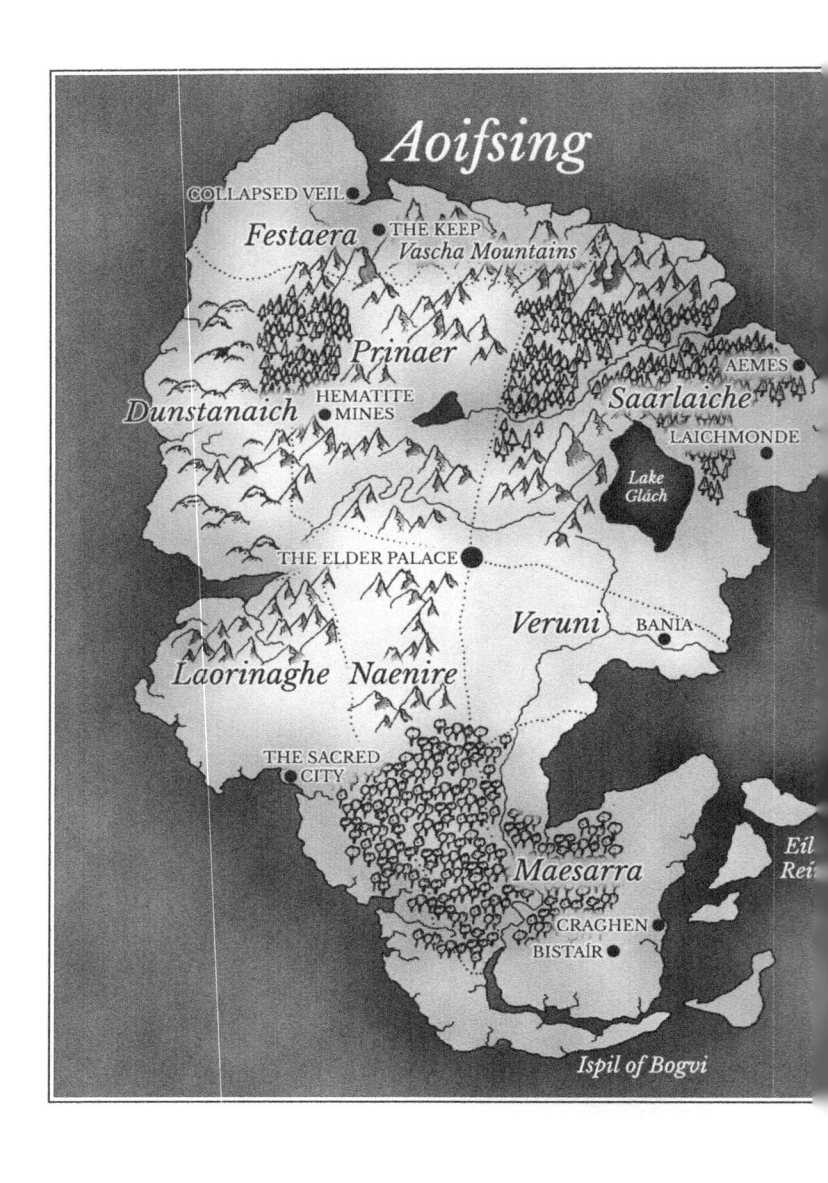

Aoifsing

- COLLAPSED VEIL
- *Festaera*
- THE KEEP
- *Vascha Mountains*
- *Prinaer*
- AEMES
- *Dunstanaich*
- HEMATITE MINES
- *Saarlaiche*
- LAICHMONDE
- Lake Glách
- THE ELDER PALACE
- *Veruni*
- BANIA
- *Laorinaghe Naenire*
- THE SACRED CITY
- *Maesarra*
- CRAGHEN
- BISTAIR
- Eil Rei
- *Ispil of Bogvi*

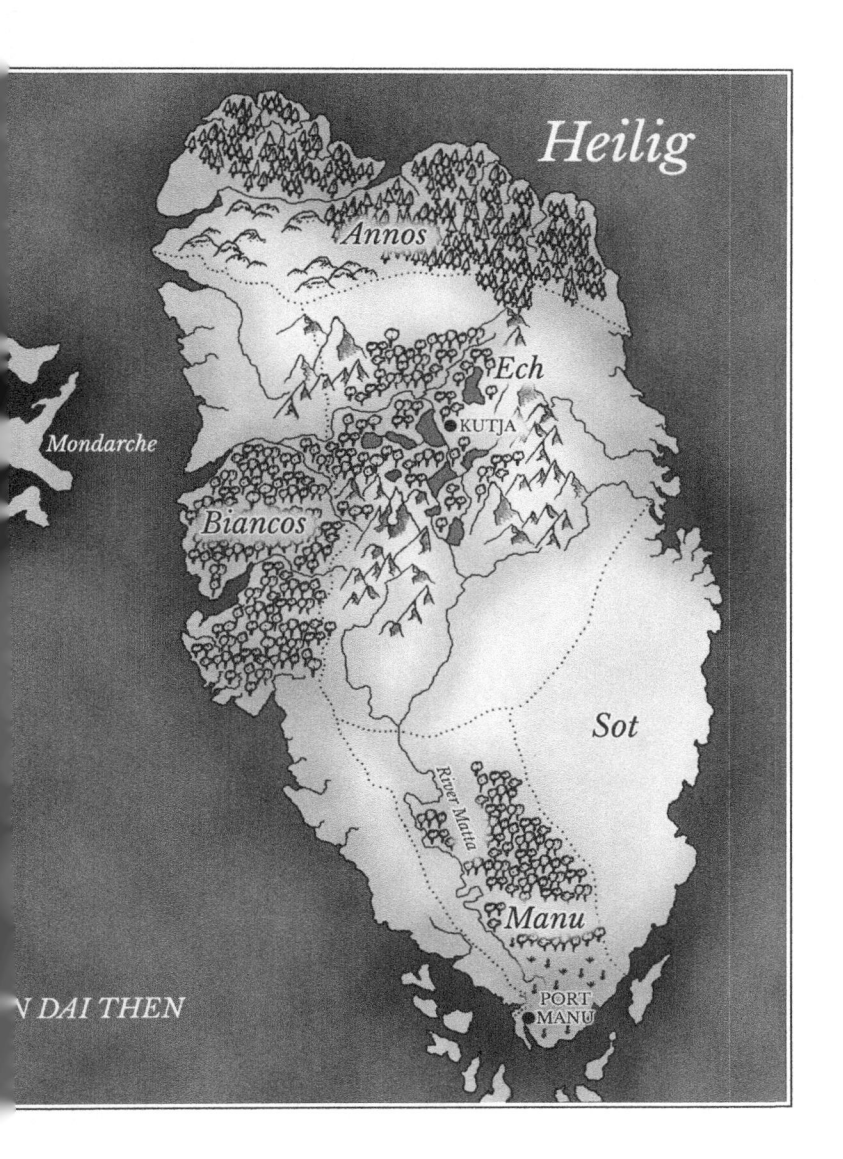

Heilig

Annos

Ech
• KUTJA

Mondarche

Biancos

Sot

River Matta

Manu

N DAI THEN

• PORT
MANU

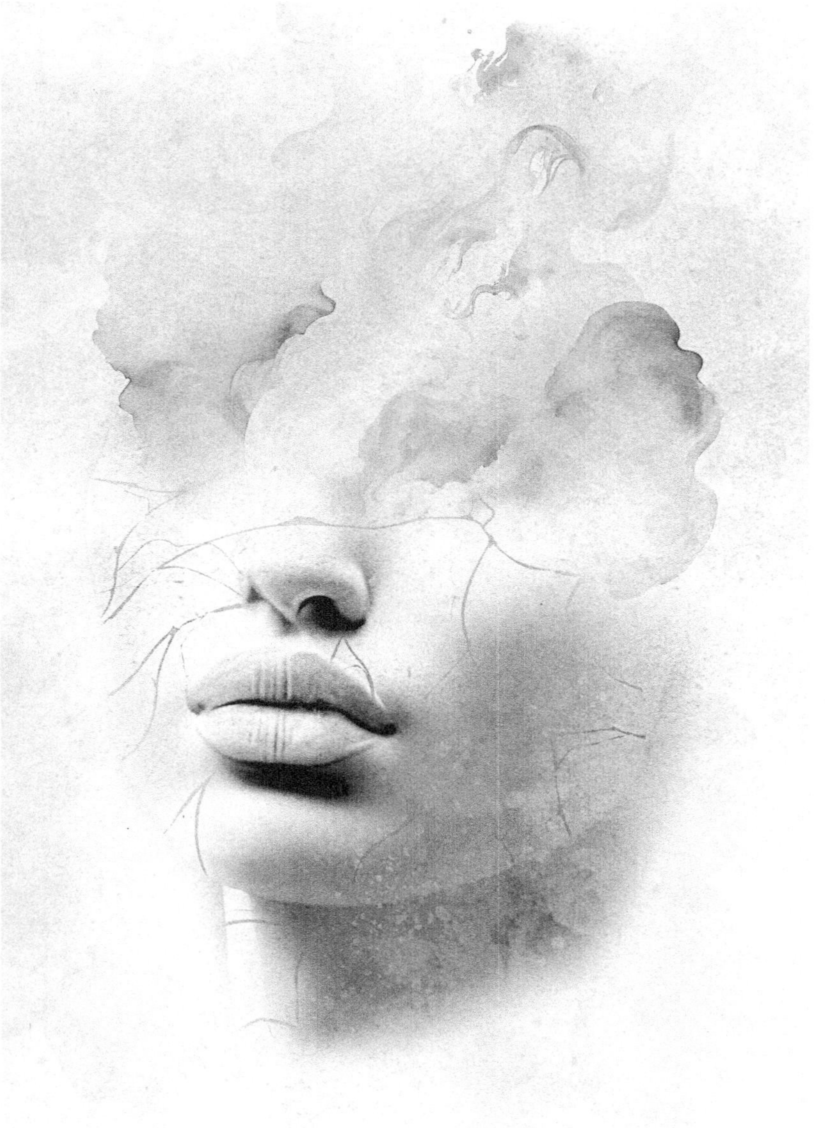

Part One

Chapter 1

Saski

Home. It should have felt welcoming. I should have wanted to be there. Yet, that wasn't the case at all. Dragging myself from the sea and onto the shore in the south of Biancos, I lay my cheek on the warm sand and tried to let the reality of being back in Heilig after almost eighteen months away sink in. Knowing I needed to get off the beach and find clothing before someone spotted me was the only thing that made me get up. My powers were drained from four days at sea. Four days of giving myself over to my powers in order to move through the vast open ocean in flight from Neysa's return to Aoifsing. My body moved with the telltale signs of fatigue, and I knew I needed to eat and rest before moving on. Could I get a hawk to one of my brothers, I might take the barge. In that initial moment, though, rising from the waters, a female born of the sea, what I needed was to get off the strand. It would not do to be seen stark naked with my siren nature on full display.

Cadeyrn met me on the beach the day I left Aoifsing. Before they all left on some half-cocked rescue mission to save Reynard. I would have gone too. Had they asked. But no.

Neysa was back from the human realm, and the last thing any of us needed was for me to be tagging along like a third wheel. Or fourth as it were. While I appreciated them informing me of what had been happening, it pissed me off that Silas hadn't had the nerve to come himself. I assumed the kiss I gave Cadeyrn wasn't delivered to Silas, but a small part of me, mostly that small part of who I used to be, enjoyed the idea of kissing Cadeyrn. Who knows. Perhaps he was stand-up enough to tell them. I doubted it. The problem was that I was supposed to have been by the docks waiting on a ship. Instead, he'd found me on a small beach, stripped bare, ready to plunge into the water. Only my family knew about this aspect of my gifts. My nature as a siren.

The sea called to me and I to her. Like Silas and his sister, moving through water was effortless for me. They knew about my wind affinity, but I had always kept my aquiline affinity secret. Sirens were never trusted, and it wasn't something I wanted out in the open. In my defense, I hadn't used my siren ability since I was very young. I didn't particularly like being able to lure others without their consent. I *did* have a moral code. It was why I made such an effort to challenge myself with males.

Gods, I was tired. Every muscle and limb ached, and my eyes were heavy with fatigue. From the depths of the sea, I had pulled a handful of pearls, black and perfectly round. Sneaking into the town on the seaside, I kept to the shadows until I reached a home with clothing hung on a line. Directing the wind to blow toward me, I found myself in possession of a linen shift and breeches. Not interested in thieving, I left the pearls in exchange for the clothing. These would replace the items tenfold and likely feed the family for a month. Arik and I used to dive for pearls and leave them on doorsteps around Yuletide. It was our little secret. Pavla found out, and she and Ludek came up with a whole business plan to cover a different village each season. Arik and I dove and brought them to shore, while our siblings delivered the pearls to homes. We became a tale spun throughout Biancos. Whispers of the bounties of Rán, Goddess of the Sea, ran rampant. Gods, we did that for at least twenty years. Thinking of Pavla—of softer times—pinched my gut in a most unpleasant way. I shook the memory from the barnacles of my mind and donned the clothing.

I hated shifts like that which I nicked. They always seemed like clothing to keep females in a place of subservience. I was never one to acquiesce to male power. So, I pulled on the breeches and tore the shift until it was hip length, belting the torn off hem around my waist. There. Time to find a hawk.

Biancos enamored me as a child. Its dry, windblown coast and seagrass which caught the dawn and dusk light as though staring through citrine, was true Heiligan magic. We had a holiday home a bit farther north than where I came ashore. Summers were often spent there, and Mother would go when she needed to privately mourn Ludek and Pavla's father. It now seemed so similar to Maesarra since I had seen Aoifsing. And I hated it. I hated that it felt like where I'd spent nearly a year with Silas. No matter how I looked at it, in that year, I had been with Silas. I never scented another fae on him. It was the two of us and the ghost of his mate, I suppose. The sooner I could get home to Kutja, and forget Silas, the better. At least that was the lullaby I sang myself.

A seaside inn welcomed me with its wooden sign blowing in the breeze of the oncoming storm. I had no money, and stupidly had given all the damned pearls for this godsawful get up. Still, I walked in. Not many faces turned, yet the innkeeper narrowed his eyes at me, saying he didn't want any trouble. I wasn't even armed. How many times in my life had I felt the need to say "I am not angry. This is just my face"? I was thoroughly over it.

It was warm in the parlor. Though the breeze blew in, the air was heavy and thick with late-summer ripeness. A male sat on the floral wing chair, reading a novel, booted feet propped on a stool. I slumped into the chair opposite, earning a glance over the book. He did a double take, then brought his eyes back down.

"I take it you're awaiting transport?" he asked mildly, eyes still on the book.

I cocked my head to the side, debating answering.

"Your brother is in Munde. I can send word."

"Who might you be, sir?" I asked.

He smiled, still looking at his book. The innkeeper looked over, curious about our conversation. I flicked my fingers, and the sea breeze became a full gust banging the shutters open, sending the innkeeper round to the windows and away from us.

"Dorn," he answered. "One of Eamon's squires. Though I hate that title, don't you?" He put the book down and looked at me, shaking his head. "You could use a room."

"I could use a lot of things at the moment. Why is my brother in Munde?" And the better question. "Why are you here?"

"Waiting for you, of course. Little brother was securing the lands. This was his last stop. He and Eamon thought to send me in his stead, with his regards. Your mother sent word that you would come through here. And here I am. And here you are."

"As simplistic as it all seems," I said to him, "what is your purpose here? Little brother could have come himself. Or Eamon for that matter."

A devilish grin came over him. His handsome face held a wide mouth, curving up at the edges, giving him an edge of alarm that was only heightened by a scar from his top lip to the side of his nose. Deep-set charcoal eyes shone with delight at my appraisal.

"How'd I rank?" he asked, leaning forward.

"Pardon?" I crossed one leg over the other. Oh. No wonder the innkeeper looked at me strangely. I had forgotten shoes. Fighting the urge to squirm, I met his eyes. "Ah. My brother presumed to send me a companion?"

Those upturned lips poked a bit higher.

"Dorn? If you have a room here, I would very much like to bathe and sleep whilst I wait for my brother to arrive."

He stood and offered me his arm, which I pointedly refused, yet I followed him upstairs and into a bare-bones room. There was a double bed with a worn quilt, a wooden chair, and a table with an ewer of water. Gods, I was thirsty. I drank the entire pitcher and stripped out of the clothes to bathe.

"You may follow and tend to me, squire."

He pushed off the wall and prowled after me. His dark eyes watched me bathe before reaching for me. It felt good to have someone pleasing me, yet I couldn't help the tears that threatened as I let him touch me. Gods above, I really sunk myself by falling for Neysa's mate. Sometimes I wanted to kill her. Truly kill her for having them both. Then, the rational side of me knew it wasn't her call either. So, Silas did with me what I was doing with this male. The thought didn't sit well, and for the first time in my life, I felt dirty.

I SLEPT the full night and most of the following day. Dorn procured me a new set of more suitable clothes and riding boots.

Once I had eaten three bowls of fish stew with surprisingly fresh, seeded bread, we set out. It was late afternoon, but I never minded riding in the evenings in Heilig. Until the phantomes plagued us, the dark was a welcome place. I would often set out at night to be at one with the Goddess. It struck me as we rode that I always felt connected to the Goddess Heícate. Though I was not on the best terms with Neysa, she was the heir to the Goddess to whom I was most deferential. The sun set as we rode, and the bursting of lights seemed to welcome me home. I truly had no idea how far we were from Munde, and I didn't care enough to ask. In fact, apart from thanking him for the clothing and agreeing it was time to ride, I hadn't spoken to my companion at all.

"Have I displeased you, Your Highness?" he asked.

I nearly rolled my eyes. I hated titles. Did he displease me? No, I supposed not. I told him I was simply wanting to see my brother. Munde was on the river Matta, which would take us home to Kutja. Riding harder and faster, I had begun to see the trails of colors from the energy explosions. Opening my arms, to the horror of Dorn, I invited the energy to barrel into me, filling me with revitalizing succor. Dorn suggested we camp, but I insisted on pressing on, finally arriving in Munde just past dawn. Though worn down to my tiniest fibers, I pushed through the home where Arik was staying, and threw myself onto his bed. He jumped, yelling, until he realized it was me. I was sobbing, not even waiting for the door to close. He knew. Of course, he knew. I could feel the *I told you* so bubbling up from his throat, yet it never passed his lips. We knew each other well enough to know when to press our luck. I had brought it all upon myself. I knew it. He knew it. So, I cried with the only one I would ever cry in front of, and once the tears were shed, I sat up.

"We have a situation," he said, groggily. "Are you ready to be queen, sister?"

Chapter 2

Cadeyrn

Corraidhín appeared in front of me, face wild, blood coating her blades. All around us, ash rained from the explosion of the Bania seat of power. There was no sign of my mate, Corraidhín's brother, or Cyrranus. What's more, I couldn't feel Neysa's power at all. Something had a damper on it. Etienne sacrificed many of his own guards in that combustion, all to make certain that we lost ours as well. The estate was a dead zone. Even the enemies left here were unwilling to fight. Everyone stood in stunned silence. A whiteout peppered with debris left all of us fae in a confused cease-fire.

Then I caught it. The faint scent of Neysa's blood and sick. I yanked my cousin, and followed the scent, crossing the grounds toward the outskirts of the city of Bania. Once the scent was gone, I started to sprint. We scaled walls and fences. The light was fading, and as every structure there was made of some type of pink clay, the city was aglow in shades of coral. My eyes were burning with the color around us and the sweat running into them. Why couldn't she have just told me where she was? The last I'd heard was her screaming for me to get out of the manor. The manor that tuned to ash within the breadth of a minute. We were there to rescue Reynard, and I'd lost my mate, my cousin, Reynard, and his partner, who was the representative to Maesarra. I'd only had Neysa back for a few days when we went off on this chase. And once again, we were apart.

Streets dipped and rose in steppes and hills, lined with everything from businesses to crofters' cottages. Situated at the bottom of Veruni, Bania was the largest city in Aoifsing. It was a center of commerce, sprawling in every direction. We searched for hours. Corraidhín finally put a hand on me to stop. We both bent over, breathing hard. We were in the city center, having circled back here from the eastern edge of town and the docks. Courtyards in front of offices met the streets. Behind each was a row of cottages, pink with tiled roofs. A fountain bubbled before us, birds lazing about on the water. The air was not moving at all in the city, as though it were holding its breath. Sweat ran all over me, panic creeping in. Corraidhín looked into my eyes, apparently at a loss for words herself. We kept walking, aimless and silent, traipsing Bania looking for our family. Neysa counted her inhales when anxiety crept in. I was counting the times I had touched her since finding her. I counted the times I had seen her smile, the tips of her tapered ears turning pink when she did. From the moment I saw her at the table in Richmond, finishing her Pimm's, to the cautious whispers of our hands in her flat, the night in the forest, and the one damned night in Bistaír. The night I wanted to take away her trauma from the human realm. Before I started to act like an ass over her seeing Silas. I would give anything to touch her. I'd almost had her back.

Night fell, light coming on in windows and streetlamps. Each row of homes and city gardens seemed to hint that she was behind one of the tidy entryways. In the distance, a lonely figure stood, covered in a hood, lifting her hand to us. Exhaustion pulled at me, and Corraidhín's plodding steps suggested it pulled at her too, as we dragged ourselves to the female. There was something familiar about her, but I couldn't place what. Hairs on my arms raised in alarm. The streets were an eerie quiet, so at odds with the colorful city. The female wore a stern look yet smiled slightly with genuine warmth. She beckoned us to follow down a few streets and into a home tucked away in an alley that ran between shops and cafés.

Her door swung open to a neat room painted shades of blue with white furniture. Once inside, she lifted her hood, letting us see her face fully. Amber eyes sat round and watchful on a face which seemed to flush from golden brown to sunset tones with her movement. She removed her cloak, and her bronze-flecked dark hair fell down her back. Corraidhín gaped at her.

"I am Elíann, aunt to your mates. I believe I may be able help."

Neysa

I WAS MOMENTARILY SO stunned about Etienne bringing Solange back that I nearly let go of the scraps of power I still had. Etienne thought he could keep all of our powers girdled in this hellhole of a room. Though ill from the aphrim wound on my arm, and the multiple head traumas I'd received from Etienne's soldier, I could still gather bits of my magic. Reynard's nostrils were flaring, his chest heaving in and out as he pulled at his bindings. The bindings his father had fastened on him. Silas hadn't taken his eyes off me. I smelled my own vomit on myself, mixed with my sweat and Silas's. The scent of

Reynard's crusted blood reached me from the other side of the too-small chamber. The room was damp and uncomfortably warm with no air circulating. Had this once been a normal house? Flashbulbs were still going off in my vision, causing me to blink repeatedly.

"So, what say you, whore?" Etienne asked, crossing an ankle over the other as he leaned against the plaster wall. Silas yanked at his chains, snarling through the gag in his mouth. I needed to stand but didn't trust myself just yet.

"What does your wife think about you wanting to bring back your dead daughter?" I asked, thinking about the notes Silas had found in Francois's room. Another wave of nausea crested, and I fell forward, bile emptying onto the gritty floor.

He waved me off with a look of disgust.

"From what I've learned," Etienne answered, picking at a tooth, "sacrifices must be made to bring one back. The Goddess requires penance. Blood for blood. What better sacrifice than she of the same blood?"

Holy Gods. Reynard squeezed his eyes shut. The one swollen so far, it blistered outward. We weren't healing.

"I suppose it's your family, not mine," I said, flippantly, though my heart was screaming for Reynard. My friend who was just a game piece to his father. "I don't really care what you do, so long as I can get my mate back."

He grinned at me, white teeth flashing in the fading light.

"So, you are content to have just one mate again?" Etienne asked.

Wait. What? I looked to Silas.

"You see, the whole purpose of arranging the marriage between my Solange and Cadeyrn was to bring about a new generation of fae who could have power over all. It doesn't suit me one bit to have you shackled to Cadeyrn."

I laughed in his face. Like hell I would let Reynard's bastard of a father take Cadeyrn from me. Take him and attach him to Solange, who'd already tried to kill him when they were married nearly two centuries ago. Scraping myself from the filthy ground, I almost crawled to Silas, pulling up on his legs. Too many blows to the head made me sluggish. Silas's heart was going a million miles an hour. Slowly, so that there was no reaction, I allowed a trickle of my power to leak from me into Silas. His body twitched.

I was going to say hang in there again, I told Silas. *But it seemed in poor taste as you are actually hanging.* His eyes were looking down at me, though they still remained translucent. Probably not the best time for a joke in poor taste.

"So, let me get this straight," I said to Etienne. "You want me to get you the clock and hand over my husband so you can bring your dead daughter back to birth my mate's children?" I couldn't help the venom that came out of my mouth. "I look forward to killing you slowly, you sick fuck. Cadeyrn will never go back to Solange."

He giggled maniacally just as Reynard had years ago, then turned to elbow his son in the face. I screamed. I didn't know how many head injuries it would take to kill a fae without his power, but my guess was that we were nearing that mark.

"You see," Etienne cooed. "A few years back, I took a lovely concubine. She required, like many wild beasts, years of breaking before submitting to me."

My fingers tightened on Silas.

Etienne motioned to the guard to leave. "Eventually though, she came around, and has been loyal ever since. She is currently swaying your mate to be in his trust. They should be here shortly. Now if we only had that clock, we could start the countdown . . ."

"Why would he ever trust her?" I demanded. His serpent's smile was slow before he responded.

"Because she is your father's sister."

Shit.

Corraidhín

The only time I had seen Elías, Ewan and Neysa's father, was in a portrait in Bistaír. Though merely a rendered image, it was representative enough that I could easily see that this female was his twin sister. That alone did not encourage my trust in her. I mean, Konstantín was Saskeia's brother, and that didn't go very well at all. By the Gods, I was tired. Cadeyrn, poor thing, was burning from the inside out. Both of us were nearing the bottom of our power wells. We sat on the white sofa and waited for Elíann to explain.

"I was on Eílein Reínhe, the Queen's Isle, when Ewan and Neysa were born," Elíann told us. She was their nursemaid and was sent away with Ewan to the Elder Palace. "He arrived there as a foundling. I arrived not long after, looking for employment. So as to not look suspicious, you understand." She tried to take care of Ewan as she had on the isle yet was forced to become a concubine for Etienne. Her face became guarded telling us this. A look so much like Ewan, my stomach squirmed. "When Ewan was perhaps ten or eleven," Elíann said. "I was sent away, and I knew from chatter as I traveled, that Analisse reported to Saskeia that I had died."

Cadeyrn pinched his nose.

"Yes, yes. That's all well and good. However, Auntie, how can you help now?" I asked, since my cousin seemed to have lost his bloody voice.

"I know where Etienne has them. I saw his son just this morning when I went to feed him."

Cadeyrn stood and paced the room, then went through

the house looking for something. He stormed back in, his hair a sticky mass cresting his head like an onyx wave.

Elíann pressed us. "We must go soon. Reynard was poorly this morning, so I'm quite sure he will be far worse now. Plus, the other mate has been beaten."

Cadeyrn and I growled. There was something off about this female. My gift was prodding at her and feeling less than positive about this whole situation. Cadeyrn's demeanor told me he was not buying the whole story either.

"Why are you here? In Bania?" he asked.

"It was a way for Etienne to keep me hidden."

Cadeyrn told her to take us to them and looked at me as if to say *We are all well and truly fucked anyway*.

We followed her through the city to a hovel of a house not far from the docks. Mold grew from foundation to eaves, insects stuck in the green muck like rotten amber. She knocked, and a guard let us in. At the back of the home was a room with no airflow and a horrible lack of magic which stole my breath just like when we cross to the human realm. My eyes immediately found Silas's. He was hung from a wall, chained and battered, only his eyes retaining his power. Neysa was wrapped around him as though trying to have every part of her touching him. Even from where I stood, I could see the dilation in her pupils and the injuries she had taken. Cadeyrn started to rush toward them, but Etienne stepped in his path, a stone held before him.

"Ah, ah, Cadeyrn," he said and turned to Elíann. "Thank you, my dear, for bringing them to us in such a timely manner. Be a love and bleed my pathetic son a bit more."

Reynard was barely alive, his wrists torn open from the weight of his body pulling on the iron cuffs. Cadeyrn had me worried, as he was stock-still. I'd known that Auntie was dodgy, but we'd had little choice. I tried to look to Neysa, but her eyes were unseeing. *Bloody hell*.

"The spell, my dear?" Etienne asked his concubine. Elíann handed him a leaf of paper, a dagger, and held the stone while Etienne grabbed Cadeyrn's arm. I yelled. Neysa screamed and lunged for them, but Etienne was quicker and slashed clean through Cadeyrn's leathers, his blood dripping onto the stones. Neysa's scream turned into sobs, rasping in harsh bursts from her throat. The words "I just got you back" hung like extinguished lanterns.

"I just got you back," Neysa rasped again with her eyes fully black.

Darkness swelled in the room courtesy of our injured princess. For a chamber devoid of access to our powers, it seemed Neysa was able to cause a bit of trouble after all. Etienne tsked, unseen in the glittering dark.

I swore to all that was good and holy—and all that was terrible and naughty—that if I died in this hovel, I would be the biggest pain in the ass ghost that ever was.

"Now, now, little whore," Etienne cooed. I moved to my brother in the dark and pulled the gag from his mouth, and then from Reynard's. "We had a deal. Cadeyrn is Solange's. He will be very happy. Don't you worry. You may go once you tell me where the clock is."

"Whatever you have done to my cousin," I said softly. "Undo it now or there is not a festering corner in any realm where you will be able to hide. You have no money, no allies, nowhere to go."

"Oh, but I do. I have the chosen one. The Battle King. A fae for the ages to father my grandchildren and make us the most powerful family in Aoifsing history. Isn't that right, Cadeyrn?"

"That is true," my cousin answered. By the Gods. He was spelled. Neysa's breathing was ragged. She also stunk like infection and sick, and I wasn't certain I could handle much more of the smell. "It will be lovely to have Solange back, Etienne. Our children will be Gods."

The black air built in the room. Its headiness was near suffocating.

"You have missed one minor detail," Neysa said, her voice like broken glass. "My power adheres to no one and nothing. I am the heir to the Goddess Heícate and nothing can contain me."

When she stopped, Silas broke free of his chains and lightning sparked between him and his mate. Guards began rushing into the room. It was far too small in there and far too bloody dark to fight in close quarters without killing one another. Neysa must have thought the same as she lit the room to near blinding. Her power hadn't been truly used in a year, and it was obvious her grip on it was touchy. Silas reached for one of the guards, but Neysa snarled that he was hers. She struck the male with the discarded chain from my brother and ran him through with her sword before bashing him on the head. Her rage had us all take pause. Take pause and *not* notice that godsdamned Etienne had slipped from the room. Cadeyrn still stood there like a giant bloody column. Then just as quickly, he was gone. He disappeared into himself. Silas swore. Neysa was about to turn her blade on Elíann, but I called to her. Auntie's intention was suddenly clear to me.

"Neysa, wait," I said. "Don't. Not yet."

She growled at me and gnashed her teeth. Her eyes were untamed.

"Brother, I think perhaps you may need to step in."

Silas took out the last two guards and dropped his sword before walking to his mate. Gods, I wish they would figure out this madness between them. Going against this Gods-inflicted nature was killing them all. He put his arms around her, prizing her fingers from her blade, whispering in her ear. She calmed with him and went a bit floppy. Hmm. I think perhaps she was quite wounded.

"I swapped the stones," Elíann said. "Earlier today. I brought the one for the spell home with me, having swapped it for a crystal with negligible powers. Cadeyrn isn't spelled." Which meant that my cousin had gone after Etienne. Silas and I whooshed a breath, and I looked to Neysa, who was completely passed out in my brother's arms.

Shit.

Chapter 3

Saski

Any wards on the property had been rendered useless. I supposed she had no concurrence with any magics used to protect the palace and its grounds. The horses had moved to the very edges of their stables, concerned, but not in a state, which I found interesting. Darkness spilled from the stables, mingling with a tragic kind of keening wail that made my heart ache even more than it was. Not that I would admit to my heart aching. When Arik said we had a situation, I really didn't think this was the issue. We took the barge back upriver to Kutja, making decent time with both my twin and me commanding the currents. I found it hard to look at Dorn, and Arik kept pestering me for details. I grabbed him by the throat and said to leave it alone.

Basz and Ludek were standing in wait when we arrived. Basz began explaining, but Ludek put a hand on his mate to pause. My brother walked to me and took my face in his hands, pressing his forehead to mine.

You played a tricky game, Saski, he said to my mind through his oraculois ability. The ability to speak mind to mind. *I am sorry for your pain, but I see it passing. Chin up.*

I wanted to have him embrace me and tell me I was as good as Pavla and suited to rule, but there were too many around. I tucked my chin once, then held it high, asking Basz to continue. Ludek's mate—and our personal guard—led us into the stables. I had seen the beast once on the beach just before she and Neysa died. I couldn't look at her when we boarded the ship, leaving her behind. I had felt loss for my cousin's *baethaache*. As we approached the *baethaache* in the stables, I drew in a breath. She was magnificent. Every scale gleamed with a different color, like the moonlight reflecting off water. Her power shimmered around her just like Neysa's.

"Why have you not sent a hawk informing them?" I asked.

Basz cleared his throat. "You are queen, Saski. We await your decision. We were uncertain as to your . . . inclinations." That stopped me in my tracks.

"You worry that I would keep her *baethaache* for my own gain or spite?" I asked, incredulous. Arik coughed. They looked to each other. "You as well, Ludek?"

I was building an anger that wouldn't suit the position we were in, so I worked to calm myself as I strode for the beast. She had died to protect Neysa, and it was she who made it possible for Neysa to be brought back. I knelt before her, my sword at my feet in deference. She huffed almost a laugh. Snarky thing.

"Do you wish to see Neysa?" I asked her.

Her eyes lit up and she shifted, knocking the wooden stable wall, making the chains and bridles all clang together.

"She is alive. Because of you. It has been some time, but I know she still mourns you."

The beast shuddered as though it were sobbing. Ludek was behind me, his hand on my back.

"I shall send for her," I told her and stood to walk out. Gods.

MOTHER SAT in the center seat, the five governors from each land in Heilig surrounded her. Silas was correct in thinking I should have come back sooner. I felt as though I was walking into the snake pit. My brothers and Basz flanked me, thank the Gods. Arik explained on the way home that it was simply a council meeting, wishing to express support for me as queen and to sort through the muddy details that Father had so gloriously mishandled. However, walking in and seeing the assessing faces of the governors, I was sure there was more to this. Mother held a pinky to her lips—our secret sign that she was here for me and loved me. She did this with each of us, having never told Father. When Pavla's body was found, we were told her pinky was pointed up, touching her bloody lips.

"Governors," I said, pulling up my confidence. "I hope I did not keep you waiting long. What a day it has been."

"Majesty," Varno began. "It has been quite some time since we have seen you. Tell us, how is Aoifsing? You must be well acquainted with it after spending what? Eighteen months there?" Varno had the darker olive skin like my brothers and I did. Our mother's Sot coloring. I remember years ago, in a heated night, he and I made some hasty promises to one another that faded away with the sunrise. I hadn't seen him in some time, but his blue eyes still twinkled with mischief.

"Well acquainted, my lord," I said, a wicked smile confirming exactly what he was pressing for. I could not have cared less what they thought about me. Couldn't I? "I assure you, having been exposed to all that I was, I am more than ready to assume my position here alongside my brothers." The council looked to each other. Mother sat back and folded her arms across her chest. Oh, I would hear about this later. Mother's viper tongue would surely lash out at me. "I intend to rule Heilig with both of my brothers as my equals."

"Are you abdicating?" Cassia from Manu asked. Whipping to face her, I met her dark stare head on. She squirmed slightly under my eyes, shifting and pushing back at her cropped jet hair.

"No. I am expanding the seat of power. A house that rules from an isolated throne is vulnerable. One with support and structure will flourish. It is written and contracted, ready for you all to sign."

A laugh sounded from Terin of Annos. He was a smaller race of fae. Almost childlike, with soft hair and skin, but his appearance hid the cunning and spite he carried. "You cannot handle it, Majesty?"

A collective sharp intake of breath washed over the room. I crossed one ankle over the other, and leaned down onto the table, looking into his youthful face.

Varno chuckled from beside me.

"Here I thought I was being kind and saving you lot from dealing with me alone. Do not mistake, Terin. There is nothing I cannot handle."

While the gathering of governors was in a rather informal setting, I knew better than to assume this was a casual call. Thankfully it was cooler here than it was in Maesarra, though with the room so full, tensions so high, I fought to not pull at the neckline of my jacket. Dorn moved a chair behind me, quickly bowing before moving back to the shadows of the receiving room. He was useful, I supposed. I sat with feline grace and crossed a leg over my knee, straightening the skirts of my jacket over my skin leggings.

"Now, governors, please. Let's get down to it. Why have you made such haste coming here?"

"Saski," Varno began. Mother sucked in a breath. "Majesty." He quirked a smile. "We have all been informed of how you aided your cousins and were involved in breaking the enchantment on our weapons. You have our gratitude. Though it must be difficult for you, given your father's role in the matter." My brothers shifted ever so slightly closer, Basz's shield snapping up around us. "Relax, I'm only voicing what Her Majesty has asked."

The sun was dipping low, copper streaks spearing in through the cathedral windows, alighting on Varno's skin and eyes. I waved for him to continue, dust particles spinning in the hazy glow.

"The princess's *baethaache*," he said. I swallowed and raised an eyebrow. "It is our request that it not be returned to Aoifsing."

I laughed and sat forward, meeting the eyes of each governor, finally settling back on Varno. A flush crept up his neck under my stare. "The beast is not a family heirloom. She is a part of the princess. Their souls are entwined." Neysa's soul had a complicated loom of knots with that of her beastie and her two mates. That unwelcome pang of missing godsdamned Silas swirled in my gut. "Your request is denied. There are no grounds for holding her here, and to do so would not only breed bad blood between our lands, it would be criminal."

"Do you stand against your council, Majesty?" Cassia asked.

Dull throbbing pushed behind my eyes. I had always liked Cassia, though now I fantasized briefly about using that depilatory cream with which Neysa had threatened me on Cassia. Perhaps Cassia wouldn't even care if her hair fell out. The throbbing intensified, and I longed for a bath. "I was under the impression it was a request, Cassia, not a verdict."

"It is the duty of the council to act with the well-being of Heilig in mind," Terin said, voice pitched high. "It would do to have some leverage with Aoifsing. Especially while their ruling bodies are in such flux."

"We do not need a hostage, Terin," Arik said, and I heard Ludek begin to speak as well.

"Agreed," Ludek chimed in. "There would be no benefit in holding the beast here. In fact, returning her would seem in better graces, thereby almost indebting us to the princess and her mates."

"You have been unusually quiet, Eamon," I drawled. I always drawled with Eamon. I think because since we were children, I was always teasing him. First with fighting, then as we came of age, with my body. It was really no wonder Neysa and Corraidhín despise me. Eamon was sweating. I cocked my head and looked at him. Arik leaned in too, and finally grabbed him by the collar, demanding to know why his power was leaking out of him in rivers. I had been curious as to why his father, the governor of Ech, had sent him. The governor had always been a thorn in my father's side, though they appeared thick as cream.

"My father," he wheezed, "has taken the beast."

It was Arik who stood to his full height, towering over all of us, and announced, "This was an act of treason. You will all be kept here under guard until we determine who and what is making a stand against us. A member of our family was abducted from the palace grounds." My brother was shaking beside me, his eyes on his best friend. Both were in a stand-off, devastation behind both sets of eyes.

Our guards left the room, and by the shuffle of boots, soldiers were fanning out in the halls and the property in search of the elder Eamon, and my cousin's *baethaache*. I believed this was what Neysa once referred to as a clusterfuck.

REALLY, we needed to have gotten a hawk up immediately. Eamon's power could have cloaked and moved the beast quickly, but not without needing to stop for some time. Plus, the *baethaache* was as stubborn as her mistress. Mother and my brothers trailed me as I made my way to a hawk. They were arguing in tense whispers. I knew what they were saying.

"It looks bad," I said.

Ludek nodded.

I scrubbed at my face, needing to bathe and sleep. "If I tell her she was here and now she's gone, it looks as though I had something to do with it. Exactly how they wanted it to seem." Walking into my chamber, I slumped onto the chaise at the foot of my bed. *What if... What if I went back to tell them? If I returned and explained, then perhaps...* My line of thinking trailed off. Was I hoping to see Silas again and masking my own want with this?

If you do go back, Ludek said to my mind, knowing precisely what I had been thinking, *it will reflect poorly here. I am not telling you not to, sister.*

I stared at Ludek, having missed him terribly. Memories of our pillow forts when we were children came back to me. Ludek and I would hide behind a cracked-open door, waiting on unsuspecting passersby to push the door further open. Before they had a chance to step away, massive piles of cushions and cuddly toys would tumble upon heads. Ludek and I would run. One time we had set the trap for our nursemaid, but Father walked into it. He backhanded Ludek and scolded me. Thinking back on it now, my hands were shaking in anger. Father had never truly treated us as equals.

"We have to destroy the clock. I must see it done," Ludek said to us.

"I hate that fucking clock," Arik said. Mother slapped his shoulder. "Ow, Mother."

"Leave us," Mother said to the males. I braced myself for a

lashing. Gods. I was the queen now, and I still hated being reprimanded by my mother. My brothers filed out, Ludek glancing back at us, eyes wide. I began undressing, readying for a bath. It was early, but I was travel worn.

"You have fallen in love with the other mate," she said.

Why did everyone call him that? It was awful. Coming from Mother, it pissed me off more as she herself had two mates.

"How irresponsible, Saski."

My blood boiled. "Pardon?" I stood naked, facing her. "I won't listen to this, Mother."

"I blamed her—Saskeia. Then Neysa. I blamed them for not coming to our aid. For killing Pavla. When it was your father. He killed them all. He betrayed us all. It is time for *you* to make things right in Heilig, Saski. Promise me."

"I shall try."

"You shall," she corrected, eyes boring into mine. She watched me pull my dressing gown around me and loosen my braid. I was too tired to bathe. Unexpectedly, she embraced me. "You will make it right. And I shall help." With that, she left the room. I lay back and was asleep before I shut my eyes.

FOUR TIMES in my century of living, I had known sheer, unadulterated fear. The first was as a youth—perhaps twenty or so. Pavla and I were stirring up trouble in a resort town in Biancos. We had been drinking and invited a few fae to a bonfire on the cliffs. I was dancing and heard my sister scream. When I looked around, she was nowhere. Like Ludek, Pavla's gift was in oraculois and gauging intention and feelings. She was strong in a warrior sense but had no physical gifts. So, when I located her, she had slipped from the edge of a cliff and was clinging to the rocks, swaying above the crashing surf. My fear-induced power had a wave of hard air slam into her from behind and lift her to me.

The second time was two years ago. When Ludek came into my chamber, from the look on his face, I knew. In that moment, the fear of being without my sister hardened me. Shaped my wild ways into wickedness. They say that the same boiling water that softens the potato hardens the egg. I became the egg.

The third time I felt fear was seeing Father and Sonnos pulling Silas by a chain around his neck. I knew then I loved him, and the prospect of seeing him die struck me with a vexation of my entire being. Even though I knew Silas wasn't mine to love, I would have done just about anything to free him. To save him.

So, you see in my eight decades, three points of real fear made it fairly uncommon. Waking in the predawn hours to clawed hands over my face and knees pinning me to my bed filled my body with razor sharp panic. Fuses ignited within me, setting each part of my abilities on high alert. In the dark, heat swelled, making my body instantly sweat under the beast above me. It snarled quietly through its black, shimmering maw, as though not wanting to be heard. Once I was able use my nose, I recognized his smell, though I wasn't certain I should have been relieved. The beast's clear seafoam eyes kept me pinned, while his body shifted, hanging in a balance between male and beast. It seemed the shifting took something out of him, giving me a split second to manage my horror and flip him over.

"If you wanted to be invited to my bed, Cadeyrn, you had only to ask." I had air at my back, helping me keep him pinned beneath me.

He snarled, heat flaring, and I noticed, not without a bit of smugness, that he was stark naked. "Where is she?" he growled, the sound coursing through me.

"Here I thought my kiss brought you all the way across the sea to me." I pulled myself over him and folded my arms across my chest. The curtains around my bed blew closed, the door clicked to lock. "By *she*, I assume you mean your mate? However did you lose her this time, Battle King?" I didn't know why I even said that. He had never done anything wrong to me, and if I were honest, he was suffering more than I was with the mating bond between his mate and Silas.

He sprung forward, ripping through my power, clear eyes filled with green fire. "You want to play, Saski?" His voice was a low bass, tumbling between us like a boulder. Any semblance of strength I had was no match for the endless imperium that was Cadeyrn. "Want me to seduce you and tickle your confession out of you, pretend I'm not seeing my wife?" He prowled to me, grabbing the back of my neck and sniffing the length of my throat, pressing his bare chest to mine. Teeth scraped along the taut skin, his nails digging in. "Or I could tear out your throat and find her myself."

I swallowed and placed my hand on his face.

"Cadeyrn," I said, voice like a lap of water. "I am not your enemy. Sit back and listen to me. Unless you really want to have a tumble . . ."

He bared his teeth. Was that a no?

I pulled my dressing gown from the foot of my bed and covered myself. He pulled the sheet around himself, realizing he was naked.

"I can smell her beast. I know she's here." A sliver of defeat shone in his mask of dominium as he said that.

"She was," I admitted carefully. Then I told him. With the curtains on the bed closed, the heat became insufferable, yet we needed no eavesdropping ears. "Well, now we have to figure out how to keep you hidden. I've already gotten shit for falling for your cousin." He raised a dark eyebrow at the admission. "Why again are you here, Cadeyrn? Surely you didn't scent the beast from across the sea."

He shook his dark head and put his face in his hands. I had a feeling Neysa was going to continue to hate me.

CADEYRN

PERHAPS I HAD ALWAYS BEEN able to see behind Saski's facade and that was why her demeanor never truly bothered me. From the very first time we met, and she started goading Neysa, I knew it was an act. One that dug a knife into my mate and twisted it deep. One that I hadn't foreseen damaging us. An act, nonetheless. So, as I sat there, in the far corner of Saski's bedroom, both of us near to bare, I didn't care. The past two weeks I had been in and out of my *baethaache* form, tracking Etienne and allowing him to lead me to Heilig.

When Neysa and Ewan decided to take on the lupinus outside the Elder Palace a couple of years ago, she'd said she needed to do it on her own. She didn't want to risk anyone else. I finally understood the need. I didn't want her anywhere near that godsforsaken clock, and I was willing to risk us to keep her away. I knew in that split second when I decided to disappear with Etienne that there was a possibility I would be putting Neysa's love for me at risk. Whether or not Elíann told them she switched the crystals, or whether or not they believed her, I wouldn't have known. The only comfort I had was that if this destroyed me, I knew that my mate and Silas had each other. What I hadn't anticipated was that, once I arrived in Heilig, the imprint of Neysa would be so strong. It took me a full day of wildly tracking the impression to realize it was Neysa's *baethaache*. And that she was alive. Though the outcome may not change, it was imperative the beastie got back to Neysa, regardless of the internal protests of my own *baethaache*.

The chamber was stale as though no one had bothered airing it in the time Saski had been in Aoifsing. Apart from that, it was a fair representation of the female. Sensuous fabrics and hard lines from the pitted spires of her bedposts to the heavy silk that fell from the posts and windows. She sat on the velvet chaise in nothing but her thin dressing gown, occasionally forgetting to turn off the act. I rolled my eyes every time she tried to pull the vixen card on me. I wasn't impressed. Just as I wasn't impressed when she'd kissed me on that beach. I knew she was a siren as soon as I saw her dissolving into the foam of the sea. Why I didn't tell Neysa about the kiss, I didn't know. I didn't want to hurt her. And the more immature, male reason—I knew Neysa was nearly as relieved to touch Silas as she was to see me. Then there was that human who followed us. Gods above, if I didn't know any better, I would think my wife was a siren as well for the way she has us all drowning in her wake.

Dawn was fast approaching. Though I needed rest more than anything else, and by the deep circles under Saski's eyes, she did too, we needed to move on our problems. Saski left her chambers to retrieve her brothers. Ludek walked in, bleary eyed, having no idea why Saski pulled him from bed. Arik was more alert, though he was being physically pulled by his sister, a pile of clothing in her arms. I stood, pulling the sheet tighter around me, and caught the clothes that were tossed my way. The brothers were openly gaping at me, Arik blatantly sniffing the air. I scoffed and moved to the bathing chamber to change. Thankfully what she pulled from Arik's closet was a simple set of fighting leathers, and while slightly tight, at least they fit my height. Now I knew how Neysa felt, always at someone's mercy to find fresh clothes. Something deep and hot ached in me thinking of her. Thinking that she must be feeling betrayed and angry. Wondering if she felt betrayed enough to bed my cousin. Knowing it wouldn't even have been a betrayal, and none of us could come to terms with the arrangement. The fire in my gut smoldered. I'd spent so much time in my *baethaache* form, I hadn't even spoken to her. Another lie I told myself. I refused to speak to her from my *baethaache* form, and I had refused to make the time when I had been out of it. I knew quite well what kind of useless male that made me. I had never been good enough for her anyway. As I walked out of the chamber to join the others, I had an arm wrapped around my middle, trying to kill the pain. Fucking Ludek saw right through me and closed his eyes once in acknowledgment. I shifted my cold mask back into place. Saski wasn't the only one with a facade.

"So, Etienne thinks you are spelled and on board with bringing his dead daughter back to bear your godlike children?" Arik asked, incredulously.

I raised my eyebrows and quirked my mouth in confirmation.

"That's a glorious spectacle of fuckery, my friend," he said with a whistle.

I pulled my hand through my hair.

"And Neysa thinks you are spelled as well?" he pressed. "You just left?"

Saski hissed. I glared at her.

"I thought that the quicker I left with Etienne, the more realistic it would seem. I was hoping Elíann would tell them. That they would know."

"That's quite a hope," Saski said. "I should think a prayer and an offering would go along with that hope."

"Saski," Ludek warned.

"No, Ludek," Saski shot back. "You went after her, Cadeyrn. Brought her back across to be with you, and now you've just left her? Thinking it was for everyone's benefit? Did you not think that perhaps you should have left her there in the human realm to continue to heal? Rather than reopen the wound?"

"You are saying this out of concern for your cousin? Or because you are pissed off she is back with mine?" I asked softly. She lunged for me, Arik pulling her back. I would have taken it. I deserved it.

"And are you truly here because you cannot handle her being with your cousin?" Saski's words fanned the flames in my chest. "Did you think you could, but seeing them again together made you realize theirs is a bond tightly woven?"

"I think . . . perhaps," I answered her honestly, "we are arguing two sides of the same coin." I fell onto the chair. "I just need to know she will be safe. If she's near that clock—if any of you are—it won't end well. If I can get to it and destroy it without involving anyone else, then there's a chance . . ." I choked and cleared my throat. "A chance for her to be happy. I'm sorry. That doesn't work in your favor."

"No," she said, crossing her arms over the black dressing gown. "It does not. But I understand. And I will help you."

I looked up at the steel resolve on her face and had to smile. She was wearing a look so similar to Neysa.

"I almost wish I had been born to be a farmer," Arik muttered.

I knew the feeling.

Chapter 4

Neysa

We healed eventually. After almost a week, Reynard was quieter, though slowly coming back to himself. Our soldiers were looking for Cyrranus. I prayed he'd made it out of the manor. My head was still a bit dodgy, so I stayed down, mostly curled against Silas. Strange dreams marred my uneasy sleep, much like they had in the human realm. I hadn't heard from Cadeyrn, and I had a feeling I knew what he was doing. If he truly wasn't spelled, then I thought he'd gone after the clock. The alternative stung too much to think about. Deep down, I felt he went because seeing me back here, and the bond with Silas still a living thing between us . . . it cut him. And I hadn't known how to suture it.

It was before dawn when I woke without air. My lungs were constricted, cold sweat breaking out over my whole body. An ache in my chest had my eyes stinging with tears, and though Silas was asking me what was wrong, and was trying to hold me, I seldom let him touch me anymore. I bolted from the bed in the room we shared, tearing through the inn, down to the docks in nothing but a chemise. He followed, of course.

I paused at the water, my hands on my knees, ignoring the stares of the dock workers and sailors who had long since begun their day. Glittering darkness unraveled from me in gratuitous ribbons. I couldn't breathe through the anxiety. I could feel him. As though he woke with me.

Cadeyrn. I breathed. *Please.* No response. I sunk down on my rear and yanked at my hair.

"I'm going after him, Silas."

He put his hands on my shoulders.

"He's gone after the clock. I know it."

"Perhaps, he really doesn't want you to be near it. I know I don't."

I looked up at him over my shoulder and saw the softness in him. "I feel that something is wrong." I hated the weakness this brought out in me. "It's like . . . like I can't hold myself together."

"You miss him," he stated simply.

"Yes, of course. But this is more. Like I'm a boat that keeps taking on water. I'm trying to patch myself, but I can't. I need to get to him. I need him, Silas. Something in me . . . something is physically missing. I can't put my finger on it."

He sat next to me on the filthy deck, pulling my legs onto him. "Then we go. But I won't—" He cleared his throat. "*Trubaiste*, I won't let you near the clock. Be aware that I will do whatever it takes to keep you away from it." His eyes had a fierceness in them; his mouth set in a hard line I normally only ever saw on the battlefield. "If it means knocking that hard head of yours again, or jumping onto the fucking clock myself and letting all my power be taken by it. I will not allow you near it again. Understood?"

I nodded, my eyes filling, and put my hand in his hair, pulling him close as a vision took hold of me.

Running though ruins and towers. Lights around me. A necklace shaped like a bird with topaz eyes. Screaming. Wing beats. My head thrown back, body wrapped around Silas. Hands entwined, tattoos pressed together above our heads. Saski, screaming into a pillow, pulling her legs in tight. The sea, churning and beckoning. So much blood.

I held on to his shoulders, gasping from the vision. I was up and off the ground, being carried to the inn through a flume of water. Silas had seen the vision. I was again unpracticed at not projecting them to him and Cadeyrn. Ever so gently, he laid me down on my bed. I swallowed and pulled him to me, burying my face in his neck. Shields of mist and darkness pocketed us as we shared our gifts. He lifted me to him, sitting up, his mouth found my neck, and he bit down as I threw my head back. It was as much a solidification of this mating bond as I would allow. Consummation was not an option for me. I would have only Cadeyrn in that respect. But Silas and I needed a primal conjunction which made our bond stronger. We all needed to be at our strongest.

With that bite, a piece of my world, like a puzzle, clicked into place as we lay together, shaking. It was intimate. I couldn't deny it. And I felt his reaction to me just the same.

"Silas," I whispered.

"Don't say it, *Trubaíste*. Please."

Pushing closer, I took his face in my hands. He moaned and clutched my waist.

"I think," I began. "Without me, you and Saski . . ." He tried to pull away, and I locked my legs around him tighter. He laughed a little, shaking his head.

"Perhaps. But there is no *without you*. I love you. Like I have never loved another. I know you aren't mine to love. Not really. But it doesn't change the fact."

"She loves you, Silas. Truly loves you."

He cocked his head at me.

"I think you two . . ." It pained me to say it. "Are well suited for each other."

He was quiet, moving hands along my body, keeping his eyes on me. I pushed away slightly, keeping some distance between us. "And if Cadeyrn doesn't come back?" he asked, forcing my stare.

A lancing, searing pain had me seeing spots. He knew it would. It was why he asked.

"If he leaves and cannot be redeemed from his beast, or the clock destroys him? What then? You're fine with me being with Saski?"

I pulled back farther, as if to extricate myself.

He growled and refused to let me go. "No. Do not run. Not from this."

"I don't run from you," I said, lifting my chin. "I want you to be happy. I refuse to believe he isn't coming back. I refuse it."

"Then we go find him. And address the other issue when we find him."

I turned into my pillow, hoping to get some sleep, when there was a thunderous knocking on the door, followed by a stern voice.

"There is an inordinate amount of darkness and mist coming from this room, you lot. It's making everyone nervous."

"Not for you to worry about, Corraidhín," Silas called. I giggled into my pillow, our shields dropping.

She pounded again, the door opening due to a crap lock. I pulled the cover up over my head as though that would help.

"By the Gods. I thought you'd never do it. Don't worry. I won't tell Cadeyrn. Though of course he will know. And there's nothing to be ashamed of, because you're mated too. But, you know, you both needed it."

Slowly, I pulled the sheet off my head and looked at her. She tilted her head and puckered her rosebud mouth at me.

"You don't know what you're talking about, sister," Silas growled.

I knew she was sensing something, but with Corra, it was always a hard call. The leaking-boat feeling remained in me, despite the pounding in my head being gone. A space of emptiness right where—

"My *baethaache*!" I shot upright, the sheet coming off, and Silas gathered it up.

"Your tits may be smaller, but they're cuter," Corra pointed out. "Mine will probably be awful once the babies are done with them."

I shook my head and looked down at my chest, wondering if fae healing extended to keeping perky breasts. What a strange thought to have at a time like this. Silas shrugged, looking his fill as well. I elbowed him.

"Och, *Trubaíste*, I stare at them all day. What's with your wee beastie?" he asked quietly, knowing how her death affected me.

"She's alive. I think. I feel her absence. But not like she's dead. Like she's missing from me. Trying to find me. Perhaps in trouble."

Corra continued to stare at me. "Elíann has something to tell you, Neysa. Perhaps when you're done with my brother, you can come to Reynard's room." She turned on a heel and walked out, slamming the door.

What the hell had that been about? I moved to get up from the bed. A roughly calloused hand stopped me.

"Not just yet, aye?" he said, using those eyes and that rugged, friendly face. "We may not be mated in the sense of having sex with one another, but we are bonded. And I don't want there to be anything between us that makes you feel like you have wronged Cadeyrn."

I looked at him. From the face I knew and loved to the

body that that could turn the heads of the Gods, and smiled while I held his hand, then drizzled my essence into him.

"I don't think either of us would survive if this bond hadn't been solidified."

I touched the scar on my neck. A matching one from Cadeyrn, given under very different circumstances, adorned the left side. "I guess the Goddess always gets her way, huh?" I asked, huffing in resignation.

Silas gave me a sad half smile, which landed like a gut punch. I was always going to hurt both of them.

Elíann knew that Reynard's father had been in contact with Lord Eamon, the elder, governor of Ech. Though all Etienne's assets had been frozen, he had an under-the-table deal with Eamon regarding retrieving the clock.

"Etienne knew Ludek was who you trusted with the ancient timepiece, so he forged an alliance with Eamon," Elíann told us. "He has a lumber company out of Saarlaiche which has never used his name. That would be how he travels to Heilig."

Silas slammed a fist down on the table. Reynard smirked at the violence, and I hoped he was becoming more of himself. I went to the bathing chamber in our room and curled myself into a ball in the lukewarm tub water. And I cried. I put up a shield of darkness so Silas couldn't hear me. I didn't want him thinking I regretted it, but I felt like I had let Cadeyrn down. I always told him I chose us. And I did. This was more complicated than I could have imagined. For all the love I felt for Silas. The magnetism. The mating bond. I wanted Cadeyrn. I wanted *us*. Only us. In the tub I held myself, clutching my stomach and my swollen chest, and tried over and over again to reach Cadeyrn. My thoughts to him were like beating on a vault which refused to open. I couldn't have come back here—come so far—only to lose him again. The thought of not getting him back had me hiccuping and tearing the skin around my fingernails, only to watch it knit back together. After a time, I washed and left the tub, pulling down my shield. The door pushed open, Silas standing against the frame. He knew. He knew me too well. His eyes followed me as I dried and dressed.

"I don't regret it," I told him, touching the wound at my neck. "So, don't look at me that way. I wanted you to."

"We can leave in the morning and look for him," was all he answered.

Chapter 5

Cadeyrn

We packed a decent amount of provisions, yet I found I needed to hunt everything I ate. Some base, primeval need to kill. My companion winced as I beheaded the game. It was a kind of wild boar with a thick hide and nasty great tusks. We traveled much in silence, scouting and tracking. Picking up Eamon's trail here and there where he would have come out of his shield to regenerate his magic. Saski kept her weapons sharpened and clean, taking the time each evening to sing the oiling cloth over her curved crescia blade. Gods, I wished she and Silas could make it work. They were so alike.

Were I to choose the nonlinear progression of time, as we had discussed weeks or maybe even months ago, would I have been subjecting those I care about to a fate determined solely by my choices? Would I create a trap within a parallel dimension just like our conversation that odd day when Dean had appeared in Bistaír? Or would their own choices fit into the ultimate outcome? I almost wished that wily Dean character were here to help me pick apart my ideas. He was surely going to fade away, and it would be one more person to add to

Neysa's guilty conscience. The night began to play its symphony of creature sounds, seemingly in concordance with the fading light. It was as though a bow were being played over the lines of light jumping between the pockets of colorful energy. I marveled at it, not disguising my awe.

Saski raised an eyebrow, telling me the sounds were almost like a sixth sense wherein there was an overlap between the lights and sounds that manifested in a movement which could be felt within our minds. It seemed that even our senses and perception of reality and experiences around us were relative. There was no concrete realm to ponder.

Sleep claimed me under the lullaby of this new sensation.

The realization that I was tracking the clock hit me in my waking moments. I bolted from my bedroll and grabbed my twin swords, strapping both on my back, then kicked Saski's boots to wake her as well. How this would play into the fucking thing's dynamic, I couldn't know, but the fact that I hadn't known until that point left me uneasy. Could it have activated the countdown due to my tracking? Had it been activated when Ludek hid it? Was it all in my head, and I could simply have chosen to disregard the godsdamned thing altogether? Saski noticed me staring at her and demanded to know why. I shook my head.

"I refuse to listen to, acquiesce to, or even entertain anything to do with that clock," I said more to myself than to her.

"Congratulations," she said. "You've made a choice."

I cocked my head to her.

"I said . . . back in . . . wherever the hell we were when I first saw the clock, that we had to decide. It had to be based on our own decisions. You lot didn't really listen to me. To me and Ludek it was obvious."

Bloody fucking hell. She was right. Between our intrinsic

gravitational "otherness" and the hatefully simple notion of making a choice, she and I could nullify the clock's power.

"Is that why Ludek wouldn't tell me where he hid it?" I asked her. "Even though he knew I was the one to destroy it? Because I had to come to terms with making the decision?"

She nodded and swallowed, sensing the heat rising in me. "So, what will you choose, Cadeyrn? It is yours to decide."

We packed the rudimentary camp we had and stalked off. She kept a wary eye on me, casting glances here and there.

"I choose to find Neysa's *baethaache*," I said, breaking the silence. "I choose to find the clock and make certain it affects no one ever again."

She tsked and sucked on a tooth.

"What?" I demanded.

"Choose to stay alive, you stupid ass," she yelled at me. "Choose to keep your mate. Keep you two together. Regardless of Silas. Regardless of pain or anything. Choose. As she chose. As she tells you time and again, she has chosen."

I stopped and raked a hand through my hair. She threw up her arms in frustration, and I grabbed the back of my neck.

"Don't be so godsdamned—"

But I cut her off. "She solidified her mating bond with Silas, Saski."

She stilled at my words.

"I felt it. The day I arrived at Kutja. It had to happen. I knew it would."

She was looking me dead on, not blinking.

"Neysa chose that," I said, wanting to throw up. Saying it aloud. Admitting it, was close to my undoing. My head spun in an endless tide of blank thoughts. As though I could not function on any level, thinking of my mate with someone else. I felt, in that moment, so dangerously close to losing all sense of my fae self and giving in to my most primitive, beastly nature. "She chose that," I said again, swallowing the thickness in my throat.

"No," Saski said, voice soft. "She didn't."

I laughed, dark and without humor. "Well, I know my cousin, and I know he wouldn't—"

She cut me off. "That's not at all what I meant. Gods. For someone as bright as you, Battle King, you can be incredibly dense. I meant that she never chose the bond with him at all. It was forced on her. And she's fought it. Or haven't you noticed that? She never chose him. She chose you. Do you think what happened changed that?"

"I don't know!" I flared out and singed a tree with my power. Claws extended and retracted from my hands, the tips of my fingers remaining black and leathery. "I don't know. Maybe it does. I won't know."

"No, I suppose not," she said with pursed lips. "Because you left her."

"I did not." I meant it to be a definitive, but my rebuttal only made me sound petulant. Perhaps I had been a child throughout all of this rubbish. Perhaps I was the oldest fucking child in existence. Or perhaps I had no protocol for how to react when it felt like all the realms had come down upon me. Like I would gladly welcome the blanket of death rather than live within the incarceration of this heartache.

She walked off angry.

"Did you say to her," Saski called back, "that you were leaving to take care of a problem, and that you will see her soon, my darling? No. You let her think you were spelled and were going to go jump back in bed with your dead fucking wife. Your head must be a bloody great mess, my friend. And this is coming from someone with quite a slew of internal issues with which to deal."

"Then, what, oh great seer, shall I do to rectify my

mistakes?" I asked, hoping she actually had an answer. My boots stomped the wet leaves as I walked after her.

"Make. A. Fucking. Choice. Choose her."

"I have!"

"You chose the female. Not you two," Saski insisted.

I wanted to kill her. Burn the fucking land to the sea. I chose Neysa every damned day. She was the only thing I wanted.

"You keep thinking you are misbegotten and unworthy or some asinine inner dialogue, Cadeyrn. Choose to come back. Choose, you stupid fucking prick. Because I can't have what you have. So just fucking choose."

There was a stream nearby, its rushing a cooling tether to normalcy. The heat in me was threatening to burn us all alive in this jungle of energy. The singular roar of a beast reverberated through the trees, bouncing from the far rock faces. My *baethaache* clawed from inside in response, and I took off at a sprint. Saski kept close and pulled me into the stream, wrapping herself around me as we became the water itself. It was fascinating unbecoming and knowing I was not a conglomeration of transferred particles, but a readapted form of being with an unadulterated consciousness. The change was quick enough, and we reappeared on the mouth of a riverbank which was foaming from the spill of a waterfall. The roar sounded again, closer this time.

"Thank you," I breathed. She nodded curtly. My beast kicked from within me. I tamped down on the need to break free, gathering my wits about me. We searched for a relatively easy climb to the top of the falls, grabbing for purchase on boulders and vines. After a time, I realized that Saski could have become the waterfall and gone to the top without me. Yet, she stayed on, keeping beside me on the climb.

It was at the summit of the falls that the roar became a scream. Indignant and painful. My *baethaache* tore from me as it never had, flying to Neysa's. Male expletives and the sound of whining steel filtered down to us as we scrambled the last several meters. Eamon and Etienne stood, a sickly, invasive shield coated Neysa's beastie, my own covered in my own shield to protect it. The two males were backed against the tree line, positioned between my *baethaache* and the two of us. Saski grabbed my jacket.

"Think. Choose." I was barely above my beast, eyes all but seeing her, fire coating where my shield should have been. It was then that I felt it.

Ticking. Throbbing and expectant. They had found the clock after all.

Neysa

I REALLY HADN'T WANTED to resent Heilig in and of itself. I resented it in so far as it was, quite literally, a royal pain in my ass. It took us about a week to sail across from Bania, landing off the coast of Biancos. We rowed a small craft to the sandy shore where, the previous year, I had closed the Veil and paid with my life. The location itself had me shaking with trepidation and memory of battle and combustion. Silas was pale-faced and wouldn't let go of me while we made our way across the beach, in and around the caves and tidal pools. We searched within the shadows of the cliffs and between tidal islands, from the first rays of morning light to the bronze ticks of sunset. She wasn't there. Neither was Cadeyrn, but I didn't expect to find him. I knew what he was doing. If I didn't think about it, I could compartmentalize the gutting ache. I had always been good at that. Evening had us building a small fire atop the dunes, huddling close to fend off the haunting this place manifested. I twisted in my fight for sleep, seeing phantomes on the beach. Hearing the pop of my aneurysm over and over again. Hearing my *baethaache* cry. Hearing Cadeyrn screaming through the flames and pandemonium of battle.

Choose. The word kept ringing through me like a giant gong was being hit in my psyche. A missive from my subconscious. What was I supposed to choose? What did it mean? As we left Bania, Corra pulled her brother aside, holding his face close to hers and whispering something I couldn't hear. She maintained her cool presence with me, not offering the warmth I was used to in my friend. *Choose.* Surely not between them. That was not supposed to be my fate if I was meant to have or need both mates. Though, to choose, I had always chosen my husband. I would always choose us. Were he to be gone . . . I didn't know what to choose. The thought had me holding my stomach. Flutters of fear pushed against my fingertips.

From deep in Heilig, a pull, not unlike that of the tourmaline in Peru, coaxed me awake. I pushed at Silas and sat up. He was rubbing his eyes, obviously not sensing any danger. His presence always calmed me. I laid my head on his chest and tried to zero in on the pull. Hoping it was my *baethaache*. With fingers interlaced, we pushed them into the soft ground beneath the reeds of seagrass, combining energy to find the lure. For hours we lay there, pouring ourselves into the earth, allowing it to meld with our own power to show us the way. As we had done before, he and I allowed our gifts to meddle and play with one another, finding an ending and beginning in the life force connecting us. In the connection was a link to the path she had taken. Not scent alone, but a sort of light trail of her being. I grabbed at Silas and pressed a kiss to his mouth in confirmation. Along that trail, we moved toward the essence of what was my *baethaache*.

Nearly as soon as one crosses from Biancos to Ech, the sweeping dunes become forest, then jungle. Not dense and bug ridden, but lush and jewel toned, imposing a feverishness in my body. The air was filled with heady florals and birdsong. The humidity allowed for Silas to partially dissolve and pull the two of us faster through the boldly colored rainforest. When a stream became accessible, our progress was quickened even further, and so we had to camped overnight just once.

The desperate roar of a beast stopped us in our sodden tracks. Silas regained himself to grab my hand, and we set off at a breakneck speed in the direction of the call.

I'm here. I'm coming, I said to her.

Choose. What in the actual fuck does that mean? What voice is telling me that as if it were a book being shoved against my chest? Sounds of rushing, violent water came from beyond the beast as we tore through the jungle. A waterfall. We were coming from the opposite side.

Singing steel and the cyclonic vibration of movement so fast it was of no particular adherence to nature sounded. Then another roar. We pressed on, my thighs and calves burning with the exertion. Exploding from the jungle proper to the flat plain above the waterfall where the river fed, I was struck dumb. Cadeyrn and Saski were fighting Etienne and another male who looked similar to Lord Eamon, Arik's friend, along with a small faction of soldiers. Driving the force back was Cadeyrn's *baethaache*, completely separated from his male form. Silas was as shocked as I was, judging by the sharp intake of breath and the way in which he grabbed my waist as though to keep me back. Etienne's speed made his a viable force, but all he was doing was continuously striking and hiding behind his soldiers, not caring whether they fell beneath the blade of my mate or my cousin. Blood soaked the ground water. It was two against twenty or so. The other male kept close to my *baethaache*, a glistening abhorration coating her essence.

Cadeyrn took a knock to his thigh, and I screamed, causing him to snap his sight onto me. Until that moment, he hadn't seemed aware we were there. Anger flared from him. Shock, devastation, disgust. I was blinking rapidly, not able to grab ahold of any of the warring, negative emotions emanating from his face. Etienne sped toward a particularly knitted canopy of trees and ferns. The other male took the opportunity to remove the shield from my beast and attempt to run his sword into her heart. Cadeyrn's beast whirled to him and, with one gnash of his scaled snout, took the head of the male clean off, blood dripping hideously from the maw of the *baethaache*. I chased Etienne, Silas joining his cousin and mine in the fight against the soldiers.

Neysa, no.

I nearly stopped at the sound of Cadeyrn's voice in my mind. It had been so long since I'd heard it, I almost sobbed. Yet I ran still.

I can catch him, I responded. My reply was stubborn as my boots tore across ferns and bramble.

Etienne was in my sights, a couple hundred meters ahead, darting through the canopy and its mossy boulders which stood sentry. The heavy boot fall of my husband chased me, gaining on me. Another pair, softer, close behind him. Saski. Silas brought up my other side, reaching for me. I turned to him, confused. Cadeyrn swung his sword at chasing soldiers, maiming and killing those within spitting distance of us. I lurched forward to take off again, but found heavy hands on my shoulders. Silas.

"Not letting you near it. Can you feel it, *Trubaiste*? I am not letting you."

I tried to wiggle from his grip, but a ferocious snarl ripped behind me. I turned, expecting to see Cadeyrn's beast, but found my mate there instead, the snarl having come from him.

"Just listen for once!" he growled, hatred and anger in his

eyes. I was pinned to the spot with that anger, indignant power spewing from me in protest. A soldier came up behind. Before I could dodge the attack, Cadeyrn grasped my arms and a hard wall of air from Saski threw me. Threw me from the canopy, quite a ways away. Cadeyrn's heat followed to where I landed with a crack and thud, my arm bent at an odd angle, blood running into my eyes.

Snarling erupted from where I had been seconds earlier.

"Stop it, you two," Saski yelled. "Cadeyrn, let's go. We need to end this." The snarling stopped. Before the soldier who was creeping up on me had a chance to draw his weapon, Silas ripped his head from his armored body. As the male fell dead, Silas crouched before me, assessing my wounds.

Why? I managed to say in my mind. I didn't even know who I said it to. Cadeyrn? Silas? I pressed to standing, Silas growling at me to stay down. I growled in his face, saying I needed to see Cadeyrn. He half carried me, my broken arm wrapped about my midsection, to the thicket where they had all disappeared. Coming through the natural boundaries of the clearing, Silas and I both gasped at the sight. Etienne had activated the clock, its monstrous ticking a common sound effect in my nightmares, haunting me in the human realm and beyond. I couldn't even take the bus in London for lack of stomach for the ticking sound it made.

Choose.

"Shut up!" I screamed. "Just shut up. I don't understand. I've chosen, godsdammit!"

It was then that I saw it. My mate and my cousin were fusing their own powers together as though bonded to one another. From that visual fusion, they pulled back from each other. It seemed oddly familiar.

"Is that not what you and Ewan did in Prinaer?" Silas asked to my ear. Oh Gods. It was. They were opposing the gravitational force of the clock by issuing a force of their own.

With each step away from the other, they sped, building speed and strength of power. Etienne reached for the clock, interfering with the g-force being created. It wavered, interrupted by the intrusion. I pulled from Silas, who could have sat a building on me for the lack of give in his hold. "You're not going near it. Not on my life, *Trubaíste*," he said with no room for argument.

Though the static force between them wobbled with Etienne's advancement, he did not reach the clock. Instead, once within the confines of their force, Reynard's father was torn apart.

I did not look away. I was happy to see the violent end of the male who raised Solange. Who abused and was willing to sacrifice his wife. Who gave over his son to be tortured. Who beat and tortured Reynard himself. I was happy to witness his end and be able to one day tell my friend that his father would plague him no more. I watched the skin tear from his body, the blood spray in thousands of individual droplets as Etienne's body shattered. What that made me, wanting to watch, I didn't know. I didn't care. I was myself. Darkness and light. Strength and vulnerability. And I chose myself.

A visible, audible crack in the realm detonated as the two fae I watched took it upon themselves to make certain this timepiece was never used again. The moment the clock became a confetti pop of magical shrapnel, both Cadeyrn and Saski blew backward meters upon meters. The explosion matted the grounds, leveling all plant life and anything in its path. What was once a plain within a rainforest, filled with emerald-green waxy leaves and bright blooms, was now a wheat-colored butte reminiscent of Southern California. Within the confines of Silas's shield, I screamed and screamed. Once the dust had settled, he and I wordlessly ran in opposite directions. He to my cousin, I to his.

The impact where Cadeyrn hit the ground was so great,

his broad form was plunged into a couple of feet of solid ground. Trees crisscrossed over the hole where he lay, like a trap set by armies in wait. *No. No. No.*

Cadeyrn. Please. Be alive. Please.

I dug under gnarled roots and exploding pockets of energy that winked around him like psychedelic pixies. They spun, like shards of glass. His eyes were open, staring blankly above him, body still. I choked and spluttered, pulling at his shoulders. If he was gone, this all would be for naught. If he was gone, I could never explain to him what he meant to me. That what was between us was greater than any construct built by a God. I swore and choked, pleading with the universe to allow me to show him that I would bleed the realms dry for him. For us. Because in the end, the two of us was all that mattered.

Arms came around me and wrapped me against him, his chest finally lifting, shallow and strained. A sob escaped me. I let loose the horrible, racking pain in me that compounded every day in his absence. This one male I had chosen to spend my life with. The one I wanted and needed above all others. His scent wound into me, trickles and eddies, flying through my veins like blood. I released mine back, filling him with all I was. Everything I had. Between us, a glow settled. Neither dark nor light, but serene and understanding.

Chapter 6

Silas

It was instinct that had me pitching off to get to Saski. She was thrown so fucking far, just as Cadeyrn was. There was no telling how broken either of them would be after that explosion. Or implosion. Whatever the hell it was. I just knew *Trubaíste* would get to my cousin, and I had to get to hers. Letting my gift pull me in the direction of her power, I ran full speed, noting the broken branches and wet foliage along the path she had traveled. When I saw her, I had a brief vision of Neysa on that beach in Biancos—mostly blue and shattered. Saski's legs were thrown over her twisted back, and droplets of water ascended from her body. Each drop like the slow ascension of her soul. In the strange way of this land, the movement of water through the thick air made a sound like notes on a piano, the notes in turn brightening the air around them with a pop of color. Pinks and purples like so many of the flowers around us. I swore and dove next to her, knowing she wasn't completely gone. Not yet.

Like a child, or a babe with a mobile, I began swatting at her water droplets, swearing at her to wake up. We needed a healer there immediately, and the only one close by may have been just as poorly. The only thing I could think to do was to scoop her up and run, as fast as I could manage, back to Kutja. Or any other village or town I might stumble upon.

Silas, Neysa said to my mind.

Fucking hell. I could hear the tone of Neysa's voice and knew it wasn't golden on her end either. I didn't know if I could spare the time to get to her and save Saski as well. I ran and concentrated harder than I ever had, to try to break into *Trubaíste's* power to let her know what I was doing and that I would send help. Something snapped in me. A yawning in my gut had me terrified. Terrified for what was happening around us. To Neysa. To my cousin. To Saski. Fuck.

Trubaíste, I said to her. *I have to get her help. I will send someone back to fetch you both, or I will come myself.*

I understand, Neysa said back.

I could have puked. Of fucking course she understood. No one would understand more. *I thought you would. I'll come back for you.* Every word I spoke to her in my mind was strained.

I know. Save her, Silas.

Along the stream, I was able to move us through the water, Saski's natural affinity and mine allowed for easy transport through the ripples. How had it never bloody occurred to me that she was a siren? Wind affinity. What a whole lot of bloody bollocks that was. Thankfully, Kutja wasn't very far from where we had been, especially in relation to the sheer number of rivers, lakes, and streams there were in this land. Gods, I'd never seen so much water outside of the ocean. I suddenly missed my sister quite a bit and wished she were there. Of course, if she were there, she would likely punch me in the face and tell me to save my fucking mate and cousin. Hell.

Ludek came tearing from the palace gates, his mate and

Arik a distance behind. I pushed on past them all with a growl, not slowing until we were inside.

"Where do I lay her?" I snarled.

A healer was waiting just inside the courtyard, telling me to lay her on a wide bench. I hadn't changed the angle she had landed, so when I laid her down, she was still a horrible, crumpled ball.

Arik was stock-still, frozen. I didn't know if he was about to throttle me. Ludek placed a hand on me and the other on his sister. The healer was working quickly, running hands and stones over Saski's body. Over the queen of fucking Heilig's body. I walked away and threw up. Basz was calling orders to soldiers and ordering a guard contingent to where we had been. It felt like hours, yet must have been mere minutes, but the healer was able to straighten Saski's legs and arms. Each crack of her joints hit me with a wave of nausea. I walked to the back of the room to empty my guts. I felt like I had the first time I walked onto a battlefield. This time, the horror was over losing someone I cared about. We moved her to a stretcher and transferred her inside to her bedchamber. I needed to go back to my cousin, but refused to leave until I knew she would be okay. Ludek pulled me aside.

"She will live, Silas. Because of you."

Half of me felt relieved. Half of me felt like I had committed the greatest betrayal in history. How could I have left them there? I didn't even see how bad Cadeyrn faired. I scrubbed at my face, not knowing what that made me. Ludek touched my shoulder and forced me to look him in the eyes. They were the same shape as his sister's, though where Saski's were mossy green like Neysa's, his were a deep brown that seemed to soften each time he spoke.

"This is my fault," he told me. "I forced Cadeyrn's hand. I apologize. I knew what he needed to face. I knew what you all did. I wasn't sure what it would take, but I knew not facing it would kill you all as well. And if Arik and I lost another sister . . ." He trailed off, voice catching.

I wanted to hit him. I wanted to beat him and scream. But he was right. In fact, there was no part of what he was saying that wasn't spot-fucking-on. Which made me want to rip my hair out.

"We'll find them. We'll get them here. You made a hard call, Silas," he said, and the rhetoric started to get old.

"You can spare me the fortune cookie mumbo jumbo, Ludek. I get it. I just feel like a right piece of shite for it."

"I don't think the fortune cookie phrase is something I understand."

"Nor do I, brother. Nor do I. But Neysa says it and it seems to be fitting to the climate of our conversation, so I used the phrase. I didn't particularly care for the outcome."

"No, I should think not. What is a fortune cookie?"

"Fuck knows."

"Ah."

Saski groaned and exhaled from the other side of the room. The healer left, promising to return shortly with more tonics. Ludek and I watched her go and made our way to the bedside. Gods and shite, she was a mess. Color had come back to her face, but it was still bloodstained and pinched with the remnants of pain. Ludek took her hand and stroked her palm, no doubt speaking into her mind. I couldn't pry my eyes away from her. When hers finally met mine, Ludek squeezed her hand once more and left us.

I didn't know what to say. I didn't know if she could speak either. So, I stood, staring at her like a fucking hatter, sorting through what was going on in my head and heart. She closed her eyes and fell asleep while I sat on the edge of her silk-and-iron bed and watched her. The healer came back in, humming to herself while she administered a tonic that didn't even wake Saski. She told me contact was good, so I put my filthy hand on her arm. Then on her shoulder, my fingers aching to thread through her hair and tell her something. When I pulled them back, not wanting to get her any dirtier, I felt a twitch and stilled my hand on her arm again. I knew the healer would be back in to clean her, as she was still half clothed, soft cloths and bandages covering wounds and anything one might want to keep private. I felt the urge to pull the blankets up but knew she would bite my head off for doing so before she was clean. I'd never known a female to take as many baths as she did. Bringing my eyes back up, I realized she was looking at me lucidly, her cheeks damp.

"Are you in pain?" I asked. My voice was like rust. She scoffed and rolled her eyes, but immediately grabbed her head from it. I fished in my bag for the peppermint oil I used on *Trubaíste* and put a bit on a wet flannel from the side table.

"Cadeyrn?" she whispered.

"I don't know." My fucking voice broke answering. She reached for my hand and held it. I kissed it quickly. "Neysa is with him." She breathed in relief.

"You could have left me there."

"No," I said, locking eyes with her, "I couldn't."

There was a commotion in the distance. I listened in, but it was Arik bursting through the chamber door that told me my cousin was here.

"Go, Silas," Saski told me. Arik said he would stay on, and I slipped from the room, heading toward the noise.

HOLY BURNING HELL. In the salon on the ground floor, next to the library, Cadeyrn was laid out on a bed, someone, likely Ludek, had the forethought to bring in. *Trubaíste* was laid on a curved chaise near him, their hands still clenched together. She was fighting for air, while his chest hardly rose and fell. I knew I'd started shaking but knelt beside her.

I had done this. I chose to save her cousin. I left her behind. Injured. Knowing she would give anything to save Cadeyrn.

I had to keep him alive, Neysa said to me. *I gave him my breath.*

Bloody. Fucking. Hell Realms.

"Let me give her mine." I spun to Ludek. To the healers. To Basz. Anyone. "Let me fix her. Can I? I did this." I was pounding Ludek's chest.

The healers shushed me, and I swear I could see Neysa roll her eyes. She hated shushing. I curled myself around her, letting my gift merge with hers. It felt awkward here with so many others in the room. What we did was an intimate act I would never want witnessed by others. Not sexual, but something born from the desperate clutches of magics wielded by meddling Gods. Yet, I knew it was what needed to be done. Little by little, my power drained from me, and filled her. It poured into her veins as hers filled mine, bringing life to us both. She held me tighter and allowed me to push my power further into her. A long, solid breath rose in her chest, blossoms of color staining her face at last.

Thank you.

I just pulled her tighter in response. "I'm sorry. So sorry," I whispered so only she could hear.

Love's a funny thing, isn't it? she asked me. I pulled away and widened my eyes at her. She smirked, and I didn't know if I wanted to kiss her or slap her.

Ludek coughed, hiding a laugh.

When I got back to Saski, she was sitting up, trying to refuse a tonic her brother was pushing on her.

"She might be better behaved after a bath, Arik," I said, attempting to swagger in, as though I hadn't just had the wind knocked from my sails.

"Then, I shall call her handmaiden and have a bath drawn for her like the child she is." He placed the tonic on the side table. I took it up and sat.

"If I promise to bathe you, would you drink your damned tonic, Your Majesty?"

The door clicked shut. She snarled softly at me and drank it. The whole damned thing. I ran her bath and took a moment to wipe myself off before I went back for her. Most of me was covered in a layer of filth. Her long golden legs swung over the bed but were too shaky to stand, so I joked about her needing to be carried like a child as well. She stifled a moan as I sat her in the huge tub and began to wash her.

"You've an entire forest in your hair," I said, plucking leaves and brambles from the deep brown locks. She shrugged, allowing me to scratch at her scalp and untangle the mass. "They are back. He will live. He's . . . still not awake. But Neysa gave him her essence."

Saski stiffened, then looked to me over her shoulder. I was twitching my mouth like Ewan does. She reached to it, running a thumb across my lip.

"Stubborn ass," she said. It was my turn to shrug.

"Surely you're not surprised?"

"That you're stubborn, or that you chose to save me?" she asked, voice shaky, her thumb dropping from my lips.

"That I love you, you wicked thing."

I took great, sick pleasure in watching each emotion and expression flow across her face, then turned her back around to finish washing her hair. I could feel the temper rise in her as I kept her turned away from my admission. I rinsed the rest of the washing-up liquid from her hair, knowing she was itching to say something.

"Well, I shall believe *that* when I see it."

I snickered quietly, knowing it pissed her off more, but pulled the necklace from my jacket pocket and fastened it around her neck, laying the silver bird across her warm chest. She spun in the tub, cursing the discomfort it caused, and I snickered again into my hand. She looked down at the jewelry, the topaz eyes glinting in the light coming through the window. I honestly didn't know if she looked more comical, half enraged in her tub, naked and bejeweled, or more beautiful.

"It has your eyes," she spat.

At that point, I really was trying to not laugh at her. She had to rein in her emotions, so she was acting out like a petulant child. Allowing her seductress siren bullshit to leak out, she all the while tried to seem indifferent. I leaned over and narrowed my gaze at the bird. Gooseflesh erupted over her flushed brown chest, the bird rising and falling with each breath.

"Huh," I said. "Never noticed. I bought this for you ages ago. If you don't like it, I can take it. As it has my eyes. Maybe give to my sister."

She harrumphed and tried to stand, swaying on her feet. I grabbed at her and wrapped her silky dressing gown around her body. She muttered that it was the wrong dressing gown, and this one was surely ruined now that it was wet.

"Apologies, Your Majesty." I deposited her back on her bed and started to walk out.

"And where are you going?" she called in her princess

voice. My back to her, I pressed my lips together, trying to not laugh.

"To tell your brother I didn't have better luck with your behavior."

"I was surprised. That's all."

"Well, Majesty. I reckon you need to rest. Once the surprise has worn off, you can send for me." I was nearly in the hall when she called back.

"I told you I can share, Silas. Question is, can you?"

Well, that sobered me the hell up. It was time for a drink.

Chapter 7

Corraidhín

I should have been back in Bistaír a week ago. I hated leaving my family this long, and Ewan was out of patience. You see, the issue was that I simply couldn't leave Reynard behind. With Elíann. In the weeks since everyone had left, Reynard became less and less himself. The torture he had endured since his capture, and the emotional trauma of his captor being his blasted father, corroded his good nature. His mother and Cyrranus were still missing. I had scouts out all over Aoifsing and no one had heard hide nor hair of him. Was that the phrase? I tried to get our friend to come back with me, but he became enraged as I'd never seen him.

If I was being honest, it frightened me. Not for myself, of course, as I could take the weasel down with the moisture from a glass of water. No, I was frightened for him. I never knew the kind of love and need for another as I have now. Not until I met Ewan. If I were to lose him, I was quite certain that there would be no being in this realm who would be safe from my wrath. Well, apart from my children. And possibly my brother and cousin. I guess I shall include Neysa. I digress . . .

Poor Reynard lost his partner over a century ago, and only a year ago found love in another. I simply could not imagine the anguish he felt. And I simply refused to give up on him. I also refused to think about my brother and cousin and their mate. Because there was no way they would come away from their mission whole.

These Goddesses propagate their grand ideas for all of us and never understand the destruction they cause. I am not saying that my brother and Neysa do not have a connection beyond Heícate. No, we all meet and foster connections not quite in league with our plans. However, to thrust upon them both a bond neither asked for? That was an immeasurable cruelty. Try as I might to come to terms with it, I simply could not. I despised what Heícate had done to my twin and to Neysa, and perhaps this was unorthodox, but I sided with my cousin. All three of them suffered with this mating bond. As had Saski. However, no one suffered like Cadeyrn. Cadeyrn who could often be a prick of the first degree, but whose only mistake was loving Neysa with everything in his being. I truly did not know how he had handled any of this. Though, I supposed he had fucked off to Heilig or Gods know where in a bit of a tantrum and arrogant male hunting fit.

Reynard, Elíann, and I moved to a home within Bania so we could be more comfortable than we would be at an inn. I corresponded daily with my husband, and each evening, before I fell asleep, I pondered leaving and going home. Gods, I missed my babes. Reynard and I sparred in the back garden of the house. He was reluctant at first, preferring to sulk.

"Yes, darling, I'm quite sure Cyrranus will be happy to come back to a scrawny, malnourished male. I know I would be livid if, when I got back, Ewan had let himself go. Gods! Can you imagine? Oh! Did you ever hear about that human king, Henry?" I asked, pointing my blade at the one near him. Reynard groaned and agreed to pick up a sword. We made our way out to the walled garden. "He was a young king and had six wives. Six! Not at the same time, of course. Though I have seen stories like that as well. Mostly in compounds with hideous prairie dresses. Anyhoo, Henry started out quite dashing, but it seemed that with each subsequent wife, he got fatter and fatter." I shuddered. "Point being, darling, don't let yourself go. Cyrranus will want to see you as he last did. Whole and handsome." I winked at him.

He paled but nodded. And so, we sparred and trained a bit each day. We searched the city and outskirts. A hawk arrived early one morning whilst I was out running.

Corraidhín,

I have been going over ledgers and noting ships' registers. There are recent regular departures from Bania as well as the Sacred City in Laorinaghe. I've sent word to Yva and her fellow representatives. I believe it imperative to find out what is being transported. The numbers haven't added up. If you can, look into it. I shall keep you informed. I should hope you will be home soon.

Yours,

Ewan

Once back in the house, I read the message to both Reynard and Elíann. She explained that Etienne and Arneau had hands in so many businesses, but Ewan's trade embargo tied those hands significantly.

VERUNI WAS a province populated by many *noíchera*. As was the case with Lord Dockman, *noíchera* prefer to live and travel by night. These fae have gifts and magic which are only viable after the sun sets. With that in mind, Reynard and I suited up in our torn, singed leathers and set off for the docks of Bania. He deliberately slowed his pace for me, as I would have needed to become mist in order to match his speed. The pink cobbled streets dipped down, feeding to the lower part of the largest city in Aoifsing. As large as the harbor was, it fed into a river before meeting with the sea twenty or so kilometers out. We picked out the ships with scarce crew and searched the area. Two boats sat, their sailors casually pacing along the dock before the vessels. Both boats were not huge, yet presumably large enough for a sea voyage rather than the many smaller ones here which were used only within the bay that stretches between Saarlaiche, Veruni, and Maesarra. Between us, we watched the bloody ships until they pulled from the dock and made slow passage from the harbor. Reynard slumped back, a defeated look on his face.

I began to sit with him yet noted a single flash of light in the distance, coming from each retreating ship. My hand grasped Reynard's jacket and hauled him up. Mist enveloped the ships, making them now invisible to the naked eye.

"Oh," I said, quickly trying to figure out the best way to move us down river.

"I'm ready to hear what you're thinking, Corraidhín."

"There was a pirate once," I began. "I saw a documentary about him." He pushed his gloved hands into his eyes and inhaled. Why does that always bother everyone? "Listen. There is a land in the human realm called Louisiana. It is a place that sits below sea level at the bottom of a bigger land. It is full of marshes and rivers which lead to a great bay. Or a gulf. I don't quite remember. I had once been curious to go, but my brother showed me the large insects and these horrid, long-snouted beasts which live in the swamp, and I decided perhaps it wasn't for me."

"Corraidhín."

"Yes, yes. Anyway, the bay or gulf, at the time, a couple of hundred years ago, I think, was a route to many great trading places. This pirate—LaFitte, I believe was his name. Regardless, he took over a small, seemingly innocuous island in the gulf. Or bay. What is the difference between the two?"

"Corraidhín."

"It's a relevant question, darling." I tutted. "The island was the first land a ship might pass whilst heading toward a very large trading city. His men would intercept ships from the island and steal all the goods being transported. Just as quick, the treasure would be transferred to smaller ships and run upriver to hidden estates, then sold. It was a brilliant operation. The smaller ships were able to duck into awful thickets of gnarled root trees within the water called man-groves." I shuddered. "Just awful. They could hide in those spots and be unseen by military patrol."

His annoyance faded as he caught where I was going with the story. I saw the moment the idea hit home. His almost-translucent eyes lit up. "You think that those ships we just saw leave will meet with additional ships downriver and switch goods?" he asked. I nodded and patted his cheek. "Good thing, hellcat, you can move as fast as I." With a wink, he ran.

Oh, thank the Gods. The weasel was back.

That single flashing fae light kept a steady pace as the ship eased along the riverbank. Just before the river emptied to the bay, there was a jog in the direction of the light. We moved with it and watched as a much larger ship met with the one we had tracked. Males were disembarking both watercraft, meeting along the soft shoreline. I started to fizzle to mist so I could get closer, but Reynard whispered, "What happened to the pirate? LaFitte?"

"He pushed his luck one too many times, and the privateers were said to have surrounded his ships as he attempted to escape. But no one really knows where he went when the ships went down."

He nodded as though that were enough to hear, so I moved away from him, praying he didn't do anything stupid like my brother would do. Or Neysa.

One male hauled a trunk from the ship we had tracked. From it he pulled what was unmistakably, aphrim skins. Treated and cured, ready to be made into fighting leathers and ropes. Anything that needed to be of the best quality. The male from the larger boat signaled for one of his males to open a crate sized like a wardrobe. I moved closer, nearly shadowing the party. Inside the crate were hundreds of steel weapons. Mainly blades and steel arrows.

"This is our second shipment of steel," the male from the larger vessel said. From his accent I knew he was Heiligan. From his manner of dress, I knew he was not an ordinary pirate, but a well-commissioned privateer or military sailor. "While the skins are useful, it is not all our agreement settled on. The governor's patience is wearing thin."

"We are en route to procure the rest. You shall have the other goods twofold when we come back around. If the weather holds along the coast, we are looking at a month."

"Then we shall meet back in a month."

The goods took a couple of hours to transfer between boats. The *noíchera* harnessed their magnetic power, linked to the moon, to move the trunks and crates. I pulled Reynard farther into the cover of trees along the riverbank.

"The larger ship is from Heilig. The smaller one had aphrim, so I would bet it traveled from inside Maesarra on the river. They alluded to other goods needing to be picked up. The boat is heading along the coast, and the captain said it would be to its destination and back within a month.

"Festaera?" he asked in a whisper. I tapped my finger on my lip, thinking.

"Perhaps, but the Heiligans brought steel with them. Festaera normally does not sell off its other resources."

"Yes, but with the embargo . . ."

"True. We have one chance to figure this out." The night pulsed around us. I stared him in the eyes, knowing I was about to have one incredibly enraged husband.

"Then I suppose a-seafaring we go?" he asked.

I moved to him and did my best to cloak him in mist as we sped onto the *noíchera* ship. Gods, I did not care for that manner of travel.

Chapter 8

NEYSA

"It's not over." I pulled Ludek out to the hall where the metal tiles lined the walls with depictions of Heiligan history. He agreed. "What else do you know, Ludek? I'm not game for more surprises."

"We have five governors from our lands sequestered in chambers here," he admitted.

Oh great.

"Saski announced she planned to rule jointly with Arik and me. There was a bit of a fuss. That was when we found that Lord Eamon had taken your *baethaache*. Cadeyrn arrived that evening. He and Saski went after her. They tracked the clock."

"And?"

"And we now have to contend with essentially incarcerating our nobility. I suspect we are on borrowed time."

"Isn't that the theme," I said drily. He laughed, squeezing his chocolate eyes shut in a brief admission of exhaustion.

We walked together to the stables where my *baethaache* and Cadeyrn's were huddled against each other. They stood and sniffed wildly when I came in. For a moment I simply stared at them. Their scales and fierce beauty. These beasties stood as substantial proof of Cadeyrn's and my bond. They were the darkness and shimmering light inside us, where our souls braided. I could feel how conflicted Cadeyrn was. I understood why. Why he had such trouble with the connection between Silas and me. I knew the situation was destroying him. Moment by moment, he was fading from this bond. What he didn't see, or refused to see, was that while I didn't feel whole without Silas, without Ewan, without Corra even, my wakeful nights in the human realm were haunted by my want and need for my husband. Only Cadeyrn.

Ludek touched my shoulder as he walked past me while I gathered my thoughts. My beastie's eyes seemed to smile at me. I grabbed a damp flannel and gently wiped her down, cleaning the wounds she had received in the fight. When she was clean, I kissed her snout and turned to Cadeyrn's. He huffed and rolled his eyes. I burst out laughing. Of course, it would be a cheeky little thing like my mate.

"Alright, you. May I clean you up as well, or will you tell me you can do it yourself as Cadeyrn would say?"

He pushed at my hand and flipped the flannel on top of his head baring his teeth in what I took for an encouraging grin. However, he still had bits of soldiers between his teeth, which was slightly off-putting. Even so, I began wiping and cleaning him, enjoying the repetitive motions nearly as much as the beast did. The flannel swooped under the wing joint, and I polished the catchall lines where the tendons stood out from the leathery skin. Each brush of cloth brought a snore from the beast. Ludek sat on a hay bale, telling me about each governor and his or her family. Like my brother, Saski and Arik had no desire to rule. Ludek would accept wherever he was placed, content to be of service to his lands in the capacity which best suited the land itself.

"What is it *you* want, Ludek? You seem to always acquiesce to what others want."

"The difference is that I am happy. My family, my mate, my desire to serve. I know I am essential to Heilig. That knowledge brings me comfort. So, whether my siblings decided upon a parliamentary rule or a modified monarchy, I will stand behind it."

"And do you foresee one outcome over the other?" I stroked the sleeping beasts as I asked, knowing Ludek would sense the reason behind it.

Before he could answer, a battle cry sounded from the far side of the palace grounds.

"Oh, for the love of all that's holy. What now?" Ludek cried.

RIMMING the outer edge of the palace grounds was a vanguard of soldiers. They pushed at the perimeter of wards which had physical demarcations in flowering hedgerows and willowy trees. Silas came up behind Ludek and me, Basz stepping toward his own soldiers. The wards were still strong, so it would seem the soldiers were aware that they would not be getting in. Impressively, palace guards and warrior types filled the grounds quietly and quickly, their numbers too many for me to count from where I stood. Clapping and shuffling of booted feet multiplied from every nook and cranny of the grounds. A quick glance upward revealed the flowering vine-covered grey battlements and turrets were lined with archers. The fortifications and military presence was humbling. Even my mother did not have this kind of response on her isle. Though, that was more of a personal choice. One which most likely led to her demise. I worried about how Ewan was handling it all.

A male stepped from the line of opposition soldiers, pointed features and jet-black hair that shone blue in the sun. Arik joined his brother and moved forward.

"Patricius," Arik said tersely.

"You are holding my sister and the other governors prisoner, Arik."

"They are detained, yes."

The line of soldiers slammed spears into the ground as one, causing a rumble, and made me jump. I was so tired.

"This is how your sister chooses to begin her reign?" Patricius asked, razor-thin brows high.

"My sister was ushered into a governors' meeting as soon as she arrived home, where we were played for fools as Eamon abducted my cousin's *baethaache* from our property. It is well within our rights as peacekeepers in these lands to detain the governors until it is clear whether anyone else had any involvement in the matter."

"Has Eamon been found?"

"He is dead," I answered. "He was about to drive his sword through my *baethaache's* heart. My mate's own *baethaache* killed him." There was a murmur.

"And you are?" Patricius asked, his nose pointing down at me.

"Neysa Obecan Bowden, princess of Aoifsing, heir of Heícate, and cousin to the queen of Heilig."

Silas squeezed my hand.

"Apologies, Your Highness." He turned back to Arik.

I nearly fainted from the return of oxygen that rose so swift in me. I'd never declared myself quite like that before. Of bloody course it had to be when Cadeyrn wasn't there with me. We had never even discussed whether I would take his name. He so rarely used it, though everyone seemed to know

Bowden. I wanted that piece of him a part of me just as my father's name was a part of me.

Patricius went on, none the wiser to my inner turmoil.

"Well, surely it is time now to release the others?"

"My sister, your queen," Arik spat, his usual arrogance replaced with anger. "Is barely awake, having been gravely injured in the attack. My cousin's mate is still unconscious. You will understand that our priority has not been to tend to the governors, who, I assure you, are not lacking comforts. If you would like to speed things up, Patricius, help us find how far-reaching Eamon's organization is. For there were plenty of soldiers under his command."

As the two males spoke to one another across the invisible barrier, I narrowed my eyes, and leaned to Silas.

Look closely, I told him mind to mind. *Patricius and his officers are wearing aphrim skins, correct?*

Aphrim were native to Aoifsing and not Heilig. Trade only recently having opened between the two continents, it was rare to find someone in Heilig donning aphrim. Much less, a whole company of officers. Saski had never seen the skins before seeing mine the first time I'd been in Heilig.

"It would seem so," Silas answered. I said the same thing to Ludek in my mind. His nostrils flared as he pursed his lips. I saw him whisper to his mate, Basz nodding once. I retreated a casual few steps, Silas and Ludek with me. Silas's eyes were on the weapons the soldiers carried. He was assessing the details, and I felt his power reaching and crackling.

"Those males have shiny new steel, Ludek," Silas remarked.

"Cassia's land is Manu. They have an abundance of steel and brass."

"I'd like to see Cassia's sword, if that would be all right with you lot," I said to Ludek and gestured to Basz who was nonchalantly standing in front of us, listening closely.

Arik permitted Patricius to cross onto the grounds and come inside to see his sister. His soldiers backed to the river's edge and set up camp while we went inside the palace, no one bothering to voice the fact that Cadeyrn should have been with us. Angry and unhinged with him still under, I was so pissed off he took it upon himself to destroy the clock. I was upset he had been there with Saski. I was bitter that I had been back in this realm six weeks, and half of that I had been without Cadeyrn. The only thing I wasn't angry about was the fact that Silas was in love with Saski. Because I wanted him to be happy, and I was genuinely happy for them. Even though I knew she kissed my husband before she left Maesarra.

My knees threatened to give out on me, a desperate sort of exhaustion pressing into my movements, so I walked to the garden bench where Saski had been sharpening her knives last year. After sitting heavily, I unhooked my jacket and rubbed the shoulder that still burned every so often. It was as if a phantom blade sliced into me just to keep the memory of that day in the Festaeran caverns alive. The scar was jagged and raised, running from my shoulder down the bicep. Had I still been in Aoifsing and had fae abilities, there would be no scar. However, fae healing would never erase the emotional scars of that day. Of all the days leading to it. I knew I would come to terms with my mental health at some point. Once we could rest, I told myself.

"Dead on your feet, *Trubaíste*. Come, you're about to plant that pretty face on the ground." Silas lifted me and leaned me against him as he sat. Ludek lowered beside me. I hadn't realized I'd fallen asleep. Rubbing my eyes, I sat up, reaching for the sword Ludek held. As soon as my fingers met the hilt, I saw images.

Ships sailing. Running through ruins and a tower. Wine being poured. Laughter. A face far in the background. I was trying to focus on the face, but the wine bottle came to light faster. The same bottle Yva had brought me in Laichmonde. Finally, Cyrranus, bound to a chair.

My body was rejecting the energy expenditure. There was too much lately. Emotionally and physically, I was having trouble keeping up. I slumped forward, head dangerously close to the sword.

"I'll take that, cousin." Ludek held my face in his hand and looked at me with his warm, intense eyes. "I didn't see what you saw, but I do know that if you do not rest, you will be as poorly as your mate." He gave me a knowing look. I wrapped my arms around my middle, pressing a hand to my gut.

"I know my mother imported steel from Heilig a few years ago," I said with a yawn. "I don't recall seeing any trade agreements for it recently with any of the provinces in Aoifsing. Do you have any knowledge, Ludek?"

"The trade minister dissected the trade with me a few months ago when I was trying to ready for Saski to come home," he answered. "The only goods that were regularly being shipped were the nuts from Saarlaiche, moonstone pearls, and wool. Manu suffered after the Festaeran steel incident, as we put restrictions on sale and trade."

I turned to Silas. "The ledgers. Etienne and Arneau were stripped of land and title, and we removed all weaponry. Were he still trying to run an organization, he would need weapons."

"Aphrim skins," Silas said through clenched teeth. "But we seized them all, along with his property." He paused. "Ah. The ones from the battle in Bania. Surely that wouldn't be enough to trade for foreign steel and transport." Silas pulled at his chin.

"Not at all."

"So, we need to suss out who the fuckers are who are skimming aphrim and where they got them," Silas was thinking aloud. "So far as I know, there is still a moratorium on breeding the nasty buggers, so whoever is trading has their hand in the pants of someone already in possession of aphrim."

We knew Etienne's aphrim had been seized, and there were monitors on the other four main aphrim farms in Aoifsing. There hadn't been unchecked herds since the battle in which Paschal was killed. Even the herd in Bania were from Etienne's farm.

Though my mind was muddled with lack of sleep, bits of human world history came back to me. During World War II, in the human realm, French vineyards suffered greatly. Many were razed and, in essence, left for dead. Others, during German occupation, were under the thumb of those who were referred to as Wein Führers. Wine lords. These vineyards and wineries produced a commodity in an era that had little with which to bargain. In fact, while the French made very little money on it, the Germans were able to use the French champagne as currency with neutral countries, or any willing to turn a blind eye. In a world where no one trusted concrete currency, champagne was a valuable trade item. Could aphrim have become a black-market commodity in this realm of shifting allegiances where legions of steel had been spelled?

"In my vision, I saw Cyrranus being held in a room where wine was being poured. The wine was the same as Yva brought, Silas. I couldn't see the faces of any others in the room, but they were all wearing the Manu steel." I began to explain to them the liquid currency of the Second World War, feeling almost like Corra talking about her documentaries. "I think . . . perhaps there is an under-the-table operation going on with someone in Manu and Laorinaghe."

"And you think Cyrranus may have figured this out as well?" Silas asked, turning the Manuan sword this way and that.

"Question is, who can we trust to tell us the truth as we start digging?" I wondered aloud.

"Someone who needs to redeem himself," Ludek said with a thoughtful tap of index finger on chin. "I'll find Arik and go speak with Eamon."

We stood to head inside, my eyes catching on a wandering peacock-like bird as it sauntered around the garden, oblivious to us. Rather than shades of teal and blue, it was gold and silver with bright green eyes. Silas seemed transfixed by the glamorous bird. His hands were clenched at his sides as though the chandelier of feathers brought back a memory. Had I the energy, I would have asked what was vexing him. Every fiber of my being was exhausted. Buzzing began in my feet and turned to a throbbing in my legs as I stood still, slightly swaying. Our departure to Manu would be that night. Cadeyrn wasn't awake, and Saski wasn't in a state to leave. Ludek squeezed my shoulder and walked in. Silas was looking at me curiously.

"I'm so tired," I admitted. "You must be as well."

He shrugged and said he would rest when it's over. I knew that refrain.

"Every time I think it's over, something new and horrible happens, and I'm separated from Cadeyrn. How many times, Silas?" I pleaded with him.

He pulled me in close and laid a hand on my cheek. "Stay here, *Trubaíste*. I can go."

"No," I replied, leaning into his touch. Needing to be touched and held. Wanting so much for it to be Cadeyrn. "I need to go. I have seen the room and I may have another vision. Will you stay here?"

His brows pulled into a single dark line. "Of course not. I will come so we can figure out this shite and get you back to your husband."

"I meant after." I looked up at him. "You and Saski."

He blew out a breath. "Fuck knows. This place is a long way from home. And a queen probably won't want to have a nobody like me tagging around." He gave me a lopsided grin.

"First of all," I said, grabbing at his collar. "You are not a nobody. I'm quite certain she knows that as well. Second of all, home is where those you love are."

"I know," he whispered. "It's complicated, aye?"

Yes, it certainly was.

"Let's get you some tea and see a man about redemption." He winked and pulled me toward the garden doors. I stopped and squeezed his hand.

I'd be okay with it, I told him. *If you stayed. It's complicated, but love is never a small thing. And my Gods, I want you to be happy.*

He wrapped me in a hug so tight, I was pounding on his back for air.

"It's an opportunity, Eamon," Arik said, exhaustion pulling at his every word. Each of us must have been dealing with our own particular trauma stemming from the past month. Arik always seemed to let things roll off him. He was the steadying pillar to his sister's volatility. I was quite sure I had misjudged them both. An error on my part to be sure. It seemed that such a betrayal by his best friend had deflated Arik. "Show me you haven't been involved with all of this. Show me these years of friendship haven't covered up having a hand in my sister's death. Of Saski's . . ." He swallowed, choking on the possibility of losing his other sister.

"I haven't," Eamon said, pleading with his eyes. "I swear it, Arik. Ludek?" he begged of his best friend's brother. Ludek looked at him without an ounce of pity. Ludek, who had already lost his twin sister, Pavla. Who, hours earlier, was faced with the possibility of losing his other sister.

"I only found out when Father planned to send me to the meeting," Eamon swore. "After, Father had me stay when you went to Manu, Arik. I didn't know why, so I sent Dorn. I was uncomfortable with being told to stay. He only told me when he said he wasn't going to the meeting."

"Then help us make this right," Ludek said. "We aren't children anymore. This land is ours to protect. All of us."

Eamon nodded, his eyes never straying from his oldest friend. Between us, we hatched a plan to track down the smugglers and, hopefully, find Cyrranus.

Hawks launched from their perch outside our connecting doors. Corra and Ewan should receive them in Maesarra within a couple of days. Corra and Reynard should have been home weeks ago. They should start putting feelers out on Laorinaghe, keeping an eye on trade and wine production.

THROUGH THE RIVER passages along the Matta, I stood on the side of the barge watching the colors and lights twinkling along the shore as we traveled south toward Manu. The first night on the barge, I had curled up in my bed and tried to quiet my mind. It hammered on all night, pestering me with questions about what we would find, how long before we could get back to Kutja, when Cadeyrn would wake. *If* he would wake. Though he was alive, there was something in his birthright, his countenance, that nudged me. As though he were a God who slumbered. The kind of slumber spoken of in temples and sung round campfires. Fair Endymion slumbering for eternity, visited nightly by the Goddess of the moon. Could that be why I was destined for two mates? Had Heícate known Cadeyrn would fall into a sleep for lifetimes? I refused that notion. Cadeyrn was power unto himself. Healing personified. The heat to my cool darkness. Without him, my world would be cold and his would burn out. A moored ember from an eternal flame.

Yet, he slept still.

My breathing caught time and again as I splayed my hands across my stomach, like I could hold it all inside. I knew Silas waited outside my door, but I needed to start pulling myself together without him. It wasn't fair to anyone involved, especially since he had Saski. I wondered how Reynard was, and when they got home to Bistaír. I wondered how Ewan was getting on with the babes and Dean. I worried if Dean was sick. I worried about Tilly now that Dean was in Aoifsing. By morning, my body trembled, unable to regulate my temperature from lack of sleep, and I slurped down tea until my head pounded.

The last night on the barge, I stood watching the shore go by, trying to relish the beauty of Heilig. My family's land. However, it just seemed like a siren itself, luring you in with its beauty, then killing you. Before we left Kutja, I had tried to hold Cadeyrn. Tried to tell him where we were going. I hated to leave him. Again.

At some point I must have fallen asleep on the deck, as I woke with the dawn, my head on Silas, a blanket over us both.

"Sorry," I said, pushing up. He helped me sit straight.

"For what?"

"You felt the need to come out here for me. You could have slept comfortably."

"Course I could have," he said with a stretch. "I would rather be out here with you." I squeezed his hand. "Looks like we are close to town. Best get yourself some breakfast or we will all suffer."

I rolled my eyes at him and smiled, feeling more nauseated than hungry.

Arik and Eamon led us through the tight streets of Manu. It was a smaller city, but highly populated as the bordering lands were inhospitable to settlement. Marsh bordered it on the west, ocean to the south, and the dry lands of Sot to the east. Buildings were stacked and some even spread across streets, yet it wasn't the oppressive crowding of many cities in the human realm. We walked for hours, keeping to the shadows until we reached the far side of town, close to the badlands that separated Manu from Sot. The sun dipped parallel to the horizon, casting us all in an impressionistic orange glow that made everything seem like it could be okay if you didn't look close enough. A paint-splotched blur of optimism. In the past three years, that early autumn time brought about some kind of profound change. Realizing the date had me stumbling on the street. First it was when I asked Caleb for a divorce. The next year it was my night with Silas. Finally, last year, being thrust through the Veil. All were events that happened within the same couple weeks, year after year.

"*Trubaiste*?" Silas caught my elbow.

It's just the date. The time of year. It took me by surprise. Nausea roiled in my stomach. It had been sloshing all day.

"Ah, weel. Let's not worry too much. There's been some good at this time of year too, aye?" He winked. I elbowed him.

"Always thinking like a male." I heard Arik snicker, obviously catching my meaning.

"Who knows how long it would have taken my cousin to pull his head from his arse if Mabyn hadn't been so . . . magical for us."

"You're not wrong," I admitted. My cousin openly laughed at that.

Eamon motioned for us to duck into an archway which led to a courtyard. Two guards stood by a door covered in an iron grate. Their eyes went wide when they saw Arik.

"We require entrance," Eamon spoke. The guards looked to one another, clearly at a loss for what to do. It was one thing to be guarding a facility used by your governor, and another to stand against your prince. Arik raised an eyebrow at them.

"Do you have families?" he asked, hand on his sword. They nodded. "Comply and we will make sure no harm comes to them." A double-edged promise. The two males unlocked the grate and the door beyond. "Lead us please."

"Yes, Your Highness." They walked ahead, Eamon and Arik following, Silas behind me, making sure there were no tagalongs. The hall led to stairs which wound in a tight climb. At the top, the guard knocked twice and opened another grate, waiting for who- or whatever was behind the door to answer. A female with golden skin and nearly black hair opened the door.

"Honestly, you two. A pretty prince comes to town, and you forget your loyalties. Oh well, then. I suppose you should all come in." She stepped aside, hand on her sword, and shook her head. The flat was small, almost lived-in when one looked at the living area and its comfortable seating. Arik sat and propped his boots on the low table. The flippant prince once more.

"I appreciate the compliment," he addressed the female. "Though, perhaps you should reassess your loyalties. Regardless, we seek a male who has come from Aoifsing." Magic crackled as she raised her hand, and Silas grabbed it, throwing up his own shield around them.

"Ah, ah. None of that, lass," he said with a smirk. Thumping sounded from the back of the flat. The sound of wood on wood, like a gavel striking. Eamon and I walked back.

Cyrranus sat, hands and feet bound to a chair against the

far wall. He was bruised and unkempt but seemed otherwise okay. I ran over and began to unfasten his bindings, then Eamon and I helped him stand. The room was filled with wine and crates. A barred window looked out onto a dry dock where a wagon sat, ready to be loaded. Several males were turning up. We rushed back to the living room.

"I assume there is a shipment either coming in or going out." Arik was now standing, pinching his fingers together and releasing them. Each time he did, the female gasped for breath. He was controlling her airflow. "Answer, love," he said to her. Her eyes bulged, then she sucked in a breath.

"Ship leaving. We've loaded it with Manu steel."

"Where is it going?"

"Laorinaghe," Cyrranus said, voice quiet and scratchy from disuse. "It came from Bania. After the fight."

The female seemed to wrestle with something. "It's leaving within the hour," she said.

Do we get on the ship? I asked Silas. We locked eyes.

"Cyrranus and I will go," he said to me.

"I will as well," Eamon said. "Arik, you must return to Kutja. Do not back down from the governors." Arik was clenching his fists. He looked to me.

"I go where you go, Silas," I said, knowing this could be the biggest mistake I'd ever made. The clenching in my stomach agreeing with that thought.

"Fucking hell."

"Arik. When Cadeyrn wakes . . ." I cleared my throat. "I don't know. Tell him it's okay. That there's a reason it's never easy. That in this realm and the next, he is my carving on the tree." Arik nodded at me once.

Silas turned to Arik as well and spoke. "Send a hawk to my sister telling her where we are going. Tell your sister . . . don't smash the eyes." We all looked at him in confusion. He shrugged. "Let's go catch a ship."

Chapter 9

Ewan

The hawk landed just as my arrow hit the target. Corraidhín should have been here weeks ago, and I hadn't heard from anyone. I was practicing and training daily whenever I wasn't ensconced in matters of state and children. They missed their mother. Efa often placed a fleshy palm on my face to project an image to me of Corraidhín.

I pulled the note from the hawk and stroked its feathers in thanks.

Your Majesty,

The instrument which we sought has been destroyed. Both my sister and Cadeyrn suffered grave injuries. Cadeyrn is still unconscious. Your sister, Silas, and I uncovered a trade scheme between one of our lands and someone in your province of Laorinaghe. They seem to be illegally exchanging Manuan steel for Laorinaghan wine and aphrim skins. Neysa and Silas have commandeered the transport ship to Laorinaghe. We also located Representative Cyrranus, and he is safe in your sister's company. They have asked that I send this message to you and

Her Majesty, Corraidhín. I shall return to Kutja immediately and see to the care of Cadeyrn.
With best regards,
Arik

Bloody hell. I pulled at my hair and dropped my bow to return to the house. Where was my wife? I started to panic, throwing open the doors to my study. Bloody Dean was sitting at the small writing desk, annotating texts. He turned when I walked in. He was a nice enough male. I didn't know why he was still with us, unless he really had no intention of trying to cross back. My sister was a magnetic force when it came to males. That aside, I couldn't imagine what she must be going through with her mate unconscious. Why she chose to leave on the ship and not stay with him had me worried. They hadn't had a moment's peace together.

Dean pushed his glasses onto his nose. Perhaps Cadeyrn or another healer could fix his eyes.

"We have a situation," I told him.

"I get the feeling you lot say that often."

Cheeky bastard. I handed him the message and began to write a message of my own to send.

"So, who would be behind the trade on this end?" Dean asked.

"There was a candidate. One who opposed what we are trying to build here. He wanted no part of a multi-head governing body."

"Why? Was he in favor of ruling himself, or was he fearful of the meritocracy you have begun?"

I stopped and looked at him.

"Forgive me, Ewan. I mean to say that government is a fickle thing. You lot have chosen to broaden the spectrum of how this realm has been ruled for millennia. Yet, as well-intentioned as this path is, it is a system choosing representatives based on what your family deems useful and worthy. I'm not saying it is wrong. A greater number of larger governments have been constructed differently and failed. It may be the best alternative for Aoifsing at the moment. However, opposition is expected. I simply ask whether this fellow had qualms regarding the system, or his own narcissism."

I didn't know and I said as much. I honestly felt that my sister would have been better equipped to handle this mess. I was beginning to see why she was friends with Dean. Or whatever they were, as he clearly carried a torch for her.

So much had happened since that meeting that I had to get Dean and two others in to help sort through the rubbish of my office to figure out who the other candidate had been. When we could not see straight any longer, I dismissed everyone and called it a night. None of us had eaten, and I was ready to see my children. Ama had put them to bed so I crept into the nursery and sat next to the cot they shared. Their hands were pressed to one another, and I wondered if Efa told Pim stories in his mind, like a picture book. Perhaps Neysa and I once had as well. Not one of our family was truly accounted for. I couldn't make sense of how it all happened this way. It seemed like once Neysa was back, we could all move forward. And yet here I was, sharing my manor with a human, wondering where in the realms my wife, sister, and everyone else I knew and trusted were. Gods above. Floorboards creaked.

I slowly stood and made my way to the door. I knew by scent and his heavy steps it was Dean. Fae moved far quieter.

"Sorry, mate," he whispered, as I slipped into the dim hallway. "I think I've found it. Jurus of Laorinaghe. I believe it is in Reynard's hand this is written, and he organized the meeting, correct?" I nodded, taking the list.

"How do you know this is Reynard's hand?"

"He draws flip books on the corners of papers. I found one that had his signature a while back. This one, if you see, is a glass of wine being poured from a bottle." I thumbed the corner and let it fall in place, watching the sketched bottle, pour into the glass.

Last I heard, Reynard was healed. So, the fact that he and my wife were missing felt like a hot knife in my stomach. Where were they? It's likely been a week or so since the ship left Manu. Going that route would take close to three weeks if I remember correctly. I thanked Dean and said we should both get some sleep and start fresh in the morning. Just as we came to the open landing of the staircase, a servant came to the base saying there was a female shivering on the back stoop, asking to speak to me. I put my head in my hands and swore. Dean clapped me on the back and said he would see what else he could find on Jurus.

The female sat huddled against the worn wood prep table in the immense kitchen. Her hood was pulled up still, and her hands were shaking. The servant prepared a cup of tea, and I pushed some bread and leftover bits of meat at her. She picked at it and looked up at me. Though the kitchen was still fairly dark as it was the middle of the night, there was a glow in her eyes I recognized and couldn't place.

"Forgive me, *allaíne balaíche*," she said, calling me her beautiful boy, and my heart gave a great thump. She pulled back her hood, her bronzed hair falling in matted knots. "I had no hawk, and left Bania as soon as I could."

I sat hard on a wooden chair. "Naní?" I asked in disbelief, recognizing in her voice when she called me *beautiful boy*, as she had when I was a lad. I hadn't seen her since I was maybe eleven or twelve. She was startled.

"Apologies," she said quickly. "I assumed Corraidhín told you I had been with her." With the exhaustion tearing at each of my mental threads, I was internally slipping down a steep slope. No, she hadn't told me.

"Where is she?" I croaked in a panic. "Where is Corraidhín?" A few of the males I had seen lurking earlier could be heard in the hall outside the kitchen, weapons being drawn should I need them. "Nanί?"

"Your Majesty, forgive me, but I am called Elíann and I am your father's sister. Your mother sent me to the Elders to watch over you. I was with your wife and the other in Bania. She and Reynard went out after you sent her the message. Perhaps to the docks. They did not return. I waited two days and decided to make my way here."

My eyes focused and unfocused on the candle burning between us. It cast shadows on the walls, giving depth to the intricate painting on the tiles around the large oven. The light dappling through the woven baskets hanging above us made eerie striations across the counter. A sense of apprehension prickled under my skin like the split second before one begins to sweat. Though early autumn, Maesarra was still quite warm, and I was stifled in there.

"You are my aunt?" I asked her.

She nodded.

"You left me. I was a child alone and you left me."

"I was taken by Etienne and kept captive. I was only able to get away when he had your sister and her mate captive. He was convinced he had broken me. I have missed you every day, *allaíne balaíche*. Every day. Forgive me for taking a fortnight to get here."

Over two weeks. Elíann had traveled as quickly as she could with no funds. My mate had been missing for over two weeks. Within minutes, the palace was buzzing with soldiers being directed to various locations. I wanted scouts on every road, every waterway and mountain pass, and a small faction headed back to Bania. I made myself sleep until just past dawn before saddling a horse to head to Laorinaghe. Ama brought the children to me at the door. Before I kissed them both, I asked Dean to keep researching and to make sure they were safe by whatever means. He met my eyes and nodded, sucking in his cheeks. Efa held her hand to me. I pressed it to my face, closing my eyes. Images of Neysa on the sea and Cadeyrn asleep came through. Then images of her mummy.

"I am going to get Mummy, my darling. I love you, *aoín baege*." My little one sniffed but simply laid her head on Ama, while Pim began to howl as I walked out the door.

Gods help us all.

Chapter 10

Cadeyrn

Oppressive solitude blanketed me as I pulled up through the fog of consciousness. There was water. A fountain must be either in the room or just beyond a wall or door, but no sound of fae nor beast interrupted the gurgle of water.

Neysa, I tried in my mind.

Nothing. As though the word bounced off a blank wall. After a time, I opened my eyes, saw the tin ceiling and ornate crown molding above me, and knew I was in the palace in Kutja. Heat flared through me. I tried to call out to my wife, my voice shattering on the words. In clearing my throat, I sat up and loosened my neck. The last thing I remember was harnessing the clock with Saski and getting blown back. Before that . . . before that, Saski had thrown Neysa. Thrown her. She was headed to the clock, and it would have killed her. But I remember something about that horrifying me. Beyond the fact that she was injured from the throw. I couldn't pull up the memory. I tore at my hair, sorting through the events before I'd been knocked out, but nothing came back to me. Saski and I had known Neysa couldn't get near the clock.

There was naught but a towel around my hips when I stood, wobbling like a fawn. I staggered to what I assumed was a bathing chamber. Every step across the slate floor must have sounded like a pack of aphrim with my crashing into furniture and dragging my bare feet. Gods above. The water in the ewer was fresh, so someone must have been tending me whilst I slept. I drank the entirety of it, and it smashed when I tried and failed to place it back on its delicate stand. My strength was coming back in unseemly spurts, my healing kicking in. Finally, someone came through the door and promptly left like a crab backing into its shell. I didn't see my trousers anywhere, so I sat leaning against the bedpost. Arik walked in and he had certainly seen better days. "I shall get you clothes. Please sit."

I counted my breaths.

"She is on a ship. With Silas and Eamon." He told me it had been nearly a fortnight since they left. Saski came in and sat beside me quietly. I grabbed her hand and squeezed.

"You chose," she said.

"I need to eat and leave," I rasped in lieu of responding to her statement. She nodded. I saw the necklace she wore and knew it was one that had been in Silas's pocket and satchel for months now. "He does love you."

"That's what he claimed," she said drily. "Pretty statement for an ugly reality."

I couldn't argue.

"Neysa left me something. I don't know what it is. She said you would tell me when the time is right." She reached into her pocket and pulled out a bead. I picked it up and looked closely. It wasn't a bead.

"It's an *araíran-aoír* nut seed. It seems to have a magic coating. It was one of the gifts from the mystics."

"Silas drones on about the trees," she said with forced boredom. I could hear the smile in her voice though. "He said that we are due east of Aemes, and it's funny that where you and he were born is directly in line with where Neysa's family is from."

Arik looked closely at the seed.

"Tell us how to plant it," he said thoughtfully. "Silas gifted us a machine to grind the nuts. Said it had been Neysa's design. Ludek has it."

And so, I told her. Food was brought in as I spoke of the trees and the harvesting, all the while, pushing back the feeling that something was wrong with Neysa. More than wrong. My skin started to burn, wanting to shed my fae form and tear across the skies to get to her. Acid pooled in me, thinking she might not want me. To have this sort of love. This bond. To have it and have the possibility laid out before me of losing it? I had sustained more injuries in my lifetime than I could count. Gutting, drowning, burning before I knew how to use my own damned powers. I'd broken ribs and been impaled. Yet, the greatest pain I had known is losing Neysa. Sitting in Heilig with her halfway across the realms, logistics she chose, I was unequipped to handle this pain. I needed to be in my *baethaache* form and fly free to find her.

Arik left to find clothes, though I didn't bother telling him I wouldn't be using them. I stood by the doors to the balcony and looked to Neysa's cousin who had willingly sacrificed herself. She looked sad and resigned, reminding me of my mate so long ago in that frozen forest in Bulgaria. I walked to her and took her face in my hands.

"If he told you he loved you, he meant it. If I am not mistaken, the only other female who has heard that from his mouth, apart from Corraidhín, is Neysa."

A tear slipped out, and I knew she was angry for showing the emotion. So, I pressed my lips to her forehead once.

"I'll give him your regards."

"I really do share," she said and laughed. A laugh came from me as well.

"I, however, truly do not. There is one mate for me. Take care, Saski." With that, I let my anger and emotion take over and I became the beast which lurked within me. I called into the night, and a second set of wings fell in formation with mine as we soared for the coast.

I COULD HAVE FOUND the ship as it sailed the seas. Neysa's beastie seemed to try to push me off course to do just that. I snarled at her, flying harder in the direction we were going. In my state, the distance could be covered in a few days, and it seemed imperative to get to Bistaír.

Guards scattered and fell back as both mine and Neysa's *baethaache* crashed into the lawn outside the main house. Grass and gravel shot like shrapnel in our landing. I was yelling for Ewan, not realizing that though I was becoming a male once more, my voice was still but a roar. My head whipped to the door to see that puppy-eyed Dean standing slack mouthed, holding Efa. She squealed seeing me and Neysa's *baethaache*, who tromped over to the toddler and let her pat her snout. If I hadn't been in a piss-poor disposition at the moment, and completely naked, I would have stopped to marvel at the scene. And laugh at Dean's terrified face. Instead, I pushed into the manor and made straight for my rooms to bathe and change into leathers and armor. The boy still held Efa when I emerged.

"Sorry, mate, she was insistent that I wait for you."

Efa had one hand cupping the small rabbit her auntie had given her, pressing it to her puckered mouth, hiding a smile.

The other hand she held out to me. I lifted her from Dean, sighing at the warmth and weight of the child. I had missed these two.

"What is it, lass?" I asked her, touching her nose. She pressed a hand to my face, and I tried to not wince at the clamminess of her touch—like she was close to dissolving into mist. Her parents really needed to be home when she did that for the first time. Gods above.

Images flooded my mind of Ewan and Dean searching through papers. Elíann in another room. Ewan leaving. Pim crying, missing his parents. Then questions. Images came forth and her little olive eyes scrunched together in concentration. Neysa. Silas. Saski. Corraidhín. I placed my hand over hers and tried to send back images. I didn't have answers for her. None that she would welcome nor understand. Hell, I didn't understand what was happening either. However, I sent her images of Neysa in my arms. Of Corraidhín holding the two babes. Of Silas making a face. She was amused, but behind it, unsettled. She was far cleverer a child than I could have imagined. Briefly, painfully, I wondered if Neysa and I would ever have a child. If she could forgive me for waiting so long to choose us. Forgive me for going after the clock.

"I must go, lass. I'll have your father back with you soon." I began passing her to Dean, but stopped and considered, savoring the innocent scent of her and the trust she placed in me. "*Mis caráed*, Efa. You and your brother. Never doubt that." *My heart*, I told her. It was my job to bring this godsdamned family back together again, and I didn't want another child thinking they had grown up unloved and left behind. I couldn't look at Dean as I pushed through the heavy front doors, turning slightly so my swords didn't catch on the frame.

According to the guards at Bistaír, Ewan left the previous evening. If I rode hard, I thought I may intercept him. I'd not slept since Kutja, but I'd be godsdamned if I let Ewan take on the trouble brewing in Laorinaghe on his own when his children waited at home. And where the hell was Corraidhín?

The coastal road was the most direct, though perilous at times as it switched back and forth around hairpin turns obscured by crumbling rocks. Still, I knew the road by heart. The sea below crashed relentlessly against the cliffs, sounding like the song of Saarlaiche, calling me home. Whilst Neysa was across the Veil, I stupidly began putting plans and promises together which I figured were of no use. Now, she was here, more or less, and I could show her, yet we were once again separated. We hadn't even had one night alone together since being back. Apart from in the wilds coming back from Prinaer, so forgive me for not counting that. I needed to be with her. To touch her. To be inside her and see the shimmer that covers us when we find pleasure in one another. Above all, I wanted to please her. More than I had before. More than she believed possible. And still there was that gnawing feeling of there being something mortally wrong.

After sleeping one night, the push north continued, and I slowed above the Sacred City, trying to feel for Ewan. It was less than clear if Yva or her cabinet had anything to do with the smuggling scheme, but I doubted it was the female herself. She was a friend to Neysa and had kept in touch with Corraidhín after my mate had crossed. Pressing a coin into the hand of a city guard, I asked him to find Yva and tell her that her friend's husband waited outside the city walls.

"Your servant, Battle King," the guard said with a bow. So much for anonymity.

Stone walls surrounded the city which was built on a slope down to the sea. An olive tree grew beside the wall perhaps a mile from the city gates. I waited beneath it, devouring the little provisions I had brought along. My shoulders sagged seeing the Laorinaghan representative walking to me, my wife's brother by her side. I clapped Ewan on the back, stupidly glad to see him alive and well.

A DAY's ride from the Sacred City was a town called Bacchíus. It sat, much like many inland towns in Laorinaghe, on the edge of many vineyards. Laorinaghe was known throughout Aoifsing for its wine production and quality. Bacchíus was little known to me, as it was smaller and less built than the other vineyard towns. In fact, coming into town late in the evening, it was apparent the abode had fallen into disrepair of late. Few fae lights lit the streets, illuminating the potholes in the cobbled thoroughfare. Buildings were boarded up or shabby enough to not invite a second look. I had us cloaked as there were no three fae more recognizable at the moment than the king, myself, and the wild card representative for the province. No one was out and about anyway, though dim lights shone in windows here and there. Yva insisted she had been informed that Jurus sent her a congratulatory bottle of a rare vintage from this area. It never seemed suspicious until now. Why the shabbiness of the town if it produced expensive wines?

It took less than twenty minutes to walk the length of the high street and end up in the vineyards themselves. Vines were laden with heavy grapes, begging to be picked. The autumnal equinox had just passed, so surely in the morning, pickers would be out harvesting the wine grapes. I could have done with a glass of wine right then myself. I searched my memory for the last time I'd had that either. The night Neysa and I arrived in Bistaír and she told me of the trauma she sustained in London. That she thought I would judge her for her trials made me pinch my nose.

Noise to our right had the three of us turning on a heel. A shadow slunk around a dilapidated building. Yva froze and sniffed the air. The shadowy figure peeked back around, glancing this way and that, then ducked back into the darkness.

"It can't be," Yva whispered. She stepped forward, and I put a hand on her arm. "I need to see him. Closer." She took off, spinning in her momentum like she does. Ewan and I followed at a clip as I tried to keep the cloak on us all. Running through a back alleyway, we came to the rear of a building. A tower rose from the side, cracked and ominous. Stairs wound around the outside of the tower, covered in vines and nearly impassable due to rock and crumbled bits of stones on every step. I looked up to see the figure was running up the structure. There was a walkway to the side of another building. Perhaps this had once been a turret to a manor house?

Yva didn't hesitate as she took two and three dodgy steps at a time. We followed the male who was keenly aware of something closing in on him from behind. I nearly told Ewan to wait at the bottom, but a glance over my shoulder told me he would not appreciate being told to do anything. I actually snorted. He looked just like Neysa when she was set on something.

Damn it, Neysa, I thought. *Where are you?* I wondered when we would get it together. Wood cracked under my boots, pulling my head back to the current situation.

I don't think I'd ever walked on a less soundly constructed footbridge in my life. The weight of all three of us had it swaying, bolts popping. Once inside the next building, the male swung a wood plank. Yva whirled in a cyclone of speed as I sliced the beam in half with my sword. The cloak fell, likely because I was exhausted. Utterly bloody knackered.

"It *was* you," the male said, eyes locked on Yva.

Sconces lit the two levels that were visible from our vantage point. In the low light, it was obvious the male was Yva's brother. His short honey-brown hair was the exact shade of Yva's, skin the smooth tawny shade of the Laorinaghan fae. Both had their whiskey eyes locked on one another.

"Ylysses? What are you doing here?"

The male's eyes were frantic taking us all in. Just as quick, I realized we were completely surrounded. Guards in layman's clothing stepped from alcoves and crates, doorways and corners. Godsdammit, I should have insisted Ewan not come.

"Leave," I hissed at my cousin's mate.

"Not a chance, brother," he responded.

"You have a wife and children, Ewan. Go. Please."

"Don't be a prick, Cadeyrn."

The guards herded us farther into the building, which I soon realized was an old manor home, in much better shape on the inside than the outside.

"Ylysses," Yva said sternly. "You better start talking, because right now it seems you are involved in an illegal scheme and these males are threatening me, your king, and Cadeyrn Bowden."

"It wasn't enough being a palace guard?" Ylysses asked, sweating. "You had to show the world my inadequacies and become a representative? You left me to work the fields!"

"Oh, brother. No," Yva said quietly.

"I have contacts to powerful people as well, sister. Here I have made a living for myself."

"Ylysses, call them off and we can talk," Yva pleaded. "I have missed you these months. I kept sending for you."

Ewan and I took defensive positions, back-to-back, slowly angling ourselves between Yva and her brother. It was becoming rapidly obvious Ylysses was beyond reason.

"I think not, *my lady*," he sneered. Ylysses drew his blade.

Yva whimpered and held her own aloft.

"Ylysses," I said. "Don't do anything stupid. This is your sister. Tell her the details of what this operation is and who else is behind it, and we can work out a deal. Think, my friend."

"I am no friend of yours, *Battle* King," he said, spitting.

An arrow shot up and Ewan pushed me down, saving me. Ylysses ran, and Yva took off after him. Arrows rained down, and based on where they landed, I knew there was only one archer. Cloaking myself, I ran for the bottom of the grand staircase and followed the sound of whining arrows.

My blade drew across the neck of the archer, his last arrow dropping in a limp arc. I grabbed the quiver and bow, releasing several arrows as I backed to the stairs to cover Ewan's descent. Five were down. By my count, at least ten to fifteen remained, but there were so many dark corners, it was nearly impossible to know for sure. Yva was parrying with her brother, guards circling them. Ewan met me, and as I picked off the circling guards, he wielded his twin swords, cutting down anyone in his path. We fought for an hour, maybe more, before it was finally down to three guards and Ylysses. We were more than evenly matched, but all three of us had taken a few blades to our extremities. I was blinking my eyes repeatedly, trying to refocus as my power and even basic strength were failing me. It was a wonder I hadn't burned out already.

"Ylysses, where is Jurus?" I called.

His laugh cut through the sweat-thick atmosphere.

"Jurus? Who knows. He's a pawn. Lower than me on the food chain."

"Then who?" I pushed.

"Etienne."

"He's dead. Try again."

Ylysses's face dropped a fraction. "His wife," he tried.

Ewan swore.

"Yes, but that little bitch won't be a problem much longer," a voice droned from the recesses of the room. I spun and flicked a dagger right where the heat signature was, knowing it hit its mark. I didn't care anymore. A body fell.

"By the Gods, Cadeyrn," Ewan said with more of a reprimand.

I wiped at my brow with the back of my hand, the leather brace catching on a cut I didn't remember receiving. "It wouldn't have ended any other way, Ewan." I walked to the male and kicked him into the light. He was still alive. Barely. "Arneau," I said to the male. "Not at all surprised you're involved, though surprised you ascended the ranks."

He spit at my feet.

"So, you wouldn't like me to heal you?" I squatted down, pulled my dagger from his abdomen, and wiped it off on his jacket. "Francois?" I asked, a light tone to my voice, checking my cut in the reflection on my blade. Not too deep. Just irritating.

"Not far . . . from here," he gurgled, choking on his own blood. "I can show you." He pulled at my jacket, begging me, while I held the dagger to the minimal light, making sure the blood was gone.

"Yva," I called to her. Ewan had Ylysses's arms bound behind him, Yva's sword at his throat. "It's your province. Shall I heal him?"

"We can find her on our own," she answered. "Kill him."

"What? No." Arneau pleaded.

I raised my hand, and he struggled to crawl away. "Where is she?"

"She's already dead!" he spat.

Oh, for the love of Aoifsing. I snatched his ankle and pulled him back, but an explosion rocked the front of the manor, throwing me hard through the back of the room.

Chapter 11

Neysa

Two weeks into the sea journey I couldn't rein in my panic anymore. Sitting on my own, at the stern of the ship, gave the others a reprieve from my quick temper and jumpiness. Silas was twitchy as well, and I wondered how much of it was from walking away from Saski.

He also may have sensed what I had been through and knew. Perhaps they all did. Or perhaps I hid it well, though I bled for nearly the first week straight when I knew I had lost the baby. Babies? I'm sure it had just seemed like my cycle. Really it was no surprise. There was nothing conducive to pregnancy in what I had done in the past two months. The injuries alone were abortive. I just wish I had been with Cadeyrn when it happened. But he was still unconscious in a foreign land, and I had left him there. Left him and miscarried our child. Or children. I supposed I'd never know.

According to the captain, who was still unconvinced we wouldn't slit his throat as soon as we came to port, we were three days out from the Laorinaghe coast, and the shipping lanes would be more congested. The winds this time of year gave us an extra push toward Aoifsing. It was as though the sea itself hurried seafarers along in early autumn to allow them safe passage before the stormy grip of winter. Or so the first mate told me. I liked hearing the fae sea lore, and a handful of the sailors aboard were more than happy to entertain me. The males here were merely hired hands in this smuggling scheme. We were all four spoiling for a fight, thinking it was a full-on pirate ship, chockablock of distempered swashbucklers (though none of the three males with whom I traveled knew the term). However, only the captain really knew what was being exchanged. The crew simply followed orders.

While I was alone, I spun bars of electricity around me like a cage. I knew it frightened most of the crew and our males. Apart from Silas who just walked right through and mussed my hair. I was staring from the back of the boat into the distance, enjoying seeing other vessels bob in and out of sight occasionally. Another large ship began to come in a bit closer, utilizing the lane. I felt Silas, though he was just a whisper in the cut of waves.

"Not much longer, *Trubaíste*," he said.

I nodded.

"Are you ill?" He bent over and looked at me with concern.

I had been eating and sleeping normally, but I knew from a quick glance in a rusted mirror that I had dark circles, like half-moons, under my eyes. Plus, my overall disposition was crap. I shrugged. He didn't need to be burdened with it, and I didn't want to open the floodgates of emotion.

He growled slightly before saying, "We have barely spoken. Are you angry with me?"

Oh. I looked up, and he started at my face, staggering back a foot or so. I guess it wasn't fair to shut him out.

"Not at all. Silas, I—" But then I saw the ship come closer, the sailors on our boat started scrambling. I thought I really would lose my shit if we were attacked by pirates. I mean, really. Silas jumped and looked over the side as the ship came closer.

"Fucking hell!" he yelled. I realized that closer inspection revealed Corra and Reynard, arms bound, being held close to the railing. It really was a bloody pirate ship. Holy smoking hell. A gangplank was lifted across the space between boats. A well-dressed male, presumably the captain of their ship, walked over to ours, where he met with our captain. Silas was seething, and Cyrranus didn't take his eyes from Reynard. I could have sworn Corra winked at me, so I had one eye on the captain, one on my friends.

"Morning. It seems we have some interests in common," the pirate captain began.

"Such as?" Captain Haesting questioned. Eamon stepped beside me.

"We encountered some stowaways on our vessel last week. They insisted they were to meet a ship coming from Heilig, which would be carrying all sorts of lovelies for us to sell when we drop our package off."

"If you are referring to the two hanging from your port side," Captain Haesting responded, "I cannot help. I do not know them."

"Ah, then we shall kill them and take control of your vessel anyway." He whistled, and swords were drawn.

I looked to Corra, who was inches from having her throat slit, and she pulled the water from the sea below and drew it up in a wall between the boats. In one move, she flipped, dissolved into the seawater, and, dragging Reynard with her, flooded our deck with the force of a rogue wave. Chaos ensued as my friends rematerialized from the surge of water. Multiple planks were used to span the distance between the two boats, and males were climbing over. Some used magic and could float, some could shield themselves from our blows.

"I cannot flood the ship as it is filled to the brim with aphrim skins, and that would be a shame."

"Hello, sister," Silas said as he tore his sword through a pirate.

"Hallo, darlings. Be a love and help us get rid of this lot so we can join you."

I laughed as I spun, sliding between two males as they jumped onto the deck. The movement pushed out my self-pity.

"I think we should invite them to the party, don't you?" I asked.

She winked and drowned a group of three before they stepped foot on our boat. The four of us backed up. Silas and Corra linked their mist magic, while Silas and I projected our shared electricity toward some of the aggressors. Sparks, steaming water droplets, and burned flesh rent the sea air. Conduits and electricity working in tandem was an impressive show of force. Our crew were not fighters, though two remained unruffled and steadfast, holding their weapons.

At least thirty buccaneers from the other ship swarmed our boat, filling the starboard deck. Males climbed from the bottom of the ship as well as over. We stood four abreast, waiting for as many to board as possible, then Silas and I merged our power together, creating an electrical storm that met with Corra's wall of water. Cyrranus and Eamon both made for the enemy captain. Out in the open ocean with our gifts, it was really no match at all. Once they were all done, and only a few dirty males remained on the other ship, we had our crew tie them up whilst we transferred the aphrim skins to our hold.

Sunset lingered, and as night peeked through, dampening the sky, the air became more and more chilled. We were finally back on track, spearing for Laorinaghe.

I went to reclaim my spot at the stern. As the last trunk

was dumped into the hold, Cyrranus caught sight of Reynard coming up the stairs. He threw down his sword, and shucking off his armor, stalked to my friend. Grabbing his face, he claimed his mouth without a care for who saw. Reynard pulled him back against the wooden wall of the hold and didn't break the kiss. I looked away, exhaling and muttering a prayer of thanks to whoever allowed them to return to each other. I wanted to cry. Cry for my mate, for my babies, for myself. Wanted to let it out as my hormones had been begging me to do, but not yet. Not until I was alone. Not until I wasn't a burden to anyone else. I touched my empty stomach and drew my shoulders back to walk away.

"Oh, darling," Corra said, her voice shaking. I spun, thinking she was hurt.

"Are you okay?" I asked, frantically. She hurried to me and took my hands.

"How far along were you?" she asked. Corra always knew.

I bit my lip and tried to look away.

"No one knew?"

"I didn't want to be a nuisance."

"You were with children." Silas was closer than I thought, his voice coming from right behind me. "That's what was wrong." He tore a hand through his brown waves.

I nodded, attempting to pull from Corra. I couldn't do *emotions* right then. I needed to get away. Be alone.

"How far?" Corra whispered.

"Just over two months. I think. It was only—" I choked on the word but refused to let the sob come out. "We haven't been together since . . ." I cleared my throat and chanced a look at Silas. "The first night in Bistaír. Excuse me." I yanked free of her iron grip and walked around the other side of the ship and down into my cabin, wishing I could swim to shore. Silas's voice carried as he told his sister that their cousin was still in Heilig.

I had forgotten how much the aphrim skins reeked. The musty hold held the gamey scent. They were cleaned and ready to be made into clothing, ropes, even wagon coverings. Like a leather shop, they retained the oily musk of the beasts. Coupled with the unwashed stink of the bound pirates on deck, it wasn't easy drawing a fresh breath. I walked through the hold, peering in crates until Reynard found me. He hopped on the top crate.

"Hello, Kitten."

"*You* always look like a cat, perched up on things."

"Mmm. Yes."

"Welcome back. You were a hell of a male to find, my friend," I said with a genuine smile echoed in his musical laugh. He was happy. Something long overdue him.

"By my count, you were slightly harder to find, Kitten. So, allow me to be the welcoming committee. Haven't seen those claws in over a year."

"I missed you, Reynard." And so, I told him how he had been the voice that saved me that night in London. He squared his shoulders and gave me a cocky smile that I had never seen on him.

"We have saved each other, Kitten. Come. Let's get some fresh air. The stink of the skins was never something I could take. That fruity musk." He made a gagging sound which I believed was authentic.

We walked up onto the deck. Cyrranus called to Reynard who winked and disappeared so fast it was as if he hadn't been there to begin with. I looked out to the water, the darkness so complete, only the froth of white from our ship broke the inky intensity.

"*Trubaíste*," Silas called to me. "You didn't trust me to tell me?"

He was hurt. I knew he was hurt. I squeezed my eyes shut, then took a deep breath. "Of course, I trust you."

"You didn't want to be a nuisance," he spat.

I kept my mouth shut before I said something stupid.

He looked at me, and realization seemed to dawn on his face. "Ah. You didn't want to confuse my feelings for Saski."

"I just want everyone to be happy." Independent of our forced bond, Silas and I were connected. We loved one another. My love ran a different course to his. Our primal urge to be with one another years ago, and even the urge that forced us to share our gifts, was that of a Goddess who had too much power. What ran even deeper than that, I'd come to realize, was my fierce protection of Silas. My soul-deep wanting for him to be happy and safe. Loved. Though romantically, that love was not from me. I just didn't know how to address that yet. My breath came in a choppy stutter.

"Come here." He pulled me to him and held tight. "You know, I myself am a wee bit concerned for your happiness," he teased, though the undercurrent of feeling was far more tenuous than amused.

I snorted against his chest.

"So, let us make a deal, aye? I promise to be happy, if you do the same. Stop worrying for all of us, and live your life, by the fucking Gods."

"Deal," I agreed, squeezing him tighter, not sure I could keep my end of the bargain. If Cadeyrn would ever have me back with all we have been through.

***

We pulled into port near the Sacred City and sent word to Yva to dispatch guards immediately. Reynard told us of the vineyards, saying he had gone to fetch provisions of wine for the Elders and his father many times. Cyrranus agreed, and so we headed out of the city, though none of us were sure where to actually begin our search. Silas had compiled intelligence on all the candidates and said Jurus, the one we did not vote into Laoringhe, was the owner of a prominent winehouse. It seemed a good place to start. At least until we could speak with Yva and Arturus, to whom we sent hawks. I was one hundred percent certain Yva had no hand in this, and Corra agreed, as they had kept up correspondence while I was in the human realm.

Gods, I was filthy. Even though we had bathed on the ship, none of our clothes nor our hair was fully clean, and I could discern the faint smell of blood on everything I wore, reminding me of what I had gone through. Early morning through the remainder of the day, we trekked through the inner Laorinaghan hillside to Bacchíus, the town where Jurus's winery lay. We arrived just past moonrise, though the sky was cloudy, the moon barely visible. Through the marbled shadows over the buildings and street, we could see that the town was a wreck.

"What a pisshole," Silas commented.

"It has certainly fallen in stature since I was last here," Cyrranus said, far more refined than any of us. Reynard agreed.

Every building had seen better days. It was as though no one lived there. In the whole town, perhaps only three or four windows were lit. The farther we walked, the worse for wear the structures appeared. In the near distance, we could see the vineyards, vines heavy with grapes, swaying slightly in the chilled night air.

"It seems unlikely we would find anything of note here, much less anyone having the kind of coin involved in this operation," Silas said, pulling at a rotten piece of wood that hung from a rusty nail in front of a doorway to a once-stately townhome.

"Perhaps we move on to another town?" Eamon offered. Corra stopped and put her hands on her hips.

"Wait," she said. "I once saw a documentary."

Silas groaned at her.

She backhanded him on the arm. "It was during one of those big wars in the human realm. In France."

"That's what I said," I told her. The males crossed their arms almost in unison. "Champagne and wine in general became a liquid currency to use between warring nations."

"Yes, yes," she agreed but hurried on. "What I watched showed how some of the wineries hid their vast cache of bottles in what appeared to be abandoned cellars. They had their children catch spiders to spin webs across doorways and pile rocks to make it look as though the building was crumbling. Doing so hid the main stashes of good wine from the German soldiers who had commandeered the vineyards and wineries. The Germans were making money from the wines, whilst the poor sods who owned the vineyards, and those who worked them, made nothing. They even transferred dust from rocks and such, and covered door- and windowsills to look like they hadn't been opened in an age. All so there might be something left of their businesses and livelihoods once the German occupation was over."

"I remember reading that as well," I said. It was how some of the smaller wine houses in France survived the war. "So, you're thinking that the town has been made to look as though it is in a state of fallen grace, when really it is hiding its bounty?"

She made a face suggesting it very well could be the case.

"Do we look for the most shite bucket of a building and start there?" Silas asked. I said it was worth a shot.

Our feet dragged, reluctant participants in a bit of wild goose chase. I wondered at the fae response to blood loss and hemoglobin levels. As Ewan told me a couple of years ago, fae were sensitive to iron. We typically had too much of it in our blood. He and I did not, so would that make blood loss more dangerous to me? Would the miscarriage have put me in the anemic zone and that was why I was so very tired? Or was it simply that I had not stopped? Not had a chance to recover from anything. Not had a chance to be held by my mate and listen to the rhythmic thump of his heart against my ear. The song our blood sang when we were together, nothing but his scent wrapped around mine. The world was not perfect. Far from it. In his arms was the only perfection I had encountered. As we walked through that splintered excuse for a town in the wine fields of Laorinaghe, I knew it had been some time since there was only the two of us. A Goddess had looped my tapestry to two mates, unaware of how it would fray the fabric of my connection to both. I had to fight now to be once again worthy of the love I knew I had with Cadeyrn. The love I wanted and would do anything to save.

At the very edge of town, looking out onto what was surely once a manicured lawn that spread to the vineyard below, was a manor house that had every shutter hanging, every door boarded, and even a crumbling turret on its northern side.

"Bingo," I said, wondering if I had ever, in my entire life, used that term.

"What's that?" Eamon asked.

"Oh! It's a game that old human ladies play where they call out numbers and letters and—"

An explosion sounded. We knocked into each other, tumbling in a mad heap on the lawn like bocce balls on a Sunday in June. Ash rained, and the roof groaned, the front of the manor house blown clean off. We all stood in stunned silence, wondering whether we should go in yet, but a pain in my head like I had hit a wall myself had me on my knees. *Cadeyrn.*

Reynard hoisted me up as I started blurting nonsensical orders at everyone. They looked to me like I was raving. Debris flew up from my heels as I ran to the house, hearing Silas swear behind me. Reynard darted ahead, his speed enviable. We were stepping gingerly through the rubble when I scented my mate. It was coming from the very back of the manor, but the entire house was so gutted, I could only make out shapes.

"Fuck it all to never." I heard Silas yell, pushing past me, Eamon and Cyrranus on his heels. A body lay in pieces near me, another a short way away with a sword lodged in his throat. It was then I saw that Yva was sobbing over the body, and behind her, Corra sprinting for him, was Ewan. He stood, wavering slightly but saying over and over that he was fine, and crushed Corra in an embrace.

Where was Cadeyrn? I looked everywhere, knowing without a doubt, that he was there. Silas took my hand and said to my ear, as there was noise everywhere, "I'll find him. He's here." And he kissed me on the cheek before darting off.

Then I saw him. Leaning against the balustrade, blood coming down his head, but his eyes were steady and on me. He raised a single hand. A sad, resigned smile graced his mouth. I couldn't move. It was suddenly so clear what I needed to do, that I couldn't wait a moment longer, and I knew I was going to royally piss off everyone in this room.

I need to do something. I'll be back as soon as I can. I promise, I said to Cadeyrn.

Then, as everyone was distracted with the situation, I ran. There were stables behind the house, as shabby and unkept as the rest of the town. Reynard caught me up as I mounted a horse. I told him he could either come along or leave, but I needed to go. Together, we tore through the night, heading to the center of Aoifsing.

Chapter 12

Cadeyrn

Where she had gone, I couldn't guess. Something wasn't right with her, and I suspected it had something to do with us. The way Silas took her hand and kissed her cheek. Something was wrong, but I couldn't spare the time or headspace to figure it out. If I did, I would chase her or collapse under the weight of needing her, and it seemed neither was the answer at the moment. Cyrranus sought me out and gave me a hand getting up.

"Reynard went with her," he assured me with a pat on the shoulder. It was good to see him, and I said as much before returning to the carnage around us. Yva was wailing over her brother. I pulled her off, trying to hold her. She buried her face in my chest and screamed. It was her sword that had killed him. The explosion caused it to happen. She was shaking, and finally turned and threw up.

"What in the name of all the fucking Gods are you lot doing here?" Silas asked me with a snarl.

"Same as you lot, I would wager." I could see his point though. There were bodies absolutely everywhere, and most, it was obvious, hadn't been killed in the blast. "We need to search the town. I believe Francois is here. She may be dead, but she seems to be a big part of this operation." I said it quietly to my cousin and Cyrranus. They started walking away. "Is she okay?" I asked to Silas's back, my hands shaking. The particles in the house spun around us, wights in the dark, taunting me. "Neysa, I mean. Whatever happened, I just want to know that she's okay." And I did. Beyond my own needs, I wanted her to be safe. The sounds of Yva's wails, groaning woodwork, and the faint down of ash reduced to a white buzz, insignificant to my state.

Silas stopped amidst the flurry of ash and put a hand on my shoulder. I couldn't read what was in his eyes, and I refused to try.

"She will be, brother. Where the hell did she go?"

It was a valid question. I shrugged and told him what she had said.

"By the fucking Gods, that one." He paused as if listening to something, then pressed his lips together and walked off. It didn't do any good having this scandal of the century whilst my head was a furious tangle of figuring out where my wife was and if she were okay. If I sent a hawk to her, she'd ignore it. I knew her well enough. If I followed her, she would lash out. Any instinct at all I had, would be wrong. I had to trust that events would play out as they were meant to. Even if I wanted to tear myself apart in the meantime.

The roof was creaking, more and more plaster raining down as we hurried out, even dragging Ylysses's body with us. We left Ewan and Corra with Cyrranus on the lawn, while Silas, Eamon, and I searched this godsawful, creepy town for Reynard's mother. I looked for heat signatures, which wouldn't help if she were dead. Smack in the center of what was the high street, was a haberdashery shop. Heat pushed from inside, and I felt for anything to heal. Once my gift found something, we pressed into the shop, removing the fake boarding from the doorway. Inside, nailed to a velvet chair, was Francois. She was barely conscious, bleeding still from the hat pins that held her to the chair cushions. Small cuts were all over her legs and arms near arteries, as though they had been made over and over again, allowing her to bleed out slowly, then heal. Cyrranus removed the pins while I tried to heal her.

"I did it for him," she said, pulling on my jacket.

Silas prized her fingers off the material, telling her to let me heal her.

"My boy. My heart. I knew I failed him. I wanted to take a part of his father's horrible existence and make it into something for him. Before I died. Did he know? Reynard—did he know I loved him?"

"He did not," Cyrranus said without an ounce of pity. I was surprised at the ire in his voice. "He believed himself unworthy of love because all he knew from your family was pain."

"Hell, man," Silas said.

But Cyrranus was right. I knew the feeling. I wanted to destroy anyone who'd made Neysa feel that way. If I ever met Caleb—and Gods willing, I never would—I'd pull his balls through his mouth. Francois coughed blood down her dress. She was whiter than usual. I honestly wasn't sure I could heal her. I suspected she had given up.

"I loved them both. I knew. I knew Solange was not true hearted."

I had to snort at her. That was an understatement.

"She took pleasure in others' pain. I warned her that her soul would pay consequences for her evil. I knew she was wrong from the start. Like her father. But she was my child. Etienne, he beat Reynard. He beat me. Anywhere that couldn't be seen. When his funds were seized, I used Arneau to help me establish this business so I could give Reynard what should have been his. I fear I caused you all more trouble. Has he found the clock?" She coughed violently, and ribs cracked in succession. Shit. I couldn't keep up with her injuries.

"He's dead," I told her, my voice colder than I'd meant it to sound. She closed her eyes and seemed to melt. "I will tell you what. If you can hang on, I can heal you, and you can tell Reynard yourself all that you have shared with us." She nodded, slipping into unconsciousness. I worked on her the remainder of the night, falling asleep myself at a point.

By morning, reinforcements arrived from the Sacred City, helping us to clear the town of struggling accessories to the smuggling scheme. While I slept, I had seen Neysa, tossing in her sleep on the forest floor. I had seen blood and emptiness and couldn't fathom what would have made her leave like that. For the moment, we had work to get done, and getting back to the Sacred City was paramount. Arturus organized bringing in new workers to tend the vineyards and clean the town back up, as structurally and interiorly, it was still in shape. I personally needed to get the hell out of there, so I escorted Yva back to the palace in the Sacred City. We placed her brother's body on a pyre near the sea that evening. She watched it burn with squared shoulders and a lifted chin, tears running down her grave face. I would wager Yva was one of the stronger fae I'd known. As strong as my family even. It was no wonder she and Neysa got on from their first meeting. Especially since their initial engagement was the two of them fighting outside this very city when an impostor had assumed Lorelei's position.

"I didn't even know Neysa was back," Yva remarked, as we walked through the wrought iron gates into the palace. Cyrranus walked with us, everyone else had gone in already. Bougainvillea blossoms blew around us, tossed about in the sea breeze.

"She came back, and we instantly left to find Reynard. It's

been . . . a shit storm," I admitted, dragging a hand through my hair. She huffed.

"I saw her come into the manor. Where did she go?" Yva's question was valid. Just as Silas's had been, though I literally could not make myself answer, so I shook my head. She changed the subject. "Is your home coming along?"

"Yes, thanks," I answered, my words little more than a rasp. "I shall head there once we sort this mess out." My home. Our home. Though I didn't know if I would still have a wife with whom to share it. Something was so very wrong, and neither of my cousins were at all forthcoming. My stomach had knots in it I'd never known could hurt quite so bad.

"Please take a shipment of wine with you," Yva offered, breaking my dark train of thought. "You're going to need it." She punched me lightly on the shoulder and moved forward to speak with Arturus.

Waves crashed behind the palace, a faint smell of the pyre drifting to us as the wind shifted. To avoid another pyre, I went to check in on Francois and see how she fared. Not much was holding her in this world. For Reynard's sake, I hoped she held on longer, but apart from him, I didn't care whether she passed away or not. I had no love for the female, even in light of her revelations. She was as cruel to Reynard as his father was, and I could never understand being blessed with children only to treat them as such. Still, I owed it to Reynard to keep her here as long as possible.

COMMOTION GREETED me as I entered the chamber that was set up for Etienne's dying wife. Cyrranus was holding someone back, their feet scuffling on the floor. A crop of pale gold hair showed behind the Maesarran. Silas filed in behind me.

"Reynard," I called. The scuffle ceased. He walked to me, hollow eyes and drawn face. We walked to the hall.

"Neysa told me to come back," Reynard told me in a rush. "She saw my mother. In a vision."

I stared at the pale fae, and I started to shake.

"She's fine, Cadeyrn." He and my cousin shared a look, and I was trying to count my breaths to not react poorly. My temper would serve no purpose in this.

"Your mother is not long for this realm, Reynard," I said, far calmer than I felt. "She is waiting for you. To tell you something."

He sucked in his cheeks and tapped his boot repeatedly. Cyrranus placed a hand at his lower back, the gesture causing Reynard to drop his shoulders in resignation. They knelt beside Francois. She whimpered upon seeing him and repeated everything she had told us. He nodded continuously, tears streaming from his eyes. The sun set, and darkness crept in. Servants lit sconces, their footsteps quiet as they tidied after us. The labored breathing from Francois quickened. I should have been able to heal her, so it was evident to me how the strength of the heart and spirit can affect the body. And her strength of spirit had passed.

"I forgive you," Reynard whispered.

She sighed, and in the breeze that flit through the open window, I felt her body stop working. Her son and his partner stood and left the room without a backward glance. It seemed we were all done there. I stopped into the war room, where we had all planned the battle of Prinaer, and looked at the map. Silas came in, Corraidhín and Ewan behind him. I stared at the map and measured distances. From the desk at the rear of the room, I pulled paper and pen, scribbled, then folded the sheets into envelopes.

"Give this to Neysa. Please." Ewan took the note, intercepting my handing it to Silas.

"Where are you going?" Silas demanded. His sister looked at me, and understanding lit her eyes, though she looked sad.

"Away from here. From this . . . mess," I half snarled, half sobbed, not even embarrassed at my emotion. "Just away." I couldn't do this anymore.

I walked out and left the city, eyes blurred and unseeing.

Chapter 13

Neysa

Ainsley Mads waited on the edge of the Prinaer border, sitting around a fire with her band of unusually hairy fae. I knew they were waiting for me since my approach had been allowed. Nothing moved into their compound which they hadn't approved. Riding hard for two days made the fire, with its sparking embers, look like heaven. I just wanted to get this over with. Refusing the ale, but taking whatever food was handed to me, I sat amidst the Prinaerans. Ainsley had known I was coming. How, I didn't know, but her connection to her province was strong, and the energy of the crystal mines here must have something to do with it. She didn't press me for details apart from my assurance the clock was destroyed. Anger simmered in her still for the friend and commander she'd lost in the caves of Festaera. No one was untouched that day.

Cramping and shaking made sleep uncomfortable, since my body was still adjusting after the miscarriage. Halfway through the night, Ainsley and another exceptionally tall female, draped in a fur asked me to follow them away from the camp. The other was a healer and sensed what my body was going through. She sat me against a smooth-trunked tree and held her hands over me, feeling for the loss which still needed to purge from my body. I focused on her lined face, rather than the feverish shudders tearing through me. Her ears were longer and more pointed than most of ours. Her hands moved over me much like Cadeyrn's did when he healed. I should have stayed with him. Had him heal me before I came here. Though my reason for coming was sound, my thinking and timing, perhaps, was not.

Once the healer was done, she led me to a stream to wash. Even in the dead of night, I could see the clots of blood and mucus rinse from my body. Ainsley brought me a spare set of clothes that were, of course, far too large. The shaking subsided, all remaining tissue and excess hormones in my system having been released. Remnants of the children I would never know had left me for good. Their vacancy was a pool of self-hatred for my stupidity in leaving Cadeyrn.

Though I was exhausted, we set out before first light and arrived near the Mads compound by nightfall. Chimneys puffed, woodsmoke and roasting meats permeated the air. I had told Silas, mind to mind, as I left that explosion site, that I was taking care of something that would help us all find our happiness. And to trust me. Cadeyrn, though. He had seemed ready to say goodbye from the moment our eyes met. My thought to him had been met with a sickening resignation. Yet, I knew this was what I needed to do. If Dean had been around for me to ask, I knew without a shadow of a doubt, he would agree. Memories of sitting in cafés and bookshops with him, discussing the Goddess and nonlinear time came back to me. Would Dean cross back? Would I see him again? Had he become ill or was it too soon? The only vision I'd had recently was of Francois, which was why I'd sent Reynard back. Really, he needed to go back to Cyrranus. They were past due to have their time together.

Autumn was damp this deep in Prinaer. Perhaps most of Aoifsing as well. Rain hammered on the wooden roof of the main hall while we finished up the evening meal and watched Ainsley's grandmother take a seat at the front of the hall. She was ancient looking and as calm as still water. The room of loud, burly fae quieted and turned attention to the female.

"Three deer were born of a strong herd, having lived in the forest for many generations. Of the three, one was a hart, the others, strong bucks who became essential to the herd. The forest was once a place of peace and tranquility, not often peppered with hunters or famine. However, before the new additions to the herd, it was a perilous place to be a creature of good. The herd overcame many trials, striving, against the odds, fire and flood, hunter and predator. For years upon years, the three deer kept their herd safe until it was clear they had to leave and establish themselves among the many creatures of the forest who did not have protectors."

Sleepy-eyed children were now wide awake, listening to the elder Mads spin her tale. I was lost as well, dazed by the fire and the low song of her voice.

"These deer sheltered smaller creatures and became known as protectors of the forest, blessed by the Gods themselves. One summer, a fire storm came to pass in the forest, wreaking havoc on all the creatures. For a time, the three were no longer in favor. Still blessed by the Gods, it was a long, long while before the Goddess showed her hand and introduced the deer to their true purpose in this world. For each it was a trial of the heart and spirit. They knew that even if they were to separate, their familiar bond was so strong, it would always lead back to one another. And so, they went their own ways, finding others to include in their bond, thus strengthening the realm. The Goddess was present among them and would always listen to the sincerities of their hearts."

"Were they ever back together again?" a small child asked.

She looked to be about eight or nine, but she sat with legs tucked in, her thumb firmly pressed in her mouth, so I assume she was in reality much younger. These Prinaerans were so large, it was hard to tell.

"Oh, yes, Lottie," the elder Mads answered with an encouraging smile. "Family always finds its way back to one another. It was because of their separation, that the herd could expand, changing the forest and its wonders forever."

I made my way to the sleeping quarters Ainsley provided me, barely kicking off my boots before falling into bed. Family always finds its way back together. What if one of them makes a terrible mistake and forfeits her right to the family? Would she be removed from the unconditional breast of family? Lullabies and children's stories swam through my mind as I drifted off, hoping the Goddess still held me in her favor as well.

TOO NERVOUS TO EAT ANYTHING APART FROM a tea so strong it could put hair on your toes, I washed and dressed. From my chamber, I headed to the edge of the compound where the temple to the Goddess Kalíma was located. Before entering, I used the dagger Cadeyrn had given me to slice my palm as I neared the threshold. The dagger with its engraving of *Chanè à doinne aech mise fhine. Mise fhine allaina trubaiste.* I am no one's but my own. My own beautiful disaster.

Somehow, kneeling in that temple, those words took on an almost sinister meaning. Had I only been thinking of myself this whole time? Garnet droplets sunk into the earth at my feet as I crouched to trace a circle and placed an onyx stone in the center, drawing a heart with beastly wings. It amused me how that image had started, and it made my heart clench thinking there was a very real possibility that I had used up every chance with Cadeyrn I had been given. There is only so much one heart can take. Regardless, I left my plea to Heícate outside the temple to her sister, Kalíma, and took the stone steps slowly, bowels somewhat liquid at the task before me.

The temple was exactly the same as the two times I had previously been inside. Gilded walls reflected the only light in the pitch black embracing the room. I knew where the pool lay to my right and strode for it. As had happened the first time, the instant my fingers met the water, I was enveloped by the pool, suspended in the womb of The Mother.

"Child. You have returned." The voice of Kalíma echoed, everywhere and nowhere at once.

"I came to ask a favor," I said carefully.

She laughed, distant and musical. "That is a thing of risk, my child."

"I would like to be freed from my mating bond to Silas. Only Silas." There it was. I finally said it out loud.

"That was a gift from my sister. You are her heir. Not mine. Should you not take it up with her?" That sounded quite a bit like "go ask your father" to me. Still, I persisted.

"I have made an offering. I understand the gift," I explained. "I do. It is not for me that I ask. It is for Silas himself. And Cadeyrn. And Saski, whom Silas loves. We are family and will care for each other until time itself ends, but to be caged by a bond that has only hurt us all seems counterintuitive to what Heícate would want for the realm."

She was quiet, though around me, the water thrummed with thoughts.

"Do you not love him?" she asked, voice louder than before.

I took a shuddering breath.

"I love him so very much. And though I know he loves me beyond the confines of our bond, it is the bond that wedges us apart from Cadeyrn and Saski. I know it is selfish for me to want Cadeyrn only. To want to need him only, but my heart is true in its desire. I want for us all to be happy. To be family and not caught in a drowning cage of bonds."

"Perhaps your mating bond with Cadeyrn should be severed as well?" she asked, dark ripples suggestive in her question. Bile rose in my throat, cutting off my air. Pounding in my head and dizziness took over. It would be one thing if Cadeyrn could no longer take me back. But to have our bond stripped again? I didn't know if I could handle that.

"Please. No. I just don't want to hurt either of them anymore. Even our child—our children have lost their lives." I choked. Constriction knit my insides together. As though the walls on my body were closing in as I tried to not fall apart over the miscarriage. Her glittering black face leaned in, inches from mine in this place that was yet wasn't. Her many limbs waved in every direction, before she disappeared into the void again.

"If it is a cage you truly feel you have been encumbered by, I cannot allow it to be so. I can see the altruism in your intent. The personal want and need as well," she added. "But what is love without that desperate want of another's soul? I wonder at the worthiness of the other female. He of the Forest has been eyed by the Gods. Just as your Battle King." Her limbs rode ripples of energy and water. "You have chosen the Battle King?"

I have. A hundred times over.

"Without a doubt," I told her. "He won't . . . forget me? Silas, I mean. He is a piece of my heart." *Like the air that I breathe*, Silas had told me once how he needed me.

"You certainly are brazen to make so many stipulations. I have conditions of my own." She appeared finally before me, her dark skin shining with gold flecks, many arms waving and holding items. "I will release your bond to He of the Forest."

"Without disrupting my bonds to Cadeyrn," I countered. "Both the mating and the *Cuiraíbh Enaíde*." She threw back her head and laughed, arms waving. I wasn't taking any chances on that.

"Clever child. Lucky for you, I have no interest in severing your bond to the Battle King. I abhor cages and cannot allow a child of mine to suffer the shackles of bondage."

Okay, well I think "shackles of bondage" was a bit of a dramatic stretch describing my relationship to Silas. I did love him after all.

"However," she went on, "as the bond was made by my sister, it is more complicated to alter. So, I shall require something of you."

I stood to my full height, my chin high. If she asked for my first born, I may turn the temple into an electric light show.

"You shall be my heir as well."

Oh. Shit.

"You have already sworn to protect this realm as the heir to Heícate. Swear to me now, you will stand as heir to the children of the realm."

"I want to live my life. I want to bear children and provide the kind of love and attention to my husband and family that I have not had the luxury of bestowing yet. I want to think that after our deaths, Cadeyrn and I will find one another in the next realm. If I am heir to you as well," I told her, "I shall be bound to an eternity of your making. I cannot accept. I thank you for considering." Thinking I would be immediately cast from the pool, I prepared for the landing. Yet there was nothing but silence and another thrumming in the water.

"The next realm is what you make of it in this." She leaned in and whispered in my ear. A feeling like thousands of worms rolled through my veins. "You can fulfill your promise to me and to my sister, while being yourself. So kind in her dark way, Heícate thought that having both mates would make your fate easier as it has done for her. But no," she said cocking her head to the side, arms waving like an octopus. "You have found how to love and be a pillar to the realm without needing the second mate. And they would both love you without the bond. Clever child," she said again. "I swear to release your bond from He of the Forest, and though I must insist you be my heir, I swear to not interfere with your life and afterlife."

"Or that of my mate. And Silas. Or any of my family." Again, I was not taking any chances. She cackled again.

"I swear to not interfere with the lives and afterlives of your family, mate, and He of the Forest. You have my word. I do not break my word."

"And you have mine." I swallowed, thinking this could be the stupidest thing I had ever done.

"Be free of chains, Pure One," she called as I was thrown from the pool, skidding my cheek along the rough floor. A ripping sensation tore through me, making me scream and thrash on the ground. In moments it was over, and I knew the bond with Silas had been removed. I felt sick. Even emptier than when I had walked in, if that were possible. But I knew this was what had to be done.

When I emerged, Ainsley was waiting for me, sharpening her broad sword while sitting on a fallen log. She was so tall, her knees reached her ears.

"Is it done?" she asked. I nodded, having no clue how she knew. She pulled a satchel from behind her and whistled for a horse. "Take Sleípnyr. He is a quicker horse. He is my gift to you. Fly like the spirits, Neysa."

"Thank you for your help. I appreciate it more than you could know."

"We are females 'less inclined to bullshit,' Neysa," she said with a smirk, reiterating what I had said to her the previous year when we first met. "You are worth helping, and I believe in the world you and Cadeyrn are trying to create. Go with the Gods, my friend."

I bowed to her, and accepted both the satchel and reins of the, tall, smoke-grey horse with eyes like green fire rimmed in a circle of red. I held my hand to the beast, allowing it to nuzzle me. His velvet head leaned into my touch, and he gave a snort of impatience.

"And will you help me get to my mate, friend?" I asked him, stroking his powerful sides and tightening the saddle. He held his head high and lifted a foot as if to say he would be honored. Without another delay, I hopped up into the saddle and kicked his sides to take off into the forest toward the Sacred City of Laorinaghe.

SLEÍPNYR FLEW THROUGH THE PROVINCES, making double the time I'd made on the outbound trip. We camped one night, my eyes refusing to close, though I sorely needed the rest. By the time we galloped into the walled Sacred City, I was nearly falling from my stoic mount. To the city guards who stood at the gates, I asked to speak to Yva or another representative in residence, or even Xaograos, who had been so attentive and kind when I was last there. I was accompanied into the city and to the palace doors where all three representatives and Xaograos waited for me. Yva looked like she had seen a few sleepless nights herself. They ushered me inside, a groom taking Sleípnyr to brush him down and pamper him.

Thank you, friend, I said to the horse, knowing, without a doubt, that he could hear and understand me.

We came to a fairly cozy sitting room with terrace doors

which opened to the sea beyond. I breathed in the sea air, needing to steady myself. Yva told me of Cadeyrn and Ewan's finding the manor house and clearing it of insurgents. She also said, finally, Arturus grasping her hand for support, that her brother had been a large part of the host. And that she had killed him. She did not weep, but rushing despair rolled off her.

Colorful glass cups holding tea balanced on the trays brought in by serene-faced palace workers. We ate pastries filled with meat and sweet cheese, biscuits studded with pistachios and candied dates. I knew Cadeyrn wasn't here the moment I saw who met me at the gate. The disappointment was a tactile thing I didn't want the representatives having to see. Once we had eaten, Yva asked me to take a walk with her on the beach. As we strolled, she pointed to the rock where I had flipped.

"When you crossed," she explained. "I thought it would be a fitting tribute to impound a sword in the rock to memorialize you. Not only what you have done for Aoifsing, but for you as my friend."

I laughed and looked closer, asking how they got the sword into the rock.

"We have a guard who comes from a family of fae with stone affinity. He was able to magic the sword into the rock. There is a picture of it in my office, dedicating the rock to you."

I was touched beyond what I was capable in that moment of showing. "Do you know where he has gone?" There was a plea in my voice I couldn't hide. "I feel that perhaps you do and will not or cannot say. I understand if that is the case."

She pulled from her cognac leather jacket a folded piece of paper and handed it to me. "One was given to me, one to your brother. I haven't read it, so don't ask."

My heart was thudding so loud I knew she heard it. The faintest trace scent of my mate remained on the paper, dizzying me further. Hastily written on it were two strings of numbers. 38.640388, 34.846306.

I was faced with a swift urge to punch something. I wanted to start throwing knives and flipping over the damned rock again. In touching the numbers, Cadeyrn's face came into view, tired and perhaps... devastated. I couldn't tell.

"I don't know what this means," I said through gritted teeth. I pushed the paper at Yva, and she read it.

"These numbers are insignificant to you?"

"Yes! Completely."

"Perhaps, you could scry?" she asked.

Why hadn't I thought of that? We left the beach, and I was shown to the room we stayed in two years ago. Yva brought in a bowl and salt, handing me a crystal pendulum. It was an amazonite, which is helpful for finding lost things. I didn't know if my husband counted as a lost thing and said so, but Yva told me she didn't want to bring a rose quartz and have me bite her head off for bringing a love stone. Fair enough.

We had a board with basic directions on it such as north, south, east, west. Once I began scrying, the crystal swung excitedly as though it were happy to see me. I asked basic questions to feel for its answers. Placing the note with the numbers under the pendulum, I asked what these numbers meant. It swung in a dizzying circle over the paper, and stopped dead over the top number, 38.640388, then slid straight over to the north marking on the board. I noted it in my mind, but was confused, and rubbed at my face with my free hand. Maybe north was rational, as he would likely be headed back to Saarlaiche. The pendulum spun again, stopping on the bottom number, 34.846306, then scooting to drop onto the east marking. East? Heilig? Maesarra? If Ewan had been given the same note, then I would have bet Cadeyrn was not with him in Bistaír. Dammit, Cadeyrn. He had shut down our mental link. Or maybe I had. I didn't know, but I knew I couldn't reach him, and I was bone-tired. I slid my back against the plastered wall and slumped.

My fingers itched to ask if he still wanted me. If he still loved me enough to let me back in. The answer was not something I wanted to be given by a stupid crystal. What I had done to him—to us—was horrible. After the situation with Silas, then leaving him in Kutja, then the final bit where I took off for Prinaer. I did it for us, yet retrospect had me seeing how unbelievably illogical it was. I broke the connection with the crystal and cleared the objects, controlling my urge to throw them all.

Where are you? I asked, knowing he wouldn't answer.

The question was carried away by the sea breeze coming in from the open terrace doors. If I had indeed worn out my chances, where would I go? I could stay on with my brother in Bistaír, but really, that wasn't my life to live. Starting over in a world still so unfamiliar to me was nearly as unsettling as the thought of being thrust across the Veil. Yva knocked and entered in the morning, finding me curled on the floor next to the terrace. She brought tea and fresh clothing. I snorted.

"You hardly have to be procuring me clothes now, Representative."

"Oh, but I want to help, *friend*. Just don't complain about them." She sat next to me on the tiled floor where we drank in companionable silence for a time. "Take the coast road. Follow it south. Scouts say they saw him head that way when he left."

"Where does it go?"

"South."

I rolled my eyes at her answer.

"It traces the coastline. It's breathtaking and dangerous, just like you." She nudged my arm with her elbow. "Now get dressed and get out of here."

"I may end up right back here begging for a job," I grumbled. She scoffed and threw the clothes at me. I slid into the grey riding breeches, donned the fitted blue shirt, and threw the grey riding jacket over, before strapping on my various weapons. Once my hair was braided back and I had forced down food my anxious stomach was not keen on having, Sleípnyr and I headed out on the coast road.

SHE WAS NOT JOKING about the road being breathtaking. It was a drop of hundreds of feet into crashing waves just a foot's length from where my horse trotted. I rode all day, pushing into the night, but finally had to give in to make a hasty camp. As I drifted off, the stars twinkling above, the ocean crashing relentlessly below, I tried once again to open my mind to him. When my words bounced back to me like a phone line gone dead, I fell asleep singing to myself, Rhia's song.

If I loved you more than life itself
If I brought you brightness to your day
Would you tell me you would light the skies?
Would you tell me I could stay?
If stayed with you and made you mine
If I could braid my soul inside of thine
Could we stay forever thus entwined?
Could we never see the end of time?

THERE WAS no birdsong or dawn light which woke me. Waking found me shivering and listening intently. Pounding in the air, like thunderclaps. Sleípnyr was at attention, blowing steaming breaths into the dark morning. It sounded again.

Not thunder. It was wingbeats.

I stood and walked to the cliff's edge. Smudged against the

still mostly dark sky, was a shape flying. I knew it was my *baethaache*. I called to her, and she flew in closer. The horse was nudging me, though not in a frightened manner. He seemed eager. My beastie flew close but squawked and darted through the sky, toward the south. I pulled up my ramshackle camp and mounted the horse who seemed ready to bolt after the beastie. We followed her for hours, but in the late afternoon, she disappeared from sight. We continued on, but my hopes, which had raised quite a bit, sunk low again. The day warmed so that when we stopped to eat an apple each, I changed from the jacket and shirt to a loose camisole, no doubt meant as an undergarment and not to be worn in public, but I didn't care. It was handkerchief-thin cotton with delicate straps, and probably looked wholly absurd with my twin swords strapped across my back. Though again, I was alone.

In the distance there was a squawk Sleípnyr seemed to know how to follow. He turned off the main coast road which veered left and had run inland for the past few miles. Down we rode on another road that dipped and descended with cypress and olive trees lining the dirt. Along the road we thundered until we reached a house. Or I assumed it was a house. There were gates, but the iron barriers were flung open as though not expecting to be needed defensively. *Must be nice*, I thought to myself. I tried to turn my smoky stallion around, but he indignantly drove his hooves into the ground, trotting onward, even glancing back at me as if to say "Yeah, what?" Stubborn ass. He snorted.

The house was simple stonework plastered over in white. Climbing vines were planted at the base of the house yet were not mature enough to have taken the risky climb along the walls. Each window was large and bayed like it couldn't let in enough light. A terrace surrounded the entire building on the second floor, creating a shaded porch for the front door. I slipped off Sleípnyr to knock on the door, though I didn't even know what I was going to say. I didn't know why I was there, apart from the fact that my tenacious horse wouldn't turn around. I would just ask for fresh water and directions to Craghen, I supposed. It seemed the most plausible. No one answered my knock. When I turned, I realized the damned horse had wandered off. Wonderful. I called after him in a hushed yell, but he didn't respond. My senses were on overdrive, making me jump thinking someone was near me. A hoof print was in a patch of mud on the side of the large house, so I followed that way. What I saw in coming around the corner had me standing wide-eyed.

There were dunes and a wooden deck that walked over them down to the sea. The water was clear and calm, lapping at an incongruous mix of rocky shore and white sand as though it simply couldn't decide which personality it needed to take on. The horse was still out of sight, so I looked round the back of the house. Lounges and tables, small seating areas, and hammocks strung between trees lazed about in the temperate breeze. Someone's beach house or summer getaway. Wistful feelings touched my subconscious, reminding me of lazy days and plans Cadeyrn and I had made.

New wood creaked under as I made my way to the dunes to take one last glimpse of the sea before leaving to give Sleípnyr a piece of my mind. Cresting the dune, I cried out. Cadeyrn was less than two meters in front of me, soaking wet and shaking seawater from his hair. My stomach dropped. His face moved through emotions like he was processing whether I was indeed standing there or whether I was a grey lady, moving through Gothic halls. I scanned the area, looking and sensing for the presence of any other fae.

"What . . . what are you doing here?" I asked. He stood up taller, as though readying for a fight.

"Swimming." No discernible emotion graced his response.

He was wearing only a sort of trunks which clung to his lower body, chest bare. Questions waltzed through my mind, never settling long enough to make it past my lips. *Shall I leave? Do you hate me? Have I ruined us?* There was no good place to start the conversation. So, being me, I went headfirst into the biggest reveal.

"I went to Kalíma's temple," I blurted.

He looked startled but said nothing.

"That's where I went when I left Bacchíus." *I wasn't leaving you*, I thought, though never actually said.

"I see." He walked past me, avoiding brushing my arm. Sparks of pain burst in the space between us. My pain. His pain, trying to hide itself under resolve. I stood there still, staring at the sea, wishing I could let it take me with it when the tide receded. It must be a relief to have a gift like Saski's and be able to give yourself over to the pull of the current.

"Did you find what you were looking for?" he asked, a few paces away. It took several attempts to answer.

"I had her break the mating bond with Silas." I faced the sea, readying to leave.

"Pardon?" he said through his teeth. I repeated myself, still facing the sea. "Why? What did you offer in return?"

I waved him off, trying to breathe through the panic creeping up. I knew my adrenaline was spiking when my instincts told me to bolt and keep running. Keeping my gaze locked on the rolling ocean was the only thing grounding my feet to the spot.

"I am her heir as well as Heícate's," I revealed. "I don't really want to discuss this at the moment."

"No? Then why have you come?"

I couldn't read his reaction. But I hadn't come. I didn't even know where I was.

"Why did you have her break it?" he pressed. "When you had just solidified it?"

I did turn at that, looking at him with confusion. My hand strayed to my stomach. To my empty womb. He followed the motion, jutting his head forward as though sensing something. Eyes wild but his face softened.

"You . . . were with children?" His voice was pitched high yet came out ever so quiet.

Tears spilled out of my eyes. I nodded.

He stood straighter and pulled me to him. I collapsed, finally letting it out. Sobs carried on for long minutes. Calloused palms rubbed over my back. "When? When did you lose—them?"

"On the ship. I wanted you there," I sobbed. He held me against him, his wet chest soaking through my camisole. "I wanted you with me." He kissed the top of my head.

"Does Silas know?" he asked, stroking my hair.

I nodded.

"Was he okay?"

I looked up into his face. "What do you mean?"

He swallowed.

"Cadeyrn?"

"The babes. Were his?"

I pushed back to look at him, hugging myself and shaking. "I never—" I cleared my throat. "Silas and I never—"

"I felt it, Neysa," he whispered.

"We merged all of our gifts, letting them flow through each other. He marked me." I touched my fingers to the scar at the curve of my neck just above the scar from the arrow in Biancos. "It was a solidifying of our bond, yes, but it was not a consummation. The children were yours," I said through a racking sob.

He shuddered and stepped to me again.

"I shouldn't have left, but I thought I could see this through. I just want us to be together. I understand if you won't take me back."

He forced my chin up to look at his face. His nose was red and swollen, tears adding to the overall wetness on his face. "I am sorry I wasn't there for you."

I had never heard his voice like that. Clogged and croaking. His glassy green eyes were becoming heavy and red rimmed as well.

I tucked my chin again, holding my stomach as though the pressure of my arm would kill the stabbing hurt.

"But, by the Gods, Neysa. I am yours. Every ember of my being is yours. I just want you with me."

I dove forward into his arms and cried. Clomping hooves and shuffling talons sounded behind us. We both laughed to turn and find Sleípnyr and my *baethaache* standing side by side, watching us. What a sight they were.

"Come inside. I can stable your horse while you bathe." He gestured flippantly up the stairs. "Third door on the right upstairs is the bathing chamber. There's a dressing gown on the door." He ducked back out to care for my magnificent horse.

"Thank you, Sleípnyr," I whispered.

Chapter 14

Neysa

Wax, recently dried plaster, lemon oil, and sea salt scented the house as though it were new. Every floorboard and crevice I passed in and out of the bathing chamber was spotless. What was this place? Even the dressing gown hanging from the door seemed new. The nearly transparent powder-blue cotton was just a whisper of cloth on my skin after my bath. Before leaving the chamber, I stood staring at my feet, not knowing where to go. Where to meet him. I wished he would meet me at the bathing chamber so I didn't wander, feeling stupid. When I was a child, I was separated from my father in a large store. As I was prone to panic, I ran circles around the shop, blindly looking for him, feeling rejected and alone until he found me and held my shoulders, telling me it was okay. Breathing steadily, I closed my eyes and felt for a tether to my mate in this strange place. A spool of ribbon in my subconscious unfurled. The ribbon led me from the chamber back down the stairs until I didn't need it any longer. I could feel him. Scent him.

Autumn sun had begun its unhurried dip into the horizon in the early evening hour. The white walls glowed with painted streaks of light coming through the bay windows and the French doors which spanned the entire back of the house. The doors were thrown open to the deck, making the house seem as though there were no inside nor outside. Cadeyrn stood, having presumably bathed himself, in slightly loose trousers and a soft cotton shirt, the sleeves rolled up. He had one hand grabbing the back of his neck, the other, it was obvious to me, had recently pulled through his dark hair repeatedly.

"I poured wine but thought . . . I should examine you first." His tone was careful.

"A healer at Ainsley's took care of me. She cleared"—my voice broke a little—"the remaining tissue from me, then healed me completely."

He nodded.

"But I would feel better if you made certain." My feet were quiet on the dark wood as I made my way to him. Above all, I wanted to feel his hands on me again, and form the magnetic draw between us. I knew he felt the same. He placed gentle hands on my stomach.

"May I?" he questioned, hand on the tie of the dressing gown. I stood still while he undid the tie and lay both palms flat on my abdomen. His magic seeped into me, exploring and singing with my own. He knelt, keeping his hands on my stomach, and after a time, I felt a quiver from his fingers as he shook.

Slowly, I put my hands on his head, threading my fingers through his thick hair, and held his head against my stomach.

"I wouldn't have left Bania," he said, breaking the silence. His damp cheeks pressed to my empty womb. "If I had known. I wouldn't have . . ." *You were thrown from the clock*, he said in my mind.

"And had I gotten closer I still would have lost the babies. I would have died as well. I was gravely injured in Bania too. I've had loads of time to think, and the fact is, from the moment of conception, we have been running. Whether trekking to find Reynard, or being beaten by mercenaries and Etienne, or facing the clock and a ship of godsdamned pirates. There was no stability for me to carry the children to term. Look around. I still don't even know where I am. We aren't ever in a solid home."

He pulled his head back and looked up and me, peridot eyes piercing and tragic, still spilling tears. I touched his face and he stood, pulling the two sides of my dressing gown closed with trembling hands.

"This is your house. Our house. I built it. For you. While you were gone." He motioned with a hand. "Across the Veil." Shock must have been evident on my face. "Yva gave me the land, and I built the house for you. Because even if you never returned, I wanted you to know that you had a home somewhere. A beach house." He smiled shyly.

"This is ours?" I didn't take my eyes off him. My beautiful male.

He pressed his lips together and said it was. A home. One that was made for us. This was ours.

"Thank you," I said, grabbing his shirt in my fists. *My whole heart, Cadeyrn. My whole heart belongs to you.* He wrapped arms around me and pressed his nose into my hair. Desire shot through my veins, yet my body was processing both his and the Mads's healing. I needed to sit and to rest, if only for a few minutes.

We watched the light sink into the sea completely, the air cooling. Our bodies pressed close on the settee, cuddled under a blanket, sipping a thick white wine which seemed appropriate for both the location and season. It coated my tongue like salted caramel and pear.

"What were the numbers?" I asked, remembering the note. It had occurred to me somewhere along the ride here, that they seemed to be coordinates. He pressed his lips to my temple while I slipped my hand into his shirt and stroked his stomach. Gods, I missed this. His breathing caught, keeping him from answering. His fingers played at the skin along my neck.

"The coordinates for Cappadocia," he admitted. I turned to look at him, endlessly amused. "I didn't know what to say to you. I didn't want anyone reading what I would say, and I wanted you to know . . ." He shrugged. "I guess that I love you. That I missed you and needed you. That there has never been a small moment between us. So, I wrote the coordinates for where you let me kiss you the first time. I knew them because Silas and I tried laying the longitudinal grid of the human realm over this one—which doesn't work by the way—and I had the location for where you were taken memorized." Heat crept up his face. "Quite absurd, really. Looking back, I was very tired and confused."

I laughed against him, kissing his chest.

"Show me the rest of the house," I said, letting my hand dip into his waistband, fingers walking slowly south. He purred and set his glass down and, moving out of my touch, gave me a lopsided grin that did about twelve million things to my body.

The kitchen was large and bright, cases of wine stacked in every corner. Gifts from Laorinaghe, he told me. There were two mudrooms and an office with twin desks that looked out on the water. Three rooms and accompanying bathing chambers dotted the ground floor, all with a crate or so in them, but no furniture or anything of note. He stopped at the foot of the stairs and pulled me to him, his hands going into my hair.

"May I kiss you, wife?" he asked.

"I might kill you if you don't, husband." I arched into him, not seeing straight anymore. His lips hovered over mine.

"I'd like to see you try, lady." Our lips met, parting

instantly for each other. I tasted the wine and salt on his. The essence of the male who was mine. From the meeting of our mouths came the unfurling of the wings of our *Cuiraíbh Enaíde* as our souls rebraided. He pulled away first, eyes glazed over, breathing heavily. "The rest of the house," he said, almost to himself. I giggled and took his hand to go up the stairs. Halfway up, he stopped, his head dropping to my shoulder.

You don't have to say anything. You don't have to turn around. I just . . . Neysa, every time I see you, it's like seeing you for the first time. You're so beautiful in every way. That's all.

I squeezed the hand that held mine, thinking I felt the same looking at him. But I really did want to see the rest of the house.

The hallway upstairs I had seen, noting the four doors on the right. Having been in the bathing chamber, I knew they faced the front of the house, looking out onto the front lawn and, in the distance, tide pools. A single door was on the left. At the very end of the hall was a small seating area. There was minimal furniture anywhere in the house, but those chairs I recognized from our rooms on Eíleín Reínhe. Easily recognizable were the tufted, raw silk cushions and spiraling carved driftwood arms and back, studded with moonstone pearls. Between them sat a tree trunk, polished and topped with brilliant blue sea glass.

"The tree was the first I cut down on the property."

"Did you build this whole house yourself?"

"Gods no. I did some. Cut down trees. I was always cutting down trees." He laughed. "I helped lay the foundation and some other bits here and there. The glass I made." He ran a hand through his hair. "I was angry. Silas and Saski were doing whatever, and I just couldn't get past it. Missing you. So, I came out here once the walls were up, and set fire to the sand. So now we have a table."

"From what I've tasted of desire, I hold with those who favor fire," I murmured a line from a Robert Frost poem, touching the glass top. A phantom heat came off it. He pulled me back to the top of the hall to look into the first room. It sat empty, not terribly large, but spacious enough with high, vaulted ceilings. He stepped further in, placing a palm on the wall. Shimmering followed, and without warning, there was a set of double doors. Cadeyrn ushered me through to another bedroom so large and spacious, with two alcoves which would perfectly fit beds. It was like a Victorian nursery. I leaned back against him, allowing his strength to coddle me.

"If it happens one day," he said quietly, arms encircling me. "Then yes, this could be a nursery." He pointed to the far wall. There's a room over there for a nurse if we choose. Otherwise, I don't know, we can store your endless supply of socks in it." I huffed. "If it doesn't happen, know that I am happy with you alone for all time." I was nodding, a lump in my throat. "Oh, and it's cloaked to everyone but the two of us for now. I can expand the spell later on."

As we left the room, I put my hand against the wall, a vision slamming into me.

Splashing in the sea. Diving from a rock face. Firelight dancing off bare skin in front of the fire in Aemes, Cadeyrn's face close to my belly. Children's laughter in this room, just outside of my sight. Crystals of every variety alight.

"You're impossible to surprise," he said, pulling me from the room, having seen my vision. We took the last door on the right. Upon our entrance, hundreds of crystals illuminated. The sun had set outside so the ephemeral glow was enchanting. Shelves lined the walls, clustered with crystals and books. "Ewan knew what I was building. He sent the crystals. I kind of thought we might like a settee or lounge in the middle, but it's yours to play with. I just tried to not have it be totally empty."

He was rambling while I was spinning in circles, absorbing the energy. When I was filled with the fortitude of the stones, I reached out and held Cadeyrn's beautiful face in my hands and allowed the energy to spill from me into him. His head threw back and body arched into me, hips pressing against mine. His hands splayed over my sides and yanked me so there was no space between us. The line of him matched with mine, pockets of energy bursting in ecstasy and rolling along the highways of magic existing in our bond. I kept allowing my gifts, amplified by the harnessed force of the stones, into my mate. His face was not of this world when he looked back at me. I was tingling, encasing us in electricity.

You haven't shown me our bedroom.

He backed me from the crystal library, across the hall, and threw open the only door on this side of the hall. The sight of the room stole the electricity from me. I was so awestruck, Cadeyrn laughed.

"It's up to you to decorate. I just brought in a mattress." A mattress which sat on the wood floor, surrounded by sheepskins, and topped with a cloud cover of duvets and blankets. What took my breath away was the entire back wall made of glass. Some spots were doors to the terrace, some hinged windows, but there was nothing to impede the view of the sea beyond. Darkness filled the glass, but in his mind, he showed me what it looked like first thing in the morning. The chamber was large enough to have a seating area and desk, dog beds, whatever we wanted. Our bathing chamber was off to the side, the exterior wall made of glass as well.

"Why didn't you tell me sooner?" I asked. He was fidgeting with a crank on a windowpane, propping it open to allow the breeze inside. "You even said we should start over. You never mentioned this."

"This is where I wish I had a chair to dramatically slump into." He opened another window.

Calm waves danced on the shore outside. I crossed my arms over my chest.

"Saski told me I hadn't chosen us. I argued with her, but she was right. I chose you," he insisted. "You kept telling me you chose me. But you were *mated to my cousin*. And you loved him. You love him. I couldn't see how you really chose me—chose us. At the clock. When you showed up, I was feral. I had chosen when we approached it. Finally realized you had chosen us, and I had been so pigheaded I never accepted it."

"You realize Saski likely told you that so she could have Silas, right?" I teased him.

"That's not funny. And yes. That did come up. You're a fiendish little thing, aren't you?"

I smothered a laugh and opened a terrace door, slipping the dressing gown from my shoulders so I could feel the ocean air on my skin.

A low growl came from behind me. I looked over a shoulder at him.

"Join me then," I said, voice husky, jutting my chin at his clothes. Over my shoulder, I watched him prowl closer, eyes gleaming. His shirt came off and he stood behind me, pressed in close. "I would love anywhere I am with you, but this house—this home—is beyond perfect."

I put my hands over his calloused ones on my low belly, wanting to feel them over all of me. His teeth worried at my earlobe as I twitched back against him, feeling the demand pressing into me. I was beyond talking. Circumstances had us stretched at the seams since the beginning, fighting for this time together. Time alone. His hand moved up and held my breast, the other hand over my throat pulling me gently back to his mouth that traveled along my jaw.

"38.640388 north, 34.846306 east," I stuttered.

He rumbled, shifting the press of him further into my

backside. I felt him smiling as his mouth kept along my jawline.

"I suppose that was the exact location you destroyed me by kissing my jaw like that." And Gods had he ever.

"Let's just say it was a destructive night," he responded, voice closer to the shuffle of water over sand than male. His hand cupped me and pushed me back into his readiness, fingers playing where I wanted them most. It was every part of us I had missed. Every shared look and glass of wine. Every conversation under the cover of darkness. Every time he touched me in comfort or desire. I moved against him in both directions. Desperate for every inch of us to connect, I pushed into him, his body behind me, fingers slipping along me, in me, my vision spotting.

"It has been months since we have been together," I breathed. "I'd very much like to destroy you again." Months of longing for him. For this. For us. He paused, hands shaking.

"Annihilate me," he whispered in my ear, the tickle of his breath moving every follicle of nerves in my body as he turned me, lifting my legs around him.

We were falling toward the mattress, hands in each other's hair and over chest and shoulders. I wanted to feel every crease of skin, every cut of muscle, and roughness of stubble on his face. From the fingers that traced me, I sensed he felt the same. There was nothing in any realm like the feel of his lips on mine. His face hung just before me, black hair tipping slightly over his forehead, making the hypnotic crystalline green of his eyes pop. My thumb brushed his eyelids, and he slipped into me, our bodies meeting flush. My head hit the pillow as his teeth grazed my throat in a primal scrape on the taut skin.

We moved together, a stride only the two of us would ever move within. I pushed up into him, pulling back and pumping forward, my hips leaving the mattress, making him growl. Months without him. A year separated by realms. Every slick bump of us against each other echoed the distance forced upon us. My open hands grasped the duvet as I rocketed through my climax and sat up, still filled with him, and bit down on his neck. He roared and found his apex, then bit down on me, pulling blood from the wound. His healing gift wound around us and knit together the broken skin. He moved as though to pull away.

"Stay," I said, kissing his chest. "Stay, please." In me where, once, we created lives, which I lost somewhere over the sea. "Stay in me."

"Of course." Fingers stroked my face, full lips brushed over my cheeks and mouth. Heavy-lidded eyes watched the rise and fall of my chest, where it teased his own. His mouth dipped to my chest, lips dusting over the tips of my breasts.

"What if I hadn't found you?" I asked in a whisper.

"You would have found me. Just as I would always find you. The only way I'd ever let you go is if you asked it of me. *Misse caráed, misse trubaíste, misse bás á aimserre, misse baethá, am bryth.*" A kiss over my heart.

"My heart, my destruction, my death and power, my life, forever." I repeated in English what he had said in the aulde tongue. Vows as binding as any we had said on the beach in Craghen. He held me close, our bodies still entwined, not breaking the perfect fit of ourselves until the sun rose like blaring trumpets over the horizon.

Ispil of Bogvi, or Isle of the Gods, was the southern-most part of Laorinaghe. At the top were villages and farms while somehow the bottom was uninhabited until now. To the east was the open sea, while to the west was the narrow strait separating Laorinaghe from Maesarra. Perhaps only a few miles across, we could take a boat and be to Bistaír in hours. It was the channel side I could see dotted with tide pools and impossibly inviting swimming holes.

"There aren't poisonous sea snakes and angry mermaids in there I have to worry about, are there?" I asked as we stood on the flat red rock that hung over such a swimming hole. The water was clear to the bottom, casting a teal glow around us. I had no swimming costume, of course, so I was trying my hand at swimming topless in naught but my knickers.

"Not that I have encountered, but creatures seem curious about you so, who knows?"

I whacked him on the bum and took off running and flipped into the cool water. As my head broke the surface, I heard Cadeyrn splash beside me. He came up with a giant grin that had me returning the smile. His large frame cut through the water neatly as he swam off. I followed, knowing I was far less graceful, but being in the water sparked something in me. He ducked into a cavern and waited for my reaction. Ledges of the same red rock, perfect for sitting, lined the cavern. Oyster shells clung to the roof and walls like bog-standard barnacles. However, they were anything but standard.

"Moonstone pearls," my husband said to me, as we tread water. "They were always assumed to be only on Eílein Reínhe. I have found them in every cove and cavern here, and clustered on the sea floor. At high tide, the sea level rises so the caverns are submerged."

I pulled up on the ledge and hoisted myself over to have a closer look. The shells shimmered like moonlight, unlike regular oysters which were grayish and bumpy. These caught every reflection of the water, turning the cavern into a room of flickering sunlight. Each time I thought I had mastered my awe in this place, I was humbled again. Waking in Cadeyrn's arms to the cleansing light that only comes off the ocean in early morning, I had been giggling like a mad woman. Seeing the tide pools and being on the beach helped to heal more in a day than the Mads healer did a week ago. She said the miscarriage wouldn't affect my fertility, and when I questioned how long before I might be able to try for a child again, she looked at me like I was crazy. No delay she told me. I was fae. Not human.

While I marveled at the moonstone pearl oysters, Cadeyrn floated on his back, eyes closed as though relaxed for the first time. The marvel was no longer the shells, but the gorgeous beast floating below me. I sat, legs dangling in the water, and watched his face, remembering how I stared at him sleeping that first time in Barlowe Combe and couldn't have looked away—or looked back—if I'd tried. He turned and dropped out of the float to swim over.

"My beautiful monster," I said with a quirk of the mouth. He pushed up on the ledge, an arm either side of me, our bare chests nearly touching.

"My beastly Goddess," he returned with a heart-stopping smile. The one that creased his eyes and seemed to refuse to contain itself on his face. With every rise and fall of our chests, my breasts brushed him, and I was wondering if I had enough oxygen to swim back. He blew once in my face, clearing my head, and jumped back into the water, swimming away.

Catch me.

You little shit, I called after him in my mind. Laughter bounced from the cave walls, but he dove and swam underwater where I couldn't see him. From the cool dimness of the cavern to the bright sun dancing on the water, I swam, looking for him. A rock splashed near me, having been thrown from another cove a hundred meters away. I swore and swam as quickly as I could toward the cove. Inside were thousands more oysters and, sitting on a smooth rock on a sandy bank, was that beautiful monster, dripping wet. He smirked, sensing that I was a half second away from licking every drop of seawater from his skin.

"Took you long enough," Cadeyrn drawled. I had to admit I liked it when he turned up the arrogant facade. I knew he wasn't ego driven, but he was well aware of what he did to me physically, and it would be an outright lie if I said it didn't turn me on.

I trudged out of the water and strode for the back of the cove, ignoring the heat coming off my mate. Scratches marred the ceiling and wall, and there was an impression in the sand. I touched it and a vision like a snapshot came to mind of my *baethaache* and his, curled up here.

"Seems this is the beasts' lair. Occasionally," Cadeyrn called over his shoulder. "They like to sneak off here in the evening." He was still sitting on the rock, watching me.

"You have separated yourself as well?" I was suddenly saddened that I didn't know this large part about him.

"In Heilig it happened, but I think my injuries caused it to reverse, which I don't understand. I became the beast again. That's how I got to Aoifsing. Once I arrived here and your beastie was here, I separated. They have no inclination to be apart now."

"That's actually quite cute," I said, still sad I hadn't known. My head hung as I looked around. Pressure built behind my eyes as tears threatened.

"What's wrong?" He hopped off the rocks and walked to me, taking my face in his long fingers. I saw my feelings reflected in his eyes too.

"I've missed you," I told him. "That's all. I've missed us. So, so much."

"I missed you too, *Caráed*."

I pushed onto tiptoes to kiss him, once again struck by how fiercely I loved him, and how he was mine. The thought must have crossed to him, because he lifted me and lay me down on the sand, our wet bodies pressed together. I tasted salt on his skin everywhere my lips moved along his torso and legs, and everywhere in between. Back to our lips fastened to one another, I placed my hand over his thundering heart and breathed in. My magic found his and stitched together so tightly, we drew apart gasping. From my hands, I could summon heat, and he crackled with electricity.

"This is new," he remarked.

I drew heated lines down his stomach, sending a growl through the cavern. "Now you know how I feel," I teased.

He responded by pinning my arms above me, encasing us in a shell of sparks.

"You're a quick learner."

A laugh vibrated on my chest as he trailed heated kisses over me. As we made love, our gifts flowed back and forth, no longer his or mine, but unconditionally ours. The sand beneath us turned to vibrant blue and green variegated glass. After, we stood, staring down at it.

"Now we have the top to a dining table," I said.

"It'll be a right pain to get that up to the house." As we pondered the logistics, the sound of *baethaache* squawks pierced the silence. We swam from the cove and cautiously made our way atop the red rocks again. I threw my camisole over my bare chest as Silas pulled a boat ashore.

Chapter 15

Silas

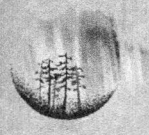

There was enough turmoil in our family alone without dealing with what was going on in Laorinaghe. As bad as I felt for Yva, her brother must have been a complete tosser thinking he could carry on with the scheme for much longer without someone taking notice. We were in the Sacred City for a few days after, all of us hoping *Trubaiste* would meet back up with us. Alas, Cadeyrn handed notes to both Ewan and Yva and fucked off to Gods know where. Ewan and my sister needed to get back to the babes, so it wasn't right for me to stay. I knew Neysa wouldn't want me here. She would be mind-fucked that Cadeyrn wasn't there when she got back, though. I think deep down she thought losing the babes was her fault. As though my cousin would ever bloody think that. He would likely blame himself. I wasn't sure he would be wrong, but what was past was past.

I took my time getting back to Bistaír, letting my sister have time on the road with her husband. Reynard and Cyrranus accompanied me the first day, then split off for Craghen. I had to meet up with them soon enough anyway before I headed home to Saarlaiche. For the first time, I knew it would feel empty in Aemes and Laichmonde. Though it would all be comfortable and familiar, my family wouldn't be there. There was a possibility Cadeyrn would have returned, but I doubted he would leave his mate to shift for herself on the road of that great distance. In fact, I made a mental note to kick him into the next lunar cycle if he did.

Arriving at the modest castle in Bistaír, my entrance was drowned out by my sister hissing and pounding a wood-paneled wall. Following the sound of her anger, I rounded into the sitting room. She had a sword to the throat of that lanky shite, Dean. A guard was standing sentry over Elíann. Ewan looked torn between trashing the room and yanking his wife away. The children were screaming like birds of prey, trying to get out of the arms of a nurse unsuccessfully keeping them held back. I sauntered in, stood next to my sister, and crossed my arms.

"Corraidhín," I drawled.

Dean had a look of near to shitting himself as his eyes shifted to me. A bruise bloomed on his cheek, his glasses cracked and askew. I reached out and straightened them before taking a long sniff. Ah. "Seems he has been uncloaked as well then."

Corraidhín pressed the sword against his throat at my comment, a thin line of blood seeping out. Elíann whimpered. Dean did not, to his favor. He pursed his lips and looked skyward.

"Let's start by explaining why you cloaked yourself, and why this was all kept hidden." Ewan adopted his commanding tone, sounding every inch the ruler he thought he wasn't. However, there was a pocket of hurt in his voice. Dean was breathing heavily from his nose, chest rising and falling close to my sister. "Silas, escort him to the settee please. My love, you can step away now."

"They were here with our children, Ewan," she hissed

through clenched teeth. One of said children broke free, toddling to his mother at enviable speed. She picked up Pim and held him close, breathing him in with her eyes closed. I deposited Dean on the settee harder than perhaps necessary, hearing the wood under the upholstery creak.

"Please," Elíann said, trying to move past the guard. "It wasn't his fault. He didn't know."

"What a crock of shite," I spat. "Then it's a coincidence he met Neysa and followed her back here?"

"Would I be allowed to speak on my own behalf?" Dean asked, a bit cockier than he was in a position to be. "It's all well and good that I am to be mistrusted at this time. However, this woman—female—who is pleading my case is a stranger to me. I would very much like for you to hear me out. Where is Neysa?"

"Not your concern," Ewan barked.

"Is she okay?"

"Tell your tale," I commanded. I didn't know whether Neysa was okay. I didn't think for a minute Cadeyrn was okay, and what they needed was to be together and mourn the babes, yet they were separated once more. Something inside me began to burn. I wondered if I had eaten something dodgy.

"When I met Neysa," Dean began, "I didn't know whether she was brilliant, or crazy, or both. I wanted to be near her more than anyone I'd ever met." Dean ripped his cracked glasses off and squinted while he spoke. "We were friends. When I said I wanted more, she told me her tale. All of your tale, I suppose. She was in love with a ghost she had said. While I wanted to dismiss it and conclude she was truly mad, two things stood out. One, she had too much detail and emotional attachment. No one who was as insane as she would have to be in order to believe her tale could function in everyday life as she did. She was too keen, too good at her career, too amiable. Two—memories—bits and bobs from childhood, flickered in my mind during her tale and in the days after. I was the youngest of my siblings by more than ten years. We look nothing alike. My father left before I was born, so everyone assumed I was a product of an affair. My mother, Tilly, as you know her, thought the sun shined out my bum. But I remember hushed explanations for why I was as fast as I was or explosive in my movements. When I saw Cadeyrn in mum's shop that day, not only did I know him based on Neysa's description of him and the way he reacted to me, I knew I had seen him before when I was a child. It all started to make a sick kind of sense. So, I tried to follow them. The rest you know. Somehow, I feel as though I belong here. Though I don't know how. Did you or Cadeyrn have any sordid affairs thirty-four years ago?"

I snarled, spittle flying onto his lenses.

"You would like that, wouldn't you?" I spat. "To be able to throw it in her face if either of us were your father. The answer is that I have had plenty of sordid affairs. None of which resulted in you."

"And you know this how?" he sneered.

I hit him. So help me, he just couldn't keep his mouth shut. Gods, I was really losing it. And what the hell was burning in my gut?

"I know this because you are *my* son."

Dean turned to Elíann, pressing a hand to his mangled face. "Come again, love?" he asked her deathly quiet.

"You are my son," Elíann confirmed.

"I am my mother's son. And you are not my mother, madam," he seethed. Dean looked at all of us. We, who had scented the parentage.

"Tilly found me near the Veil. I had come across pregnant, in hopes of finding my brother, Elías. He was not there, and I went into labor fighting off Etienne's cronies who had followed me. I had escaped him for a time, so he didn't know about you. I had hoped . . ." She sniffed. "That I could stay with my brother. Or at the very least, leave you with them. Safe. I just wanted you safe and away. I knew how cruel Etienne was. I had known Reynard as a child and saw what his father had done to him. By the Gods, child, I would rather have died than see my children go through that."

"Children?" Dean asked.

"You had a brother. He and I both slipped into the other realm whilst you were birthed, yet Tilly found us and was able to bring me back and save you."

Dean had his head in his hands, shaking it back and forth.

"I made her swear to care for you. Her husband was leaving her, and she was so tender with you. And with Leím, though he was no longer with us."

"Leím. My brother. What was my name?"

"Deánvar," she sobbed. He bobbed his head.

"You tried to take me as well," Ewan said softly. "I remember. I was young. You told me to pack up and leave in the middle of the night. I made a fuss about Haven—my dog—coming, and it drew the Elder guards."

"I'm sorry, *allaíne balaíche*. I tried."

Corraidhín moved to stand by Ewan. Efa tugged his trousers and he picked her up. She placed her fleshy palms on his face and babbled. He coughed a laugh and kissed her. I wondered what she had projected to him. Gods and shite, I needed to sit down, but I couldn't back off that mess yet.

"So, I am your cousin, Ewan? And Neysa's? And Reynard's brother?" He shuddered a bit. We all nodded at once which looked really fucking stupid. "Christ."

The burning in my gut became intolerable. My sister looked to me with concern, as I must have been dissolving a bit. I shot her a look saying to keep it quiet, then excused myself to my room, where I fell to my knees the minute the door shut.

I'm sorry, Neysa's voice said to my mind. Fire flowed through my veins.

What in all the hell realms? What had she done now? I felt like the air had been pulled from me and the vacuum of nothing in me threatened to swallow me alive. Our mating bond. It was severed, and I was shaking and cold on the floor of my room. Corraidhín came in and pounced on me.

"Oh," she said. "What has she done?"

"Shhhhhe . . . ended the mmmmating bond with mme." My teeth rattled against each other, and my sister covered me in a blanket, wrapping her arms around me. Fuck, I felt like I was a lad.

"Is she alive?"

Oh. Fuck. I felt for the threads that bound us, surprised they were still there, even though the bond clearly had been removed.

"Yes. Sshhe's in bbbetween rrrealms, I think."

"Where is Cadeyrn?" she asked, a steel tone to her question.

"Fuck knows." I must have dropped to sleep, because the next I knew, I was in bed, and Ama informed me it was two days later.

"The problem with Neysa is that she thinks she can solve everyone's problems," Corraidhín intoned drily. "I told her months ago she needed to figure out how to deal with both of you. I didn't mean this."

"Well, she certainly figured it out, sister."

"I don't understand." She held up a finger. "Let me ask

you this, darling. You two had finally consummated. Was it the babes? Were they yours, Silas?" she asked quietly.

"We never did. It was different for us. So no, the babes were Cadeyrn's. As they should have been. She has always chosen him. Them. And I would never try to fuck with that."

She was thoughtful. I took it as a bad sign.

"Do you think she's well?" I asked.

"I don't know, darling." She grabbed my hand.

"I nearly stayed. In Heilig." I made myself look at her in the eyes. "With Saski. I love her. But I couldn't leave Neysa."

"And now? Your bond is gone."

"No," I whispered. "The mating bond is gone, but I can feel every thread that links me to her. We are still very much connected. Almost like the connection I feel to you and Cadeyrn. Just not that desperate need. Is it fair? To Saski?"

"Saski will take you no matter, brother. She is besotted. Whether it is fair depends on your love for her. Will *you* be satisfied?"

A hawk landed in front of me where we sat on the top of a small hill overlooking the estate that was Ewan and Neysa's birthright.

SILAS,

Neysa is safe with me here. I hope you are well, as I know what has happened. Please come join us so we three can speak plainly about all that has transpired. Cross the straits between Maesarra and Laorinaghe, near Onnadh, and land at the end of the Ispil of Bogvi. There will be a white house. Safe travels, brother.

Cadeyrn

. . .

Corraidhín and I exhaled at the same time. I gathered myself and prepared to leave.

"Neysa blames herself for losing the babes," Corraidhín called after me. "Blames her love for you and thinks all she has done is wrong."

"I know she does," I said and walked away.

They walked me into the white house together. We three were oddly silent. They were both sopping wet, so Cadeyrn left to get towels. Neysa threw her arms around me, making me feel a bit awkward as she was wearing knickers and a top that left nothing to the imagination. I gently pulled her off me, and a flash of hurt crossed her face, reminding me of when she would take a rebuke from my cousin when he was under Bestía's spell. Fucking hell, I didn't want that. Instead, I took her hand and we sat on chairs that were placed just on the edge of the room, where it spilled onto a deck overlooking the beach. Bloody hell, this was a nice house.

"What did you have to do to break it?" I asked carefully. How horrible was it being bound to me that you would risk Gods-know-what to be unbound? Before she answered, I knew. "The Goddess?"

A nod. The encounter came spilling out of her mouth, and images and bits of the conversation with Kalíma came through our mental bond—which was not severed. I growled and tore at my hair, my face. She sat up straighter as though she had been slapped. I looked at her sitting there, beautiful with wet hair tumbling down her shoulders, the white top completely see-through from seawater, showing every bump of her breasts and belly, every freckle standing out on her face. "For me?" I growled again. "You went to her for me?"

"And Cadeyrn. And Saski," she said. "None of you deserved this mess." She gestured wildly in the air and pointed to herself.

The burning remained in my gut, and I was shocked that there were fucking tears coming out of my eyes. I think the last time I had cried was when I landed on a pointed hilt of a sword when I was twelve. It slid between my ribs and nicked my lung. Cadeyrn joked that it was the sword of the Goddess Kaeres come to claim me for being an insufferable arse of a child. My da roared at him to never say such things, which, by my count, was the only time Da sided with me.

"And you? What about you?" I asked, knocking at my nose with a fist.

"Silas," she said moving to me on her knees. She knelt between my legs.

I batted at my eyes and flinched but let her lean into me.

"I didn't need to be bound to you to do what I am to do in this realm. I did not trick either of us out of feelings we have had. I wanted to be free of what might keep us from our happiness. I do not love you less, as perhaps you do not love me less."

I snorted at her.

"But I want to be with my husband. I want him to know that he and I are the foundation for all we are to do and become, forever more. I am in love with *him*. And to have you bound to me is cruel to all of us. And you are in love with Saski. She is not a fling for you. Now we have our chances at happiness."

I knew I was dissolving a bit more as the fucking tears kept coming. Gods and shite.

"It wasn't your fault. The babes." I touched her flat stomach, and she covered my hand with hers.

She shrugged.

"No, *Trubaíste*," I said, a hair's breadth from her face. Those almond-shaped eyes tried to look away from me. "It was not your fault."

Cadeyrn came back in and wrapped a towel about her shoulders. He had pulled on a pair of trousers. I looked up at him before standing.

"It wasn't yours either, you stupid fuck. And with the way you two are at it all the time, there's no question there will be another *turtarh é slighe* quite soon."

Cadeyrn coughed. Neysa looked bewildered.

"I don't know how to translate that," she admitted. Cadeyrn and I laughed.

"It means *turtle in shell*," he answered. "It's a fairly rude way of saying *pregnant*, putting more emphasis on how the deed is done. I've never really taken a shine to the phrase."

She looked embarrassed. My cousin said he would get us something to eat and "By the fucking Gods, something strong to drink." I heard in his voice the relief of being with her. I knew in a million fucking years he would have moved realms to keep her from going to the Goddess for this. I knew he would have sacrificed himself, her love for him, anything to keep her out of the Goddess's clutches. However, he couldn't keep her away. Despite the guilt he wore, he was whole again with her. She was whole again with him. In this bloody amazing house with its realm-load of magical wards.

After a few bottles of that fantastic Laorinaghan wine, Neysa asked me what it felt like when the bond severed. It was like she had been waiting all day to ask. I looked at her, with the golden light of sunset casting depth to her face, she shined like a Goddess. Saski didn't know, but when she was near the sea, and the sun shone on her, she radiated a light that could have turned the Gods to mortals. Huh, funny I should think of Saski then. I supposed I had to answer, though Cadeyrn looked uncomfortable.

"At first it burned. Within me. Then it felt as though everything in me had been stripped away. I was a hollow ache." Her face crumpled.

"Corrosive," she whispered. Cadeyrn's hand shot to his hair. "Everything. All that I do is corrosive."

"And what do you feel now?" Cadeyrn asked me. I was drunk, and we were being honest for the first time in years, so I told them.

"A bit lost. I am *croíbriste am caráed*. But," I started to continue, but she asked what it meant. *Heartbroken*, my cousin told her. "But more settled. Not frantic as I was. You?"

She smiled weakly. "Settled, yes. You see," she whispered and drew a line in the air, looping the three of us together. "We are always bound to each other. There is no God capable of changing that." The trail she made with her finger left a stream of light which slowly dissipated.

"Really, you just don't like being told what to do," Cadeyrn teased her. She whacked him and drew him to her. I swallowed a lump watching their lips meet, but I was thinking of someone far away. Interesting.

"I also thought there was a reason Saski and Silas were so drawn to each other. And I look forward to hearing all about it," she said to me with a wink before falling back against him. "Saski might share, but Cadeyrn does not."

He laughed quietly against her, making her chest bump up and down. I tried to not watch that. He ran his mouth along her neck and jaw, and that was when I said good night. She mumbled something about the first door at the end of the hallway past the kitchen, but there was a loud thud as, presumably, two bodies hit the decking. Just like rabbits, those two.

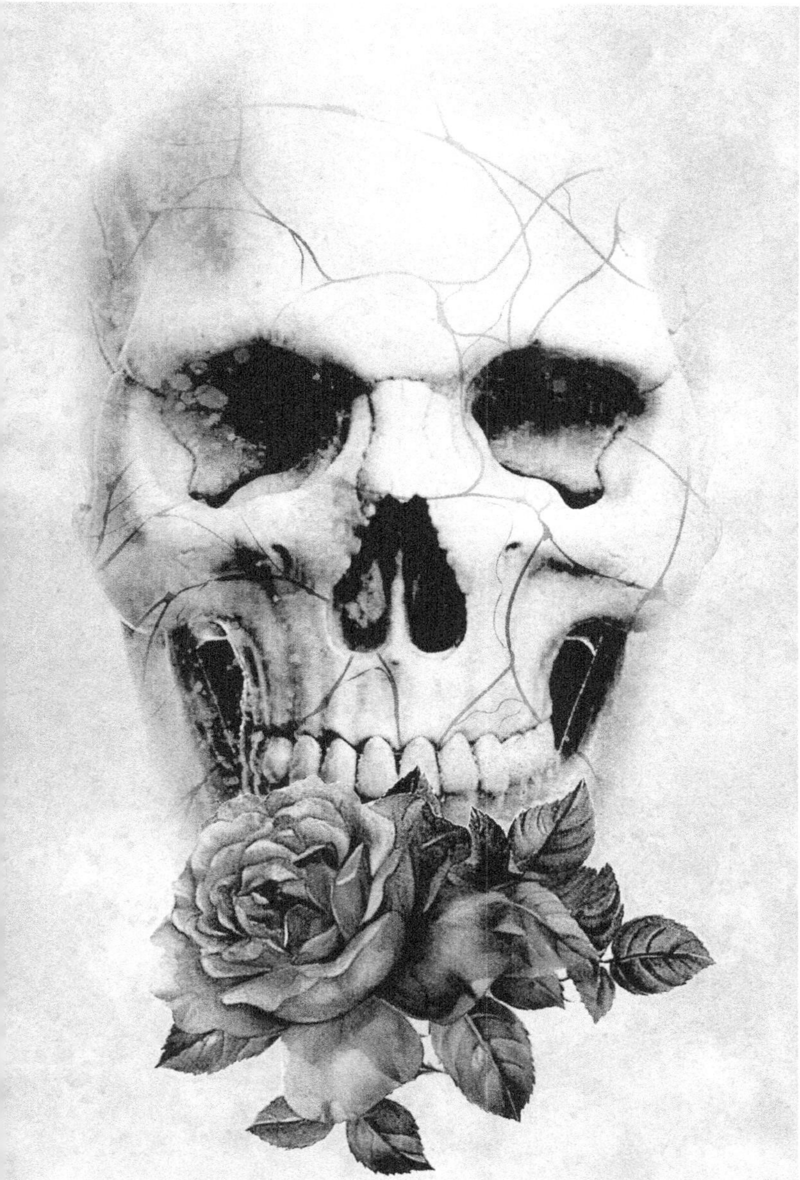

Part Two

Chapter 16

Yva

Fires covered several vineyards in the north of Laorinaghe; they had started a week or so ago. It began with scouts reporting smaller farms and wineries battling the flames on their own. Once townspeople were talking, word spread that it was no mere coincidence that vineyards were ablaze, especially since it had been just under two months since the wine scheme was uncovered. At least once a day, I wondered why I accepted this position. It had cost me my brother, my freedom, my peace of mind, and sometimes, I think, my chance at happiness. Arturus told me I was young still and just as the winds shift, so could fortune and despair.

Over a year ago, when I had heard the news of Neysa's disappearance I was crushed. More so than I thought I would be. Our friendship had a wild start to it, but she was someone I genuinely adored. Her crossing seemed like the augury of the end of times. She came to Aoifsing like the missing brick in a wall that was meant to fortify us forever. She and Cadeyrn shook the realm with the sheer strength of their passion and magic. When Corraidhín wrote to me telling of the horrors which came to pass in the Festaeran caverns, I had all but sequestered myself for a week. I had lost a friend. Perhaps my only true friend. However, it was the realm that I worried for. Cadeyrn was fading more than most realized. I would see him now and again, building a home for his missing mate on the land I gifted him. The care he put into the house broke my heart. He was a thing of beauty, casting a line of his soul into the sea, wishing himself away.

It is because of their own peace that I did not want to bother them with the problem of these fires, though I knew it was only a matter of time before I must inform Ewan. On the desk at which I sat, looking toward the sea, was the stack of mail I was trying to ignore. A familiar scrawl caught my attention. I plucked the grey envelope from the stack, pulled the stiletto blade from my hip, and sliced it open, releasing the scent of bay leaves and blackberry wine.

Representative,

I heard rumors of late indicating you may have some issues at hand in Laorinaghe. The sailors in Biancos taverns are saying land is on fire and perhaps there is someone seeking retaliation for the schemes we uncovered recently...

What was he doing in taverns? Arik often wrote to Arturus and me, making an effort to keep diplomatic avenues open between us. After the meeting in Laichmonde last year, Arik spent weeks with us, getting a feel for our ways and systems, aiding in matters of state. He seemed so much the pretty prince in his flashy finery and arrogance, but he had a crystal-clear head for diplomacy and the academics of intrigue. I appreciated his humor and willingness to listen to my complaints. It was almost as if I had a brother again, though Ylysses was never one for depth of conversation.

... I have been touring the vastness of Heilig, meaning to campaign for the system of change my family and I wish to implement in our lands. You would be amazed to hear the sordid opinions of folk in taverns. For instance, Olde Jym (I

must capitalize the "O" in Olde to illustrate the fellow as a mascot of the general population of those with ale-fueled verbal bowel incontinence), who works on the dock in Manu, was glad we leashed the corruption in his city. Why you ask? Well, he believes that my sister is his soul mate, and he intends to do all kinds of things to her, those of which a brother cannot fathom. Speaking of soul mates, consider yourself fortunate to never have to marry to appease the rules of court. Yes, yes, I know I do not have to, as we are on a path to dissolution. However, it has been strongly suggested by all the governors that I maintain the normalcy of times past and unite my family in Kutja with another Heiligan land...

As a child, like many children I would wager, I wished I had been born of noble stock. The food and riches were alluring. Aristocracy did not have to worry the harvest would be poor and scrounge for food all winter. Nobility were taught how to wield and control their magic. My speed and ability to create what Neysa amusingly called a "whirling dervish" of momentum caused me to smash into things all the time as a youth. The gentry would be tutored to master their gifts, correct? As a mature female, I realized no one was exempt from problems. At the suggestion of having to be forced to marry someone I did not know or care for, I would abandon my position and live in solitude.

... In a Biancos tavern this very evening—I continued to read Arik's letter—*a haggard-looking male who may have once been good-looking, sat opposite me. He would down a mug of ale and cast a glance over his shoulder at a female who was constantly wiping her nose on her soiled tunic. A wet, sticky stain grew by the minute. Each time he turned back around his expression was sour. After he drank four ales, I finally allowed my curiosity to get the better of me. From the anonymity of my hood, I asked why he looked at her after each drink as though expecting change. He sighed and drank a fifth tankard, belched*

in a most impressive manner, and said, "My boy, that is my wife. After each drink, I hope she gets better looking so that I might enjoy taking her home."

Suddenly, I was quite sober. I myself drank my own mug and vacated the tavern, having a go at a belch of the magnitude of the haggard fellow's, yet I find it is not in my physicality to release with such vulgarity. Tell me, Representative, as you are of both disciplined and loyal nature, yet wonderfully untamed, would you have me marry for statecraft?

Your servant,

Arik, Prince (though not for long) of Heilig, Hand to Queen (Gods save us all) Saski, and your Friend and Liaison in all things gloriously boring between Laorinaghe and Kutja.

I SAT BACK in my purgatorial wooden chair and smiled. Perhaps I had another friend as well. If tavern chatter in Heilig was of these blasted fires, then I supposed it was time to inform the other representatives and Ewan. At that exact moment, a large cat hopped onto the ledge of my balcony and swished its tail, looking directly at me. My own eyes narrowed suspiciously at the creature.

"How in the realms did you get up here, *Cathe Sídhe*?" I asked her folding my arms across my chest.

She merely swished her long, fluffy tail, regarding me with a quiet solemnity. Fur the color of burnt sugar covered her body, disrupted only by a patch of snow white on her chest which resembled the shape of a crescent moon. Eyes of warm brown stared back at me. The palace sat on the edge of a cliff, fifty meters or so above the sea. It would have been a feat of acrobatics for her to have gotten here by happenstance. *Cathe Sídhe* seemed an appropriate moniker for her, as only a cat of supernatural powers could have appeared here. As though tired of my delayed invitation, she executed a graceful hop down from the ledge then sauntered into my office.

"By all means," I said, gesturing with my hand. "Come in. Can I get you some tea?" Or something stronger for myself, as I clearly was speaking to a feral cat.

She noticed a Yule bough draped over the fireplace and promptly swatted it with a clawed paw.

"Bah! None of that. If you are to be a nuisance, *Sidhe*, you are not welcome here."

She shrunk back from my tone momentarily. Then, as cats do, she seemed to roll her eyes and move along. A quick rap at the door preceded Xaograos coming to tell me I had a visitor. Before Xaograos finished, Arik strode in and flung himself on my settee.

While I stood with arms crossed, the prince of Heilig lounged on my teal velvet settee. He had a forearm across his eyes in a dramatic shrouding of his expression. The door clicked discreetly behind Xaograos. Dusty boots stayed planted on the floor, but the clothing covering the rest of Arik's long body looked fresh and as extravagant as ever.

"Do you tell your tailor to put as many rivets and ornaments on your clothing as possible?" I asked by way of greeting.

"There's a cat in here, Sonnos."

Said animal decided that was a summons and leaped to the rolled arm of the settee above the prince's head. He moved his studded leather arm to gaze at the cat. It slid down next to him and purred, curling its body into the crook of his neck. When I'd woken that morning there had been a violet streak in the sky that had me thinking it would be a strange sort of day. I hadn't been wrong.

"I have only just received your letter, Your Highness. Yet here you are, far from home. Am I to think you are fleeing a proposal?"

As he seemed content to be cuddling the large caramel cat, I walked back to my carved wooden desk and flicked through more correspondence. The dark mahogany around the office seemed to eat the sunshine coming through the window. A boon in the height of summer, yet in the early winter as it was, the room felt dark.

"I was remiss in my letter not to ask if I could be of assistance with your fire problem."

"The great kingdom of Heilig has sent its prince to fight Laorinaghan fires? You could have sent another letter."

He swung his leg over and sat up, making the cat yowl in protest.

"You would have told me you have it under control, and it would have been awkward, as I still would have made the trip." *Cathe Sídhe* wound between Arik's trousers, looking at him with big eyes. He reached down and scratched her head.

"So now we have an official Heiligan response to an internal crisis of which I have yet to inform the king or any cabinet members. Has Queen Saski sent Ewan anything?"

"Do you realize your cat has your exact hair and eye color, Sonnos?" He succeeded in distracting me. The cat was now blinking at me innocently, and I had a sneaking feeling it was here for a greater reason. Bringing myself back to the diplomatic issue at hand, I tapped my boot in a rapid staccato on the clay-tiled floor. Arik sighed and ran a hand over the cropped dark beard which lined his cheeks and jaw. Finally, his olive eyes met mine. "I left a note for my sister when I left Manu. She should have received it a couple of days ago. I came alone."

I wasn't certain whether I should be relieved or not. On one hand, it did not implicate me in withholding information from the greater system of government. On the other . . .

"Are you running from something, Arik?" I sat next to him.

"Oh, thank the Gods you dispensed with the titles."

"Arik?" Gods, he could run jest around a fool. He placed a gauntlet-covered hand on my knee and looked into my eyes.

"I came for you, Sonnos," he whispered, leaning in. I punched his shoulder and rolled my eyes as he sat back, laughing. "Really, I was sick of playing pretty prince to the Heiligan sycophants who cannot distinguish their golden-hided asses from the holes in which they squat to shit. This seemed better use of my time and effort." The cat jumped up between us and licked its paws. "The cat . . ."

"I don't know what this *cathe sídhe* is doing here, Arik! It showed up five minutes before you did."

He stroked his jaw again and murmured that it was curious. A knock sounded at the door, followed by a female guard whom I had seen best two males in the sparring ring the previous week. She handed me a note. Arik stood leering over my shoulder.

I turned to him and snorted. "Are you my shadow, Prince?" He snorted in turn and pecked my cheek. I elbowed him in the stomach and read about three fires being controlled, but another, far to the north on the border of Dunstanaich, had doubled in size. Soren, the Dunstanaich representative, was calling for aid in keeping it contained to our province. I turned and quickly scribbled a note to Ewan, handing it to the guard to send off to Bistaír. Once she had gone, I sat again and wrote out messages to each representative in Aoifsing, Ainsley Mads of the twin provinces, and with a huff of resignation, Cadeyrn. Once finished, I snapped at Arik to do something useful if he insisted on staying. I immediately felt awful for snapping. He sucked in his cheeks and his nostrils flared a bit. I had insulted the prince of Heilig. Me. A nothing guard from the fields of Laorinaghe. He turned away and shifted his stance.

"Fine," he bit out. Then he shifted again and removed his gauntlets, throwing them to the floor where the cat instantly seized them. The gauntlets were followed by his leather riding jacket. Confused, I did not wish to further insult him by demanding just what he was doing. One long leg lunged laterally, and he reached over it, turning in an arc and landing on the opposite leg. What was he doing? Dancing?

"Your Highness," I said in a scolding tone. He snorted and unbuttoned his shirt, tossing it to the cat as well. The furry invader was plopped right down in the white material and watched the prince swaying and prancing. "May I ask what you are doing?"

Arik turned to me, shirtless and bare to the hips. His deep golden-brown skin nearly matched my own. While my hair was honeyed like the *cathe sídhe* beside us, Arik's was as dark as black coffee. A smattering of it on his chest led to a thin line running between the valley of his abdominals before disappearing into his riding breeches. I was not thinking about what that trail would feel like under my fingers. My peasant-stock fingers, calloused from years on a bow.

"I'm being useful, Sonnos," he answered, taking off his boots.

"Do you need some privacy, Prince? I believe we have different views on usefulness at the moment."

He laughed, walked to me, and flicked my nose, before making to unbutton his trousers.

"That's quite enough, Your Highness," I said, hurriedly. My hands were on his, dangerously low, keeping him from undoing his button, and he laughed again.

I pulled my hands away, my knuckles brushing the stiff strands of hair under his belly button.

"There," he said with a chuckle. "I distracted you for a moment, did I not?" I blew out a breath and turned my back on him. "Feel better?"

He was right behind me, and his bay leaf and crushed blackberry scent came over me. The last thing I needed at the moment was the prince of Heilig making me aware of how long it'd been since I had been with a male. So no, I did not feel better. A little unhinged. Not better.

"Yes, wonderful; thank you, Prince. Kindly redress before your shirt is ruined by that *sidhe*."

Arik smirked and took the letters from my desk. They turned in his hand and blew out the open balcony doors, scattered in every direction by the wind. My eyes were wide and incredulous.

"Relax, Sonnos," he said quietly, leaning over the railing, bare chest touching the iron which wrapped the stone. His dark features cut a striking contrast against the wintery grey sea. "I have sent them all on to those they were addressed."

"You can do that?" I asked. "I mean, you have that kind of power?" He regarded me for a heartbeat, then shrugged. It was an almost humble gesture, so I said, "Thank you."

"I was just trying to show off," he said with a flippant wave of his hand. I laughed and leaned over the rail with him, watching the late afternoon sun glint on the waves.

"You're very serious," he pointed out. "Is that what it takes to be a head of state?"

"I have no idea what it takes. I am the daughter of farmhands who was good enough with a sword and bow to be admitted to the Palace Guard. No one took notice of me until Neysa. Now here I am, pretending to know how to run a province."

The sun was lowering into the early winter sea, a chill

creeping off the water. Though not as warm as Maesarra, Laorinaghe was more temperate than most of Aoifsing. All around the Sacred City, tidings for Yule were being prepared. The cat joined us on the balcony and rubbed its furry body against Arik's bare shoulder and arm. I shivered.

"That *sidhe* seems to really like you," I remarked. He stroked its head, small sweeps of dark hair showing on his hands. I hadn't noticed that before. The cat yowled at me and butted its head against Arik's bare chest. I quelled an urge to smooth my hair.

"It feels for me, as you pay me no mind, Representative."

I shook my head and wondered if his sister was as much of a flirt as he was.

"I am sorry about your brother, Sonnos. I lost my sister" —he swallowed—"Pavla. I may be an insufferable cad, but I love my siblings. The pain in losing Pavla . . . it doesn't go away. So, I am sorry for your loss."

I was nodding my head over and over again. No one talked to me about Ylysses. I surely did not bring him up with anyone. Arik's sentiment surprised me enough that I responded.

"I wish he had died with honor," I admitted in a voice I'd almost wished would wash away with the breeze. "It was my sword which killed him, and he died dishonorably, Arik. That haunts me."

He faced me, elbow still braced on the rail. "Do you sleep?" He reached and traced what I knew were dark circles under my eyes. "I couldn't sleep after Pavla's death. Then a couple of months ago, when Saski was nearly killed . . . it all came back. That's why I had to be away. What of your sleep, Sonnos?"

"It has been some time since sleep has claimed me fully," I answered him honestly. "It is not something I make known. I would appreciate your discretion." I didn't need anyone knowing anything beyond that I was the pinnacle of health. Many here in Laorinaghe were not convinced I was the appropriate choice for their representative.

He hooked his thumbs in the top of his trousers and lifted his shoulders.

"I can help," he said carefully. "I have . . . an ability. One which might help. I couldn't use it on myself or Saski, but it helped Ludek and Mother. I would ask for your discretion as well."

I raised an eyebrow and asked what he could possibly do to help.

"I am"—he cleared his throat—"a siren. Of sorts. I have never told anyone that. Only family knows, so please—"

I walked from the balcony and waved him off. I was not in the mood for further teasing.

"Put your clothes back on, Arik. I have work to do. I leave at first light for the Dunstanaich border. Playtime is over." What was he playing at? I rang a bell for a servant. Arturus and I were due to dress for dinner with the nobility and wine merchants. "Dinner is at seven. Arrive in whatever capacity you see fit. We will be dealing with privileged folk and discussing the issues of our province burning."

"Sonnos," he called just before I walked from the open door. I stopped and made myself turn around and give my most stone-faced glare. I may be lowborn, but I wasn't naive, and I didn't appreciate be treated as such.

He looked at me a moment then said, "You have my word."

Another day of feeling worse, for the night I spent unable to sleep had me seeing only the stark purple under my eyes. Healers hadn't helped. Each said she could give me a tonic to release me to sleep, but because it was my mind's inability to surrender, I would wake in the early hours, expelling anything in my stomach. What good was magic if it couldn't aid in something as basic as sleep? Soren had sent a hawk whilst we supped with the gentry that evening. A page came to me at the table where I sat between Hira, Arturus's wife, and Arik, who was being treated as the guest of honor.

"Most of us have warded our properties at this time, so the dangers are minimal within the boundaries of our wards," Forli, from the family with the largest wine estate in the province, explained. "We must find out what the motive is here. Are we even safe to leave?"

"I assure you, Forli," Arturus began, "when we ride out in the morning, the full extent of our combined efforts will be utilized. We will determine who and what is behind this."

I opened the messages, angling each note to my right where Arik sat. Hira was chatty and had a host of gossip-mongering friends, so I wanted to keep my correspondence from her prying eyes. Her husband personally explained to me the necessity of making certain his wife heard only what we wanted her to hear. My elbow wedged neatly between me and Arik's hip where I felt the hilt of a curved blade. I respected that he came armed to a state dinner. Not the showy, heirloom sword dangling from trousers, but a personal blade, fitted discreetly under the ornamented jacket he wore. He caught my eye looking at his hip and winked, pointing back to the letter.

Soren had his scouts in Dunstanaich detect possible warding fields which were containing the fire to the Laorinaghan side of the provincial lines. They would be sending samples of the soil and rock scrapings so that we might determine for ourselves the type of warding magic being used. This would keep us from heading out in the morning.

"Yva, love," Hira cooed, leaning into me. "I am never used to seeing you in your finery. What a marvelous dress." She fingered the midnight-blue silk of my fitted sleeves. "That neckline! More daring than I thought you would be."

As though she knew me. I had given Neysa my best dress the night Lorelei's doppelgänger was unmasked. I missed that dress. I angled the note further from her by lifting my shoulder. "Thank you. I shall give your regards to my dressmaker."

Arik peered around the front of my gown and then leaned across to address Hira, pulling her gaze from the messages.

"I agree, Hira. I may visit her so that I might bring back a gown for my sister. She tends to favor the same styles and I think perhaps, if she were to see Representative Sonnos this evening, she might ask to see the dressmaker." His interference afforded me time to tuck the note into the fabric of his jacket, as well as open the next message. Arik squeezed the top of my thigh once in acknowledgment. I felt a rush of heat in that brief touch which, frankly, irritated me. I did not need to be *feeling* anything. I had enough distraction with my lack of sleep over Ylysses. I turned my eyes back to the message.

Representative Sonnos,

We recently heard rumors of the fires. Scouts are in the area at present and have been instructed to wait until your party arrives. This is an Aoifsing problem we shall face together. Laorinaghe is not alone. Should you require specific aid, do not hesitate. Corraidhín asked me to let you know that sleep surpasses pride. I hope you make sense of the meaning.

Regards,
Ewan, Bistair

. . .

Slipping the second note into Arik's jacket, I sat back and straightened the neckline of my gown, checking the opal buttons that ran from the center of my chest to the dropped skirts. Of the twenty-eight fae present, I knew only a handful personally. Most regarded me with cool respect, which I understood and so did not rise to the frost. Keeping the major producers from panicking was the top priority of the dinner. I grudgingly admitted to myself that having the Heiligan prince here added a note of authenticity to our plans for fixing the dilemma.

"We have been given full support of the king and all provinces," I announced. "I have been personally given details of how to determine who is causing this tragic inconvenience, and I assure you, I am a shark on the scent of blood. Laorinaghe is my home, and I will not let it down." We made our way out of the dining room onto the terrace for date wine to conclude the evening. The new moon shone no light, so the twinkle of small lanterns was all that illuminated the terrace. I couldn't help but be amazed that I lived here and served the people and province I loved. The nights of not sleeping made me forgo the date wine and stand in the shadows, almost too tired to mingle. Arik caught my eye across the patio where he stood among several high producing vineyard owners. He noticed as soon as I did, a golden-haired male sidle up to me. Opening my mouth to greet the male, whom I did not know, I was silenced by the blade he slipped into my stomach.

The night spun in running streams of lights as I fell. It was an odd sort of dull pain. Feet ran in all directions.

"Don't let him leave," I garbled, blood coming from my mouth.

"Keep quiet, Sonnos."

I was vaguely aware of guards filing in and tittering gentry sobbing whilst shuffling out. Arturus was standing under guard next me. Arik knelt, his shirt off again.

"Why are you always half naked around me, Prince?" I slurred.

"He is trying to keep the blood loss to a minimum, Yva," Arturus said.

"Now stop talking, Sonnos, or I'll need to remove my trousers next."

"That could be a diplomatic fiasco," I said before slipping from consciousness.

Chapter 17

Corraidhín

A month. That's really all the peace we'd had. Ewan's scouts in Laorinaghe reported the fires to him a week ago. It was clear they were trying to deal internally, so he left it alone for the time being. Despite the space he gave Laorinaghe, Ewan had readied his vanguard to move as soon as word was given. Yva's hawk arrived the day we were hanging Yule boughs and allowing the children to play with jingling bells. The tone of her message had me discerning a bit of her emotion, and I felt it necessary to have Ewan tell her to get some sleep. I also wanted to send Dean to Laorinaghe. Let someone else deal with him. Ewan found me cruel toward the puppy dog male. I just didn't know why he was still with us. Though I supposed he was family.

My brother was back in Saarlaiche. He stopped for a night to gather his things, but after the time he spent with Cadeyrn and Neysa, Silas felt his place was home in Saarlaiche winterizing the orchard. I didn't know that what Neysa did was the right thing. It was not for me to say. I did, however, see that my brother seemed less frenzied. Perhaps, if he managed to see his own worth, he might go to Saski. Then again, there was always a strong possibility that both of them were finding comfort in another's bed and would never come to terms.

"Pim, no, darling," I scolded, pulling his little fingers from the bough.

"I'll take him," Dean offered, taking my son's hand, and leading him away. I was always confused when Dean did things like that. Then again, he was quite kind, really. So, I didn't know what my problem with him was.

"Will you be going back, Dean?" I asked before thinking better of it. The room fell silent.

"I don't know. I feel I should stay and find out who I am. Plus, we haven't a clue whether I can go back."

"Don't you miss home?"

"Corraidhín," Ewan scolded me as though I were a child.

"It's okay, Ewan," Dean answered. "I do. I miss teaching. I miss my books. My mum. The months since July I had spent with Neysa, so if I am being honest—please don't judge me for it—I am quite conflicted. We had a good thing going. It would never be romantic. I see that now. For the love of God, I would never even assume to interfere with what she and Cadeyrn have. But we were friends in a way I hadn't been with anyone. I miss that. I don't know if I can make friends here. If I can be as uncomplicated here as I was there. Yet, there is the saying, 'You can't go home again.' It's true. Nothing will ever be the same. So, Corraidhín, I really don't know. I am a bit lost, I'm afraid." He laughed. "And I've spoken far too much."

Pim had been listening to him with intense concentration. Finally, my toddler son tugged on Dean's hand, bringing him down to his level.

"What is it, lad?" Pim put his arms around Dean's neck in a hug. It had begun to occur to me that my son inherited my abilities to see intention. In this moment, I was fully convinced. And godsdammit, I felt rotten for Dean.

A servant came in explaining there were two females at the

gates asking to see me. When she told me their names I squealed and had them brought through. Ewan stood by me, curious. When Stea and Belleza came in, I launched myself at them. We three yipped like a pack of wild animals. Ewan coughed discreetly behind me. When I turned, he had an amused expression on his face. I felt myself blush, which was uncharacteristic of me, so I settled myself. Stea was the more classically beautiful of the two, fine boned, with fair features and blue eyes. Belleza though, looked much the same but for the omnipresent suggestion that she may be about to eat you alive. The sisters seemed no worse for wear having been on the road. Even their silken copper hair was untangled. I had the brief intense desire to run my hands through Stea's locks. Oh, I must not think that way. Hm.

"While my wife seems disinclined to introduce us, I shall welcome you. I am Ewan." He held out his forearm to clasp with each female. Stea leaned in and brazenly sniffed my husband's neck. She hummed in appreciation.

Ewan stiffened, and to his credit, stepped forward and pinned her with a stare and crooked smile. It was what I called his Neysa look. She got it just before someone was going to be rather injured. There was a crackle of power in the air. "Dean, please bring the children to meet our guests." Ama walked in with Efa, Dean with Pim. "Mine and Corraidhín's children, Efa and Pim, princess and prince of Aoifsing." Ewan never used titles, and I rarely saw his hackles rising. A shot of raw desire ran though me because of it. Both my husband and Stea snapped their attention to me.

"Pleasure to meet you all," Belleza said, trying to tone down the situation.

We moved from the front hall to the drawing room, which was still half strung with evergreens. The sisters had been on their way to their parents' for Yule when they came close enough to Bistaír and thought to drop in and say hello after all these years. I told them of course they must stay the night.

Ewan, whose arm was draped over my leg, flinched but said, "Of course," with the most pompous, Cadeyrn-like disregard I had heard from him. Ewan asked how we all met. I did think I had mentioned Stea to him. We had been most open about our past lovers. I, of course, being much older, have had far more, but I was rather surprised at his list. It was a game of ours once. I described how I took a past lover of mine, and he described his own experience, and we reenacted it. Good fun. Surely, I told him about Stea. We had been together for quite some time. Well, for me at least.

Roughly fifty years ago, I had to leave the human realm. Truthfully, it was because of the aesthetic of the time. I could not stand the styles and horrid clothing. The men of the human realm wore atrocious polyester trousers with wide bottoms. It was so bad, in fact, that each time later on, when I tried to watch a documentary on the time—the Vietnam War, crime dramas, and such—I ended up turning it off because, truly, the people were so hideous. So, I left the males there alone and returned to Aoifsing. For a while I stayed in Laichmonde and tried my hand at various things. I helped Baetríz, Lina and Magnus's mother, with her jewelry business. I learned apothecary tricks from Lina. I holed up with a ruggedly handsome orchard worker in Aemes. When I returned from that tryst to my flat in Laichmonde, I sat on my ass for a few months, missing my brother and cousin, and sculpting the muscles in my arms. The women of the human realm at the time were either too large or too thin. None trained, so they had no muscle tone, and I think that being there for so long made me resentful that there were so many beautiful women with useless limbs. A shame. So, I trained until my arms were precisely cut. They are no longer like that you see, because I have not the patience for what it takes to maintain that level of sculpting. However, I will best any human man in upper body strength.

It was during that time in Laichmonde that I met Belleza. She ran a couturier shop, custom making clothing, saddle bags, boots, and so on. I ordered a new set of leathers to fit my growing biceps. She told me that her sister was working on her own body the same. We met the following week for a training session. She filled great sacks with sand and rocks, and we used them as weights. I found myself watching the way her cheeks would brighten when she lifted heavy, or the rise of her chest when she pushed the weight up above her head. We tiptoed around the obvious for weeks. I didn't know why. Normally I just took what I wanted. I think perhaps I liked her partnership in our physical goals more than I wanted her body.

We were all out one evening. Silas was in town, so I dragged him along to meet my new friends. I didn't think Stea had any interest in males, but Silas's presence sparked a jealously in me I wasn't used to. So, I kissed her in front of everyone at the watering hole to which we had come. She danced with me and pulled me close and kissed me back. Eventually we went back to one of our flats. I couldn't quite remember. All I could think about was my hands in her copper hair and getting my mouth on her. She melted into me, her fingers pushing my arse into her. So, we spent a few months in each other's company. Eventually, I had to return to the human realm, and I was bored with her by then anyway. We didn't really get on apart from coupling. In the years since, I had seen them both a few times for drinks. Our time had passed, of course, but it was quite nice to see them. And she did look lovely.

As we told an abbreviated version of our first meeting, eliminating the coupling of course, as no one needs to hear that, the sun sunk lower.

"Corraidhín has of course left out quite a bit," Stea said,

earning an elbow nudge from her sister. "There were weeks I could barely pull my head out from the under the covers, Corraidhín kept me so busy."

It was not in my nature to feel embarrassed for myself, but that did light a spark of something regrettable in my being. Ewan's skin was hot to the touch, though his face remained impassive. I did think if it had been me and not my husband in this same situation, there would already have been bloodshed. Actually, yes, quite sure someone might have been maimed. Or killed. I did think I was rather violent when it came to my husband. Ewan's collected demeanor had me wanting to take him upstairs. I mustn't let that desire out, or it might confuse the situation even more.

By full dark, there was a tangible tension in the room. Dean, whom I would thank profusely, brought out a bottle of wine and poured us all a round to ease the stress. Ewan clapped him on the shoulder when he sat. Stea told me she was still in her muscle-building mode, and she had nearly perfected her shoulders and biceps. Before I could think wiser of it, I told her to show me. You see, my husband was not a jealous type, but when Stea pulled off her top and sat there in naught but a lace band across her breasts, the room went still.

"Madam," Dean said in what I assumed to be his professorial voice. "I suggest you take into account that you are sitting in the private home of the king of Aoifsing."

"Have I made you uncomfortable, Your Majesty?" Stea asked, full of mock innocence.

"It should take a great deal to make me uncomfortable, Mistress. However, I find disrobing in my sitting room for the purpose of rekindling a past affair with my mate, uncouth."

"Darling," I said, my hand on his knee. "I'm quite sure she means no offense."

Ama appeared and handed Ewan a note which arrived

from Laorinaghe. He scanned the print quickly, handed it to me, and walked out with haste.

Your Majesty,

During a dinner with our gentry, there was an attack on Representative Sonnos. She was stabbed in the stomach. Our healers are working on her as I write this. The perpetrator escaped by particle transference. I shall write more when there is news.

—Arturus

I HANDED the message to Dean, immediately calling for a hawk. Stea stood.

"Corraidhín," she said, her hand on my arm. "Can I help?"

"How fast can you ride?"

"You tell me," she answered with a smirk.

You see, comments like that were why I just couldn't get on with her for very long.

I SENT her off to Craghen to retrieve Cyrranus and Reynard. There was something about the stillness in Belleza I felt put off by. Rather than spare the time to sort it out, I had Ama show her to a room and I mentioned to a guard to keep watch.

Ewan was in his study, writing to everyone concerned. Saski needed to be made aware that he was doing all he could as well, seeing as her brother had been in danger. I sent off my hawk and told him such. He grunted at me and continued folding letters, handing them to a waiting staff member. I stood, tapping my foot until the final note was handed over, the staff gone. My husband remained turned from me, and I had a roiling in my gut I didn't care for. At my touch, he tensed and reached for the pen. It was only to give him something to do. Even without my gift I could see that.

"She has to go, Corraidhín."

I said I sent her to fetch the males in Craghen.

He swore and yanked at his hair. "You trust her? Because I don't. No one in their right mind would come into someone's home and behave as she has. When she returns, I want them gone. Immediately."

"We cannot turn them out in the middle of the night, Ewan."

His eyes bored into me; his cheeks flushed in anger.

"Don't be a jealous buffoon."

"I do not know what a buffoon is, but it's not about being jealous, Corraidhín. She's actively trying to bed you. In front of me. It is untrustworthy."

I placed a hand on his heated cheeks and moved closer to him as he spoke.

"When someone knows you are committed to another and they pursue you, it is a red flag on their personality. Someone like that has little integrity, and by the Gods, Corraidhín, if there is one thing I will not excuse in someone, it's a lack of integrity."

He had a point. Regardless of my friendship with Stea, her behavior was lacking in principle. I may swim in the sea of grey morality, but trustworthiness was of import to me. Still, I attempted to appeal to his nature as my mate.

"And yet, I want only you." My hand slid down him. He shifted his eyes to mine, and he lifted my shirt overhead. I had become quite fond of lingerie in the human realm and had scores of it in my houses. The white triangles of floral lace I wore allowed a veiled view of my assets behind the material. Ewan drew fingertips over the lace, still pursing his lips in anger. I released him long enough to step from my trousers. Matching white strings of ribbon and lace covered me. He was wound as tight as a clock.

"And can you tell me it wasn't desire I scented on you earlier?" He laid a hand on me, slipping fingers into the sides of the lace. "I had a flash of the two of you in bed."

"I have a very good memory," I said breathless, wondering when he started having visions. "The desire was for you." His face was still stony and splotched with red. "Only you."

"And do you regret not having breasts to fondle?" He pulled his fingers from me and kneaded my breasts through the lace.

"I have no regrets, Ewan," I said, looking at his structured face with his olive-green almond-shaped eyes, and his nearly crimson lips.

"Then why has she gotten you so hot this evening?" He stepped away from me, crossing his arms over his chest, and I was stunned. "I could feel the want in both of you."

I was getting angry.

"When I was with Stea briefly all those years ago, I was searching. I know now, boy, that I was searching for you. So, yes, I remember the feel of taking her to bed. It excites me that I had that time with her, and that now and forever all I want is you between my legs, and to see your eyes looking up at me. If you wish to continue to be upset with me because of my past, then it is up to you. I will not stand here, offering myself to you, any longer."

It was silent for a beat too long. I moved to gather my clothing. Ewan knelt before me, stilling the hand that reached for my shirt. He pulled my face to his and kissed me, lips hungry against mine. I pulled him on top of me and he moved deft fingers until I broke, begging for more. Though I had no desire to stop, we could hear boots downstairs, and we knew it was time to get back down. I paused at the door and called back to him, where he stood washing in the bathing chamber at the back of his office.

"Later this evening," I promised, "I will show you the only things on my mind. They all center around you. Prepare yourself, *husband*," I told him. He smirked, eyes narrowing in amusement and well, if I must admit, love.

Chapter 18

Reynard

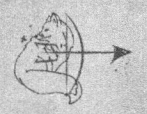

As a representative of Maesarra, Cyrranus was given the lease to a home in Craghen. In the beginning, he balked and protested, saying he could afford his own house. Once we returned there after I had been taken hostage by my dreadful, now-dead father . . . Once we found one another on that blasted pirate ship in the middle of Saen Daíthaen, the Sea of the Old Gods, he changed his mind. That hellcat Corraidhín made certain in all my healing after being tortured, in all my misery from not knowing if this male I loved had been killed or was being tortured as I had been, that I kept my strength. She told me Cyrranus would only want me back whole, and so I trained harder. She regaled me with stories of some rotund human king named Henry who had eight wives. Hearing about his festering toe wound was enough to keep me fit.

Once the ship was cleared of pirates, and Cyrranus and I caught sight of one another, his hands were on me, and his mouth was on my face, my neck, my ears, promising a lifetime. Promising everything I never had with another. Promising a home together. Well, we moved into the representative's quarters that overlooked the small harbor in Craghen. Which is where I was the evening we heard of the Laorinaghan problem.

Dinner was finished, Cyrranus ushering guests from our home while I made my way out to the grassy lawn behind the house. It was a flat stretch of green that dropped at the end, sloping down a gravelly hillside until it met private docks of the harbor. Voices of servants and grooms carried on the warm breeze. Pulling at my cravat to attempt to loosen the day, I hopped to the retaining wall on the southern-most end of the garden. A couple meters off the ground, I was able to tuck into the shadows and look to the sky, the new moon keeping it dark, allowing the stars to shine brighter. I wasn't at my best that evening. Sometimes I found it harder to shut off a century's worth of reactive theatrics. This evening had been one of those, and I pushed too hard with one of the area nobility. Cyrranus was a surprise candidate for representative, so I should be more tactful in my approach to the fae we entertain, since they were always scrutinizing him. As I said, it was no small thing to flip such ingrained behavior on its head.

Once atop the clay wall, I yanked the cravat clean from my neck and let my head hang back. Hearing a heavier shuffle of boots and a grunt, I smiled to myself. He was never one for stealth.

"You make it difficult to find you," Cyrranus said, hoisting himself over the lip of the wall. "We do have lounge chairs." He too had pulled the neck of his shirt open and mussed the tidiness of his owl-feather-brown hair. I purred.

"I like being on top," I said, bending my knee, the sole of my boot resting against a tree behind me. He chuckled, the sound shaky and dark. In the shadowed night, far from the servants' eyes, or the comfort of the home that was perpetually just a tad too warm, there was a pregnant lull.

"Like moss on a boulder?" he teased, stepping closer. His

frame shifted in his shirt, moving toward me in the hidden pocket of evening.

"Only if you are the stone beneath me. Let's see if you can fill that role, darling." I reached between us. His body, larger than my own, fell against me, legs on either side of mine. I could feel him pushing into me. "Mm, yes. If I must be moss, you have fulfilled your role." His chest rumbled against mine. I grabbed the hair at the back of his head and pulled his face to my neck. Teeth worried at the tender skin where my neck and shoulder meet. Memories rushed in of his marking me, incisors tearing my skin as I lost myself completely in his arms. The night we knew for certain we were mates and not just lovers.

"I'm sorry for my antics," I said, hardly any breath in me. "I remembered that couple from when I was young."

"He was a shit-stirring boil on the arse of Maesarra. Think nothing of it," Cyrranus responded. I pulled his head back to look at me, and found I had nothing of import to say.

Hands fumbled with breeches. When lights flared from the house, hoofbeats punctuated our interlude.

"We have company," I breathed, bad naturedly against his mouth. We stopped our movements, attempting to catch our breaths. "I can string a bow from this tree limb and simply take out whoever it is."

He laughed against me, taking a deep breath.

"Representative Maison!" a female called from below.

"By the Gods, I cannot go down there like this," he whispered, gesturing to the evidence of our tryst. "Who the devil is it at this hour?"

"I have come from Bistaír to fetch you," she called.

I knew she could neither see nor hear us. We were but a presence. "Go run toward the harbor and back up. I'll take the measure of her."

I skipped off the wall before he agreed. Before she knew I was coming, I appeared behind this copper-haired female.

"Weel, weel," I crooned in the voice that made people think I was a few marbles short. "With biceps like those, Starfish, I might make an exception to my general preferences."

She whirled, a pair of knives in slender hands, her grip showing veins running the length of the forearms. My foot came up and knocked the blades in a hair's breadth of a second.

"I seek the representative. I've news for him." She briefly explained knowing Corraidhín, and at once I knew there was a history there. I led her into the receiving room of the house where Cyrranus waited, iced water in hand. She looked between us and had the gall to laugh.

"Now, Starfish, don't be cheeky. Say what you need, lest I put an arrow in your arse and my mate boots you out the front door as I've the feeling Ewan wished to do."

Cyrranus looked at me curiously. The female took a breath and swept her braid back over a shoulder.

"There is a crisis in Laorinaghe. One of the representatives has been attacked in the palace. The prince of Heilig was also in attendance."

I circled her while Cyrranus asked for more details and had a servant send a hawk to Ewan and Cadeyrn. Something about her piqued my predatorial instincts. Cyrranus noticed and kept her talking. The leathers she wore were new and hand stitched so intricately it put the needlework of my father's aphrim clothiers to shame. I ran a finger up her bicep —it was twice the size of my own, though half the size of the male with whom I shared a bed.

"Why were you sent? A hawk would have been faster." I was standing before her in a blink, lucky arrowhead pressed to her throat. It was the arrow I had initially shot at Neysa in the jungle so long ago. Not the one which struck Corraidhín, but the first I shot. I'd had a clear line to the spot between her brows, which I decided last second to make a warning instead. I kept the arrowhead, because had I not, my life would be so very different. I would be the same unlovable miscreant I had been, and the realms might not even exist. I may have saved the female, but she sure as hell saved us all.

"Corraidhín sent me," the midnight rider said. "I ride fast."

"Mmm. As do I. Still." I stood beside my mate before she had a chance to realize I'd moved. "You have delivered your piece. You may go." She looked aghast and crossed her impressively built arms. A breeze swept in, rustling the papers on the sideboard. I may not have a true gift, but something in that breeze contained a message of ill content. By the straightening of my mate's shoulders, I could tell he felt it too.

Sentries opened the door to the receiving room and held them for the female to exit. She shifted and blew out a breath before turning in a huff to leave.

"Starfish," I called.

"Stea," she spat. "My name is Stea Ledermaín of Saarlaiche. I am no starfish."

"Starfish are opportunistic feeders hiding behind beautiful armor. Tell me, Stea Ledermaín. Why have you reappeared in Corraidhín's life at this particular moment in time?"

She turned on a booted heel and left, heavy footsteps echoing down the limestone floors. The sentries shut the doors while I spun to Cyrranus.

"How could you have possibly known that quickly that she had been a . . ." He flapped his hand. "An acquaintance of Corraidhín?"

"Apart from the faint scent of my little hellcat on her, and the smell of desperation?" I laughed. "When I was indentured to the Elders, I had to find out all I could on Cadeyrn and his cousins. I trailed Corraidhín for a few months when she came back to Laichmonde maybe a half century ago or so. If I remember correctly, Starfish has a sister who owns a shop of some sort which was a front for something else. It wasn't anything I cared about, so I never looked into it."

"Shit."

"Mmm."

"Reynard, I hate to ask it but . . ."

"Darling, I'm already on my way. I'll head out as soon as we finish what we started earlier."

"Thank the Gods," he said and turned me around, my back pressed to his front. I gripped the back of the divan as his teeth scraped the back of my neck, and we did indeed finish.

Chapter 19

Silas

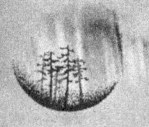

Some time had passed since I'd spent the Yule season in Aemes. Saarlaiche in winter gnawed at every bone and joint, leaking into the body with each icy raindrop and gust of wind. My cousin loved it. Neysa would too, I suspected. One could not walk to the stables or market without feeling as though frozen highways ran through the veins of his extremities. To winterize the orchards, we had to prune and cleanse the leaves, lest there be an infestation of oiphid insects. The little fuckers hid within the bark throughout the cold months and destroyed any blossoms in spring, keeping the trees from blooming. As our family had lorded and tended these orchards for centuries, we had become accustomed to that which was detrimental to the harvest. Many fae with abilities necessary for growing things lived in Saarlaiche. While we winterized, those fae were brought in to sense any oiphids, to open any blocked arteries in the root systems, in order to stop the beginning of rot.

When I left that sliver of a peninsula where Cadeyrn had built their home, I passed Bistaír briefly, and then made my way home. It was already late autumn by the time I arrived in

Aemes, so I got to work with the laborers and fae who worked alongside those in deference to the Taempchal a Glách, where the spirit of the element of greenery and growing resides. Getting my hands dirty in the orchards helped me process all the shite that transpired lately. I had a mate. After centuries, I had a mate. Yet she belonged to my cousin, heart and soul. Within that mind-fuck was the fact that I had somehow fallen in love with my mate's cousin. Yet I was here, across the godsdamned realm while she sat on her throne. She never sent word. Never asked after me, despite the mayhem I went through the past months. It was likely for the better. Who was I but a godsdamned country squire? I was no fit for a queen.

Heaviness hung in the air, indicating a storm coming from the east. Carso, the male I'd been working alongside lately, jerked his chin at me, acknowledging the weather. We wrapped up the individual tasks we were completing, loaded the tools into a wheelbarrow, and moved out of the orchard, silver and gold leaves glittering with the first drips of rain. Cadeyrn's hounds flanked my heels as we headed back toward the estate where my family has resided for hundreds of years. Neysa loves these dogs, and I could sense they missed her too. I wondered when they would come and collect them. Or whether they would come back here for a time. We didn't really discuss any of the details. I'd had to get out. I had no grudge against them. In fact, I felt content knowing they finally managed to be with one another the way they should have been from the beginning. By the Gods, I'd loved her. Loved her still? But at least we were not drowning with that mating bond. What a cluster that was. I supposed Saski never knew the mating bond with Neysa was severed. I supposed she thought she would always be second best. The problem was that if I told her otherwise, I would have to deal with the fallout when she realized she must marry an equal. I was no fucking equal to her.

Rain was coming down in sheets by the time the dogs and I entered the house. I shut the door against a gust of wind, and of course the bloody hounds had to shake their shaggy coats all over the foyer. Turning into the drawing room, I drew my knife at the sight of a figure.

"Fucking hell, man!" I yelled. "You very nearly had a dagger in the throat."

"You distracted that much, Silas? I would have thought you'd have scented me coming in." Magnus poured a tumbler of liquor and handed me the glass.

I sunk into the settee, accepting the drink. While Magnus and I had been friends since he was a lad, I knew without asking that he was here in an official capacity.

"I've had eyes all over Laichmonde like you asked," he began. "Really nothing of note."

I looked up over the rim of my tumbler and raised my eyebrows.

"Until yesterday. An old acquaintance of Etienne's was in town frequenting the clubs and stopped into a couturier shop in the Parkside District where my mother happened to be purchasing a new belt pack. She was behind the screen trying on bits 'n' bobs whilst this male rambled on. By the sounds of it, he was stocking up on leathers and haberdashery, amassing quite a bill. Said he was staying for another night and heading back home to Bania. At this point, Mam was peeking out from behind the screen, you get? You know how she likes to stick her nose where she shouldn't. She said the shop owner was peaky and seemed to be trying to speed him out the door. In the end, he said, 'We can both thank old Etienne now, eh?' And left without exchanging coin."

"So, we have had eyes all over for months now, and the only lead on anything sketchy was from your mam?"

"Should have put her on detail from the get-go, mate," he responded, tossing back the remainder of his drink.

I scrubbed at my face. Even dead and gone, Etienne was still a thorn in my arse. Question was, when did I bring others into this. I knew the couturier shop Magnus spoke of and said so. My sister had a fling with the owner's sister some years ago. I wouldn't have pegged the female for a criminal mastermind, but Etienne's reach and funds were well woven for a number of years. Centuries really. I was in the human realm most of the time Corraidhín was getting on with the sister, so I didn't have a clear idea what was happening here at the time. Gods, what was her name? I remember seeing Reynard slinking around Laichmonde when I crossed for a week or so to see my sister. Last thing I wanted was to bother Reynard with this, knowing what he'd gone through. However, Cyrranus would likely reach out to his new trade minister to see what they could find.

Blowing out a breath, I drank the rest of my own drink and set the glass on the scratched and worn oak table. As children, my mam sat us at this table to do arithmetic and grammar. There was a nursery and study on the third floor, but in winter when it was dark so early as it was this day, she preferred to bring us down in front of the fire and send our tutor home. Once, this house was filled with family. Cadeyrn's mam, and mine and Corraidhín's, always laughing and busying themselves. Something always cooking in the kitchens. My da home at the end of a long day, collapsing where I sat now, asking for just a few minutes to read a book and have tea before we fell on him. Gods and shite I missed them. If it weren't blowing a gale outside, I would have been back to the orchards, elbows deep in dirt.

"How soon did Baetríz tell you of this?" I asked Magnus of his mam's espionage.

"Soon enough I was able to put a tail on the fellow. I tried to get in with the proprietor's good graces as well, but she indelicately told me to fuck off. Bloody shame too. I've had a dry autumn, and by the look of her, she could warm a frost demon's dick in February."

I laughed despite myself.

"Magnus, you dumb shite, every female in Laichmonde knows to stay away from you by now."

"And my sister knows to stay away from you, yet somehow she keeps a fucking torch burning. If I didn't like you as much Silas, I'd have castrated you ages ago."

I felt bad about Lina. I did really. She was one of the most beautiful and strong females I'd known. I just didn't feel for her the way she deserved to be loved. Magnus knew this. Hell, Magnus couldn't keep his trousers on for a week. Dry autumn, my arse.

I hefted myself from the settee, noticing I'd gotten mud and Gods-know-what all over the leather, then told my friend I'd send a hawk to my sister and Cyrranus. It was time to start finding out what was happening in Veruni as well. It had been harder to establish a new representative there, so it has been in an oversight state, watched by the neighboring provinces. Before I reached the door, my housekeeper, Tani, announced there was hawk on the landing and she quietly told me off about the mud. I pointed to the dogs, who narrowed their eyes at me in distaste. *Take one for the legion, lads.*

From the hawk I pulled a message and put the bird on a perch just inside the door to keep the poor bastard out of the rain while it waited for my reply. I wondered if it would be a fantastic existence to be a hawk and be free to fly at will, or if I would fucking hate it because I'd be pressed into flying around in all weather for arseholes like me.

SILAS,

We have been informed of arsonists in Laorinaghe that require attention from all of Aoifsing. Additionally, Yva was gravely wounded in an attack in her palace in the Sacred City. Arik happened to be there. We are not aware in what capacity he was present, but we may require you to assist.

Yours,

Ewan

Then hastily written at the bottom:

Any information you have on Stea and Belleza Ledermain of Saarlaiche would be appreciated. They are old friends of Corraidhín's who have stopped in for a visit. However, I am disinclined to trust them. Gratitude, brother.

Well, fuck. I shoved the note at Magnus and looked about, mentally cataloging the weaponry I would take. I had made quite a mess. I would have to give Tani an extra day off to make up for the work. A screech sounded at the door, and the hawk I had perched inside ruffled its feathers in warning. Waving Tani off, I opened the solid door and pulled a note from another hawk as it hovered midair before landing inside.

Silas,

I am sure you have received notice of the situation in Laorinaghe. We were informed tonight via a peculiar rider. Stea Ledermain, whom Reynard believes to be a former lover of your sister's, claimed she came from Bistaír on behalf of Corraidhín. What's more, he is convinced Stea and her sister were running a scheme in Laichmonde around half a century ago. Reynard is trailing her on her return to Bistaír. Hope this finds you well.

—Cyrranus

The two hawks were circling one another near my feet, making the dogs growl in warning. I broke them up and snatched a pen and paper from the small writing desk where my mother used to sit. Gods, I couldn't stop thinking of my parents lately. In the notes, and to Magnus, I said I would be en route to Bistaír at first light.

Chapter 20

Saski

Luckily, I didn't have much time to moon over Silas. I was mostly a pragmatist. Did it mean much that he told me he loved me if he left anyway? I supposed so, yet there I was on my own, not in the state of mind to be writing love poems. I was neck deep in a multitude of screw-ups my father had amassed in his existence. This whole blasted place should have been on a parliamentary rule centuries ago. I was schooled from youth to run a monarchy. To flow and abide by the intricacies of state and court. To hold autonomous rule. Until it became real that I would be ascending the throne, I had acted like a child, disregarding what I have come to understand as a fallacy in the system.

Ludek sat, barely visible behind stacks of papers and files. Basz had been gone a couple of weeks, checking in on the coup in the south. In his absence, Ludek was always trying to pretend he wasn't twitching without him. It was sweet. We knew it would take years, decades even, to switch from the monarchy to a parliamentary rule, making the transition through a temporary plutocracy. Apparently, that was what Aoifsing was doing as well. I supposed Father's death was the "shot heard round the world" in this realm. I'd bet Neysa would have quite a bit to advise us of with her academic knowledge. Gods only knew what she thought of Cadeyrn and me working together on that horrid clock. We heard little from Aoifsing since they all left on the ship. Ewan sent word once the scheme was uncovered. Apart from that, well, I just tried to not think about his brother-in-law.

"It's getting rather damp in here, sister," Ludek said to me with a smirk.

I tried to tone down my affinity.

"It's a beautiful necklace."

I touched it without thinking, the grooves and striations of the feathered wings now familiar to my fingers.

"Especially the eyes." He was referring to the green topaz eyes of the bird that matched Silas's own.

"Trying to deflect your misery, Ludek?"

He laughed. "Yes. But I can feel the emotions rolling off you. Send a hawk. He was the one worried you would be angry with him."

"I'm working. Leave it alone, brother."

He chuckled and went back to his mountain of paper. If Silas was so worried, I would have thought he might have made an effort to contact me. But he had not, and here we were. Plus, I knew Neysa was pregnant since my all-feeling, all-seeing brother sensed it before they left. If the children were Silas's, there was no chance he would be wanting to come back here. As though he would want this life with me anyway. To be what? A consort to a queen who wished no part of either her birthright, or the system she governs?

"You can be anything, Saski," Ludek whispered. "There are no bonds to hold you to anything or anyone."

"We need to sort out this godsforsaken place, Ludek. Otherwise, it will be a death run with the governors trying to claw for power."

My brother stayed silent; his lips pursed. I stood and snatched the pen and contact ledger from the desk. On my way out of the room, I heard Ludek smother a chuckle. Arik was Gods know where these days, traveling around again as he'd done in my absence. It seemed he preferred to be more the diplomat than whatever it was at which I was playing. In the loggia next to the entrance to the courtyard where we all trained, two guards were facing off head-to-head. Tension cracked in the air, the two males one word from coming to blows. There was a crash of boots in the hall, several other palace guards turning the corner. The captain froze when he saw me, quickly smoothing back his cropped copper hair.

"Majesty," he said with a quick bow, the others all following suit. "Apologies for the disruption."

"Captain Umvelt. I was on my way to the courtyard. Care to knock steel with me?"

He shifted his attention to his males, their own gazes shrinking back from the orange glint of Umvelt's feline eyes.

"Quite sure those two can learn to play nice without you." I motioned to the two whose fists were still clenched around each other's jackets. They quickly dropped their hands and inclined their heads to me, tall, pointed ears catching on the strands of white hair that had come loose of their braids. Umvelt fell into step beside me, leaving the under guards to deal with the insubordination.

It was a slippery day for a sword fight. Autumn storms were blowing through nearly each evening. All the trees at the far edge of the courtyard were dropping leaves as though taking a knee in deference to my approach. Jewel-toned foliage littered the gravel, and all around us rose the smell of leaf rot. I loved it. Loved the dying sun in autumn and the way the world knew how to change its tune and release what it no longer needed. Autumn felt like the tide. Destructive, unpredictable, and a guarantee of vicissitude.

Umvelt stood, hands clasped behind his broad back, patiently waiting for me. I'm not stupid. I knew he likely had twenty other things he could be doing. He would rather be doing. However, I wanted to train with someone who was worth my effort, and I wanted to hear his thoughts on our current climate. I rolled my shoulders and unsheathed my crescia-bladed sword. The bird on the hilt winked up at me as though daring me to not think about the male who had gifted me the bird necklace. With that thought, I lunged. Umvelt sidestepped me, his glowing cat eyes almost smiling. He was a hard male to amuse, but I'd done it in the past.

"Captain," I began, "how is your beautiful family these days?" He parried as I jabbed forward, catching his blade for a split second.

"They are well, Majesty. My daughter wed last summer and is with children. My son joins your brother in his diplomatic pursuits." He crouched and swung, knocking me off balance with the back of his sword. "I believe that was one point for me, Majesty?" There it was. His little smirk, and those small, sharp incisors started showing.

I agreed and stood to pull the stuck leaves from my leathers.

"You always were a better fighter than your father. Perhaps not as good as Arik, but better than your father."

Umvelt had served my family for over a century. He was in even my earliest memories, still looking as young as the male before me. I couldn't let the Arik barb slide though. Especially since Neysa had beat Arik. Thinking a bit like my cousin, I ran at the captain and knocked his hip with the wing on my crescia.

He choked on surprise but stayed standing long enough to wrap an arm around my shoulders. I slid from his grip and jumped onto the overhanging branch. It shimmered with Arik's magic as my brother had warded the area. Umvelt spun in confusion when I dropped behind him and laid the hilt against his spine.

"Point for me, Captain."

His eyes twinkled with the pride of an instructor being beaten by his pupil.

"Tell me," I said. "Why were the Schloss fighting back there?" Schloss were typically docile with one another. They are a race of fae bred for honor and skill. It was rare for them to be unruly in their place of service.

"No one is certain yet. I had planned to find out when you requested my company. Sig and Glyn are your mother's guards, though she was not in the vicinity. I'm told she was in the salt caves with her ladies."

The salt caves had a small company overseeing them. We were raised to respect the salt. It was a place of restoration where most oraculois magic—the magic of telepathic communication—does not work. Mother appreciated being able to shut out any thoughts that weren't her own when she was in the salt. I did rather think that she was ill for weeks after she confined herself to the caves. It was likely worth having a look into.

"There is chatter amongst many folk, Saski," he told me. When he did away with the titles, I knew we were speaking level to one another, and I appreciated it more than he knew. I pulled rapiers from the corner shed and tossed him one. We fenced as he divulged the chatter. Much of it I knew. Rather than seeing the reason in forming a parliament, many viewed the move as my being a misguided youth with no head for politics. Each pang of the rapiers vibrated through my arm, urging me to fight harder. In my eighty-three years I had gleaned quite a bit of politics. I knew I'd behaved like a spoiled princess for many years, but I also knew how to play the game of state.

"The system here is flawed."

"I can see that, Saski," Umvelt said soothingly as though I were his daughter instead of my father's. My father who was a murderer and fraud. My father whom I looked up to and revered. My father who killed Pavla. I dropped the rapier on the ground, suddenly overwhelmed with guilt and loss.

"You are every bit as capable as your brothers," Umvelt assured me. "As Pavla would have been. You have my word that I will serve until my last breath."

I met his eyes, steeling my spine. Umvelt's wife was from Sot, like Mother. Their children were darker like Ludek, their hair dark and silky, laced with copper from their father. And both had his uncanny molten russet cat eyes. Gepard were his folk. Feline in nature, yet of larger stock than most Heiligan fae. As a youth, Pavla and I wished we could meet a Gepard male. Ludek told us they had tongues that felt like sandpaper. How he knew this, we could only guess.

"Thank you, Captain Umvelt," I said to him. He looked uncomfortable. "Your loyalty, guidance, training, everything. I appreciate it. I hope you know that. Please tell Amelíe I appreciate her support as well. I understand you had been dragged away by my father for many long periods of time. It could not have been easy, and I thank you both."

By the set of his shoulders and the thrumming of his heart I knew he was pleased and embarrassed, yet he bowed low and simply asked to take his leave.

Umvelt and I made our way back through the tin-tiled halls. In one direction, the hall led toward the family dining room one level up and private offices where I'd left Ludek earlier. The opposite direction ended in a small courtyard filled with fountains and ferns of every variety. Stairs to the more public areas of the palace ascended from there. I was about to turn right to seek out Ludek once again and see whether he and I could speak with Mother, when Umvelt, uncharacteristically, put his hand on my arm, halting me.

"Majesty," he said.

I turned and saw a group of mainly Schloss guards holding a half-Gepard male in tattered clothing. The male's burnt umber hair hung limply about his warm brown skin. It took me a full minute to register it was Umvelt's son.

"Gunther. Explain." Umvelt was first and foremost a captain. Had it been my son looking so bedraggled, I would have inquired of his well-being first. The Schloss holding him released his arms and pushed him forward. The captain snapped attention to them, making them shrink back.

Through sharp incisors, Gunther began to speak, moving his gaze from his father to me.

"His Highness left for Aoifsing. For the province of Laorinaghe. He made me swear to wait seven days to tell you, Your Majesty."

"And how long did you wait, soldier?" I asked, keeping my venom in check.

"Seven days, Majesty," he said with a bow. "I stayed in Manu an extra two nights, finishing what His Highness had been doing. I then took punts upstream and finally caught a carriage into town last night. It was seven days this afternoon."

"Majesty," came a deep baritone. "Captain, we found him hiding last night outside the palace walls," one of the Schloss guards I had seen earlier said to us.

"You did not report it," Umvelt answered.

"He begged me to wait until today. He was being loyal to His Highness."

"And you," I said, pointing to the other Schloss, "found out and threatened him?" He nodded. Umvelt adjusted his stance and began to speak, but I interrupted. "You were both loyal to your position and my family in turn, and I appreciate loyalty. However, next time, inform us. You may go."

They looked to each other in shock but clasped hands behind backs and marched off. Gunther Umvelt looked close to passing out. I motioned for his father to help him.

"Why has my brother gone to Laorinaghe?" Rather than answer, he handed me a letter addressed to me and Ludek, written in Arik's spidery, elegant script. It was soggy and dog-eared, but still legible.

SASKI, Ludek,

Don't be too harsh on the Umvelt lad. He's a good male, and whether or not he kept his promise, I was glad of his service to me. I have gone to Laorinaghe to see if I can be of help to its representative. They are experiencing fires in retaliation for the uncovering of the scheme this autumn. Truthfully, I could not stand another minute of preening for the nobility. Yva did not know I was coming either, so don't be pissy, Saski. I shall see you both soon and will be in touch.

Yours,
Arik

I SHOULD HAVE KNOWN that Ludek would find it absolutely hilarious. No one seemed too concerned with the fact that I could not run a dissolving monarchy when my hands to the crown were absent. Stomping in a huff wouldn't do us any good, but I found I was stomping regardless. Wind picked up within the office, and the stack Ludek had been slowly whittling down ruffled.

"Don't you dare, sister," he warned.

I reeled in my power and slumped into the chair opposite him.

"He needed a break, Saski. Remember you had been gone for a great while, and he was doing the diplomatic rounds even then."

"Yes, but now our hides are on the line, and he's tromped off to Laorinaghe!"

"Our hides were on the line when you were enjoying Silas." Ludek was rarely so blunt, and I snarled at him for it.

"You're just in a twist because Basz has been gone, and you haven't been laid in ages."

"Perhaps, but Basz will be home tonight, and I'll be well taken care of. Can you say the same thing? Your poison tongue is your undoing, sister. Watch it."

I crossed my arms over my chest and pondered whether I would be allowing myself to be seen to any time soon. The council we established was urging both Arik and me to wed to unify the lands. I felt a stabbing headache coming on just thinking about it. I watched the markings and piles my brother was making. After a minute, I joined in, trying to offer an olive branch of sorts.

We'd been working for an hour or so when there was a rush of noise from below the windows. The sun had sunk, and this far north, midafternoon was as good as nighttime. Small flares lit up the windows. My brother and I looked at each other and walked to look out of the glass. Hundreds of folk were gathered just beyond the gates, torches held aloft. They simply stood. Ludek and I watched as a guard met them. Conversation ensued between the guard and a few of the folk. The guard turned and rode back to the main gate.

"We should go down," I said, turning.

"No, Saski stay up here."

I looked at Ludek in question.

"There is so much interference in the emotion I am

getting from the folk below, but I don't feel there is malevolence from the crowd. Only a need to be heard. Still, I would keep you safe in here. The guard will bring us the news."

THE PROBLEM, I had come realize, was that not only was it difficult to switch political systems that had been in place for millennia, but dissemination of truthful information was nearly impossible. Vast areas of Heilig were provincial, the folk who dwelled in these places uneducated. In cities, misinformation spread like disease. Those in positions of relative influence or financial power were able to sway any to their cause, be it supporting our Heiligan reversal of the monarchy or playing against us as weak and doing the lands injustice. That was why Arik had been traveling round, informing our folk of the realities and prospectives for our political future.

The crowd beyond the palace gates was demanding a concrete alliance with the other lands in order to maintain the trade they depended upon for their livelihoods. Our official response consisted of assuring them we were aligned with each land in Heilig, using our governors to ensure that trade increased with not just each land but also with the provinces in Aoifsing, now that we could openly trade with them. Ludek and his appointed team of finance executives had gone through the fiscal impact of our open trade with Aoifsing and determined that it had not only expanded the reach of locally made goods, but it had also added jobs in its transport. Having a mass of folk who were, for the most part, unworldly and uneducated, laying out the details of the benefits of trade had been difficult.

. . .

Of Chaos and Haste

The following morning, I sat in the hall we used as a war room, my booted feet propped high on the carved wood of the velvet-cushioned chair beside my own. Umvelt sat across from me, watching me sharpen my crescia blade.

He had been in the training pit when I'd arrived before dawn, needing to blow off some steam before the meeting today. As he wiped the sweat from his brow while he put away his weapons, I took note of with whom he had been sparring. A few palace guards clustered, all covered in grit and sweat. We had the most culturally diverse folk in our guard and staff. From the Gepard like Umvelt himself, to the Schloss specialty guard, and the many regional representatives from various lands of Heilig, I used to believe I could never be bored with the males here. Of course, that damned Saarlaichan fool across the sea had to ruin it for me. However, across the gravel this morning, his shirt soaked through with sweat, my attention caught on a set of corded, narrow shoulders. His back was to me as he lifted the soiled shirt from his torso, exposing tucks of muscle across his dark golden skin.

"Am I too late to play?" I chirped from the opposite side of the ring. The males spun toward me, much faster than their previously exhausted countenance might have suggested they were capable of moving. Varno snorted and gave me a half smile, stepping forward.

"I must get ready for the day, Majesty. As must most of these males," Umvelt said.

"I can play for a bit," Varno, governor of Sot, answered.

"You look a bit worn out, Varno," I teased, braiding back my thick, dark chocolate hair. "Are you sure you can handle me?"

The others left the ring. Varno came closer and leaned in, his scent like new leather and wind. It had been a really long time since I'd had any male companionship, and I found I was slightly off balance in front of Varno. *Varno.* I'd had him before. We were passionate and rough, and I found I may want to take advantage of that now.

He smirked as though reading my thoughts. "I have always known how to handle you, *Majesty*. You were my queen before you were anyone else's."

Oh. My toes curled in my boots. I held his stare for a second longer, then ducked under his arms and kicked my boot into his rock-hard rear end, sending him forward a few meters. Balance caught, he spun to me, no weapon in his hands. I set my blade aside reverently and cracked my neck.

"Bare hands?" I asked, bringing fists up in front of my face.

"Bare everything, if you'd like," he answered.

Memories of Silas dropping me on the gravel surged in. He had been all over me in the garden, filling me, and just as I was about to find release, he had heard Neysa and dropped me, then ran off. I was never so humiliated in my life. And I knew I deserved it. I knew in that moment that the hell I had put Neysa through had quite literally come back to bite me in the ass. In the form of gravel and pebbles lodged in my cheeks that I wouldn't let anyone except Ludek tweeze from me.

"This ground is rough even for our history, Varno," I answered instead. My mouth went dry thinking of bloody Silas and looking at Varno. I punched out and he ducked expertly, jabbing me with his elbow. I rocked back and hooked a leg behind his, then thrust my own elbow into his chin.

"Fuck," he growled.

"Perhaps later," I shot back.

He launched forward, his head and shoulders a battering ram at my stomach. The impact had all the air blown from my lungs. We landed, and I scrabbled to roll out from under him, while trying to catch my breath. Just as I managed to slip under his arm, I felt him against my exposed waist. I stopped moving for a millisecond, heat flaring in my cheeks. He flipped me over and held my arms above my head, his chest pressing me into the ground.

Into my ear, he said, "Give me a place to be in five minutes, *Majesty*, and we can settle this."

It took great restraint to not push back into him. Instead, I slowly turned around and brought my knee up straight into his groin. He collapsed back with a snarl.

"Second floor. There is a room next to the library. Don't keep me waiting."

ONE SWIFT KNOCK preceded him opening the door. I had removed my leathers and stood in a thin black bodysuit that covered little of my chest and none of my backside, which I turned toward him. The shuck of his clothing sounded behind me, and hands that were softer than I had become accustomed to grabbed my hips. He kissed my neck, and teeth scraped along my spine.

"No teeth," I shot, in a panic. He grunted. A sob ripped from me unexpectedly. I pulled away in horror.

"Saski?" he asked.

"No. No," I said again. "This was a mistake."

He walked to me, and I saw every corded inch of him ready for me. Dark skin and that angular, beautiful face. "I can be slower," he said, reaching a hand to my face. I turned my head away from the concern in his sapphire eyes.

"Please," I said in a weak plea which made me angry with myself. "Leave me." I qualified my plea with a resounding command.

He looked at me one last time and pulled his clothes back on before leaving the room. Gods I was a mess. I couldn't even grasp whether I was more of an idiot for making him leave, or for starting to take him. I didn't have any idea whether I would see godsdamned Silas again. Would he even care if I had been with someone else? Did he care for me at all? Was he still wrapped around Neysa's dithering little finger? In a state of utter annoyance and unfulfilled lust, I yanked free a sheet of paper and pen.

Silas,

What the fuck is going on in Aoifsing? Things are a mess here. How is Neysa? The babes she carries? Are they yours? I don't even know if it would matter to me. I do know I was bent over with someone else about to take me and I pulled away, thinking of you. Take that how you want it.

Saski

I folded it and sent it from the window before I thought better of it. A hawk may have been more direct, but my magic should be able to locate his. I had to dress for the meeting anyway.

THWICK. Thwick. Thwick went the curved blade over the whetstone. Governors from three lands, Biancos, Annos, and of course, Sot, filed in. Ludek chatted animatedly with Terin of Annos. He shot me a look as soon as he saw me, eyes shifting to Varno. Just bloody great. Our trade commissioners, constables from nearby towns, and several merchants from the area took seats around the long silver-topped table. It was said that the silver came from the forest floor where the long-ago queen of Heilig cleansed the plague from our lands. Kutja. Her name meant heart song, and she was considered the heart of our lands. My hand ran over the cool metal, thinking of my cousin and her willingness to sacrifice herself for the sake of saving us all. I snorted, mockingly calling her a martyr in my head, yet I pulled a slip of paper from my leather folio. I must be feeling sentimental today, writing all these notes. Gods.

Neysa,

As it has been some time since I have seen you, I wanted to inquire about your health and well-being since we saw each other last. The babes you carry have been on my mind. I have heard that my brother is in Aoifsing, and there are fires. I do hope they are far from you. Sometimes I wish for your counsel in matters of state. We have planted the araíran-aoír seed and it has propagated faster than anticipated. We expect a small but decent harvest next year. I must be off now, as I am about to sit in a meeting regarding trade and unifying our lands. Like you, few seem to trust me. I guess I've dug that grave myself. There is a saying here, "All of me, is all of you, and all of me holds hope for all. Always."

Your cousin, Saski of Heilig

I folded the paper and signaled for a page, asking him to send a hawk for me. Before the page retreated, I looked to Ludek. Where were Neysa and Cadeyrn? My brother looked off in the distance. Basz came in then and whispered to him. Ludek held up a finger for me to allow him in my mind.

I believe they are in Laorinaghe. Though not near the fires. Cadeyrn gave Basz the location before he left.

I spoke quietly to the page and let him leave as the meeting was called to order. Varno hadn't taken his eyes from me since he walked in. I couldn't meet them. Shame, guilt, desire, stupidity, all tumbled around in my gut. When I did look up, welcoming everyone, I found the governor of Biancos piercing me with a cat-and-canary grin. I supposed it wouldn't be a meeting without a bit of drama.

"Is she off her rocker?" I screeched as we shut the door to the library after leaving the meeting.

"Saski," Ludek tried.

"No, Ludek. We are moving away from this totalitarian bullshit."

"It is not unheard of, sister, to marry for alliances."

I whirled on him, finger pointing into his chest. "So, you marry!"

Basz coughed behind me as though to indicate I may be off *my* rocker to suggest that his mate be married off. Whipping my head to him, I gnashed my teeth in a semiferal warning.

They'd listened. All the bloody participants listened, and it had been going well. We discussed the improving economy, and the socioeconomic boon of our trade being open. Ludek and the trade minister showed them the schematics on how it would continue to thrive as we moved further from a monarchy and into parliamentary rule. We amended laws that gave ultimate rule to me. To *me*. I was refusing to hold them all by the balls as we had for centuries, and they took it in stride. Even the ethical subsidiaries we used to transport goods from the provincial areas were discussed. We made it clear that we were not failing the lands. Each move being made was to empower the folk here. To give them the means to thrive.

Through it all, Varno kept his glacial eyes on me. How I maintained my cool under that stare is a mystery I may never solve. Trade documents were signed by all parties. We even had two motions signed for the initial parliamentarians to be instated. And just at the closing, the viper I had previously called Auntie Perla, struck.

"If I may make a motion myself, Your Majesty," Perla of Biancos began.

I flicked my wrist for her to continue.

"It is all well and good to begin this . . . alteration of our way of life."

I stiffened.

"However, as you have said, it may take many years—decades even—for the system of government to fully switch and become self-sufficient. His Highness, Arik, is not here and leaves us with little hope for his participation."

"Arik is tending to diplomatic duties at the moment," Basz cut in.

Perla nodded and smirked. "Just as well, it is our queen we look to in keeping with our Heiligan way of life. We believe that a union between you and one of the nobility from a Heiligan land is in the best interest of our folk."

My eyes pinned her to the spot. "And who would you have me wed, Auntie Perla?" I asked so sweetly that everyone in the room made a small sound of dread.

She looked to her right, her hand gesturing to the male beside her. "My true nephew, Varno of Sot."

Varno swallowed, a lump riding his throat.

It took all of my will to keep my power in check. I wanted to release my siren song and change all their minds. I knew I could do it too. None of them knew. None. A light wind picked up, and I stood, my brother and his mate flanking me. Varno stood as well, opening his mouth to speak.

"Meeting adjourned. Thank you all for coming. I believe we have made much progress, which is the purpose of all we are doing. Good day."

Of the three of us, none spoke until the library door had shut. Gods, I wished Arik were here. Pavla would have laughed herself hoarse and told them all to go to hell. My fist clenched on my heart thinking of my sister.

I sat hard on the chair that remained ever next to the cabinet which held the Heiligan queen's book.

"You always knew, Saski. You were raised to do this. Remember we used to talk about it as children? I knew if I married, it would be for love. You said you never cared anyway," Ludek said gently. I put my head in my hands.

"But we are changing things, Ludek. That's the point."

"They want to know you are doing what's in their best interest."

I looked up, shocked to see he agreed. Agreed with them.

"Ludek?" I whispered. "You think I need to do this?"

He walked to the window.

"Basz?" I asked of my brother's mate.

"I think you should tell them to piss off and you should go find your country squire."

Ludek groaned and rolled his eyes in Basz's direction.

"Not helpful." Ludek turned to me. "But I think you should consider committing to one of two options," my brother stated. "One: Marry Varno. He's gorgeous, he's loved you since you were fourteen, and it would appease everyone."

"Two?"

"You tell them all to piss off and go find your country squire."

"Remind me to thank you later for agreeing with me," Basz told him, a smolder in his eyes.

Ew.

A knock sounded at the door. We looked to each other. Basz opened it to Varno, who stood with his hands behind his back, eyes on me.

"Did you know?" I asked him. "Did you know that Perla would ambush me like that?"

"I had planned to ask you myself. Before the meeting. We . . ." He coughed. "There wasn't time. Things went differently to how I imagined."

Ludek stepped beside me, realizing, with that gift of his, what had happened between the Sot governor and me.

"You were going to propose to me this morning? Had you decided before we sparred? Did you change your mind and fancy a good fuck instead? Why buy the cow—"

"No! I . . . Saski," he began, but Basz growled. "Majesty. I told you that you have always been my queen. I have loved no one but you. Since that night at the dock in Manu. You have been all I've wanted. I clawed my way past my father to take his place as governor in order to one day get a chance to marry you."

Through the stained-glass panes of the windows, I looked out on the grounds where a few folk still remained camped. My folk. Those who looked to me to do what was right for them. If I hadn't stayed in Aoifsing—hadn't stayed with gods-damned Silas so long—maybe I wouldn't have fallen so hard. A few years ago, a union with Varno wouldn't have been anything to complain about. We would marry and get on with life. Take other lovers if we chose. It was how I was raised. As a princess of these great lands. It wasn't until I met bloody Silas that I realized I didn't want that. I didn't want any of it. I wanted him. Since the first time I set eyes on him. Yet here I was, a queen needing to unite her folk. And that male from across the sea was not here. Despite what he told me, the glint in his shimmering sea eyes that seemed to ripple with my siren power as though calling to me. He wasn't here.

A warm hand pressed into my lower back. The scent of crisp leather at my side. The male who had just spilled his heart out to me, stood staring out the window, quietly allowing me to think. Ludek and Basz stayed. I knew they would never leave me in this state. This situation. It was as much their business as mine.

"Saski of Kutja," Varno began and dropped to a knee. He held a ring, the diamond in the center large enough to scry.

A compressed, inevitable feeling overcame me. This was what I was meant to do for my people. Who was I to complain? Gods, it could have been Terin of Annos I was forced to marry. A shudder went through me at the thought. Ludek sniffed behind me as though he heard me.

"I would be honored to have you as my wife. To ally with one another in home and politics," he said.

I turned fully and looked at his warm skin, the color reminiscent of summer nights. Looked at his eager, wintery blue eyes and the blush that crept up his neck and cheeks, turning his coloring like the late-autumn leaves outside. At his sculpted lips, not soft and lush like the male I truly loved, but still rugged, chiseled, and attractive. Lips that had the slightest touch of pink like blossoms in springtime. His face was alight with all four seasons as he knelt, proposing to me. I held out my hand, resigned to accept.

Boot steps thundered down the slate-tiled halls, followed by an urgent knock on the wood-and-tin carved door. Basz opened and accepted a letter.

"Majesty," Basz said, handing me the message. "From your brother."

I opened it and read, Ludek at my shoulder.

Saski, Ludek,

This night, during a dinner, Yva Sonnos, representative of Laorinaghe, was attacked in her own palace. Healers are still working on her as her pancreas and liver were pierced. I will stay here to find out who is behind the attack. Our cousin, Ewan, has been informed, and there is a massive response from all of Aoifsing. I do not believe myself in any more danger than usual, though rest assured, I am being as careful as always. I trust you both will do the same.

All my love,

Arik

LUDEK LOOKED TO BASZ, an unspoken conversation passed between them.

"I will ready myself to go," my brother's mate said. He had just gotten back. I couldn't allow that to happen to them so soon.

"Basz, no." I grabbed his hand.

He smiled at me and kissed my cheek. "I may be your brother's mate, but this is my job."

"We can send others. Eamon and Dorn. We have a godsdamned army, Basz. I forbid you to leave."

He looked shocked.

"I still have final rule. Unless Ludek feels he must object." We both turned to my brother.

He swallowed and gave Basz a half smile but shook his head. Basz growled and stormed from the room. I'd never seen him lose him temper before.

"Thank you," Ludek whispered. "Every time he leaves . . ." Ludek looked down and scrubbed at his face. "I fear he won't come back."

"I will go," announced a nearly forgotten voice from the back of library.

Ludek and I turned, almost surprised to see Varno standing there. Oh, I had been about to accept his proposal. Perhaps he had forgotten as well.

Varno stalked to us. He pulled my face to his and pressed a kiss to my mouth, full of heat and unsaid words. "I will go with whomever gets sent and personally accompany Arik back."

I opened my mouth to tell him that Arik might not appreciate my sending him. I'm not sure Arik ever really liked Varno. He and Eamon used to hide from him when we were children. That, and he caught us in a compromising position while our families were on holiday in Biancos once.

"Saski." He implored me with his eyes and grabbed my hand, slipping the ring onto my finger. Its weight was significant, pulling my senses down to it. "I will bring back your brother. And when I return, my queen, if you will, in fact have me, we shall be wed."

I nodded my head, stiff and automatic.

He smiled. Straight white teeth in that sculpted mouth, and the smile lifted his eyes, the cerulean dancing.

Saski, are you certain? Ludek asked in my mind.

I've no certainty left, Ludek.

I'm sorry, sister.

Varno looked to Ludek, a question in his eyes. Ludek looked at me once more and left the room. My heart was racing, the room too small. My betrothed still held my hand, and so, pulled me closer to him, wrapping his other arm around my waist. The silk of my gown bunched where he held on, pushing my hips closer to him. Half of me wanted him. Half needed to get air, and I didn't know to which half I should throw in my loyalty. Before I thought more, his lips were moving across my collarbone, tugging my sleeves aside. Hands roamed my body. I kissed him back, yielding a bit breathlessly. We backed to the wall, and he hoisted my skirts up, hands all over me. When his teeth scraped my neck, I reared back so quickly my head slammed into the stone wall, audibly cracking.

"Shit!" he said, dropping my skirts and cradling my head. I felt it, my fingers coming away with blood. "What happened?"

"No teeth," I murmured, dazed. "I said, no teeth, Varno."

"Truly, Saski? We are betrothed. It is my right to mark you."

I stepped out of his embrace and glared at him through spotted vision. "It is my right to decide who does what and when to my body, Governor," I spat. He stepped to me, but I held my position.

"Apologies, Majesty. I look forward to having all of you. And you having all of me."

"We need not rush, Varno," I said coldly, giving him a flippant hand gesture as I walked to the door.

He looked aghast that I was walking away.

"Good day."

Chapter 21

Neysa

Trauma has repercussions more surreptitious than I would have once expected. Once a week, I spoke with a healer to cognitively learn to move past the trauma I had faced the past couple of years. As I was sure many had done, I tried to pretend I was okay. Tried to pretend that my current state of happiness could overshadow the pain experienced in the recent past. I tried and failed. I would wake in the perfect light of a perfect morning, in our perfect home, gasping for breath, sparks flying from my hands, setting fire to our bed. The dreams were a rotation of syndicated memories and projected alternates. In some, I was being beaten by Etienne and his guards, watching Silas and Reynard die before me. I would watch Cadeyrn disappear with Solange as though she really had been brought back. That dream usually had me vomiting upon waking. It was the easiest to control once the healer helped. I could step away and know that Etienne and Solange were dead. Step away and see, in my dream state, my husband sleeping next to me, his hand resting on my hip as I slept.

Some dreams I witnessed Cadeyrn being thrown away

from the clock, his body broken and lifeless. Feeling that everything we had worked for faded with his light. Again, I was able to control the dream most times. I could slip away and see us together in our bed, sometimes unclothed and still attached to one another. Silas said we were like rabbits. I supposed he was right. I couldn't get enough of Cadeyrn's body in mine. Our exchanging of life. The visible circle of light and energy that spun between us as we moved together.

The worst of the dreams were the ones I was still trying to manage. In the first, I woke, having been thrust back into the human realm, devoid of my gifts, my family, my mental acuity. I wandered the streets of London, Hamburg, Los Angeles, even Istanbul, knowing I needed to find a Veil to get home. Time moved quicker with each step I took, and I knew I wouldn't make it. In that one, as was the case when I was thrust through the Veil in that Festaeran cavern, I would wake in my bed. Wake just as I had in that forest in Northern Germany, confused and not sure which reality I was inhabiting. It took moments before I could truly catch a breath, Cadeyrn waking to use his healing gift, forcing my lungs to work.

In the last of the dreams, I was with our children. They were babies sometimes, toddlers or young children others. Some nights they were teenagers, arguing with me or Cadeyrn. Sometimes we were older and saw them as adults. Their faces were so clear. Then they were violently ripped from me. The way in which I woke was different. Often, I was covered in blood as I had on the ship from Manu. However, I'd seen the children slip away from fever, their heartbeats a thunderous missive that was replaced by a void in my ears with its absence. I'd seen them killed by Etienne, his fist or sword being their end. In the worst, my hands were choking the life from them as I screamed and cried. I woke from that dream, our bed sizzling, my husband with rapidly healing burns on his arms, as though I absorbed his powers and used them against him.

In the day I was normal. Normal for me, anyway. Once I was back to Cadeyrn, healing together, the mating bond with Silas lifted, I was settled and happy. Happy is such a trite word. Yet for perhaps the first time, I felt the love and soul-ending connection Cadeyrn and I had, and could move forward. Happiness was knowing we had the future we deserved. Unfortunately, my subconscious wasn't quite onboard.

Early mornings always presented me a chance to start anew. From even my early childhood, long before I knew I was fae, the waking hours of the day were when I could arrange my thoughts and grant myself the headspace for the day. Clear skies spread beyond the wall of windows. Behind my bed, the dawn sea below tumbled innocuously, colored a washed slate, rinsing the stones and sand in a continuous cycle. Cadeyrn wasn't in our bed when I'd awoken, so I washed up and slipped a gauzy, pale blue dressing gown around me before padding into the hall and down the stairs. Out in this remote slip of land at the tip of Laorinaghe, on the Ispil of Bogvi, no sounds polluted the morning, save the call of birds and the gentle crash of surf. Complete silence accompanied me through the house while I put the kettle on for tea and searched the cupboards for a cup. Through the bayed kitchen window, a single direct ray of sunrise pierced the dimness of the kitchen. White cabinets and black-and-white stone tiles gleamed clean and pure in that ray.

Pastries were tucked under a tea towel in a marble bowl on the kitchen island. I knew I'd said I wouldn't finish them straightaway, as we had just gotten them from a shop in the nearest town, but I couldn't think of anything else to eat. I lifted the muslin towel and scoffed at a note sitting atop the buttery baked goods, a smear of date jam staining the ivory paper.

You'll regret finishing them this soon.

Hmph. Splashing some freshly made cashew milk into my tea, I headed from the kitchen. He must have gone out the back as the floor-to-ceiling French doors were thrown open, two scaly *baethaache* lay on the wooden deck. I grabbed a cashmere wrap from the back of our oat colored sofa. Chilly air filled the living room. It seemed a bit of winter was starting to advance after all in our first Yule as a couple. The first year we had known each other, I had spent Yule with him and his cousins. We were getting ready to leave for Eastern Europe to find the missing crystals, and I was terrified of how far in love with him I had fallen. Last year, my brother and Corraidhín's children were born, and I was stuck in the human realm, curtains drawn against the festivities of the season.

Both beasties snorted a puff of steam in greeting. I reached down to pat each one, their heads pressed together, bodies curled as one, each iridescent scale like a continuous pattern moving from one beast to another. Decking gave way to flagstone pavers, dusted over in sand, meandering throughout the back lawn toward the sea. I walked barefoot toward the dunes which sloped to the beach, toward the seagrass border between lawn and dunes, before stepping onto the teak bridge. Familiar broad shoulders and dark hair faced out at Saen Daíthaen. Cadeyrn sat on the top step as the bridge turned to plank steps. New wood creaked as I folded my legs under me, offering him my cup. He reached across himself and picked up a cup of his own and gave me a small smile. Quiet as the atmosphere around us, we sat, drinking our tea. Once he'd finished, his arm slipped around my waist, drawing me infinitesimally closer.

"Did you go for a swim?" I asked, touching his wet hair. Though he wore a loose cotton sweater, I could feel the dampness of his skin beneath. He nodded.

"And a run. Were you able to wake yourself?"

I thought back to my dreams. It was the one where he leaves with Solange.

"I could change it this time. It's getting easier. At least with that dream. I could stop you by showing you that you were sleeping next to me."

His face took on the mask he wore when he didn't want me to know what he was thinking. Without saying anything, my husband pulled something from the side where his teacup sat. A pistachio and honey pastry dripped buttery flakes on my dressing gown. I grinned and took it from him, taking a bite and sighing with pleasure. He chuckled. Sunrise was nearly complete, ever-broadening apricot-tinged light swelling from our left.

"I need to train today," I said with a yawn. "It's been a few days since I really worked." It was his turn to grin.

"I was hoping you'd say that."

SWEAT DRIPPED INTO MY EYES, and I blotted at them with the back of my hand. Cadeyrn took advantage of my distraction, hooking a leg around my ankle, sending me sprawling into the sandy turf. I knew better than to complain about it being an unfair move. In a real-life scuffle, I couldn't allow myself to be distracted by anything. As I said, it had been a while since I trained regularly.

We had ordered some clothes for me, including new leathers and aphrim skins, but they had yet to arrive, save a couple pieces I found in the nearest town. Not the height of Aoifsing fashion, but simple and attractive. Today, however, I wore the riding breeches and jacket Yva had given me when I stopped by the Sacred City looking for my mate after my miscarriage. While the breeches covered my legs, as soon as I went down the knee split, my skin beneath tearing as well. Cadeyrn winced, but I snarled and waved him off, hopping back to standing. Sleípnyr, my magnificent grey horse, popped his head through the window of the stable as though checking I was okay. He had been a gift from Ainsley Mads when I left her home in Prinaer, and I could see in his twinkling green and red eyes that he understood everything I said.

"I'm fine, Sleípnyr," I told him. "Just letting your pretty face get the better of me." Both the horse and my husband snorted then looked to one another incredulously.

"You always do let pretty males distract you," Cadeyrn said, teasing.

My head knew he was baiting me to get me to fight better. However, it stung and pissed me off. I drew my narrow sword and spun it recklessly.

He sniggered. "I mean really. I watched you fight Silas years ago, and he seemed to be able to take you down with a smile."

I lunged for him, but he continued the provocation.

"Good thing you didn't fight Dean. It would have been an embarrassment to be overtaken by him. I meant to ask," he drawled, turning from me with ease, "does he do yoga? He seems like he does yoga or—" I kicked sand up at him.

Don't rise to it, Neysa. Just fight.

Our swords clashed, over, under, over, under. I was light on my feet and determined as hell now, but he had three hundred years of experience under his sword belt, and he was far larger. Pulling my blade back, I twisted and ducked, coming alongside his and knocking the tip of his blade with the side of mine. The sing of metal rang. In that ring, I was thrust into a vision.

Corra kissing a female with fiery hair. Solange running a finger down Cadeyrn's chest, then looking directly at me. Saski and Ludek staring from the window in the palace in Kutja, the glow of a thousand torches beyond the stained glass. Arik holding Yva, her stomach bleeding onto the red clay tile loggia in the Sacred City. Dean, standing in front of Pim and Efa, his arms spread wide, as though shielding them from something.

It must have taken Cadeyrn a moment to realize I was in a vision, because I was backed against the teak panes of the stable, a forearm at my throat, the sword extending from his grip. I came out of the vision with a gulp of air tasting of salt, new wood, and hay. I turned my head toward the sea, branches from an ancient looking pine tree marring the view of the surf. Sleípnyr whinnied and kicked. Once Cadeyrn saw that I hadn't fought back, he dropped his arm and grabbed me around the waist to keep me from sinking down.

"Sorry, *Caráed*," he whispered. "I didn't realize it was a vision."

Unable to speak yet, I projected the images to him mind to mind. I walked to Sleípnyr, and stroked his long snout, letting him know I was okay. He leaned his head into me.

That wasn't like my dreams. It was a vision, I said to Cadeyrn.

"It could be a manifestation of your dreams into your waking self. There is a fine line between dreaming and visions. Not that I don't value what you see. But I feel like Pim and Efa could be representing the children—our children," he said with a catch in his voice, "who you see in your dreams." I looked over at him and shrugged.

"Or they are in real danger. Why was Corra kissing that female?"

"Perhaps it was in the past?"

"Like Solange?" I asked.

"Solange is dead, Neysa. You see her in your dreams. Perhaps . . . should we call the healer?" he suggested, voice hushed.

I snapped my eyes to him, anger flaring through every inch of me. "I don't need the healer at the moment, apart from maybe to stop my fucking knee from bleeding. I need to write down the visions and sort them out. Maybe you're right. Maybe I'm seeing my nightmares in the daytime. That hasn't happened before though." I picked up my sword and wiped it off with a cloth I had in the pocket of my jacket. "I am not fragile, Cadeyrn. Healing, yes. Broken and fragile, no." I started for the house a few hundred meters away from the stables. He fell in line with me near the steps to the decking. The *baethaache* were gone. Likely in their cave down off the beach. Cadeyrn opened his mouth to say something, but I cut him off. "And if you're trying to bait me, don't ever suggest my attention strays to another male."

"I was teasing to get you worked up," he answered, cool and defensive.

"And don't make fun of Dean. He was my only friend when I *was* broken, and he may just be the only thing standing between our niece and nephew and whatever threatens them."

He put his hands up in surrender.

"And he does cycle and Pilates. Or did. Not yoga." I stormed into the house, heading for the stairs, but I could swear I heard a muffled chuckle behind me, which incensed me more.

THE SOUTHEASTERN EXPOSURE of the bedroom and bathroom windows sometimes made it unbearably bright. The bathwater was cooling, yet I lay in it still, my legs propped up on the lip of the stone tub. My knee was healing, though had Cadeyrn tended to it, the wound would have healed already. If he was right, and my dreams were bleeding into my visions, then could I trust anything I saw? His heat and rain-washed scent arrived before he did, walking to the doorway and crossing arms over his chest. My mate's eyes were pinched, lips pursed, face hard. I sat up.

"What is it?"

He pulled a message from under his arm.

"Yva sent a hawk to us and to Ewan. There are fires in Laorinaghe. She waited to inform us all as they have been trying to deal internally, but the fires have reached the Dunstanaich border now. They think it's in retaliation for the wine scheme."

"What can we do?" I asked. His nostrils flared. "What else?"

"Arik is with her."

I stepped from the tub in a rush of cool water and grabbed the tasseled towel. Afternoon sun filled the bathing chamber while I quickly dried off and slipped a sweater of Cadeyrn's over black leggings. Arik was with Yva. In the Sacred City. That was close enough to the vision that I felt it should be noted. Cadeyrn was thinking the same thing yet said nothing. I could tell by the set of his jaw, the possibilities whirring in his head.

We stood in the kitchen while he cooked dinner—a simple pasta with some of the local veg, and crisp bacon. I loved watching him cook. The same attention and precision he put into everything he did, from fighting, to reading, to making love, went into his food. Leftover starchy water from the drained pasta sat to the side while he stirred in the oil and bacon, veg, and cashew milk. He then poured the starch water into the pot and stirred, making the once-independent ingredients come together in a creamy sauce. I poured us each a glass of buttery red wine and set plates on the island to be filled. Cadeyrn took the opposite seat to where I slid onto a stool at the counter.

The meal I had been enjoying moments before turned to dust in my mouth. An intense wave churned inside me, requiring my full concentration to keep my fork from shaking in my hand. Late afternoon sun had sunk low enough that the kitchen was cast in shadow. Two lanterns were lit, a soft, warm glow illuminating the winter dark. Cadeyrn set his fork down without a sound and looked to me with a question.

"You think I'm crazy," I said, twirling the pasta and releasing it.

"No."

"A bit though. What with the dreams and now the vision. I've taken psychology. You are validating my feelings and compounding your concerns with a nugget of what you know to be true. It's wearing you down, and you think I'm slipping into insanity."

"One: I have also taken psychology."

"Wait. What? You have? When? Where?"

He waved me off. "I was bored in the 1970s and enrolled in university. Corraidhín had gone back to Aoifsing because she didn't like the aesthetic of the era. It was an interesting time politically and socially. So, I took to a degree program."

"Which degree program? What school?"

"Durham, of course. Had to be somewhat close to the Veil."

"Wow. How did I not know that?"

"You never asked. I also have a couple of certificates of proficiency from educational establishments here in Aoifsing. Point being, I understand what you are saying, and I can see how you would draw that conclusion in the conversations and events of today."

"Cadeyrn," I warned. "You're using the patronizing tone."

He cleared his throat and pinched the bridge of his nose.

"I do not think you are mad. I think the events that have come to pass with us these past couple of years, and even what you have endured before, have created a delayed stress disorder." He stopped speaking for a moment.

I knew more was to come, but I stared into my plate of Michelin-worthy pasta, wondering if he was right. How much trauma had he seen, though? He and his cousins, Reynard, my brother? They had all gone through just as much as I had—more. And yet, they didn't seem to have a delayed stress disorder.

Cadeyrn went on. "Your nightmares and visions may be sharing headspace with you. I think it might be prudent to bring in the healer once a day for a while until you can at least sleep properly."

"Every day?" I whispered. "You really do think I've lost it." Icy fingers of shame walked up my spine.

"Bloody hell, Neysa. You're a brilliant individual who has sustained major crisis. If it had been your divorce and the loss of your father alone, it would be understandable. But you were cloaked and led to believe you were a human. You found out you weren't. You were attacked in the human realm and abducted, violated, over and over. You fell in love with me, and that's a nightmare in itself," he said with a lopsided grin. "You dealt with fucking Bestía, phantomes, your mother being murdered, dying for fuck's sake, the business with Silas, the miscarriage. My love, I don't think you're mad. I think you need a fucking break."

The rest of the dinner was eaten in near silence. His cheeks were flushed, eyes bright and seeming almost wet. We tidied the kitchen together, an act of comfortable domesticity, and made our way into the living room. I nestled into the crook of his arm and stretched my legs out on the couch.

"What was the song you sang in that tent in Craghen?" he asked me, a hint of embarrassment in his voice.

"Which one? I sang for hours. Horribly, I might add."

"When I crossed to find you in the human realm," he began, and I turned to watch his face. Low-lit sconces brightened his aquamarine eyes. I traced his face with my fingers and played with the silver streak in his hair. "I looked through your phone. First, to see photos."

I smiled to myself, knowing he would have found loads of photos I'd taken of him without his knowing. Including one in Istanbul I'd snapped when we were in our hotel lobby before dinner. That was my favorite, since he was unaware I was taking it, but his eyes were wide, looking at me like . . . he wanted to kiss me. I looked to those bright eyes in this moment and asked him to go on.

"Then I wanted to know what music you had listened to when you and Ewan were headed to close the Veil."

I placed my hand on his stomach and circled my fingers on his abdomen.

"What did you find?"

"The last song was called 'The Fall of Rome,'" he said, a hand stroking the side of my thigh. "I don't think you had been singing that, but it felt like one of the songs you sang."

"It was the same band. I used to go see them in LA."

He nodded and kissed my head.

Beyond the closed French doors, a shadow dropped. We both sat up. A hawk paced the deck. Cadeyrn retrieved the message from the bird, stroking its feathers in gratitude.

CADEYRN AND NEYSA,

During a dinner in the palace in the Sacred City, Yva was attacked. She was stabbed, and the perpetrator escaped using particle transference. We are told she lives but is gravely injured. Arik was with her at the time. We don't know why there was Heiligan representation, but she had only today called for aid in dealing with the fires. I have sent word to all representatives to be on guard. Additionally, Corraidhín had visitors this evening. Old acquaintances, one of whom was a lover. Belleza and Stea Ledermain. I do not trust them, and quite frankly, I do not want them in our home with our children. Have you any information?

Yours,
Ewan

CADEYRN PINCHED his nose and ran a hand through his night-dark hair. My hands started shaking, and I folded the message in thirds, placing it on the table before me. We looked at each other, unspoken words confirming what we both thought. They may not be dreams after all.

"Do we go to the Sacred City or to Bistaír?" I asked.

"I'd rather you stay here," came a careful answer. He walked to me and sat on the very edge of the sofa, the cushion dipping, our sides pressing together. "It isn't clear whether your brother is calling on us to help."

"Yes, but Pim and Efa," I began. He placed a hand atop mine. "And Yva is my friend." My voice was peaked.

"And she is the Laorinaghan representative. Her care will be superb. Plus, if Arik is there, there may be a Heiligan response."

"So, we wait?"

"I can ride out in the morning. Speak with Ewan."

I turned to him slowly, my mouth agape. My limbs locked up, building blocks of tension settling from my toes to my jaw as I transitioned from shock at his statement, to anger.

"Pardon?" I asked through clenched teeth. He was turned away from me, looking outside. I saw his hands tremble slightly. I briefly pictured Silas trying to tell me to stay behind, knowing it would never happen. The thought must have projected because a flash of pain crossed my husband's face.

"You're right. I'm quite certain he wouldn't ask you to stay. Which, I believe would make him an enabler to potential fallout."

I was slack-jawed at the response.

He shook his head, pinching the bridge of his nose so hard it left a mark.

"An enabler," I repeated under my breath. "So, you just know better than he does—than I do—and are telling me to stay behind." Regardless of whether I actually wanted to go, at that point, I was just pissed.

"I'm not telling you. I don't *tell* you what to do. I'm asking. Because I love you. Because there's a reason there are thousands of wards woven around this property."

"Am I . . . a liability?" The horror of that possibility shamed me.

He shook his head at my question and said no, meeting my eyes. "Please, Neysa," he said, already exasperated. "I just want to know that you are safe. It's just for a couple of days. If these visions were all true, and it seems as though we are headed that way, then just knowing you are here within the wards for a couple of days more would make me immensely more settled. But I won't ask you again to stay if you truly want to go."

I stood and walked to the door, staring out the back. Truth be told, I wasn't ready to leave yet. But would I regret sending him? I twisted my fingers into the knit of the sweater I wore and chewed my bottom lip. Dean, the children, Yva, Corra . . . Solange. Cadeyrn met me at the doors and turned me toward him.

"She's dead. She has been dead for over a century." His voice was quiet.

"Bestía was dead."

Understanding dawned on him. Males could be so thick.

"I will burn my way through the Gods to make sure nothing like that ever happens. I swear it." He ripped a slightly elongated incisor across his forearm, and I watched the blood well up and dive to the washed-wood floorboards. "In this world and the next, I will do anything it takes to keep our family together."

"I don't know what my role as heir to Heícate and Kalíma truly is meant to be, but you and I—we are my concern. Go to Bistaír. Come back to me." I took his forearm and pressed my lips to the cut before it healed, my tongue sweeping over the blood that contained the bond between us. He pulled me closer and tipped my chin up to look at him. I could lose myself in his glassy blue-green eyes. We stood for moments, just being together, knowing the repercussions that occurred each time we had been separated before. I laid my head against his chest, hearing the solid, comforting thump of his heartbeat.

I was just so tired.

Chapter 22

Silas

Storm clouds spread from Saarlaiche south, keeping miserable company with me on this trip to Bistaír. Dissolving into the water was effortless in the weather, moisture being everywhere. I was making excellent time and walked past the guarded gates of the estate just past midmorning the day after I'd left Aemes. To my surprise, there was already an assembly waiting there.

"Weasel," I greeted Reynard and hoped, with a mental cringe, that he knew it was more of a term of endearment now. He smirked at me and winked, and I trailed him into the house.

We followed the voices to the drawing room. Yule boughs were strung, and hints of citrus and spice lingered in the air. I squeezed my eyes shut briefly, wondering why I was so fucking sentimental lately. My sister was speaking to her former lover and the haberdashery sister, while Cadeyrn and Ewan chatted quietly near the windows. Sucked in cheeks and a murderous glower told me Ewan was in a right foul mood. Reynard whispered that it had been the same since he arrived the previous evening, on the heels of Stea. It confused me for a moment as he kept referring to Stea as "Starfish." We insinuated ourselves into the conversation with my cousin and brother-in-law. They each clapped me on the back. I looked around, wondering if Neysa was there, but said nothing. Corraidhín caught my eye and shook her head once.

"So, this is the cocktail party before we break off and discuss matters in private?" I asked.

Reynard snickered.

"I assume all the non-family will be gone shortly?"

Corraidhín growled at my question.

"The welcoming committee here is second to none," Stea remarked.

I already knew I didn't like her. I couldn't recall whether I'd had the same feeling all those years ago.

"Cool your suction cups, Starfish," Reynard cooed, making Stea reach for the knife at her hip.

My sister put a hand on her, and Ewan looked apoplectic.

"Bottom-feeder?" Dean asked Reynard, handing me an ale and jutting his chin at Stea.

"Mm. Yes," Weasel answered. "Take what they can and eat almost anything."

Gods and shite, I wanted to laugh aloud, but there were too many murderous faces in the room. I turned to Dean.

"I've never had any complaints," Stea responded. "I don't even know what your male would do with you as skinny and unfucka—"

My sister had her hand around Stea's throat. The interloper was pinned to the wall, a Yule bough hanging over her ginger hair. "Do not speak ill of my friend," she purred in Stea's face.

A door slammed upstairs, Cadeyrn and I realizing at the same time that Ewan had gone, Dean with him. Without a word, the rest of us followed them. Corraidhín released Stea and told her to stay put and perhaps think about what she'd said.

Cadeyrn laughed first, but I couldn't hold it in either.

"What?" my sister asked when we reached Ewan's study on the third floor.

"You just put her in time out," Cadeyrn said, wiping his eyes.

She lifted her chin and huffed. "Well, she was misbehaving."

We all just lost it and laughed. I was fucking exhausted and sat on the ground next to the settee where Cadeyrn perched. He looked . . . off. Probably uncomfortable without his mate. Reynard hopped onto the side of Ewan's desk.

"I am seeing the resemblances more now." I pointed to Dean and Reynard. They spared a shifty glance at one another.

"Reynard, darling," my sister called. "I know we are all busy right now, but perhaps you could show Dean how to harness his gifts while you're here."

Reynard choked on his wine. "Hellcat, he may be my brother, but I'm not sure I would be best to teach him anything. I had a horrid upbringing."

Cadeyrn stiffened beside me.

"Have I missed something?" he asked in his cool voice. The silence in the study was fucking profound.

"Christ," Dean said. "Did no one tell them?" We looked at one another like scolded children. "It wasn't exactly *my* place to say anything."

Ewan stepped up and briefly explained that his and Neysa's aunt Elíann was Dean's mother. Etienne, his father. He was Reynard's brother and Neysa and Ewan's cousin. Cadeyrn pinched the bridge of his nose and muttered something about Neysa not being here.

"Where is she?" I asked casually. He met my eyes, and I understood before he said anything.

"I asked her to stay home. Stay safe. She's had a hard time. Lately." He was carefully picking his words, but we all were frozen, listening. "She has these dreams. And then she started having visions." He told us about them and how he had originally thought it was just more dreams. His eyes were clouded with tears. Then he described the visions and there wasn't a sound in the room for a fuck ton of minutes.

"Sorry, mate," Dean said, breaking the silence. "But do you think it's the best idea to leave her alone?"

"What are you implying?" Ewan asked.

"I . . . don't know. I just think that whether it's her own psyche working against her, or this dead wife of yours coming back," Dean said, "I feel like she shouldn't be alone."

I thought the same. My money was on all of us thinking the same. Including Cadeyrn. My cousin sat there, his arsehole mask on, nostrils flaring, but I could feel the fear rolling off him. He muttered about all the wards he had on the property and the *baethaache* with her. It all seemed secure, but something still didn't sit right. Cadeyrn's constant shifting in his seat told me he was ready to get back home.

Ewan handed round copies of the correspondence he had with Arturus and Arik. I felt a slap on my neck, and I pulled a piece of paper from it, swearing under my breath. It smelled of open ocean and something I couldn't put my finger on, but my whole body tensed. A note from Saski opened in my fingers. She must have somehow sent it with her power. I read it. I reread it. I walked to the other side of the room and read the fucking thing again.

"Silas," Ewan called, pulling me out of figuring out the note from Saski. "I need you to go to Laorinaghe and work with Arik. I received a message this morning saying there is a small faction coming from Heilig to aid in the fires. We also need to figure out what to do with the witches downstairs."

THE NOTE STAYED in my jacket, thrumming with Saski's energy. What in every bleeding hell realm was she trying to say? I was ready to kill someone for touching her, and I knew I had no godsdamned right to think that way. She knew about the babes and thought they were mine. What's more, she probably had no clue Neysa lost them. Fucking hell. Shouts came from outside, and the sound of hoofbeats and screams cut through my thoughts. Everyone bolted from the study and took the stairs in twos and threes to reach the front. Guards had the doors blocked, the captain explaining that a fire had been set just outside the wards of the estate. The males stationed at the gate had been attacked. He was shifting, transferring the weight of his shield from forearm to his back, not quite meeting Ewan's eyes. Cadeyrn and I stepped in front of him together and asked who attacked the guards.

"I was not there, my lord," he answered. Of course you weren't there, you fuckwad. I heard Stea or Bea, or whatever the bleeding fuck their names were, snort behind me like she was already out of patience. I shot her a look over my shoulder where I saw her roll her eyes at me. My sister kept excellent company then.

"Who found them?" Cadeyrn pressed.

More footsteps crowded into the foyer, and I barked for everyone to stay the fuck back. The guard looked around. Corraidhín cocked her head to the side and drew a blade, but somewhere close one of the babes wailed.

"Take the children and secure His Majesty." No one even

knew to whom Cadeyrn spoke that last bit, but I wasn't surprised when I saw Dean lift Pim from the ground and try to guide Ewan from the front room. Ewan, being Ewan, shook off all hands, trying to get back to the captain. That ginger-haired Ledermaín sore in my arse stepped up next to Ewan as though she didn't care to know her place. Her hand sat on her leather-covered hip, a half smidge from the sword at her belt. I thumbed my own blades seeing the twitch of her fingers, knowing I was not even remotely sure whether she would be drawing a weapon in support of her king or against. *Godsdammit, Corraidhín*, I thought to my damned self.

"Captain," Ewan began. The captain's eyes were wild, and he clapped his heels together at being addressed by his king. Flakes of ash floated from his epaulets. "Start from the beginning and—"

"Does he have any information or what, Ewan?" Stea said, leaning against the walnut-framed arch that led from the foyer into the receiving hall. Her fingers extended toward her hilt.

There was a sucking pause in the air, and in that second of vacuumed stillness, no one moved. We all knew something was coming. We just weren't sure where it was coming from. Stea was launched back into the hall by an unknown force. Her screeching, stunning form was a butterfly pinned to a shadow box, her arms moving about like the nerve endings of useless wings. In the mayhem, the captain of Ewan's guard dropped, his head bashed in by a blunt object, the wound bleeding onto the foyer steps. A flash of golden hair and a pretty smile told me just who was behind the slaying. Corraidhín was pulling Ewan and Dean away, but Ewan was looking at Dean, whose arms were full of toddler, but his hands were upturned, and he was staring at them aghast. The magic signature stretched from Dean to Stea.

Ah, puppy dog grew a pair. I mean, a power.

On the floor, Cadeyrn was healing the captain as best he

could, though the blood was gurgling from the guard's mouth. I pulled my short sword and walked to the sisters in the hall. Stea was knocked out and Belleza had hellfire burning in her eyes. Possibly because Reynard had her hair in his fist, his arm locked around her throat.

"Silas," Cadeyrn called. "That piece of shit assassin we let go in the forest has now attacked within the wards on both this estate and Yva's." I knew what he was thinking. Fucking hell, I didn't even know where we needed to start.

"Send a hawk to Neysa."

Chapter 23

Neysa

Saski's note came by hawk, and I was surprised at the tone of it. Her comradery. My heart ached being reminded of the babies I'd lost a few months ago. Before writing her back, I made myself a cup of valerian tea. The tea had been harvested in the light of a full moon, cleansed and packaged with amethyst in an attempt by my healer to give me assistance in eradicating my nightmares. Being alone here was stranger than I thought it would be. I was used to solitude. I lived alone after my divorce and even in the cottage in Barlowe Combe. Then again in London and Richmond when I was thrust through the Veil last year. Somehow, though, the seclusion of this beautiful home, paired with my not wanting Cadeyrn to be in danger, made me uneasy. Closing my eyes while I sat at the writing desk in our sparsely furnished office, I let the sound of the night surf beyond the doors calm me. Quiet nighttime sounds trickled in. The hum of the hydropowered fan my husband built, some sort of insect in the brush bracketing in the house, the increasing intensity of waves beyond the dunes, intermittent winds whipping sand onto the glass doors, warning me of the storm to come. I shivered, trying to shake off the arachnid legs of unease walking up my spine.

Every room, apart from the nursery upstairs, had a set of French doors leading to the outside. It was only the second night Cadeyrn had been gone. He sent a hawk that he'd arrived in Bistaír. It wasn't that far, though one had to account for the tides to cross between the mainland and the Ispil of Bogvi, and I really didn't understand the tides yet without a clear visual: high tide, low tide. So, really, I couldn't plan when to cross on my own without Cadeyrn. A fact which irked me. My mate and his cousins could always feel for a shift in the tides before they changed. A bonus to having a water affinity. I wondered if sirens like Arik and Saski could predict the tides. Saski always seemed to know the layout of everything around her. Even in a foreign situation.

Clarity had me open my eyes and pick up a pen to write Saski back. A flash of light bounced in my peripheral vision. I looked up. Earlier the sky clouded over, rain threatening to come in from the mainland. There was a charge in the air, lifting the gauzy curtain on my windows. I had yet to experience a full lightning storm here on the ocean. I felt closer to Silas thinking of it, and so I touched the nib to the paper and wrote.

Saski,

Your letter came as a surprise, but I am glad of it. Though we are far from the fires, there is something brewing here, and Cadeyrn has gone to check in with my brother and see what he can do to help. There were so many things unsaid when we last saw each other. I want you to know that I have no grudge against you. It is not my place to say anything in regard to your relationship with Silas, but I have no grudge. I cannot say much about this, as the wound is still fresh, but Cadeyrn and I lost the babes. It is a grief I was not expecting to swallow me as whole as it has done. I would not wish it on anyone.

If there are matters of state I can help with, please reach out. I may not know the answers, but perhaps I can be a sounding board for you and Ludek. Give him and Basz my love.

Take care of yourself, Saski. You deserve to be happy.

Your cousin,

Neysa

I called for our hawk, sending it off, wondering how it would fair in the oncoming weather. Typically, we kept two, but just after Cadeyrn left, one fell ill. I brought it to my healer, and she'd had the bird since yesterday, tending to its ailment. Nothing was visibly wrong with it. No injury. However, it seemed to have begun wasting at an alarming rate. It didn't occur to me that perhaps I should not send out this hawk for mere correspondence. It never crossed my mind I might need it for an emergency. I tucked the note into the carrier tube on the hawk's leg and stroked its down. It squawked and took flight as another flash of lightning lit the white caps of the waves. On the wooden deck between the dunes, the flash illuminated a figure standing still, looking at me. I gasped and stepped back into the house, shutting the glass doors, and sliding the lock. Was I seeing things? Prickles rose up my spine one at a time like a spider counting my vertebrae. Night reigned black beyond my doors. There was no longer the sound of that mystery insect. There was only constant tumultuous surf and insistent winds.

Breathe. My chest was heavy, the index finger and thumb of anxiety squeezing my lungs, clouding my eyes.

Don't be an anxious mess, Neysa, I scolded myself. *You're not helpless. Plus, you're probably just tired and worried about Cadeyrn.*

I waited for another flash, wrapping my cashmere throw

around my shoulders, twisting the ends of it around my fingers, and watched the night grow restless.

I wished I'd had the dogs with me, but they were in Saarlaiche with Silas. Or Sleípnyr, who was probably snoring in his stable. Though, who brings a horse in the house? I would absolutely have brought a horse in the house in that moment. I looked within myself and felt for my tether to Cadeyrn. We were too far away to communicate with all these wards on the property. It was as if our magical Wi-Fi was out. A phone would have been handy right about then. A quick text like,

Hey, Cadeyrn. FYI, there's a huge storm brewing rn and I'm pretty sure I saw someone outside our house. I'll lyk if it's evil or not.

Sometimes human technology did beat magic. Dammit. I was starting to lose my calm. And I was really close to bringing a horse in the house. Another flash, and the rumble that followed was angry and foreboding. The very foundation of the house rolled under me like the earthquake-proof structures in California. *Dammit, Neysa. Don't lose it now.* I didn't even have a hawk anymore if I needed one. On the tail end of the thunder came a keening wail I recognized as that of the *baethaache*. Oh, thank the Gods. They hadn't been around much today, and I assumed they'd been hunting. The wail sounded as though it was farther away than I would have liked, but it gave me some comfort. Until I heard it moving farther out. Why did we have the only beasties in existence who were scared of thunder?

The front door and back patio doors were closed, but oh Gods, I hadn't locked them. I ran through the hall and living room, arriving at the doors as the lighting flashed again. The figure was illuminated just outside on the deck. White garments and hair rose and billowed around her, dark magic shimmering. I screamed as the bolt slid home. Before I could look away, the figure lit up again, her moonlight-colored hair lifting in the static. The air around her crackled with veins of electricity. She smiled and lifted a small hand to wave at me.

Before I could blink, she was pressed against the glass, trying the handle, gnarled incisors bared at me. Cracked nails, long as talons, gauged at the glass. She was a phantom, for sure, but the deep gashes in the glass were very real. Were I to use my magic, I would blow the door to pieces. Faith that our wards would hold was all I had. She continued gnashing at me. Black oozed from her mouth where it ran down over her rotted teeth. I felt for Cadeyrn's magic again. Our inner communication wasn't working at all, and I could not figure out why our protection spells weren't working completely. The wards should have held on the whole property. There should have been nothing of either realm which could have overridden the wards. In my head, I was screaming for Cadeyrn, for Silas, for Ewan, Sleípnyr. Anyone. The rain started, fat drops splashing on the deck, tossed this way and that by angry winds, like hastily thrown projectiles. Still the figure stood there, staring at me. The same tiny, regal figure I'd seen in visions. The one who tried to kill my husband.

Solange.

Anger bubbled in me, darker and deadlier than I was ready for. No one wanted to be on the receiving end of my hate and anger. It turned me from a frightened animal, protecting her home, to a vengeful warrior, itching to engage. Solange smashed her hand against the glass, but it held without a vibration. Then she was gone. Only a shimmer of magic in the dark storm indicated anything had been there. Of course, Reynard's sister would have speed. Where she went, I could only guess. I caught my breath and went to each window and door, checking locks and feeling for the magic Cadeyrn used to seal the wards. I had been wearing loose pajama pants, but quickly changed to my leathers, knowing she wouldn't be gone long and the night would be anything but quiet. And I was ready for a fight. The forearm dagger Cadeyrn had gifted me on Yule two years ago sat comfortably on my arm. I flicked it out and in several times, checking the mechanism that made it shoot out and bringing myself to my killing calm.

Chanè à doinne aech mise fhine. I am no one's but my own, regardless of delayed stress disorder, prophetic visions, or murderous, undead ex-wives of my husband's. I tested the mechanism once more, then I strapped small swords to my thighs, my powder-coated narrow sword down my back, and grabbed a quiver of fire glass arrows and a bow, stringing it as I walked into the hall. I was not a mad woman. I was a pissed-off warrior with a realm's worth of rage which needed an outlet.

The sea was raging. Winds rocked the outside walls, the hum of constant crashing surf carrying up from the beach. Back in the living room, I reluctantly looked out the blackened doors. Was it ever a good idea to look out a dark window? I really didn't think so, yet I did it anyway. No one. Lightning flashed again, and she was standing there, a sword in hand. I jumped, which pissed me off. Before I had time to register another presence in the house, wholly different to Solange, a knife moved toward my face. I tipped my head sideways quick enough to avoid getting brained, but the steel sliced a line from my temple to ear. I spun with a curse. How another fae was able to get in, I couldn't fathom. Blood ran freely down my face, and I dropped to the ground, kicking out. Just as my boot hit the other fae, he was gone. Blinked out from very fabric of the world for all I could tell. For a split second, I wondered if I had imagined it, yet the taste of iron made it evident I had not. I backed against the wall, knocking over the bowl we had by the door. It crashed down, porcelain shards splintering into my hands.

The male blinked into existence before me. Space-time

rippled with his appearance. I knew him. He was the one who'd attacked me in Bulgaria two years ago. The one who'd attacked our camp in Veruni, stabbed Silas, and, I was now quite certain, attacked Yva.

This was meant to be an extermination. I launched myself at him, registering Solange beyond the doors, chanting with both hands pressed to the glass. She was trying to forge a key to unlock the wards. Shit. Golden Boy blinked away. Particle transference. *Just like Cadeyrn's* my mind said. If I could reach into the power of Cadeyrn's that I shared, I could reverse the particles. *For every action, there is an equal and opposite reaction.* It might be Newton's Third Law, and he may have been a human, in a nonmagical realm, but the same held true in this realm. If some magical affinity allowed him to enact particle transference, then not only could I use Cadeyrn's power against him, I could also tap into my mate's healing abilities. Just as Cadeyrn was able to heal, he was equally capable of dismantling a healthy conglomeration of cells. I could dissect the particles as he transferred. A smile wiggled its way to the corners of my mouth. Oh, was I ready to fight.

Golden Boy appeared next to me and swiped my arm with his knife. The leather took the brunt of the blade. I used the reverse transference, and he stopped his progression, hovering between being here and not. Half of his form was corporeal, half was impressionistic paint drops attempting to form a picture. A look of horror showed on his face, which I promptly shoved my dagger into. The blade slipped into his eye socket, popping the tawny eyeball from its nook. He screamed, blood pouring through his nose and mouth. I released the hold I had on his transmittal, and he left completely. I doubted he would be back but wasn't positive. I was so pissed that this invasion messed up my new house.

Leaving Solange to her ghostly chant, I walked to the kitchen and left though the kitchen door, coming round the back of the house. Rain matted my hair instantly, a mix of water and blood running into my eyes. It ran into the collar of my jacket, but I hardly noticed. I unsheathed my sword and called out to her, also willing the bloody *baethaache* to arrive quickly. Neither of them liked lightning, so I hoped they hadn't abandoned homecoming altogether and holed up somewhere. Shit. The light around Solange flickered, her form corporeal but luminescent. The very air around her looked disconcertingly similar to the Veil. Like staring through petrol fumes. She turned to me.

"We haven't been introduced," I called over the driving rain. My sword spun in that arrogant way my dad hated. "I am Neysa, Cadeyrn's mate and wife, heir to Heícate and Kalíma. You are dead."

"He is not yours," she said in a slippery singsong voice. It moved through the night between us like a child's song through a failing radio signal.

I shivered despite myself.

"He has always been mine," she screamed and ran at me, though it was more of a glide. I swung my sword, missing her by an inch as she moved aside and glided back to me with Reynard's speed. If nothing else, I wanted to put her back in the ground for what she did to Reynard. Then I wanted to burn the ground until there was nothing left of her in atom nor memory.

"The stars in the fucking sky and the Gods themselves beg to differ with you, Solange."

"*We* will be Gods," she said, her watery voice projected to me. It bounced around us, an echo in the pocket of ether. She pulled her arms back, elbows going out to the sides like wings, and thrust her arms forward. I had barely enough time to roll from the magic blast, sending a backdraft of my own magic in retaliation. Really, I didn't know why I hadn't used magic on her first. Old habits die hard. So do murderous ex-wives, apparently. She screeched and threw another wave of energy at me, though the blast fell too far to the left. I channeled the storm and hoped that in some far-off link I still had to Silas, I could piggyback on his power. As I held my sword aloft, lightning touched down from the sky and hit my blade, sending me careening back into the wall of the house. Not quite what I had hoped.

Solange cackled, head thrown back, jaw unhinged, and glided toward me in that fucking creepy way. Her essence loomed over me, choking my breath and pulling the life from my veins. No part of me was able to move from her hold. Draining. Everything in me was draining. I was a leaf losing its vitality, turning to crumbling, papery fertilizer. She leaned over me farther, her hair all over my face. That was when her teeth gnawed at my nose. Tearing skin and crunching cartilage. I screamed and pushed at the magic shackles she had pinning me. Every centimeter of my vision was filled with her platinum hair and blood-addled eyes as her ragged teeth tore at my nose. Black ooze and my own blood choked me, coating my throat.

Fight. It. Neysa.

I called the lightning once more, allowing it to not only fill me but also hit Solange with the full force of my power. She dissipated into the ozone of the storm. I knew we hadn't seen the last of her. Like Bestía, there was a spell cast, and it had to be broken. No telling how much time I had and if my strength was waning. My rage sure as hell was not. In the meantime, I needed to get the hell out of my house and warn the others about the golden-haired assassin that sliced my godsdamned face.

Sleípnyr burst through his stable and came to me as though I'd called him. He was saddled and ready to ride, and I couldn't for the life of me figure out how. He snorted, mocking me for underestimating him again. Wasting no time, I restrapped my sword on my back and mounted my beautiful horse. We took off at full tilt toward the coast road. I knew I didn't have to tell him where to go. He could sense my thoughts and direction. Plus, he probably instinctively knew which way to go to avoid being trapped at the tip of a narrow peninsula.

Without a boat, we had two options. Either go all the way up the Ispil of Bogvi, and back down into Maesarra, adding three to four days to the trek, and spend each second not knowing when and where we would be attacked again. Or, hope that we hit low tide and were able to cross the straights. About an hour up the road where the rocks jutted from the sea, should we arrive before the rise in tide, we could pick our way across the pink rocks. It was less than a mile, but dangerous under the best circumstances. Full, moonless dark in a storm with two assassins on our tail was probably the worst circumstances.

Sleípnyr's head was down, pushing faster, as though he sensed the tides. A fae kelpie, who would never leave my side. The water was slowly rising when we arrived, but he and I both pressed on. I rubbed a hand at my still-bleeding face. Salt spray kept my powers from healing myself. It didn't slip my mind that this would be a rather unfortunate time to be ambushed if my waning powers and salt were working to keep me from healing.

Damn it, Cadeyrn, I thought. *Why didn't I just go with you?*

Not wanting to put Sleípnyr in more danger, I dismounted and touched a foot down on the slick rock. We hiked together, hopping over the cracks and separations in the dark stones. My eyes were swollen, the blood from my chewed nose filling every pocket of skin on my face. I yelled for Heícate to help. Perhaps it was presumptuous of me, but I was angry and exhausted and ready to take every inch of it all out on someone. The Goddess of Magic did not answer my plea.

Still the rain came down, lightning every once in a while, showing us how far we would fall, should we slip between the rocks. Gaping crevices of endless black water churned, waiting to steal us away like greedy sentries at the River Styx. The faint silhouette of pine trees was visible on the other side, but they were still about a hundred meters away. Maybe more. My vision blurred with blood and a mix of seawater and driving rain. Muscles in my thighs burned with the constant activation. I stayed in a sort of squat, clenching my inner thighs in order to keep my center of gravity low and not get blown from the rocks. Each wind gust and back blow from a wave tipped me. Sleípnyr kept stepping back to brace me when I got knocked back. He was the one keeping me alive. With less-than-stellar vision and my entire body half-frozen and wet, I was near to collapsing. My leathers stuck to me, restricting movement and chafing my skin underneath.

Waves lapped at the cliffs, making me feel as though the rocks themselves were swaying. More memories of seismic activity in Los Angeles moved through my mind.

Sometimes the earth gripes, Little Moon, Dad had said to me years before. *Just like the foundation this house was built on, you have to roll with it.*

Sleípnyr nudged me. I touched his neck and kept on.

"I'm rolling with it, Dad," I said aloud. My words were swallowed by great dueling gusts of wind. I grabbed the reins, leaning into Sleípnyr's flank. A gap larger than we had yet crossed, stood before us. There was no other way to get over, so I threw a booted foot across.

That was a mistake.

Straddling either side, I looked at my horse, helpless and desperate. The water was rising, his hooves covered. Even my boots were weighted down. I scrambled to the other rock and slipped. Every pull-up I had ever done, each tree branch I had used as a bar on which to build my strength, helped me cling to the scruff of stone I had one blood-covered hand over. It was a mere twig. Pine or juniper. Some evergreen branch stubborn enough to grow from a rock perpetually subject to the temper of the ocean. The water rushed over me, trying to pull me down to the sea below. I yelled, but the sound was gone before it came out. Waves broke over my head, seawater going down my throat. The branch creaked in my grip before the water receded for a moment. Sleípnyr whinnied, and I heard him jump from one side to the other just as my head started to go under again. I crested to see my horse's own head coming at me, biting my jacket, teeth glancing off my shoulder. Some distant part of me knew it would hurt at some point. In some quiet situation where I wasn't actively drowning. I let go of the rock with one hand, grabbing onto his mane as he yanked me out of the crevice and onto the rock. The sky flashed bright again. I could see it was nearly a straight shot to the shore beyond. We sprinted, the water rising faster and faster. One last leap took us from the death rocks onto the Maesarra mainland.

I hit the ground in a shoulder roll, then doubled over, my lungs straining with exertion. Sleípnyr was sweating and panting beside me. He was eyeing the split seam of my jacket and torn shoulder muscle underneath. If a horse had a repentant, guilty look, it would have been his. But all I felt was gratitude. I didn't trust staying in one place for long. As soon as our breathing normalized, I patted his head and my smoky stallion and I took off for Bistaír. I wasn't shocked that things had gone awry, but I did think that if I had simply gone with Cadeyrn in the first place, I wouldn't be tearing through the countryside at four in the morning, bleeding from several places, and not really having any clue where I was. Thank the Gods for Sleípnyr. He lifted his massive head higher at my thought.

"Yeah, you. Saved me again, you did."

He snorted and picked up more speed. My legs were cramped, my back ached in ways suggesting I may not even be able to dismount on my own. The sun peeked from the hills in the distance, then lifted higher into the sky. Something in the sunrise injected a bit of optimism to my ride. We passed the villages outside of Craghen and were on the road to Bistaír at last. I'd still only been there the once, after Cadeyrn retrieved me from the human realm. Yet we were close enough that my ancestral home pulled me toward it. The closer we came, the more I felt something wrong there as well. The gates had twice the number of guards I'd seen last time. I told them who I was, though it seemed they all knew. The horse's great sides were heaving, his body covered in sweat. A groom ran to take him, and I made him swear to make sure he was okay. My body slid sideways off Sleípnyr, hitting the gravel with a painful crunch, from which I lifted myself with forced stoicism. Liveried officers swung the doors open for me, and I all but tumbled inside.

No one was in the front of the home. I stood a moment trying to gather my thoughts when Efa started howling from above. She sensed my arrival, it seemed, and was throwing images toward me. I had no energy left to climb the stairs, so I slid to the flagstone floor and tipped my blood-crusted head back against the wood. Footsteps were running, and then Cadeyrn's hands were on my face. I couldn't see him, but the horror he was projecting was palpable. I hadn't seen my face, but guessed it was a mess.

"I'll take her to my room," he was saying. Others' hands were on me too. Efa's and Corra's.

Efa held my index finger and projected images to me of things that had occurred there.

"She's quick to rat us all out it seems," Cadeyrn said to me with a forced half smile. I snorted, but even that was too much effort. One of my nostrils was blocked by dried blood from where Solange had chewed my nose.

"Is everyone here safe?" I managed.

"Yes. Silas has gone to the Sacred City, but we are all here."

"Good. Because I just had a real shit night," I said and closed my eyes.

Chapter 24

Neysa

"In her visions, it was just Solange standing there, trying to, I don't know, touch my arm or something." Cadeyrn was whispering. "She wasn't this *naem maerbh*."

"She chewed her godsdamned face." Another male voice. Ewan. They were whispering so low I couldn't catch all of what was being said. I'd only managed to tell Cadeyrn bits of what happened before my body demanded sleep. By the feel of things, I wasn't completely healed. Warm fingers curled into mine on my left, and a hand rested on my right arm. There were so many scents in the room, I couldn't tell who was with me.

"Halloo, Pet," Dean whispered. "You can keep pretending to sleep if it suits."

I did open my eyes to a pounding sort of headache. Efa was asleep on my left, her little body curled into mine. I bit back a sob.

Dean's eyes tried to catch mine, and I noted they were a fluid, deep brown now, his ears softly pointed. I tried blinking to refocus. He smiled. "Ah, that. Right now, it's all about you, Pet. Not me." He winked, then kissed the top of my head.

My head was worse than I thought if I was seeing Dean as fae. Blinking in succession was doing nothing to round his ears and was only making the creeping migraine worse.

Cadeyrn and Ewan shuffled over. I sighed and sat up, waving off the protests and fussing. I demanded to know what had happened here, and they reluctantly told me before I told my own tale. Cadeyrn swore and scraped his hands through his hair, making it stand a good four inches above his head. I would have smiled if I wasn't such a wreck. And a tiny bit miffed at him for insisting I stay behind.

"So, let me get this straight, Pet," Dean began.

"Must you call her that?" Cadeyrn asked, icy contempt in his voice.

I glared at him.

"Not only were you attacked by the same assassin who attacked Yva and the captain here, you were visited by a flesh-eating spirit who happens to be Cadeyrn's ex-wife and Reynard's sister?"

"Your sister too, puppy eyes," Reynard said, fiddling with the button on his riding jacket.

I whipped my head to him and back to Dean. Ouch.

"Sorry, Kitten," he said and blew me a kiss.

"Either that, or I imagined the whole thing, chewed my own face, sliced my own face, cut my own side, and asked my fucking horse to bite my shoulder. I suppose though, who knows, it's plausible." I was looking at Cadeyrn with ice spears in my own eyes. I knew he hadn't meant to disregard my visions, but in truth, I felt he had. At least the severity of them. The room was quiet, and Dean slipped away from the bed to stand next to Ewan. Efa wiggled, and I pulled her in closer to cuddle while Ewan told me Corra was researching *naem maerbh* to figure out how to get rid of Solange for good. At the squeeze of my brows, Ewan explained, "*Naem maerbh* are essentially the living dead."

"Zombies," Dean muttered.

"Corra spoke once of these zombie animals, and I'm not certain that would be a correct parallel to draw," Ewan said. "If they chase slow-running humans, I think it's a bit off."

"What exactly did Corraidhín tell you about zombies?" Cadeyrn asked. Ewan flushed and waved us off.

"She wasn't a zombie though," I said. The memory of her undulating form throwing the air around her into a haze while she came for my face made me feel nauseous. Almost as nauseous as hearing her claim Cadeyrn. "She was more like a ghost. But corporeal," I said. "She moved about like she was a ghost. Like she wasn't adhering to this realm, yet she could obviously inflict damage." I motioned to my healing face. "The way she chewed at me . . ." I shuddered.

Ewan and Cadeyrn shared a look I did not like.

"That was zombie-ish, I suppose. But then she was sucking me dry."

Cadeyrn coughed.

"Succubus?" Dean asked.

"Obviously," Reynard agreed. "She always was one."

That was when I thought Cadeyrn would have offered something. Instead, he looked spooked. Like he had retreated into himself and was no longer participating in this discourse.

"I guess like a succubus. I would have said vampire, had it not seemed ridiculous—"

"Pet, we are quite literally, living with the faeries. Nothing seems ridiculous anymore." I made an agreeable sound.

"She was draining my life. My life force. Breathing me in, kind of. I felt myself withering. Like when you see photos of the Dust Bowl in the 1930s." Lands once fruitful were barren. I wished Corra were there. I bet she had seen documentaries on the Great Depression. The males in the room all seemed quiet and horrified.

Cadeyrn was at the window looking out, his thoughts shut

off to me. The world began to fall away in tiles. My eyes were for Cadeyrn, and he was a marked distance from me. The healer, Cadeyrn's earlier words of having her come daily, his flippant response to my visions. It all stung. Maybe I was just so very tired. But my insides were a fuse set alight. I started to cry. It was embarrassing, but I couldn't help it. Everything in me ached with betrayal and loss. Ewan lifted Efa from the bed and ushered everyone out of the room. Cadeyrn stood, fidgeting with his hands.

"I shouldn't have left," he said softly.

"I've heard that before," I spat, pushing at my eyes.

"That's not fair, Neysa."

I laughed in a dark burst. "Is anything? You shouldn't have left? No, it's that I should have been here with you, rather than left behind like some Victorian laudanum addict in a room with yellow fucking walls!"

"I don't think I follow the—"

"No, you don't because all you read were those stupid military novels. I mean that you treated me like a helpless woman in hysterics, when I was having legitimate prognostications of what was going to happen!"

"By the Gods, you are pulling the professor card today, aren't you? I've read far more than I imagine you have," he sneered.

I swung from the bed and pretended it didn't send me spinning into a world of spotted eyesight. I had on a shirt which hung to midthigh. Blood leaked through the shoulder, and my knees wobbled.

"I have never thought you hysterical. I'm sorry, alright?" he said, eyes wide. "I'm sorry I left. You were right," he said with a . . . tone.

"I think you should go." I lifted my chin and breathed through my nose. Well, one nostril.

"What? Why?"

"Because I understand that my mental acuity is a question in your mind. And so long as that's contrary to what I know to be true, then it's a bone of contention between us."

"Neysa," he pleaded.

I shook my head and closed my eyes briefly.

"I believed what you saw. I just thought it would be safer for you at home with the wards, rather than coming here where there was expected risk. I made the mistake. I see that. I should have stayed."

"Cade! I should have come here. We should have been together. Here. I'm going to ask you something before you leave."

He lifted his eyes from the wooden floorboards, and I nearly lost my resolve to keep pressing. Those eyes were my undoing. But if I asked and he answered the way I hoped he would, then I could grab for his hand the way I saw, in the clenching and unclenching of his fingers, he wanted to reach for me. If he answered the way I wanted him to answer, he could hold me in this bed and we could figure out this *naem maerbh* thing. Together.

"Do you believe Solange attacked me?" It came out quickly and louder than I'd wanted.

He was quiet for a beat too long.

"I saw your memory," he said finally.

I smiled at him, solemn and regretful as tears rolled from my eyes. Of all the things I thought could come between us, his questioning my sanity was not one of them. He took a half step toward me. I held up a hand.

"That's not a yes. Please leave." I turned away. For what felt like long moments, it was as if those seafoam eyes imprinted on me. His voice in my head, asking to let him in. When I stayed facing the painting on the wall, a portrait of one of my mother's dogs, I heard him leave. Once the door closed, I shook and tore a pillow to pieces to keep from screaming. *Keep it in check, Neysa.*

I was starving, having not even eaten a proper dinner the previous night. I needed to bathe, eat, and check on Sleípnyr. Corra had left me some clothes, which made me snort aloud, because I was back to borrowing clothes from others. Had I come in the first place, I would have my own damned clothes. Although, I supposed I really didn't have much of my own yet anyway. I combed out my hair and slid a silver clip into the brown waves to hold it back while it dried.

I looked like hell. My eyes were swollen and red, my lips had no color. Briefly, I wondered if I could cloak myself to look better. A facade of healthy, flushed cheeks and unhaunted eyes. Then I realized I didn't care anymore. I was apathetic to how I looked if they thought I was mad anyway. Corra's slim black trousers and thin olive-green knit sleeveless top looked better than what I'd been wearing lately anyway, since my clothing hadn't arrived. I topped it with a black, animal skin jacket, and slipped on the boots. I was glad I didn't have a frumpy sister-in-law. The thought almost made me smile.

Voices were distant, probably coming from the far end of the hall, or even Ewan's study around the corner. I slipped out and walked quickly toward the stairs. Reynard appeared next to me as I took the steps. He slid down the banister, and we walked out through the kitchens together, arms linked.

"Does everyone think I'm mad?" I rounded on him as soon as were out of fae earshot.

"Not everyone, no." He kept walking in the direction of the stables. "I don't."

I couldn't breathe, so I stayed quiet.

"My father was trying to bring Solange back. She used dark, aulde magics for many years. It wouldn't have been unheard of for her to be brought back in that form. She was barely above a flesh-eating demon when she was properly alive."

The day hung between warm and slightly chilly. The lawn between manor and stables smelled of fresh grass and pine needles.

"For the record," Reynard said, breaking the silence. "I don't think for a moment Cadeyrn thinks you're mad."

I snorted.

"I am quite serious, Kitten. He may switch on his cold bastard facade every now and again, but I've always seen through him, and right now, I do not think he thinks you are mad."

"Could have fooled me."

"I think he's having processing issues."

I did laugh at that. Reynard didn't. I understood the trauma he went through in his abusive family. I knew what Solange put him through when they were younger. I understood why he didn't laugh with me.

"Well, he needs to process a lot quicker," I said instead. Reynard squeezed my arm in response.

Sleípnyr stood from his soft hay when we approached. I stroked his muzzle and kissed it. He sniffed at my shoulder and nudged me. Honestly, had he been able to hug me, he would have. Reynard pulled an apple from his jacket and fed it to my majestic horse.

"Cyrranus?" I asked Reynard. "You both good?"

He rolled his eyes and fanned himself. I laughed.

"You have no idea, darling." He pulled aside his jacket to show me a small scar where his neck and shoulder met. I had a similar one on either side of my neck. Swallowing my pain, I hugged him.

"Mates, huh? Such a handsome pair." I grabbed a brush and began long strokes on the horse's gunmetal coat. "When she attacked me, I wanted to kill her. I wanted to eradicate her for what she did to you. What she took from you."

He quirked a pale eyebrow at me. "We will end this. I won't allow her to take more from us," my friend swore.

"No one believes me, Reynard. They think I'm batshit crazy. My mate thinks I am."

"What else do you remember from that night? Let's think it all out," he suggested. I continued to stroke Sleípnyr.

"Solange had a sword, and then it was gone. It was covered in jewels. Onyx and rubies, with an inscription down the blade. I couldn't read it."

He paled looking at me.

"Tell Cadeyrn that," he whispered. "The Sword of Kaeres. It is used by those anointed by the Goddess of War and Death. Tell him. He will believe you."

I kissed Sleípnyr again, wishing I could bring him in the house, and Reynard and I walked from the stables to the fading light of day.

"But will anyone else? I can see it in their faces. They wouldn't believe me. I don't even know if they think I attacked myself, or just that the assassin did it all and I was imagining Solange. Telling them of a sword won't help. They'd say I read it somewhere."

We sat on the long grass near the stables, backs against large, rounded boulders. I picked at the grass. The sun fled to its nighttime home, and still we sat there in comfortable silence.

"I don't even want to be in there, Reynard," I admitted.

"I know, Kitten."

A figure walked over in the darkness. I stiffened before realizing it was Dean. He dropped down on my other side and pulled at the grass. Between his fingers, he held it and whistled through the blade. It was funny that the three of us were somehow related. Not even shocking. Dean jumped and said he'd be right back. I shrugged, laying my head on Reynard's shoulder. After a time, Dean came back and handed me a plate and a glass. The plate was covered in fried potatoes and cheese.

"Cheesy chips," he said, a bit shy. "Or the closest thing Cook could make. He's a right intimidating one, isn't he?"

I took the plate and began ungracefully shoveling the food into my mouth. The males were snickering. When was the last time I had eaten? At least a full day. In the glass was a red wine with winter fruits.

"Remember the time you told me your tale? We went for tapas and were drinking loads of sangria."

Reynard sighed. "Sounds delightful. Invite me next time."
I handed Reynard the glass to sip.

"I believed you then, and I believe you now, Pet."

"Thank you both. I am fortunate in my friends."

"Mm, yes. Just think, you could be stuck with ugly coconspirators," Reynard quipped and hopped to standing, pulling me up. "Let's find Ama and get you settled in your own chamber."

Chapter 25

Corraidhín

Volumes upon volumes of folklore, mythology, and history had much of the same thing to say. *Naem maerbh* could be killed only by a worthy opponent. A chosen one, if you will. If the others didn't believe Neysa before, throwing some chosen one verbiage into the mix surely wouldn't help to convince them. I could see why Cadeyrn had been concerned. I knew Neysa was troubled. I could feel it, and so could both my children in different ways. But I'd be godsdamned if I didn't stand by her. Especially after the way I'd treated her earlier this autumn. What I needed to do was figure out how to show Cadeyrn and Ewan she spoke the truth before Silas got wind of this. The last thing we needed was my brother and cousin coming to blows again. Because I knew Silas would believe Neysa. I just didn't know why Cadeyrn didn't.

Ama put Neysa up in a chamber near the nursery. She stayed out on the grounds all day running, training with Dean, and showing him the sword. She tended to her horse quite a bit. In the evenings, she took her meals in her rooms and read to the children before retiring. Cadeyrn was out of his mind.

"I don't know why she won't even see me," he rasped, squeezing the bridge of his nose hard enough to leave a mark. Six full days after she came falling into the house, her face chewed and sliced, her ribs serrated, her hands embedded with shards of pottery.

Efa had screamed. She'd sensed her coming in and screamed to get to her. It was altogether quite alarming. Six days later, and she had told my cousin to stay away. I said good for her. Though I knew it was killing them both. Ewan was preoccupied figuring out the wards, who was sending the assassin, what part of Etienne's organization was still viable, and the fires. He stopped in to see Neysa when she was with the children, and I knew the little arse only did it then so he wouldn't have to admit to her he was the main hold out on believing her. Reynard left to make certain Cyrranus was secure, so Neysa had only Dean to keep her company. Perhaps I was a coward as well, though I wanted to present a well-documented case for her. So, I stayed mostly in the library and my study.

The night fell heavy, and tensions were high all around. Cadeyrn and Ewan were reconfiguring wards for all representative homes, sharing a glass of wine before dinner. I had just gotten the children down, though I hadn't seen Neysa reading to them that evening. I joined the males in the drawing room, making notes in my book as well. Winter in our home was nearly as inviting as it had been in Aemes. I always missed our parents this time of year. The feel of the house that had so much love. My eyes were trained on the iron sconces either side of the archway. Dean walked by, filthy and wet, not bothering to speak to us on his way to the kitchens.

"Do you think there's any truth at all to it?" Ewan asked, his face still looking down at a map of Veruni. "I mean, all's been quiet here. I've not heard of anything amiss elsewhere.

Could she have injured the assassin enough to halt his mission?"

Cadeyrn made a face I couldn't decipher. Almost like he was scenting a memory, his skin going pale.

"The house has so many wards, Ewan." His response was whispered.

"As we do here," I chimed in.

"These are older. Unchecked," he answered.

"Her healer. Has she been contacted?" Ewan asked. "Did she say anything about Neysa being a danger to herself?"

I felt sick listening to them ask these questions. Before I had a chance to open my own mouth in defense of Neysa, I was beat to the task.

"She is not," came a tight, articulated voice from the doorway. Dean walked in and stood toe to toe with Cadeyrn. "She is not hallucinating." Well, well. Puppy eyes grew a pair.

Cadeyrn muttered under his breath that he knew she bloody well wasn't hallucinating, but Ewan must not have heard him.

"And you know this how?" Ewan asked Dean.

"Because I know her," the other male said simply.

"She's my wife." Cadeyrn snarled in his face, not realizing they were playing pot and kettle. Bloody males.

"That she is, mate. But you're losing her."

Cadeyrn staggered back like he'd been kicked. Someone had to say it.

"She won't see me," he bit out through gritted teeth.

"Because you are treating her like she is stark raving bloody mad!" Dean raised his voice. "She was attacked, and you are victim shaming her. And it's killing her. The same way being in the human realm was killing her. You didn't see her then. I did. I was there and I'm recognizing the signs. You've taken away the most important thing you have together. Trust."

I didn't know if Cadeyrn was going to be sick or hit Dean.

Ewan was flushed and seemed ready to go along with whatever Cadeyrn decided. Male pack mentality. Imbeciles. I stood up shoulder to shoulder with Dean.

"It's killing me too! I do believe her. I have never not believed her," Cadeyrn said.

"Then why don't you act like it?"

We all spun to see Neysa standing in the archway, her leathers mud splattered. Cadeyrn took a step toward her, and she stepped back. My gifts could see a crumbling within them both. It was like a doppelgänger of each stood, reaching toward the other. I rubbed a spot on my chest where it hurt for them.

"There were no scents on you," he said. "No traces of magic in your injuries. There should have been traces of someone or something."

"It was raining," she whispered, tears streaming down her lovely face. "Sleípnyr and I had to cross the jagged rocks in the storm." She rolled her eyes, knowing how it sounded, even though I knew it was all true. I felt that Cadeyrn knew it was true as well, so I couldn't fathom what was keeping him from saying he believed her.

"Neyssie," Ewan said to her. "We are looking into—" She held up a hand. She knew damned well they weren't looking into anything.

"I was able to tap into your power, Cade," she said, and he winced. I thought he quite hated it when she used the diminutive of his name. Although, I supposed it was always when she was angry with him. *Oh, I should come up with a particular name to use when I'm angry with Ewan. Like Ew. Or Ewie. Perhaps not. It doesn't have quite the same ring to it.*

"When I used your particle transference to reverse his," she continued. "I was able to halt his movement long enough to stab him."

"Newton's Third Law," Cadeyrn whispered. "I hadn't

thought to do that." The pride and reverence in his tone gave my ancient heart a wallop. Neysa nodded once.

"In case he shows up again, you can try that." She turned from us. "I took out his eye."

"*Caráed*," he called, his voice like rust.

"If I were your heart, Cadeyrn, wouldn't you know me like your own?" She shrugged and used particle transference to disappear before he had a chance to answer. No one seemed phased by her ability to use Cadeyrn's power. And I hoped Ewan felt like a piece of *moinchaí* shite not believing his sister when she just used Cadeyrn's ability.

Cadeyrn lurched after her, but my husband put a hand on his shoulder. Ewan was right. Until Cadeyrn believed his wife, and probably made a good show of apologizing—oh, I would make him beg—chasing her would do no good.

THE SECOND LEVEL of the house had a public study, the library, guest quarters, and a salon in which I found Neysa, staring out the window.

"I saw this documentary once," I told her. "It spoke about a time a century or so ago. Perhaps longer. Human women who suffered from migraines and cycle pains were put into hospital wards and awful experiments and treatments were done to them. They were said to have 'hysteria.'" I did a vaguely silly swish with my hands in the air. "Their husbands happily paid for this barbaric treatment."

"Corra," she interrupted. "I feel this way anyway; so why the story?"

"Oh, really just wanted to tell you I believe you, so I'm

happy to break you out of the hospital ward and deal with the males."

She smiled a bit.

"Solange had a sword," she said. "It had an inscription on the blade, and onyx and rubies on the hilt. It moved in and out of existence. Reynard said to tell Cadeyrn because it sounds like the sword of something or other. I told him nothing would change Cade's mind."

I wanted to tell her that for some strange reason, she and my cousin were thinking neither believed the other and it was like watching the same film play out with an alternate scene. Quite frankly, it made my skin crawl, but I instead chose the route of simply being the supportive sister.

I pulled her sleeve and brought her to the library, uncovering the books I had been cataloging. Opening one, the Sword of Kaeres was depicted. Neysa nodded and touched the page. Her head shot back, and she swallowed. I asked what she saw, knowing it had been a vision. She told me that just before I'd come in, she saw the apparition of Solange out of the window. She was on the grounds. The warded grounds.

"Just out there," she said, pointing to the line of birch trees which marked the bottom formal lawn, before turning into a wooded area where I often practiced archery. "Every evening since the day after I arrived," she said. "Solange has been roaming the grounds, looking at me through the window." She chewed her thumb and I swatted her, knowing that was a rather un-Neysa-like habit to form. She pointed outside.

A flickering light moved in a jerky switch foot dance right between my two favorite trees. The figure looked up at us and disappeared. I assumed it was because it—she—saw me. My jaw was open. Well, honestly, not really, but that was a thing that was said to express a great amount of surprise.

"You did not think to tell anyone?"

"I told Dean. Only Dean would believe me, so I didn't tell anyone else."

Really, I was quite irritated that she hadn't said anything to me. Though, I supposed I hadn't been at all warm toward her. Okay, I was a bit of tit to be honest. I must make amends.

In her vision, she saw Solange touching Cadeyrn, as the vision always was, but the sword was in her hand. We sat on a settee and looked through the books. I explained the bit about there needing to be a chosen one. Neither of us had any real idea of who it could be. Although, I told her, Ewan had started having visions as well. So really, we knew naught a thing.

Chapter 26

Neysa

A week after I arrived in Bistaír, I was officially introduced to Belleza and Stea. I didn't have any real feelings about them before, other than seeing them in my vision like a warning. Plus, Dean said one of them recounted, in great detail, her days as Corra's lover. No one with any amount of integrity would pursue someone else's partner. And even more on the point of being manipulative and just plain gross, no sane being, human nor fae, would elaborate on past sexual exploits in front of the person's spouse. I was absolutely team Ewan on this one, and while I may be angry with him, he had every right to be in a rage with those two in house.

I was up before dawn and made my way out for a run. It was almost Yule, and I wasn't sure I'd ever felt less festive. Perhaps last year, but I had tried to ignore it completely as I was alone in London. To think that I was so looking forward to it this year. The sisters were up and sparring on the lawn near the stables when I circled back from a six-to-eight-mile loop. I never knew how far I'd gone here, only the relative time since I'd left and how my legs felt. On this day, I could have kept running. Running out of my head, with only the pound of my feet and the squelch of mud. Though I'd promised Dean I would run drills with him before breakfast, all I could do was keep moving to kill the cancerous ache in me. Cadeyrn and I were circling a different nucleus. Like we had been kicked out of orbit, trying to pull back to one another and finding we were stuck in separate realities. As though the clock had finally gotten to us. Months ago, I hadn't thought Cadeyrn would want me back after all we had been through. He had felt the same about me. The thought stopped my feet dead. I pressed a fist in my stomach where clawing emptiness lived. Could we be working against each other now, inadvertently redirecting our orbit? Sleípnyr whinnied from the nearby stables, and I was sure he was calling me, so I walked that way.

The sisters' coppery heads were so perfectly matched it was difficult to tell who was who as they moved in their dance of swords. One had biceps the size of my thigh. I was mesmerized by the way the muscles looked each time she moved her sword.

"Morning," I said because it was inevitable I would run into them at some point. The swords halted movement. "Stea and Belleza, I presume?" Biceps walked to me. She was stunning.

"Mad Princess Neysa?" she asked, and I laughed. I mean, honestly, it was so ridiculous and rude I couldn't do anything but.

"Apparently," I responded and held my arm out to clasp elbows. "I'm not going to beat about the bush and tell you I'm pleased to meet you. Maybe you're okay. Maybe not. I will tell you, mad or not, if you threaten or harm anyone in my family, I will dismember you. If you so much as look at my niece and nephew, previous statement holds true. Are we clear?"

She smirked and the other looked a bit twitchy.

"As clear as a female with hysteric visions can be," Biceps said. I thought this was Stea.

Turning to see Sleípnyr, I flicked my hand, and the close vicinity was shrouded in white, wiping out anyone's vision but my own. I heard her swear behind me and laugh in what I took for an appreciative manner. Though, I was the mad princess after all. Through the fog of my magic, I heard Sleípnyr scream, and I dashed into the stables. Next to his stall stood a lone, shimmering white figure holding a jewel-encrusted sword. The world stopped with her that close to my horse, who was trapped in his stable.

Solange stared at me, her hideous maw stretched into a grin, each tooth a stump of black looking more like corroded metal. She pointed the sword at Sleípnyr. The red rim in his fiery green eyes flared. No one threatened my horse. Every jagged tooth on her unhinged jaw was tipped in black as though it wore rot as an accessory. The whiteout of my magic pushed in around us, making the space we occupied within it smaller and suffocating, but ripe with every strand of my power.

She glided to me, pressing my back into a riding crop and harness. Her teeth gnashed, black blood spraying from her throat. I gagged, sweat from my run and her vile fluids turning any food in my stomach to bile. Somewhere outside the whiteout of my admittedly untimely magic cast, which I was having a job undoing, was the sound of fae running across the lawn. Fumbling behind me as her teeth pressed closer and closer with unnatural strength, I was able to grab the crop and yank it from the wall. It snapped and lashed her across the neck, more black blood spraying. I gagged. There was no discernible scent, but a thickness in the air reminded me of choking on gasoline fumes. I gagged again, whipping the crop at her and catching her in the face. The crop snagged on a few of those black-tipped teeth, yanking them out of her mouth.

She let out a howl I felt in my toes. I reached my hand to her before she could move forward again, and electricity and magnetism lifted nearly every metal object in the stables and piled onto her. She knew she was in check and hissed at me, fangs stretching from her grotesque teeth, and called to Kaeres. The others yelled from beyond my white cast.

"*Bas a Tus. Mis cumbachd am bryth mis caráed am bas. Aech mas nae Pím, nae baethá,*" she hissed.

I released more and more power, the pile of steel and pewter growing with it. She stopped her chant, and I removed my hold. The white dissipated. In front of me was Sleípnyr, spooked and pawing at the stable door, a mound of tools and weaponry beside him. Behind me were Stea, Belleza, and Dean. Solange was gone. Rays of early morning sun shone through the windows and skylights of the stables. The other horses were frantic, bashing about. Grooms and stable boys came running, trying to calm the beasts. I pulled an apple from the crate near the door and fed it to my horse, promising him I'd be back shortly. Just outside, stood my family, wide-eyed.

"Mad or no, Corraidhín," Stea called. "She is fucking brilliant."

Three distinctly male growls sounded. Corra just agreed with her and walked with me, a toddler on her hip and one in hand. Every extremity pulsed with anger in me. No one witnessed what had happened. I caused a convenient white-out, and whatever followed seemed to be of my own making. I was falling deeper into this hole. It was starting to seem, even to me, that it was all my imaginings. Though the nightmarish fangs and chanting made me a bit wary of nightfall.

"She said 'Pim.' Corra . . ." I looked at her children, not knowing how I could protect them. All the anxiety I'd run from that morning built back up. Rising heat crept up my neck, making me tear at my jacket. Breaths were short pants, my eyes glassed over. I started to repeat currencies in my mind the way I always did in the human realm.

Pound sterling, euro, rupee, ruble, peso, yen . . .

Cadeyrn came up behind me. His scent made me crazed. Panting breaths had me wanting to bury my face in his chest. All I wanted was to climb on him and be held. Or for him to bury himself in me and make me forget why I was so upset. This distance was killing me. One arm circled my waist.

"I don't . . ." Cadeyrn began. "I don't think it was Pim's name." I couldn't even respond out loud.

No of course you don't, I said to him in my mind, not knowing if he still had me shut out so completely. Or had I shut him out?

"No. I mean, I think she said 'Pim.' But not referring to the lad."

I turned in the semicircle of his arm that felt both like a welcome embrace and a hot, mocking iron poker. In his free hand was the sword. He dropped it at my feet. His eyes met mine. I would have placed a wager on my eyes looking as haunted as his, but the sorrow in his broke my heart. I couldn't believe the sword hadn't disappeared with Solange. Everyone was gathered around us. I pulled from his arm. His eyes shuttered over, cool mask back in place. What did Reynard call it? Cadeyrn's cold bastard facade? I wanted it gone again. I wanted his warmth to return.

"If not Pim, then what, darling?" Corra asked him, breaking me out of my emotion. "And if you disregard your mate again, I am evicting you from my home and province." Pim and Efa whipped their heads to their mother, incredulous at her tone. She patted them both. Cadeyrn tried to reach for my hands, but I tucked my fingers in protectively, utterly terrified of touching him and having to let go. *Don't break me*, I begged to my own mind.

You're not broken, Cadeyrn responded to the thought I

hadn't realized I'd projected to him. He continued speaking in my mind. *I told you that years ago. You never have been broken. You never will be.*

"I was called by something," Cadeyrn said aloud. "Perhaps we all were?" He looked around at our family. He told us how he could hear Solange through my open thoughts. Her chant was what paralyzed him in their bed centuries ago, when Silas found her holding a blade above him.

Bas a Tus. Mis cumbachd am bryth mis caráed am bas. Aech mas nae Pím, nae baethá.

"Your death and my power is forever, my love is death. There is no protection, no life." Translating still left me questioning Pim's name. "*Pim* means utmost and resolute protection. She said there is no protection."

But she was wrong. I was able to separate her from the sword. In the legends Corra found, no one was able to do that. Chosen one or no, the *naem maerbh* was always fought with its sword. Efa and Pim both reached for me simultaneously, their chubby fingers pressing into my cheeks, over the still-tender flesh. Images of Stea and Belleza came to me, and by the look on Cadeyrn's face when I met his eyes, he saw them too. I knelt down on the grass, taking Pim in my arms for a hug. Efa scrambled down from Corra's arms, squeezing into the hug. I asked them if we should read a story together, and they all but dragged me to the house.

"Long ago," I began telling them a story while we sat on the large cushions littering the floor of the nursery. They liked it when I made up stories off the cuff. Each child would bring me prompts for the story.

Pim handed me a small squat velvet mouse with button eyes and pinky-nail-sized silken ears.

I laughed. "Yes, long ago there was a little mouse. He was neither city mouse nor country mouse..."

The door clicked open and shut. I looked up to see Cadeyrn slip in and sit against the wall by the door, knees bent. He looked like he hadn't slept in days. Shadows dogged his eyes, and though still their captivating shade of peridot bleeding into aquamarine, the whites were nearly all red. His full mouth was pinched, the dimple pulling into the stressed corner of his lips.

"The mouse roamed for years on his own, finding out whether he preferred the life of city rats who snuck about, stealing food when they could, making folk scream and chase them with brooms—he didn't care for it much—or the life of a field mouse. A life eating slow and content meals, ending each day pleasantly tired and caked in dirt. While comfortable, Mouse Mouse—"

Pim shot Efa a panicked look, and she started crying because she didn't know how to tell me what he was saying.

"Sis Sis," she was saying. Cadeyrn came over and lifted her onto his lap.

"What is it lass?" he asked.

She kept saying "Sis Sis" and pushed the mouse to me.

"Fra," Pim started in a small, careful voice. We looked at him and Efa smiled, tears drying instantly. Pim took the mouse and said, "Fra-Sis."

"Frasis?" I asked. "Oh! Francis!"

Efa clapped and Pim sat, eyes twinkling.

Cadeyrn's twinkled the same, their color matched to the pixel. I couldn't breathe seeing his smile, but I looked away and continued the story.

"Francis sought a home of his own. He built a shelter that was torn apart by a spring storm, and he had to flee in the howling wind of that stormy night. Scurrying through field and forest, across puddle and bramble, he made his way toward a warm light in a window.

"Between flashes of lightning and rumbles of thunder, Francis squeezed into the cellar of a home. He was bruised and battered, soaked to the skin under his soft brown fur, but he was safe. Once he caught his breath, he wandered the home, eventually making his way to a room with children sleeping, and a little house just about the right size for him. There were wooden fae in the house, but Francis didn't mind. He thought they made good company. For days he made the small house his home, hiding when anyone came in. The small female who slept in the room liked to leave him treats—bits of pastry and cheese, scraps of fabric to nest on cool nights.

"One morning, a nurse came in and screamed when she saw the little lass petting Francis. The nurse dragged her away and grabbed a broom to flush Francis out. The girl screamed and wailed. Francis fled his home, diving through the open window and falling for what seemed like ages. It was dark when Francis opened his eyes again, realizing he had landed in the gutter next to the house. A small face was peering at him, touching the soft spot between his silken ears. She told him he was safe, and it didn't matter what her nurse thought, she would always keep him safe with her. They returned to the warm room and the little wooden house. Eventually, the mistrustful looks the nurse gave him turned to smiling when they sat with Francis and offered him tea in thimbles and crumbs of cake on tiny plates.

"For a mouse who took many years to find his place in the world, Francis knew he had finally found a home with someone who loved him regardless of being the type of creature at which others swung brooms. And of course, Francis and his little pointed-eared girl lived happily ever after."

Efa leaned back into Cadeyrn's chest, and he brushed her

dark bangs back from her forehead. He kissed the top of her head and closed his eyes for a split second. I wondered if he thought of our children. The ones we lost. The ones that may never be. Pim stroked his mouse between the ears and said "Frasis" again and brought the mouse to his own doll's house by the window. For a time, he took the little bed coverings from the wooden fae's beds and piled them up in an attic corner. Then he dug in a bin and pulled out another squat, cuddly mouse, putting both Francis and the new mouse on the pile of blankets, then patted the roof of the house before walking to play with other toys.

Ama walked in and said it was time for naps, taking Efa, her lids half-closed, from Cadeyrn and guiding Pim to his cot. We left the nursery without saying anything. I turned toward my room as I wanted to bathe and change. Fingers touched mine. Magic danced in the space our skin met. I stopped but didn't turn around. He curled his fingers into mine, drawing my palm farther toward his. Rolling waves of anguish and want moved in my stomach. I allowed my hand to be drawn against his. He took it in both hands and kissed it, coming up next to me. The walls of the hallway narrowed, compressing each particle of energy between us. Each skipped beat of my heart. I couldn't look at him yet, thinking he truly thought I was hallucinating being attacked. But the need for touch was painful. I let myself lean into his chest, his arms going around me and holding on. He drew a ragged breath, pressing his face into my neck like the only oxygen was there. A hand laid over my cheek. Zapping and itching told me the scar was gone. After a time staying against him, I pulled away to walk to my room but held my hand for him to follow. I still didn't meet his eyes, or his face at all. He stood in the room, door closed behind him, and pulled his hand through his almost-black hair. I left him there while I bathed and returned to the room.

"She had this scent," he began. "This overpowering smell

of roses and another flower—fruity but not pleasant. I don't know. It got worse the longer I knew her, and I started getting headaches for the first time in my life. Not even my healing could get rid of them. The smell was like walking into a room choked with incense. That last night, when she was chanting over me, the perfume of her was thick, like swamp air. The flowers mixed with something dark and oily. Rancid oil, like araíran-aoír nuts when they've gone off. I had blocked that out for so many years." His bloodshot eyes pleaded with me. "When you started having visions of her, I remembered that smell. So, when you didn't say there was a scent, I thought..." His shoulders hung heavy, the muscles of his upper back pushing up against his white shirt.

I sat on the bed and pulled on my boots while he spoke.

"I thought they must be dreams, because that scent was so godsawful you would have said something. Then if you were attacked by her, that scent would have lingered on you. It was like oil, Neysa. After the day she attacked me, it stayed on me for a week. You didn't smell of anything. That's why. Why I didn't . . . I believed you. I just . . ." He walked to me and stood between my knees. His fingers played at the hair tumbling over my shoulder. "I let my own trauma convince me it wasn't really happening."

"I don't know that there's a way forward for us," I said looking down at my hands. His hand stilled on my hair. Forcing myself to look up at him, I felt a stabbing pain in my chest seeing his eyes. "We need to trust one another, and you didn't trust me. Even after hearing Yva was attacked. Even after I saw Stea."

"I came here to secure the wards. I came to try to circumvent an attack after hearing about Yva and you telling me about Dean and the babes. I had absolute trust in what you saw. I only tried to keep you from the situation."

You thought I'd attacked myself, I said to him, dropping

my eyes. He knelt in front of me, head level with mine, and took my face in his hands.

I did not. I admit I thought you saw Solange during the assassin's attack. I NEVER thought you attacked yourself. Ewan did bring that up. I'm not trying to blame him. Just need you to know I did not think that. I fucked up. I fucked up so much. This is all on me.

"When I was a child, one of my recurring nightmares was drowning. Tsunamis," I told him with a half-hearted smirk, reckoning back to Corra calling him a mega tsunami. "Falling into black water, feeling it close over me." The terror I'd felt slipping from the rocks walked its fingers back up my gut.

He must have felt it too, because he took my hands and moved his face closer to mine. The feel of him so near and the need I felt for him was crippling. I wanted him to hear the story though.

"Sleípnyr was like a foot deep in seawater. I didn't know if he could jump with the water pulling at him. We could almost see the shore, but there was this gap. This space between the last section of rocks and where we stood. The storm was awful. And I didn't know if one of them—Solange or the assassin—would show up out there. I was bleeding and worn out, Cadeyrn. I didn't make the jump."

At that admission, he tensed, and I felt his body shudder. I kept on with the recounting of events from that night.

"I knew I wouldn't make it as soon as my feet left the rock. Somehow, I managed to grab at the jagged edge. I was holding on; my hands were covered with constant waves. I swallowed so much water. For moments, I don't know how long"—The memories replayed, making me shiver. Goosebumps rose on him as well—"I was suspended there. It was a few seconds of hanging above a deadly drop between the cliffs and having the tide and waves rush in and try to pull me away from the rocks. You know that spot. It's carved from the hell realms themselves. Sleípnyr was making noises, and he finally leaped to the other side and pulled me out. He could have taken my arm off and so long as I was out of that watery hell, I would have been grateful. That horse is the *only* reason I'm still here."

Cadeyrn's dark head lay in my lap, his arms circled around me.

Confronting Solange was next on my list, and as we sat there, I told him as much. Then, I said to him that I wasn't sure what to do after. Where to go.

"A hawk for Cadeyrn," an unrecognizable voice said from beyond the door. One of the guards, I supposed. "From his cousin." We both stood, but before answering the door, Cadeyrn turned to me.

"Wherever you go," he began, "we go together. Unless you ask me to leave, Neysa, I will be here with you. What has happened to you would have destroyed a God. Yet here you stand, stronger and more capable than before." He held up his forearm, the tear his teeth had made the previous week still a raised red scar, despite his healing. He stepped away from the door and stood within my breathing space. "I love you with every part of myself. I know I fucked up. I do. But know that I do not disregard you, or what you think. Ever. I acted in the way I thought would be best, and I was wrong. I try to see clearly, but my rage over what you've been through and the fact that I love you so godsdamned much, clouded my judgment. I see that you need time. I understand. If you find that you want me to leave, I will. You are my heart. And I will do anything you ask of me." He turned and opened the door. The guard waiting was flushed to the tips of his arched ears. He passed on the message, then hurried off.

Cadeyrn,

I left the Sacred City two nights ago, meeting with a unit of soldiers from Laorinaghe, Dunstanaich, and most recently, Heilig. There are many details I would like to fill you in on, but just before dawn this morning, Arik was taken from our camp. We were in a group, planning the day, and the assassin we have seen previously removed him from our presence. It is of note that since he appeared at Bistair, the male has lost an eye. Be on alert, and if I am not overstepping, I would recommend Trubaíste *not be alone at this time. Take care, brother.*

Yours,
Silas

Chapter 27

Silas

Moments like the ones we just experienced were the type that made me wonder what kind of cock of a God was on watch. Yva was barely healed when I arrived in the Sacred City. She seemed hell-bent on not letting on how tired she felt. Though the last time I'd seen her, the dark circles under her eyes hadn't been there. The Laorinaghan company was moving out toward Dunstanaich the following morning, Arik and I added to the numbers. I hadn't even had the fucking balls to ask him how his sister fared. I had a job to do, thank the fucking Gods. Three days through the forest took us north and just outside of the border of the smallest province in Aoifsing.

I never much cared for Dunstanaich. No real reason, other than it was a whole load of sheep and not much else. Green as far as the eye could see, but not a lot of personality. Soren, its representative, was a nice enough chap for a former Elder. He had a wife, and I was told in the century of their marriage, they'd never had children. She convinced him to take a consort to keep his position with the Elders when they were relevant, though as far as I could tell, it hadn't come of anything. I'd only ever seen him with his wife. He led his company like a career soldier, never pulling rank or even raising his voice. I'd seen a few military campaigns with him, and just like his pleasant, uncomplicated province of grass and sheep, he was a pleasant compatriot. Gods knew what he thought of me.

Last time I was on a campaign, I tore through bed partners like wildfire. On this one, I was fighting to stop wildfires, and I'd not had a partner in my bed for four months. The irony was not lost on me. Looking at fucking Arik reminded me of his sister. The last night before we'd met with Soren's lot, we had stopped before sunset to make camp. Arik caught me looking at him and he laughed.

"Alas, Silas, I am not interested in males," he said with a smile.

I scrubbed at my face and smirked. I obviously couldn't even say he wasn't my type, though I'd no attraction to Saski's twin.

"She wears the necklace. Eyes are intact."

"It was not meant to be a parting gift," I mumbled.

"She's in a bind. Reorganizing our system of government. There's been some resistance."

"She's well though?" I couldn't believe I hadn't had the balls to ask before. I was such a cockwad.

"Well enough," he answered cryptically, and I found that wasn't good enough for me. I was about to see if she needed help. If she wanted me. If he thought I should go to her. But there was a rumble of boots and hooves.

Scouts came running to us saying the unit of Heiligan soldiers was approaching. Arik and I stood waiting to greet them. As the unit came through the trees and into the clearing where we camped, Arik swore under his breath.

"Why in the name of Kutja's wanny is *he* here?" he asked aloud.

I leaned in for him to tell me there was a governor of

Heilig at the forefront where I would have expected to see Basz. The governor gave Arik a large smile, showing white teeth in his dark face. Had I not been so hung up on Arik's sister, I might have had a thought about the beauty of this male and how badly I was in need of attention from a beautiful body like that.

"Varno," Arik greeted him. "Forgive me if I am surprised to see you."

"I have come in place of Basz, at your sister's request."

"Saski asked you come?" Arik seemed confused. Varno shifted and smiled in a way I found unpleasant.

"I volunteered. We are betrothed, Arik."

To outside eyes it must have looked like Arik and I both had a collective kick to our faces the way we snapped our heads back.

"Arik, you sneaky shite, I had no idea you favored males. Felicitations," I said because I couldn't quite fucking process what this Varno character had said. The governor turned baleful eyes on me but quirked a smile.

"Varno," Arik began in a tone much cooler than I'd ever heard from him. "Are you saying you and my sister, Her Majesty, are betrothed?"

"I am. We are."

I walked away. There was no reason for me to be there, so I walked away, saying I needed to check on the weapons. I needed something to do. For the entirety of the night, I stayed in an armory tent, shining and cleaning blades, stringing bows, and telling myself I was needed here and not on a godsdamned boat to Heilig. I was right though, it seemed. She needed a governor or some bullshit. No one like me. A Laorinaghan captain found me before dawn, asleep against one of the horses I'd inspected. He told me we were heading out within the hour.

Frost covered every blade of grass and any remaining

leaves. Winter was ready to pounce. Arik was at the kettle, looking as haggard as I felt. He grabbed an extra tin cup and poured me a dose of the strong tea we had to stomach on campaign. I couldn't even open my mouth to speak to him.

"It is not irretractable, Silas," Arik said quietly. Behind him, some of the Heiligans were approaching. "They aren't married yet."

"It is not my place, Arik, to insinuate myself in matters of Heiligan state. I am but a country squire."

He opened his mouth to say something, but Varno clapped a hand on his shoulder. I pulled the too-long bits of hair away from my face and tied it all at the top of my head with a piece of leather thong. Frost coated the ends of my hair as well, so I was glad I hadn't shaved in weeks. Fuck it was cold.

Our units met with Soren's, and by nightfall it was literally a stone's throw to the border. Bloody amazing it was. If I threw a stone, I would hit a rolling hill and probably a sheep on the one side. If one of the Dunstanaich fuckers threw one from the other side, he'd hit pine forest. There was no gradual change of landscape. A sad state though. Outside of the tree line on this side, the ground was scorched. We were told there had been a trading village, but nothing was left. Arik said it reminded him of the phantomes in Heilig. They would raze the villages, burning them to the ground. He bent a knee and scooped the charred earth in his fingers, feeling and smelling.

"Not phantomes. They left a scent of roses and rot. Like a putrid oil that has been doctored to be pleasant. It was all over Pavla," Arik said, sucking in his cheeks.

Something about his description jogged my memory, but I'd no idea why. We moved with Soren's lot to the next burn area. At each spot, the glách, or those with growth/regrowth affinities for greenery, took the time to work their gifts along the earth, ensuring the next growing cycle would be productive. They worked well into the night. As I'd essentially brought them—my fellow Saarlaichans—I stayed with them and slept amongst my provincial folk.

No insurgents or rogue militants were found. Sending a whole campaign for this seemed more reactive than I'd have deemed necessary, but who the hell was I to say anything? Arik and his soldiers were finishing up tea and bannocks when I moved from the glách males and females with whom I broke my fast. Varno attempted to pull me into the conversation. I kept drinking the scalding tea. Snow flurries started drifting onto us. The more Varno spoke to me, the faster they fell. My emotions were clearly getting the better of me. Soren commented on the weather being predicted for later in the day. Varno described proposing to Saski, and so help me, Heícate, I whipped the snow into his face, spilling his tea. And then there was the appearance of that same golden-haired fuckwad who had attacked Neysa when we were en route to Bania to rescue Reynard. The same fucker who hit me and dragged me to that shite bucket of a house in Bania where Etienne tied us up, and, who most recently, attacked our captain at Bistaír. The fucker blinked in front of me, and I barely had time to register he was missing an eye. Then he was gone, taking Arik with him.

UTTER FUCKING CHAOS. Soren was screaming orders. Varno was screaming orders. I was trying to tether my magic to the elements to see if I could tap into his particle transference. There was a trace, and I took off for a horse, but by the time I'd made my way across camp, the tether dropped. The first thing on my mind was that Saski and Ludek could not lose another sibling. Someone was trying, and nearly succeeding, to remove the large figures from our realm's playing board. I kept thinking that regardless of the fact that Cadeyrn wanted to keep the fight away from his wife, Neysa was alone in that secluded godsdamned paradise, and she was a key player in this realm.

"The fires are a distraction," I said, dropping a paper I had ripped from the journal I kept in my pack. The group of males standing around looked up. Everyone had been yelling at once.

"From what?" Soren asked.

"I don't know exactly," I said.

Varno snorted. I wanted to nail him in the ear with my elbow.

"Here I have listed what has happened thus far in this shit show."

Soren picked up the paper. I wished Ainsley Mads were here. She and her band of hairy hooligans would be a fan-bloody-tastic addition. While Soren read my notes, I listed them aloud for the others to hear.

"Representative Sonnos was attacked. Someone must have known Arik was on his way to her. The elder Eamon of Heilig was working with Etienne." I stopped, thoughtful for a moment, deciding I would not share the intelligence Magnus had given me, nor the revelations of *Trubaíste's* visions. "The captain of the guard at Bistaír was mortally wounded by Arik's abductor before I arrived here." I told them of the forest attack and my captivity in Bania. Soren growled in frustration. My conclusion was that either the fires were a complete ruse, or there was a deeper meaning to the use of fire. Though my money was on the distraction, and as such, this cute campaign we'd put together for the benefit of an arsonist, needed to disband immediately.

Two meters or so above the ground was the perch on which the hawks sat. I'd brought my own on a hunch and sent it off to Cadeyrn as quickly as I could get away from the others. Whilst in the middle of signing off on another note to Saski, Varno came up behind me.

"Will you be returning to your place of residence?" the Heiligan male asked me.

"I am leaving now to track Arik." I bit down on my tongue to keep from spitting the reply I would rather have given him.

"Many thanks. My soldiers could always use an extra sword. I'll be briefing the mission shortly. If you are to come with us, you can come sit in."

I chuckled at him and turned, keeping my hand over the note.

"I can work alone. If I find him, I will send a hawk."

Before he could reply again, he was called over by a couple of soldiers. My guess was that he was skilled in the sparring ring but had never seen real bloodshed. I finished my note before he walked back over.

SASKI,

Perhaps your betrothed has told you already, but if not, I regret to be the one who informs you. Arik was taken this morning. I am leaving directly to track the magic which allowed for the particle transference that took him. There have been similar attacks throughout Aoifsing. Keep yourself safe. Stay with Basz and Ludek. Secure your wards. I will find him for you. Congratulations on your engagement.

Silas

WE NOTIFIED all representatives of the abduction. Once the hawks were up, I left, pulling myself into my power and drifting with the snow flurries. Etienne's strongholds had always been in Maesarra and Veruni. I had combed much of both provinces in the past two years, and it seemed unlikely the remnants of his organization were still there. Once I'd set off, I realized that I never responded to Saski's message. Not really. It didn't matter anyway, as she was betrothed and I'd no fucking clue what to say to her beyond what I'd penned for that hawk. I would get her brother back for her. I was a working dog, after all. I could be good for something.

Smack bloody in the center of Prinaer was the Mads compound. If we were looking for allies, then Ainsley had proved herself fucking brilliant in the past. She seemed to always know when we were coming. Last I'd seen her was over a year ago in Festaera. It had been early autumn, and she and her ruffians were dressed in furs. Pushing toward the winter solstice this time around, they were barely distinguishable from bears. Ainsley's black hair was in a chaotic pile of braids on top of her head, pulling her sharp coppery features into a severe look. She was an intimidating female if I'd ever seen one. At my approach, her kohl-rimmed black eyes narrowed further.

"I was expecting . . . another," she greeted me.

I held my arm to clasp elbows with her and her second, Thurnton. We moved in from the blasted cold and discussed all that had transpired. I guzzled my ale in one go. The heavy wooden doors blew open, and behind one of Ainsley's rather impressively large Prinaeran females was my sister.

"Halloo, darling. Ainsley," she said with a nod to us both. "It's rather a cock up out there."

"Fuck the Gods and all that's holy, Corraidhín. What are you doing here?" I asked my sister.

She kissed my cheek and waved me off.

"You know we work better as a unit. Now, let's chitchat as they say on telly."

"Telly?" Ainsley asked, turning to her second. Thurnton shrugged his bloody great shoulders, making the fur shift like a waking animal.

"Oh, it's this device in the human realm—"

"Not now, sister," I said through gritted teeth. I told her about Arik and Varno. She patted my knee under the long wooden table.

"Neysa was attacked," she said quickly and launched into a great tale of *Trubaiste* and the assassin, Solange, Ewan and Cadeyrn not believing her, and I stormed outside. It was blowing a fucking gale, snow piling higher than the soles of my boots. My sister followed me out, Ainsley and Thurnton with her. I was trying to not hit something, which made me lose my full grip on my power, lightning crashing above.

"Is. She. Safe?" I asked.

"Yes, yes. Once Cadeyrn pulled the Sword of Kaeres"— Ainsley gasped—"he said he believed her. I knew he did before, but I think he's quite traumatized about his past. Anyhoo, I kicked him in the testicles for his attitude toward her and threatened his welcome in my home. Though perhaps I shouldn't have kicked him, as they do want to try again for children."

"Why are you here? I asked again suspiciously. "I cannot imagine Ewan simply sending you off."

"Pshaw. He is not my keeper." She flipped her braided hair over a shoulder and held her chin high. "And I did not care for how he treated Neysa."

Ainsley looked up as though she'd been called. There was a

rustle in the trees, and a group of her guards appeared, a figure between them.

"Fuck it all to never," I yelled and ran to Yva, who was stumbling between the Prinaerans. She was saying, "I'm well, I'm well," over and over. We moved inside the hall and settled Yva by the fire. Regardless of being healed, her body had seen great abuse and I would wager, based on Arik's hints, she slept too little to fully recharge. There was quiet as we waited to hear what she happened to be doing there. Through still chattering teeth, Yva looked me in the eyes and said she was getting Arik back.

"He came without my calling upon him. He has been a friend to me and was taken from my lands. I will not sit by and wait for anyone else to search for him. I will find Arik, and I will bring him home." In those amber eyes I saw whirling movement like the power in her swirled behind her irises. A hawk appeared on Thurnton's shoulder, and I blinked, wondering how in the realms it could do that in a closed hall. The Prinaerans read the message and passed it to us.

AINSLEY,

It seems much has transpired since my last dispatch. Due to the involvement of the Sword of Kaeres, we believe the fires in Laorinaghe to be an imposture to get us to look away from what is, in actuality, the greater picture. If you are inclined to help, I should be greatly obliged for it. My sister is convinced your lands may be targeted next. We shall keep you abreast of our findings. Furthermore, should you happen to run into my wife, do tell her she absconded with my favorite bow.

Regards,
Ewan, Bistair

. . .

Corraidhín had a shit-eating grin and smoothed the hair on Yva's head. Ainsley said something quietly to a group of her compatriots who quickly left.

"Shall we make an offering to Kalíma and find you all accommodations?" Without waiting for our reply, the head of Prinaer stalked off, her second urging us to follow.

Next to me, my sister muttered something that sounded like "For Asgard," but I wasn't sure I heard right. Without thinking, I lifted Yva in my arms and carried her with us. She stiffened, and I whispered that she need not worry. I was as preoccupied with Arik's sister as Yva was with the male himself. She pulled back, and her eyes widened so far that I laughed and squeezed her.

"Our secret," I said. She ducked her head, honey-colored hair covering the red of her cheeks.

Chapter 28

Neysa

Kitchen smells wafted throughout the lower levels of the house, drawing me in with the promise of something which included pastry. Corra told me the night before that she was leaving to meet up with Silas. I wanted to join, but she backed me into the bookcase and told me if I even thought about leaving at this time it would send the entire province into upheaval. It seemed like quite an exaggeration, but I could see how Cadeyrn might be upset. I had made myself scarce since our conversation in my room. He and Ewan were either training or planning, and I was disappointed in my brother. It seemed Corra was too. She'd stuck to me like a thorn, even finally letting Dean research with us. It made me smile hearing him sigh happily at the extent of the library at Bistaír. He was meant to be amongst books and research.

In the kitchen I found Stea and Belleza picking at leftover roast chicken, speaking with their heads together. Cook was absent, though what indeed looked to be pastry-wrapped something sat atop the oven. My mouth was watering as I'd not eaten since before my predawn run. However, in entering,

I caught the last couple words of the sisters' conversation before they knew I was there.

" . . . fuckable, yes. Worth dying for, no."

"I'd take it front, back, and everywhere in between if offered. He's bound to need it, married to her. I just need to get him alone." They giggled, but stopped when I was fully in the room. I didn't know who had said what, but I lost it. Mad princess lost it.

Singing metal announced my sword before anyone could register it, as I was quicker on the draw from my spine scabbard than I'd ever been. I pushed the sister closest to me against the ice box, shelves on either side dumping their contents. She blocked my advance, and the other sister whistled. I turned, falling for her velociraptor tactic, allowing her to punch me in the eye. A whip of anger detonated in me. I sent my elbow and the hilt of my dagger into her jaw, giving me a moment. The original one—Stea—grabbed at me with her huge godsdamned arms, squeezing me like an Amazonian snake.

"Holy fuck!" I screamed. "Have you ever heard of leg day?" I brought a knee into her groin and twisted in her anaconda grip, only to have Belleza break my nose with the heel of her palm. I sent my boot into her hard enough that she sailed across the kitchen and knocked the dinner from the oven. Cook came in yelling, and Belleza backhanded him, then flew at me just as I dropped from the Loch Ness fucking monsters that were Stea's biceps. She kicked into my ribs, and I was about to bisect her entire body with my sword, but Dean came in.

"Christ, what the hell?" he yelled and both sisters were thrown by invisible hands into the plaster walls on opposite sides of the kitchen. They seemed to be suspended a couple of feet off the ground.

I spat blood from my mouth, streams of it running from

my nose. I wanted to laugh at the look on Dean's face as he held them aloft.

"What the fuck?" Stea screeched, scrambling against the wall. Dean held his hands out and looked self-satisfied. Cook looked murderous.

"I'm still eating that, Cook." I spat more. Streams of bloody mucus dripped from my nose and mouth, seeping into the porous clay tiles and following the grout lines. Dean dropped his hands, and both sisters looked as though they were about to come at me again. I stood, significant amounts of pain urging me not to, and swung my sword. "And I will fucking kill you and feed you both to the pigs if you raise your hands against me again." It surprised me a small bit how eager for violence I was at the mere mention of one of these ginger beasts touching my husband. For good measure, I flicked a throwing star, pinning Belleza's sleeve to the window shutter, then tossed a serrated blade, catching Stea's upturned jacket collar and sending her back into the ice box. "Pigs," I said with sick malice, "will eat just about anything."

"I feel like I've heard that somewhere," Dean mused. I smirked at him through what I assume was a mangled half face.

"You are truly insane," Belleza said. Dean put an arm around me, and I heard Cadeyrn and Ewan come in behind us.

"Which of my family were you both planning to fuck 'front, back, and everywhere in between'? My husband or my brother—your king? Get the fuck out of here."

Metal sung, guards moving in from the garden doors and hall. The sisters were apprehended and pulled out through the hall. I stumbled out of Dean's grasp and fell out the garden door, throwing up the blood that was running down my throat. Snarls and growls ripped out of me from the pain the vomiting inflicted on my ribs. My face felt like a watermelon. I wanted to kill them. Overreactive? Perhaps. I never said I was the picture of grace and piety. Footsteps crunched behind me, then hands were on my back. I felt him in the swelling of my heart before he spoke.

May I? Cadeyrn asked. I tumbled to the side, crushing mint under me. Now Cook would be pissed at *me*.

I don't even think I can turn to you right now, I admitted. I would have sworn the right side of my body weighed a full stone more than the left. Lips, nose, and cheeks were too puffy and blood-logged to speak out loud.

He shifted closer and called for rags and compresses. Dean came out.

"Christ. You alright, Pet?" From the corner of my nonhemorrhaged eye, I saw him hand Cadeyrn the supplies. I moved my left fingers and gave him a thumbs up.

"I'm mfghhuggah ghiller. Lemme fugghhha ghiller," I said, clenching my fists. Cadeyrn smirked and started wiping my face. I squeaked from deep in my gut.

"Yes, Pet," Dean said. "You can fucking kill her once you don't look like you are the product of a zombie apocalypse."

Tell him I don't think I've ever heard him say the word fuck, I instructed Cadeyrn mind to mind because I couldn't speak.

He repeated what I said, and Dean laughed.

Tell him it's sexy when he says it.

Cadeyrn's eyes snapped to mine.

"I will not repeat that."

Coward.

His eyes danced at the challenge. "She says it's sexy when you say it. There. Pleased? Shall I give you two a moment?"

I started to laugh, but pain was everywhere. It seemed to take longer than usual for him to heal me, but I supposed I was a mess. Burnt orange streaks of light skated along the lines of Cadeyrn's face and the tips of the leaves in the garden. The sun sunk lower, casting more shadows through the rows of winter vegetables popping along the vines. Pain and swelling were abating in my face, so he moved on to my rib. Just as he had in the manor at Barlowe Combe after Corra and I had gotten into some serious trouble on our trip to Peru. The trip which we never told Silas nor Cadeyrn about, but came home from with several broken bones, a torn rotator cuff, and an arrow hole in Corra, courtesy of Reynard, that nearly killed her. Some things had changed so very much in the past few years. However, some things, like my penchant for trouble, never would. I supposed I well and truly owned Silas's moniker for me. *Trubaíste* indeed.

Blood and holes covered the sweater I wore, so he split the seams with his knife, tearing the knit away without having to move my arm. Dean excused himself since I was sitting in a completely sheer dove-grey bra Corra had given me. Cadeyrn chuckled while stroking fingers along my sides where the bones were cracked. I asked what was funny.

"It's a grey jumper," he answered, meeting my eyes, his twinkling and creasing at the corners. I reached up and touched his face, running my fingers along his ear tip. A shudder ran through him. "Lay back, *Caráed*. It will be easier." His arms supported me as I leaned back into the now completely crushed mint. Pressure on my back made my vision spot, and I groaned. "Nearly done," he assured me.

You were defending my honor in there? Cadeyrn asked with a teasing note to his voice.

Yours or Ewan's. Let's face it. It was Cadeyrn's. I wasn't even remotely ashamed to admit I would gladly cause permanent harm to anyone who laid a hand on my husband in violence or lust.

I must have projected that thought to him, as he quirked a small smile and whispered, "So would I, Neysa. In a heartbeat."

Raven-black hair touched my chest when he leaned over

and blew lightly on my ribs. Pain released and he sat up. I wanted to pull him back to me. Feel his hair on my chest again. Hold him until the sun set. Until it rose again. And again. Never let him go. Those eyes I loved so much looked to me with such regret, I bit my lip to keep from crying.

"How is she?" Ewan stood in the doorway, arms crossed.

"She's alive," I answered for myself. "Sorry to disappoint."

He snorted and squatted next to me. Cadeyrn took off his own jumper and handed it to me to wear. He had on what looked to be a plain black T-shirt. I didn't think I'd seen one here in this realm.

"I didn't trust them either," my brother said. "Wanted them gone. Sorry it came to this."

I shrugged the jumper on and stood, a bit wobbly.

"Did you know that Corraidhín was going after Silas?" he asked me.

I nodded and pushed into the kitchen, grabbed the food Cook had left, and began eating it with a chunk of brown bread crusted with olives. Cadeyrn made a face. He hated olives.

"I owe you an apology," Ewan said, sharing the bread with me. "Do you ever have so many thoughts going round your head . . ." He paused and looked up at the rafters where hundreds of bells and stained-glass beads hung. "So many thoughts that you can't make sense of any of them? One moment we were decorating the godsdamned house for Yule, the next, all hell broke loose."

"And both of you," I said, pointing between him and Cadeyrn, "thought the most likely circumstance was that I was totally batshit crazy?"

The mystery dinner was a type of flaky fish, layered with spinach and cream, wrapped in pastry. It was rich, so I pushed it aside after a few bites. The males began picking at it as well. I poured water from a jug.

"Well, regardless. Apart from the succubus thing that Solange is, the fires, and our friend being attacked, one of you has those females after you. Or one of them. Who knows. I mean, it's up to you. They are quite attractive," I rambled.

Cadeyrn rolled his eyes. Elíann entered the kitchen with a note. She patted my shoulder before leaving. It was a letter from Ainsley offering her help. Postscript was written by Silas saying he, Corra, and Yva were all in Prinaer and they were going after Arik.

BOOKS OF VARYING ages and conditions littered the library floor. Dean sat against a settee on the cross section of two scatter rugs. I smiled seeing him there. Always reading on the floor, his thumb just touching his bottom lip. I didn't know how many friends he had back in the human realm. We stumbled into our friendship, and it was all-consuming. It was no wonder he thought he had a thing for me. We were always connected through our bloodlines. Did Dean miss home? I suspected he did.

Cadeyrn ran a hand through his hair and fell back a few steps. Ewan told Dean of the note as I sat next to my friend and looked at the books he had in a more curated pile on his left. Notes were written in a small leather-bound journal. I asked if he minded my looking, and he waved me on. Everything was in shorthand, but it made a scientific sort of sense. Ewan asked to see as well.

"All of our names are listed here," Ewan remarked. "What are the symbols beside each name?"

Dean rubbed his eyes, reaching for glasses that weren't there. He inhaled a breath and gingerly took the journal back.

We all believed the fires were a distraction. Something to keep us from what else was happening. Dean believed, or was starting to believe, that rather than a distraction, the fires were a means to predict where we would be. They were a herding device.

"But no one can predict how each of us would react to a situation in another province. We were all in different places. Plus, what does Arik have to do with this?" Ewan looked at the journal again. Cadeyrn was peering over his shoulder.

"Someone needs us all back together," my mate said. Dean nodded. "The symbols are our gifts? What is the angle, Dean?" he asked, voice quiet and thoughtful.

A cat hopped from a bookcase. We all jumped.

"*Cathe Sídhe*," Cadeyrn remarked. The cat pranced to us and sat smack in the middle, looking at each of us in turn, swishing its ginger tail. "She is Yva's," Cadeyrn said with wonder. The cat licked its paw and yowled. "Her power signature is the same." The cat curled into Dean's lap and kneaded his leg.

My friend explained that he started following the sequencing and method of attacks, my visions, and what was happening here in Bistaír. After the fires became too much for Laorinaghe to deal with internally, Yva called Ewan for aid. The first incident was Yva being attacked, followed by Stea and Belleza arriving. Ewan called Silas down from Saarlaiche. Then Cadeyrn.

"Solange's reanimation is somehow linked to Kaeres. I looked her up and she seems like the kind of Goddess you don't want to meddle with. She can piggyback on your magic, Neysa, because of your link to your Goddesses," Dean told me. "Which may account for the nightmares."

Cadeyrn was looking at all the notes, flipping through Dean's journal.

"I haven't been able to come up with a reason," Dean

continued. "I just think that for some reason, someone wants or needs you all in one place. It seems to me this person—fae, whatever—knew Arik would be coming to Yva. Yva was attacked to lure Arik." The cat on his lap stretched and looked backward at Cadeyrn. I blew out a breath and said I needed to take a bath. Magical conspiracy theories, enchanted cats, and blood caked on every part of my upper body called for a reset.

It was well into the evening when I came out of my room. In the bath I'd gone over the ideas Dean had, thinking about what it could all come together and mean. The air had cooled considerably, and I thought this was the coldest I had been in Maesarra. Yule season, and no one was very festive. From my room I descended the back staircase to the second-floor library. My feet were bare, making no sound on the flagstone floors. The door to Ewan's study was slightly ajar and voices were coming from inside.

"I think he's definitely on to something," Cadeyrn said.

"I can't decide whether I should insist Corraidhín come home or keep her away."

"I rather think she will decide on her own one way or another, once she hears everything."

I pulled the dressing gown tighter on me and decided to keep walking and not be a creeper. The library was empty, only two dim sconces lit. I picked through the piles Dean made, careful not to disrupt his order, however chaotic it might be. Smiling, I thought about his desk in England and how it looked like a bomb went off on it. However, he knew precisely what and where *everything* was.

"He's good male."

I spun, seeing Cadeyrn walk in, shutting the door behind him.

"I know I've given you grief about him," he said, "but I like him. And more importantly, he's your friend." He dropped to a crouch near me, but not touching distance.

"He's a natural problem solver as well. I think following his reasoning is the way to move forward." As it came out of my mouth, I realized that I'd said to my mate the previous night that I didn't know how to move forward with him. "What reasoning would someone have for needing us all to be together? Apart from the possibility of wanting to kill us all in one go. That doesn't seem the motive though."

He looked through one book and shut it in what I took for frustration. I stood to look through the shelves. My hands danced along the spines, pictures forming in my mind of faces who had read from these shelves. My parents, perhaps my grandparents, others I did not recognize. A picture of elemental magics presented itself to me. I pulled the book, a vision swimming to the surface. Symbols like the ones Dean had sketched looked like a chemical equation. There was no product to the equation, so I couldn't see what the end result of mixing the elements would be. Once the vision faded, I turned to see Cadeyrn standing, staring out the window.

"What's out there?" I asked in a panic. "Solange?"

"Not that I can see," he reported and half turned with a lopsided smile. "Wolves. There are always wolves lurking."

I raked my hands through my mostly dry hair and held up the book to tell him what I'd seen.

"When I woke up in Heilig and you were gone," he said, "I kept thinking that I'd never get to hold you again on a balcony above the sea, or looking out across caves. I thought about all these opportunities we had which slipped away. I said if we found each other, I wouldn't squander them. And I did. And here we are. Not moving forward." He pinched his nose and shook his head. "You know I will respect it if you can't—"

"Cadeyrn," I said, not knowing really what to say.

He looked up, as though knowing my head was empty. It was easier to focus on the greater problem than it was to focus on ours. On why we both always felt like the other didn't need us. If I wasn't broken, why did I always feel like anyone around me was forced to constantly pick up the shards of my mistakes. Who would want that? Then again, Cadeyrn has voiced the same query about himself.

Beside the window where he stood was a tufted bench carved and inlaid with dark stones. I walked to it and propped my knee on the bench to look out. Our fingers found each other and interlaced while we stood. My eyes closed, and I leaned my head against his shoulder. His head tucked on top of mine, and we stayed for ages like that. I knew he felt the tears on my face and the hollow breaths I took, trying to keep the tears in.

When he spoke again, his voice was tight and small. "Are you saying goodbye?" It felt like the bottom dropped from my stomach. I pulled my fingers from his and turned. "Is that what this is?"

Anxiety ripped into me without warning, and I couldn't breathe. He blew lightly in my face, releasing the air.

I grabbed his face in both hands and kissed him. Kissed him like every tether to this realm was in the kiss. My lips were hard and demanding, wet from tears.

"Never," I said against his mouth. And I meant it. He held my face, and his other hand went into my hair. "Never."

It didn't matter how we saw ourselves. I saw him. He saw me. And no matter what, I would not let him go. My hands went up under his shirt, pulling his backside toward me. We moved until I was backed against the bookshelf, my hair catching in the pages of volumes. One leg lifted and wrapped around his waist; his hips pushed into me. How long had it been since we made love? Weeks. I was starved. My core pounded, desperate for him to fill me. A few books tumbled from their resting place. We smiled against each other. So godsdamned stubborn the both of us. I pulled back to look at him and stroked the sides of his face, his temples, ears. He touched my lips. My teeth scraped the pad of his thumb.

"My beautiful mate," he whispered, kissing my eyelids and the corners of my mouth. The bulge of him rubbed into me, sending thunderclaps of desire through my very being.

I dove my hands into his waistband in the back, pulling him roughly against me, causing us both to groan. I needed the friction.

"I'm sorry. Sorry for all of it," he said, head against my shoulder.

"I know you are." I stroked his neck, my teeth pressing lightly. A balance of equals. Neither dominance nor subservience, but the dagger tip upon which we danced. "I understand. And I'm ready to move forward." To illustrate that, I tipped my head to the side, exposing the spot between my neck and shoulder where his mark on me sat, the twin to his own. Rather than teeth, his lips pressed to the scar, heat and electricity buzzing from the spot, swirling around us. I pushed his head, almost begging for teeth, yet needing the gentleness of his offering. A soft kiss to show he was mine. Blood sang in our veins, calling to us to come closer. Heavy-lidded eyes watched him pull back.

He undid the tie of my dressing gown, slipping it from my shoulders. All I'd worn under was a pair of light blue silk knickers. He ran a hand from my neck to the silk, stroking me softly over the material. His eyes were misted over, dark lashes half shading his eyes as he felt the wetness on me.

"Let me," he said. His voice was barely audible. "Let me touch you. I want to erase the pain." I pushed his trousers off his hips and lifted his shirt away. My hands and mouth ran over his stomach. Lower.

"I want to feel you too," I answered. His palms gently pushed my face into his stomach, my wet hair falling over him. Long fingers kept tickling over my skin. Neither of us realized the threads between us needed this more than anything else.

We held each other, rocking together amongst the centuries of books confettied about. Every callous on his hands covered my skin, pads of his fingers pressing against where I wanted them, even as he filled me completely. Canines ran at a razor's edge along the line of my throat as I tipped my head back in climax. Tides of release undid me, still knocking against him. He paused, the fluid aqua of his eyes burning, tracing my face, chest, and where our bodies joined. Silken skin met my fingers where they trailed his jawline. His fingers pressed into me again, giving me another climax that sent the room to blinding white. Sitting, I wrapped my arms around him, kissing his plush lips, riding his lap.

His completion ripped through him in an eruption of power that met with mine, blowing the books to every corner of the room, rattling the leaded windows. I kept moving my hips on him, undone by the power in him. The power we had together. It was utterly intoxicating. Wolves howled, a chorus of hundreds from what seemed like right beneath the window and outward for miles. We sat, joined, in a rigid embrace on the floor. Every rise and fall of my chest met his. Kisses climbed from my shoulder to my ear. His incisors finally pierced the skin on my neck, and I rocketed into the bite. When my mate pulled back, my blood on his lips, I returned the marking as he spoke, still holding my hips as I rocked over him.

"*Canítau misse a tabhair am baethe. Canítau miss am baethe. Tou a misse es yn tus. Tus dál baethe a misse. A duín, am bryth.*" These words he said to me made me cry. Ugly, hot tears ran between us, my body pushing farther onto him. Arms with endless strength locked around me, forging a barrier against anything that would threaten us.

You understood? he asked.

I nodded against his shoulder. *Allow me to give you life. Allow me to live. All of me is in you. You hold life for me, for us, always.*

He kissed my forehead and pulled his fingers through my hair. I felt his cheeks raise into a smile.

What is it? I asked, shifting to look at him, our bodies sweat slick.

He groaned. *You're so wiggly. Sit still or I won't—*

I wiggled more, and he growled, hardening again.

Fine. I won't tell you.

I stopped and kissed him as he laughed, his hips bucking into mine. *Tell me*, I ordered, rolling on him. He sucked my lip into his, and I automatically wiggled again.

See. You won't stop teasing me. He was laughing and I felt him ready to play again.

Well, if you won't tell me, I'll just go to bed then. I started pulling away, and hands lifted under my backside, sliding me forward again. I looked down to where we joined. The beauty of our two bodies as one.

I was thinking, temptress, he said, moving in me again. Gods, I could do this all night. *Please don't think I sound stupid saying this. Please.*

For a minute, I couldn't think at all. Neither of us said anything, riding eddies of ecstasy. We came together, growling in soft vibrations. His lips touched my ear.

"That I feel like we have created a life this evening," he whispered. I stilled, feeling for a sign. Nothing apart from the total satiety of being with my mate. Arms and legs locked around each other. "Just a feeling, *Caráed*."

Chapter 29

Neysa

"I'm going to pretend I can't tell that you two made up all over my ancient books," Ewan said, pulling a volume from the floor and making a face.

"I could have lived without hearing that said aloud," Dean responded.

"It was Cadeyrn's fault," I said with a smile.

He reached for me and pulled me down onto him where he sat on the settee. "Completely," he growled, face in my hair.

Ewan made a gagging sound and Dean chuckled. Pim toddled between the literary obstacles, tumbling over a stack right in front of us. Cadeyrn lifted him from the floor and dusted him off before the lip wobble turned into a wail. "You're alright, *aoín baege*," he crooned, calling him little one. "We all get stumped on books sometimes. Although, you're so clever, I'd bet you could figure all this out in a heartbeat." He tickled Pim's cheek, making the little boy smile. Pim tickled his uncle's face back but stopped as soon as he touched him. Tiny eyebrows knit together, and he touched Cadeyrn's face again.

"What is it, lad?" Cadeyrn asked him.

Pim turned to me, reaching a pudgy hand in my direction. He leaned over and placed a wet, smooshy kiss on my cheek and touched my stomach. Efa came over too and climbed up. Ewan and Dean were absorbed in their searches, backs to us on the other side of the library. Efa grabbed Pim a bit roughly, making him squeak in protest. She pulled Francis, Pim's cuddly mouse, from his fist and laid the toy on my lap. To my mind she sent images of her cot, Ama, me on a swing at our home in Saarlaiche holding a blanket-wrapped bundle. She looked up and smiled, resembling Corra so much in that moment.

I lifted her for a hug, trying to hide my tears. Pim tried to take his mouse back, but she swatted his hand, making him cry. They began screaming together, and Ewan lifted them from us, breaking up the moment. I looked at my husband and bit my lip.

I thought so, he said, taking my face in his hands, my grin pushing both corners of mouth into his palms. We had created life together. The warmth between us coddled me. The world may be falling apart, but some benevolent force of nature allowed our love to create new lives within me.

"I may have figured it out," Dean announced, still on the floor, facing away from us, totally oblivious that Cadeyrn's and my world just expanded exponentially. Anything felt possible. "Well, not totally, but bit and bobs of what we need to know to get started."

"Let's pretend for a minute that we can fit you all into categories, yeah?" Dean asked us.

We nodded, peering over him as he scribbled in the leather-bound notebook.

"Here, I've got you, Neysa, as electricity. You have that spark that also affects the light in an area. Ewan, you've got that as well, though yours draws the shades down a bit, yeah?" Ewan tipped his head and Dean continued. "You've both got the oraculois connection, speaking mind to mind and all that. I'll come back to that in a bit." He was completely comfortable teaching, and I knew he couldn't stay idle for much longer. Dean Preston belonged in a lecture hall.

"Now, Ewan," Dean continued, "you inherited your mother's water affinity. That brings me to Saski and Arik," he said and drew a line from Ewan's and my names to our cousins'.

At mention of Arik, the cat fawning over Pim whipped its head to us. Cadeyrn raised an eyebrow and smirked. Pim grabbed its tail to reclaim its attention, and Ewan promptly picked up his son, though the cat didn't seem at all aggressive.

"Saski," Dean continued, "is a siren. Well done, you lot, for not picking that up."

I snorted at his jest, enjoying it when he settled into himself. Cadeyrn snickered into his hands.

"She can control others so long as she is near water. She can become water itself, as you said, Cadeyrn. You two became one."

I stiffened at that because it sounded so intimate. Cadeyrn cleared his throat and pressed a hand to my back. Dean pushed the bridge of his nose, lifting glasses he no longer wore nor needed. He drew a wave by her name and sipped at the tea steaming near him. Cadeyrn would touch it every so often, heating it back up since Dean tended to forget his tea and suffer through the cold tannins. I didn't know how many mugs he had back in the human realm, but there were always four or five sitting, half drunk, amongst his things in his flat and office.

"Arik, we think, may share that ability in one way or another. He has never mentioned it, and based on how secretive Saski was with her ability, I'm quite certain Arik's would be kept on the down-low as well. We do know he can control the wind. Correct?"

We nodded at him.

"Between both sets of siblings, there is a near full control of atmospheric and hydraulic elements." He drew more symbols. "Now, Ewan and Neysa have found mates with similar gifts. Corraidhín has the mist magic. Cadeyrn," he said waving his hand, "you've got everything, right?"

"Not electricity," he said under his breath. "Silas has it."

Dean closed his eyes once, acknowledging the elephant.

"Yes, I see how that came about now," Dean mused in a decidedly English turn of phrase. "But remember when we chose a different thread? Remember when Silas said with the clock, he saw nothing? I believe his avenue was unclear due to the mating issue." Elephant indeed. It was a whole savanna. Maybe even a few hippos and a giraffe for good measure.

"And now?" I asked, my voice pitched.

"There is a Goddess of Seas, Wind, and Water, said to have a brother of wind. Her name is Rán. Her brother has similar gifts, yet not the strength and control she has as a goddess." He paused. I wasn't sure if it was his way of engaging his students or merely to allow us to absorb what he was saying.

"Saski," I concluded. "But—"

"I think, perhaps, each of you in your family is linked to a Goddess. Or a God. And each has a consort."

"The mystics," I said. "They called Cadeyrn 'consort to the Goddess of Aulde.' So, you think Ewan is linked to a God and Corra is Ewan's consort? And that Silas is Saski's?"

Dean sat back and scratched at his face where a bit of

stubble shadowed his skin. He said it seemed like a thread to follow.

"And what about you, Dean? You are of the same lineage."

"I believe it's through your mother's lineage, hence Saski and Arik." The *cathe* looked up again. A thought on that bloomed, but I pushed it aside for a moment.

The fact that I was heir to both Heícate and Kalíma seemed to present a sort of basis of evidence that Dean's theory was a workable one. Cadeyrn said that Solange was not linked to Kaeres in life. That we knew of. So, why now?

"That's what we must find out. It seems strings have been pulled to have some of you together and—"

"Not me," I interrupted him. "When I was attacked in our home, it was an assassination. I was not meant to survive."

"It's because you are heir to all magic," Cadeyrn reasoned. "You heel to no realm. You are the biggest threat to whatever is in play."

"And Yva? She could have died."

"No, they knew she wouldn't. But it kept Arik close. They may not have even known he was already there, but knew he'd come if she were injured."

The *cathe* blinked at Cadeyrn and nuzzled his hand. We agreed we had to warn Saski, though it was imperative none of us breathed that we thought Silas was meant to be her consort. Knowing those two, it would send them running in opposite directions. Dean shut his journal and sighed.

"I'm knackered," he said. "Not sleepy. If I went to bed, I'd be awake sorting through this rubbish all night. Just tired." The three of us bobbed our heads in understanding. Complete emotional exhaustion.

"None of us has had a break," Cadeyrn said, counting Pim's toes and making faces at him. Efa was asleep in her father's arms, dark curls spilling over Ewan's jacket. He ran his fingers through her hair subconsciously.

"There's so much magic here. It fills the world with wonder and makes so many things easier. Yet, we are doing analog research to keep the world from falling apart because of some fantastical family tree and perhaps a strange vengeance. I just want to go up the pub and have a pint. Watch YouTube. As boring as that sounds."

There was an all-around grunt.

"That sounds lovely," my husband admitted. "The Peasant and Pheasant." He referred to the pub where we first met a few years back. Again, an *mmmm* sound moved between us all.

"It's the same in the human realm," I countered. "Technology keeps making everything easier, faster, more streamlined. Yet we are always connected. Always needing instant gratification. And maybe it's not Gods at play, but there are politicians and lobbyists with enough money and power to keep their finger on the trigger of some very big guns."

"It's all relative," Ewan said. "What we need in either realm is a means to unwind. Which I'm having a very hard time doing whilst my wife and the mother of our children is out in the thick of these games of Gods." Cadeyrn reached over and laid a hand on my brother's shoulder.

"I owe you a tavern night," he told him. "You too, Dean. Not all of our family gatherings should be on the cusp of Armageddon."

Dean looked down, his face flushed to the tips of his ears. No one missed that Cadeyrn had declared Dean family. I certainly did not. I playfully scratched at Dean's pointed ear.

"Don't even start, Pet."

I burst out laughing and threw my arms around him. "I won't, cousin."

Raindrops made tracks on the windowpanes like the knots in wood. We left the library understanding one another better than I think any of us ever had. The room was considerably chilled with the cold weather that had pushed in from the south and a low-pressure system building in the north. Between both was this rain which reminded me of England. I dug my toes into the duvet, watching the rivulets slide down the glass in an endless race. A fire crackled across the room, low and just warm enough to let me sit atop the bed without being bundled. A sound piqued my ears as Cadeyrn slipped back into the room after going to fetch us something to nibble. It sounded like a violin, though no one in the house played. Cadeyrn had a smirk that was threatening to turn into a full-on grin. What was he up to?

"Two years ago on Yule, I was in love with you and scared to death you'd find out," he said. I turned from the window fully, looking at him suspiciously.

"Funny, I felt the same way," I teased. He leaned over and kissed my lips once, lingering on the withdrawal. I tugged at his bare arm. He was definitely up to something. A violin note rang out beyond the door. I started to worry there would be a quartet coming into our bedchamber when I was ready to be alone with my mate. "Whatever are you doing?" I asked, rising to my knees on the bed. He stepped back and held up a finger, a quick burst of laughter coming out of him.

"Last year," he said, "was an utter tragedy. I mean, looking back, my demeanor was positively maudlin."

We were smiling at each other, giddy with whatever he was moving toward. When I first saw him smile like that, I had been injured in the library at Barlowe Combe, and Cadeyrn healed me in his own room. I told him his smile could launch a thousand ships, and Gods know I meant every word and still did. As far as maudlin behavior, maybe he was broodier, but last Yule season, I was neither human nor fae, wishing myself away.

"I pulled my blackout curtains for the entire week and tried to pretend I didn't want a mince pie." I stuck my finger into the waist of his trousers and tugged him forward.

He leaned to my ear and whispered, "Not yet." Then kissed me breathless, before stepping back, giving me that smile again. "We were supposed to spend Yule together in our home this year. That's not looking promising, but I haven't given up on a proper round of festivities with our family." He pulled my finger from his waistband and kissed the tip of it, sending a zing of want through me. "But for now, before everything goes to hell again. Which we know it will. I wanted to give you something." He lifted my hands, encouraging me to step from the bed.

I followed his lead, amused. My face was even with his chest. I halted him, turning us by placing my palm on his bare chest. Under my touch, his heart beat faster. *I used to be so afraid to touch you. I thought it would be my undoing.* I had told him something similar on the cave balcony in Cappadocia.

Every time you touch me it is my undoing, he said. "Let me give you your gift before I get too distracted." He led me to the room next to ours, which sat uninhabited, set up as a sitting room. Next to a huge, tufted armchair and footstool was a table with covered dishes. He motioned for me to sit and uncovered the first. It was cheesy chips.

"Cook told me Dean beat me to it."

I laughed and snatched one, shoving it into my mouth and mumbling that it didn't matter Dean had beat him to it. Heaven. He uncovered the next, and there sat a perfect pair of mince pies, both topped with a pastry star and dusted in powdered sugar.

He passed me one. "I hope I got the spicing right."

"You made them?"

He nodded, cheeks flushing, which always did me in. It was easy to forget the slow days. The soft domesticities this fae warrior of mine enjoyed. I sat back in the chair as he sat in the one across from me. Our ankles touched. The balcony doors were shut, but the rain was coming down hard enough it sounded like they were open. If I closed my eyes, we could have been in England. In Barlowe Combe or in the old cottage I shared with my dad.

"Thank you," I said simply.

"One more thing." He pulled a smoky quartz from the table beside him and waved a hand over it like he had years ago when it uncloaked him. Strings sounded in the distance, coming closer. The notes became a tune, wending its way into my memory. I recognized the song and slapped a hand over my mouth. I got up and searched for where the sound was hidden. A shuttered wooden screen stood in the corner. I peeked around it, and a violin was suspended in midair, playing "The Fall of Rome" by the Airborne Toxic Event. I whipped my head to Cadeyrn.

"How?"

"I spelled it to play on its own." He walked to me. "It only knows one human song. The rest are from Aoifsing and one kind of morose one from Heilig that Saski hums while she walks. Couldn't get it out of my head." He said he found a violinist who played the notes by ear, and while they played, Cadeyrn spelled the violin to record the action. "I hid it behind the screen because, in all honestly, it's really creepy seeing them hanging in midair and playing." I giggled nervously, walking around the violin in circles.

"How did you remember the song?" I asked.

"I listened to it over and over again while I searched the manor, hoping I would never mess up bad enough to lose you."

Tears spilled down my face for us. For these two flawed, fragile creatures who loved each other to a fault. I held him, swaying to the sound of the instrument behind us as it switched from a classical version of indie rock to the haunting and lovely sounds of Aoifsing. I held him until he tugged me to the plate of cheesy chips which were still warm. In the light of the fire, his eyes glowed like they had when they were cloaked by the smoky quartz. I watched the fire dance in their reflections as we ate and chatted. In one last piece of the night, he pulled a book from the basket and handed it to me. It was a book of poetry and short prose written in Aoifsing. It was my turn to lead him. I held his hand, letting him wrap his arm around my waist in the short distance we covered from the sitting room to our bedchamber. I climbed up into our bed, slipping off my dressing gown. We slid under the duvet, and I nestled against him, my head over his heart.

"Read it to me, please," I asked, giving over the book and laying my hands on his warm stomach. He breathed in one rasping breath and opened it up, reading to me until the embers died in the fire and my eyes fell closed, listening to his voice switch from reading aloud to the bass of him speaking to my mind.

And until this realm meets the next
I will claw for you
With all that is mine
I will fight for you
With the life force of a thousand
I will die for you
And in the dark, you shall own my soul

Chapter 30

Silas

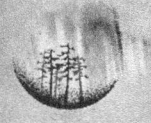

It was a strange menagerie of characters moving through the forest of Prinaer. Apart from Ainsley Mads and Thurnton, there was myself, my sister, Yva, and this *cathe sidhe* that seemed to move in and out of existence. My sister nearly flayed the fucking thing on sight, but Yva insisted it was harmless. Or at least meant *us* no harm. It appeared once I had carried Yva to her sleeping quarters that first night we all somehow showed up together—which I still say is fucking weird. Once we began our trek the following day, the *cathe* pissed off to fuck knows where, and it didn't seem to faze Yva in the slightest. She was far quieter than I remembered her being. Once the cat reappeared, rubbing its honey-colored body against my legs as I walked, making me stumble like a foal, I realized two things at once. One, it was the same color as Yva herself, right down to the eyes. Yva has that tawny hair and whiskey-shot eyes that look like sex personified, set against her brown skin. Not that the godsdamned cat was sexy. I just meant it had the same color. The other thing I realized was that the cat was searching multiple places at once. It traveled between places and times, existing where and whenever it pleased.

The thought made me a wee bit nervous since all the talk of creating alternate dimensions and time working differently with that godsforsaken clock my cousin and Saski destroyed a couple of months ago. I shivered thinking of how it nearly destroyed the both of them. Could *Trubaíste* and I have moved past that if those two died? Even being mated as we still had been, I thought anything between us would have existed behind the shadow of two ghosts. We were never meant as lovers, *Trubaíste* and I. We confused it a bit in the beginning, but when I was finally honest with myself, I loved her down to my last drop of blood. But what she felt for me was almost the same as she felt for my sister, just muddied by the shite-stirring Goddess. *Cathe Sídhe* was looking up at me like it was reading my thoughts, which was creepy as all hell realms.

"Yva," I called ahead. She looked over her shoulder at me, amber eyes exhausted. "When did the *sídhe* show up exactly?" She slowed to match my pace at the back. We all moved in an organized faction with my sister scouting ahead and moving back to us every so often. Ainsley and Thurnton flanked us, unseen in the trees to our right and left, and Yva was ahead of me with her bow at the ready.

"The day Arik arrived," she answered. "Moments before he walked into my office. The *cathe* immediately took a shine to him." She smirked telling me and I chuckled, pulling a small pinecone from the tree I stooped under and tossing it at her.

"Arik and Saski are magnetic to us all it seems," I said. "And it has naught to do with their siren bullshite." Saski was as stubborn as *Trubaíste* when it came to her nature, and never used her siren abilities, but her appeal leaked through her pores like the sea through sand.

"What did you just say?" Yva asked, stopping to turn and face me. The sound of the Prinaerans in the trees stopped too.

Yva's face paled. I thought back through my flowing thoughts of Saski.

"That both siblings are magnetic?" I asked.

"Yes, but something to do with sirens?" Her face was moving through colors like a telly in in the 1970s, pixelating between black-and-white and color. She went white then blushed, then the color drained again. Ah.

"You didn't know. I wasn't supposed to say anything. I'm such a fucking tosser," I said to myself more than to Yva. Fuck the Gods; what was I thinking? I supposed I thought Arik had shared that with Yva. She started walking ahead again, her bow hanging limp and unprepared at her side.

"Yva," I called. I was such a tosser.

"He tried to tell me," she said quietly, the wind through the pine trees swallowing a bit of her voice. "He offered to use it to help me sleep. He had been teasing me before that, so I thought he was teasing me again, and I told him to get dressed and to not patronize me. Me, Silas. Like I had any right to tell a prince to do anything."

"First, I'd like to back up and hear more about why you told him to get dressed."

She spun wet pine needles into a bundle and flung them at my face, which stung. That was the kind of thing my sister did.

"It was nothing like what you're thinking, Silas. Trust me. That kind of activity has been in a long empty patch." I knew how she felt.

"Well," I told her. "I can tell you that Arik would not have been offended. I know him well enough to know he might have been disappointed that you didn't believe him, but not offended."

She tugged on her braided hair. The crunch of our boots on snow and the increasing winds were the only sounds.

"So, they really are sirens?" she asked me. We continued walking side by side.

"That they are, the sneaky little shites. Not shocking with Saski really. She always reflected light from the water when she was near it. I had just never put two and two together. I just —" I coughed. "I thought maybe it was me seeing what I wanted to see. Don't know how Arik's abilities work, as I know they are different to his sister's, just as mine and Corraidhín's are."

She was thoughtful for a time, the snow falling on us again. It wasn't my doing. There was genuinely a winter storm moving from the north. By the wind, I would say it should keep pace with us for a couple of days, then move toward Maesarra. The *cathe* darted ahead then sprinted back to us, dropping to sit so fast Yva and I both reared backward. The *cathe* yowled and hissed, a faint stirring of snow circling its small body. My nerves were on high alert because this was all fucking creepy. If Yva's *cathe* was giving us a warning—and I was quite sure it was, as it didn't seem the type of beast to get ornery for suppertime—then we must heed. The Laorinaghan representative and I took instinctive back-to-back positions. I saw Ainsley on my side, nodding to me and backing against a tree to observe. I was hoping my sister wouldn't be back in that moment because, not only would it scare the ever-loving shite out of all of us, whatever was about to announce itself wasn't something I wanted my sister to be in the middle of. Not with Pim and Efa home, waiting on their mam's return.

A gust of motion moved through the trees ahead of us. I could have sworn there was a swath of white, but snow was abso-bloody everywhere, so the glare was hard to distinguish from anything else.

"If it's that assassin who stabbed me, I want to put him down myself," Yva muttered.

"Get in line. I have a promise to keep to him." I told him when he showed his pretty face in the mountains of Maesarra, if I ever saw him again, I'd make the way I slew his partner look like fun. And I had shoved my dagger through the other fuckwad's temple.

"Silas," my sister's voice came from behind us. Fuck it all to never. See, I knew she'd scare the shite out of me. I turned to see blood running down her face, her eyes, the same green as mine, glassy and slightly unfocused.

"Fuck. Corraidhín." I grabbed her as she fell to her knees on the snow. Ainsley was by my side before my sister's knees sunk in. For someone so large, Ainsley moved like a *paitherre moinchaí*.

"There's a village—" But she was cut off by Yva spinning into us both. We tumbled over my sister in a ridiculous pile. Then I smelled it. Oil and roses. Something like rot and cured leather. I knew that smell. The same one that lingered on the Dunstanaich border. And it clicked. It. Fucking. Clicked. My sister's wet eyes met mine. Yva was on her feet first, moving her bow in a trained fashion.

Between the trees ahead of us, right where Yva had been, stood Solange. The *naem maerbh* that was once my cousin's wife took an arrow to the neck and pulled the shaft from her moon-white skin. Oily black blood ran from the wound, staining her white gown. The stench intensified with the gush of blood. She looked at the mess curiously. I pulled moisture from the snow surrounding us and brought it up between the demon and our group. Seeing Solange with us there, I felt like a hammer was hitting my fucking chest.

Neysa had fought her alone. Isolated from anyone out in that house. That perfect fucking house my cousin built. The house Cadeyrn had built to hold a sliver of hope when he had none. This abomination tainted their house.

I felt her pushing through the wall of snow and ice I'd created. My sister moved from the ground beside me. Her magic tacked onto mine and kept pushing harder, the ice growing thicker and thicker. An alabaster hand shot through the ice and grabbed Yva.

The Laorinaghan pulled a serrated blade from her thigh holster and hacked at the hand, that rotten blood spurting like tar bubbling from the earth. The severed hand dropped to the wintery ground. Solange's other hand shot through. Corraidhín's magic was weakening, and mine couldn't hold much longer as whatever was working against us was no mere ghost. There was force behind it. A spell or a greater driving power.

"Without the Sword of Kaeres, we cannot defeat her," my sister said. Her head hung, her own garnet blood dripping into the powdery snow beneath her. Yva pulled back, half of Solange's abhorrent hand still clutched around Yva's throat. The representative spun. I yelled, knowing the strength of grip a demon would have. She could have broken her own neck in the process. Instead, Yva spun so fast, first in one direction, then another, that she created a momentum which blew through my magic and sent thousands of icicles into the *naem maerbh*. The specter wailed as the shards tore through every inch of her, inky blood like a volcanic eruption. She wasn't dead; we knew that. But she was inconvenienced enough to leave us. Her shredded demonic form moved backward through the wintery forest, arms outstretched, those black, irisless eyes locked on Yva.

"You know," Corraidhín slurred. "A decade or so ago, in Iceland—that's in the human realm—"

"There's a place called Ice-Land in the human realm?" Ainsley asked. "That's not a very clever name."

"Yes, there's a Greenland too. Which is mostly ice," my sister answered, bleeding still.

"That's even less clever," Ainsley said as she lifted Corraidhín easily.

"Yes, yes," my sister continued as I looked for where she was truly injured.

"There was a volcano. It was a well-complicated name to say. Eyjafjallajökull. Gods, I've probably butchered it."

"Perhaps, be quiet, sister, so I can sort you out?" I growled at her. It was then I noticed Yva panting on the ground.

"Yes, yes. The volcano erupted and there was so much ash that it closed airspace for weeks!"

Ainsley and Thurnton looked at me in question. I wasn't about to explain airplanes and such. I motioned for the male Prinaeran to see to Yva.

"Can you imagine how one explosion like that could change the entire world?" she asked, and her head tipped sideways.

"Was it her blood?" I asked my sister. "That reminded you of the volcano documentary? I remember you watching it the day we met Neysa." I was trying to engage her now that she seemed to be slipping into unconsciousness. Solange's blood had looked to me like an eruption. A disgusting fucking volcano.

"Hmm? Oh, yes, darling. That *naem maerbh* seems like such a small thorn in our arses, but she's become Eyjafjallajökull. Gods, Silas. I must try to remember if I'm saying that name properly. Dean would know." She touched her head where the blood was and, under her fingers, blood poured, though I'd just examined the same godsdamned spot. "Oh! I'm bleeding, that's why I feel so funny."

Nothing was funny in that moment. My insides twisted and untwisted. I didn't know if I needed to vomit or defecate Or blindly kill something. What, by the gods, had done this to my sister? I roared at the wind, my emotion doubling the intensity of it.

"She said there was as village," Thurnton said. "When your sister first arrived. She said there was a village." Ainsley and the male shared a look, and she stared off into the distance.

"The village, yes. It's . . . gone." With that, Corraidhín dropped out of consciousness, and I swore, trying to figure out just what in the hell realms was wrong with her.

More of Ainsley's bearlike fae crowded the narrow forest path we were on. I didn't know when she would have sent for them or how, but the Mads Prinaerans operated with an efficiency like I'd never encountered. A healer stepped in to see to my sister as I tore at my fucking hair. Ainsley was whispering with one of her females, and I caught the words, *eviscerated*, *Nova Thyme*, and *stench*, before I insinuated myself in the conversation.

The village of Nova Thyme, just south of here by about thirty kilometers, was razed. This was not something we had ever really seen in Aoifsing. In all the centuries I'd been alive, and in histories I'd read and had been taught, there was never the type of mass killings we saw in Heilig last year or even what had been seen in the human realm. One small thing like a volcano could disrupt the whole world. I just needed to save my sister to keep the godsdamned volcano from choking us all.

"I'm fine," I heard Yva tell the other Prinaerans. "Just tired."

I walked back to her, picking at the skin around my fingers from nerves. I had never seen Yva display that kind of power before. Most fae had magic and particular gifts, but only a small percentage of the population had gifts as strong as we do. Actually, come to think of it, very, very few, outside of the circle in which I run, had truly strong gifts. I'd seen Yva move in her cyclonic motion before. It was how she sparred. But I'd never seen her use momentum as she did moments ago. And it reminded me of when *Trubaiste* came into her power. It tired her. It kept her from sleeping. It didn't level off until . . . Cadeyrn. Ah, Gods and shite. I was not having that kind of conversation with Yva Sonnos.

"Silas, we must move to the village." Ainsley was taking

clear charge at this point, which suited me as I wasn't sure if I was abandoning this all, taking my godsdamned sister home where she should have fucking stayed, or if I should go along. I knew we weren't going to find Arik in Nova Thyme. I knew what we would find. There would be bodies in piles. Mothers and fathers covering their children, all formed in ash. It would smell of char, rose, and rot, and coat my throat and lungs like an oil slick.

"We're being herded back to the center of Prinaer." I didn't think before I said it. It just came out before I could think of why. The Mads Prinaerans all turned to me, and Ainsley waved me on but didn't seem to be listening. "I might be totally bloody off, but why raze a village in front of us? If not to push us back?"

"She's been touched by death herself," the healer with my sister said as she stood.

"What the bleeding fucking hell realms does that mean?" I yelled. The healer did not back down from my tone like most folk might. She was also a head taller than me and, with the furs she wore, twice as thick. What did they eat?

"There is no visible injury, yet she bleeds. The hand of Kaeres has descended upon her."

"So, she's dying? Are you saying my sister is fucking dying?" I was shaking, and Yva took my hand.

"Yes."

I roared. It sent globs of snow from the conifer branches. The slope of forest trembled, snow turning from powder to water, to ice. The rushing timbre of a nearby avalanche didn't even phase me.

"Get me a fucking hawk. I need a hawk. I need—"

"Pim," Corraidhín groaned. I knelt beside her. "She wants Pim, Silas. Don't let them get him. Swear it." I did and her eyes closed again.

"Corraidhín, Gods and shite. You will not die here in

fucking Prinaer. Nobody even likes Prinaer. Remember? You said it was all forest and rock and no personality whatsoever? You said—" My voice caught. "You said the Prinaerans had funny looking arses, and you would never bed one again. You can't die here godsdammit, Corraidhín. You will not." I slid my arm under her heavy head, avoiding her sword. "We will get you home. You can be with Pim."

I took her and ran. There was enough snow that I dissolved us into it and ran with my sister. We were four days from Bistaír on the fastest horse. Traveling with my gift, I could get her there in two. Perhaps I should have waited. Perhaps I should have let Ewan come. But I knew, deep down, that the only way my sister had any hope in any realm was with our family. With my cousin to heal her and *Trubaíste* as heir to Heícate and Kalíma.

I couldn't think about whether her children would grow up without their mother. I couldn't think about Ewan losing his mate, or what this would do to Neysa and Cadeyrn with all they'd endured. I moved faster than even when I'd taken Saski from that jungle pit where she'd destroyed the clock. Why must we keep running? Years of running and nothing but brief snatches of joy and the stupid banter we had to keep us from succumbing to the dimmed lives we led. Were there gods among us who truly sought our demise? The hand of Kaeres. How had my sister been touched by the hand of the Goddess of War and Death? And why? I was vaguely aware of night falling, followed by sunrise. The snow melted, and I made my way out of the storm, still feeling its pressure at my back, pushing me onward.

On through Maesarra I ran, switching from my own two fucking feet to dissolving into every river, stream, and creek along the way. My power was fading, the dissolution becoming harder and harder the more I pushed. As though in cruel symphony, I felt my godsdamned sister's magic seeping out of her and into me as she died. It was like insects burrowing under my skin and traveling through my veins. This must be what Ewan and Neysa felt after their mother died. I roared again, a continuous animalistic plea leaving me as I splashed from the last riverbed closest to Bistaír. It was still too far. I was a hundred kilometers away. Maybe more. Maybe less. I didn't know, but I was dragging my sister, my strength nearly gone, her heartbeat fading. As I screamed through the push, I heard wingbeats like thunder. I heard yelling. Someone screaming my name. More than one person. The sound of horses trampling the packed grit. The skies opened up like the storm finally caught me up and was aiding this fruitless fucking venture.

"Silas!" I heard my cousin screaming, and I nearly fucking broke down. I would never be so glad to see anyone. I yelled, my voice hoarse from roaring. Lightning went up in one last display of power before it fizzled out of me. Then they were there. Cadeyrn and Ewan, pulling her from me. Cadeyrn felt for injuries, and I was saying over again, "It was the hand of Kaeres. She was touched by death herself." Ewan raged. Trees around us flattened with the force of his power.

"Pim. She said do everything to protect Pim," I told them. They looked to one another, and Ewan took his wife and left.

Chapter 31

Corraidhín

Making myself useful was what I was good at. Our mother always called Silas a working dog. She would say he needed a job to do in order to stay out of trouble. I saw the same nature in Saski as in my brother, and I supposed it was a part of me as well. Though, I'd never admit to it. I was simply better at getting things done. I was quicker through the snow and streams than my brother, which was why I would scout ahead of our party as we moved through Prinaer on our way to Maesarra. There used to be a small city on the southern end of Prinaer, but it was destroyed a century or so ago during an uprising against the Elders. That bit of Aoifsing history had been gloriously swept under the rug—was that the phrase? My brother and cousin both fought to save the city before the fire which raged and consumed its entirety. The skeletal ruins of an ancient town were all that remained now, but there were several smaller villages in a twenty-kilometer perimeter around it.

Nova Thyme was a border town on the edge of Naenire which specialized in trading the local goods of crystals, stone, and clocks made with said crystal inside. Years ago, I sat in the cottage kitchen in Barlowe Combe with Neysa, discussing the nature of quartz. The way in which quartz worked in tandem with limestone gave it the ability, even in the human realm, to, in essence, record events. The workings of a clock, measuring the passage of time in a certain dimension, the marriage of quartz and limestone became annals of events. Tapping into that superior natural ability, which lay in bog-standard stones, required somewhat of a trick.

The storm pushing from the north created a low-pressure system in the atmosphere as I moved through the forests of Prinaer, scouting. I knew before I neared Nova Thyme that something terrible had happened there. My stomach clenched in a way it never had before I'd had my babes. It seemed every little thing had me hyperaware of my own mortality and how that might put my little ones at risk. The closer I came to the village, the more the air was permeated by a smell akin to the cheap perfumes women in the human realm wore in the early twentieth century. A heady mix of roses and musk to mask their natural odor. The way in which it mingled with cigarette smoke and exhaust from automobile oil was in line with this scent. The main difference, though, was this had an underlying scent of death. Like a fox left to rot after a hunt. It was the stench of Solange. I knew now why Cadeyrn had been hesitant to believe Neysa. It was not that he mistrusted her mental capacities. It was that this scent was so powerful and provocative that surely Neysa would have said something about it. Surely. Unless there was something in Neysa which repelled it. I must file that away for later.

With the pressure building at my back, blowing snow in torrid gusts around me, I was upwind from the smell for a few ticks. A shop at the forefront of the village looked as though it had been blown out from within, though the structure remained. I trod carefully, realizing it might not have been the wisest of ideas to search around on my own. But really, that lot would have taken far too long to catch me up here. The first shop spilled the shards of drusy and hematite which was in great supply in this region. Further investigation took me along the high street of the village, past a small temple to the element of Aedtine—fire—which I thought was a curious choice of worship in a forested area. Although, I supposed fire could be a real danger. It reminded me of a children's story our mam used to tell us before bed.

The temple Aedtine burned black smoke in a protective ring as though it had been protecting itself during whatever had occurred in Nova Thyme. All along the street, shop windows, stained glass and clear, were shattered. Then I saw the bodies. Barely cool, wisps of steam still rising from them where they lay in drifts of snow and dirt. I swallowed, realizing it was what Neysa and Reynard had described happening in Annos, in the north of Heilig.

Parents held tiny hands, clasped in a rigid clutch, resisting the final separation. Lead filled my chest seeing families, friends, and villagers all who'd met a cruel fate. Behind me, the flames in the temple burned out like a pinched candle wick. I turned, slow and controlled, scanning each building and tree, my sword at the ready. A great breath of air seemed to be pulled from the earth while wind barreled into me, the storm moving farther in. My brother and that lot must have been totally immured by it. Once the gust passed, it was as though I were watching an old film. The crystals in the village and in the whole area were replaying the events. Fuzzy images projected in the air around me of fae running through the streets, like ghosts. A few fighters stood at the ready, but much like that day in the manor in Bania, it was as if a great finger touched the center of this village and simply snuffed it out. Everything turned to ash. The bodies I could still see, and the remaining buildings, were on the perimeter and took collateral damage. It was that quick. And I knew I must really be off.

Nothing good would come of my being there. It was a cursed village now, and I had no desire to be encumbered with a curse, thank you very much.

With the snow I could be back to Silas rather quickly, but a hand came down on my shoulder just as I was about to dissolve into my power. It was then I stared into the face of Kaeres herself. Black eyes and white hair burned my vision. She smiled at me, and in that smile, I saw what she wanted. My son. I would be godsdamned if I let her have my son. So, I thrusted my mirrored blade through the Goddess of War and Death and allowed my power to claim me whole and take me to my brother.

Chapter 32

Saski

Dawn found me hanging over the side of my mattress with a wine-sore head. Queenly behavior at its finest. It had been weeks since Varno left and my brother was taken, and I was not one to wait with a smile on my face. I couldn't exactly remember the last time I truly smiled anyway. Varno never mentioned Silas being there with him, yet I knew from Silas's correspondence that he was tracking my brother as well. Something wasn't sitting right, hence the bottle of Sot wine I'd consumed in the late hours of evening.

Ludek entered my chamber without knock or preamble, which told me how well he knew I was alone. I was always alone, and marrying Varno would not alleviate that. My brother rarely swaggered, but when there was a dance in his step, I knew to steel myself for something he alone found amusing. I did not look up but kept my eyes on the aubergine carpet next to my bed. I was so sick of the jewel-toned colors of my chamber, yet I couldn't be assed to have the decor changed. I supposed as queen, I should be moving to different rooms. Unless we get more of a move on this dissolution. Now with my brother being abducted by an assassin, my hand forced in betrothal, and Gods knew what my folk thought of me in this premature state of rule, it didn't matter what color my godsdamned carpet was. Ludek sat on the edge of my bed, jostling the mattress, and in turn, my tenuous stomach. I groaned.

"Good morning, Saski," he said with an overcheered tone. I looked sideways at his smirk. He laid a hand on my back, and I realized I was still wearing the sweater I'd had on the night before. That in itself had me getting up to bathe.

"What pile of shit have I found myself in this morning, brother?" I asked, trying to pull my feet from the silk duvet.

"Curiously, sister, none that I have found. Though it's early still."

I yanked at my feet, which sent me tumbling from the bed and onto the ugly carpet. Only my brothers would ever see me in this state.

"However," Ludek began, offering me a hand. "I have an idea for you. I received a hawk from Aoifsing."

That had my attention. He handed me the message, and I read as I moved about my room, gathering clothing to take into the bathing chamber with me.

"How are you smiling after reading this?" I asked. Ludek was many things, but not one of them was cruel. "Ewan believes that whatever is attacking is trying to gather certain fae in the realm. He states that Arik and I are 'key players.' I do not see how this is smirking news, brother."

A knock sounded and I sighed, making certain I was wearing trousers of some sort. Not that I really cared. Captain Umvelt entered, his eyes on the slate floors of my threshold, hands clasped behind his back.

"Majesty," he said and cleared his throat. "I have prepared transport to Biancos where a ship is in wait." His copper hair was tied in a neat tail behind him, giving me a clear view of his striking features.

"Both of you," I said, pointing my finger between the two males in my rooms. "Explain."

Ludek nodded at Umvelt who bowed to me and left, making my temper rise about twenty notches. I began running water for a bath while waiting for Ludek to elaborate on the fact that I was clearly expected to be leaving Heilig.

"If it seems that certain ones of us are needed for whatever diabolic plan is in motion, then I should think your being there would speed things along nicely."

I scrubbed myself behind the half-closed door and dressed quickly, each piece of clothing sticking to me as I didn't have the patience to dry myself completely.

"Ludek, wouldn't it make sense to stay the hell away?"

I popped back into the chamber, and he was placing my clothing and weapons into a trunk for me, which, admittedly, was quite sweet.

"No one can track Arik's magic like you can. No one can bind her power with his like you." He held up one of my short swords, flicking the blade with his finger.

I shoved my feet into high boots. It made sense. I was never really one to shy from danger. Not really. Plus . . .

"And you'll get to see your country squire," Ludek said with a dramatic bow.

I bit my lip to keep from smiling but shook my head, rejecting the implication.

"Gods, Saski. It's okay to admit to your feelings."

"I assume I'll be leaving directly?"

Ludek tsked at me and handed over my jacket and crescia-bladed sword.

"Bring our brother home, Saski. And don't get yourself killed. Remember, Varno is the expendable one."

I barked a laugh at that because Ludek never made crude jokes. He smiled, his warm brown eyes dancing. I slung my arm around him, and we called for a servant to drag the trunk out with us. Gods. A year ago, I would have spent weeks figuring out what to bring. Perhaps I had grown a bit. As long as I had fighting leathers and my sword, I was ready to go. Such a thought.

By the Gods, sea travel was tedious. I'd taken a tonic to sleep the first day so that I was ready to utilize my powers and move us quicker. We pulled into port in the town of Craghen where I had been discovered by Cadeyrn earlier in the year. My body ached with exhaustion, and I collapsed into the wagon which was taking us to Bistaír. I worked so hard during the journey, pulling the tides and winds, that I'd barely time to register that I would be seeing Silas again. So, when I slumped onto the plush bench in the wagon sent from Bistaír, I was at once overcome with dread. He had never responded to my message about Varno. He had never said anything about my compromised position. I would have thought it was a description which would elicit *some* kind of response. I held my stomach the entire ride to Bistaír, Captain Umvelt giving me curious glances through his glowing feline eyes. I shot down his inquisition with a glare and raise of my chin.

A storm pressed in from the north, it seemed. A wall of clouds moved forward, keeping an odd sort of pace with the wheels which carried us. The gates to Bistaír were open wide as I had never seen them. Neysa stood with the nursemaid and the two children, which I thought curious. When we pulled up, she sprang forward and yanked open the carriage door, all but stealing me from the chassis. I cannot remember Neysa ever willingly touching me. My heartbeat quickened, wondering if they had news of Arik I had yet to receive. It was then I noticed Heiligan soldiers standing at the ready in an outbuilding near the main manor on the estate. For someone who grew up in a palace the size of the one in Kutja, having the royal house in this relatively small estate was rather peculiar to me. I did not understand all of the Aoifsing ways and customs. We were as dissimilar to one another as—

"Majesty," Umvelt said from behind me where he waited to dismount the carriage. I moved out of his way and locked eyes with my cousin.

"Neysa, this is my captain of the guard, Jens Umvelt."

Neysa said she remembered him from the day of the clock and intoned something under her breath which sounded like "A day which shall live in infamy," which was quite the truth of things. As the Heiligan soldiers stood in formation, I knew Varno would be close by, and I resented having to see him again so soon. Especially if he was the one to give me any sort of troubling news. Likely a very bad omen for the start of an engagement.

Neysa and I walked toward the doors of the main house when one of the children appeared by me, taking my hand. I stared at it, not understanding what the tiny fae wanted. She looked up at me with large, quarter-moon shaped olive-green eyes—eyes which matched my own—and she squeezed my hand. Truly, I had never been around children. Ever. Did they often do these things? Weren't they typically sticky to the touch? Why did I feel as though this little female were staring into my soul? I snatched back my hand, as though violated. Neysa narrowed her own olive eyes at me and widened her stance as if she were readying for a fight. At least that felt normal.

"Efa meant no imposition. She has a gift similar to Ludek's."

I looked down at the child, wondering then what she saw in me that I didn't see myself. It occurred to me that Neysa must have an oraculois connection to the child as well. My head was pounding, and I was so tired.

"As I said, I have come to find my brother. I do not want to be an imposition myself, cousin." My intent must have shown, because she looked . . . sad. "I am sorry about the babes," I added for only Neysa to hear.

She touched her stomach and gave me a half smile. I opened my mouth again, but Varno ran to us, his hand on his sword, and at the same moment, there was a rush of movement up the lawn. In a blur, Ewan sped past us and into the house, his wife in his arms. We ran after him and stopped in the sitting room where he laid Corraidhín down on the carpets.

Neysa was calling for the nursemaid and yelling for her own husband, who was steps behind us.

"Where is Pim?" Ewan was shouting over and over. The nursemaid came in, both children with her. The female child, Efa, was wailing, dragging her brother by his shirt toward their mother. Corraidhín did not look at all well.

From what I could see, she had no wounds. Her face became paler with each passing moment, despite Cadeyrn's efforts. Neysa had a hand on his back, making me wonder if they shared gifts. I refused to so much as look at Varno, even though I knew his eyes were on me.

"She was touched—" Ewan broke off, a sob clawing its way out of his throat. Efa held his hand, while her brother lay on his mother.

Cadeyrn looked up, panic in his sea glass eyes. "By what, Ewan?" he asked. "I cannot feel what ails her."

"The hand of Kaeres." The sound of Silas's voice from the adjacent foyer weakened my stance. A feeling I did not appreciate. He took a step into the room, and I knew he couldn't see me behind Varno and Ewan. "She—" He spun, brown hair falling over his face, nostrils flaring. I leaned back, allowing him to see me. His normally teasing face was flushed, wide-eyed, and tense. Every muscle in his cheeks and jaw was pronounced.

Neysa pushed Cadeyrn out of the way, laying her own hands on Corraidhín.

"Corra," she said, but her voice faded in the recess of the room. I watched Silas kneel by his sister, not sparing me another glance. If I made a fist and swallowed it whole, I imagined it would feel the same as what I was feeling in my stomach then.

"Corra," Neysa continued. "I will not allow this. As heir to Heícate and Kalíma, I call upon the Goddess Kaeres. A shimmer of glittering black rose from my cousin's hands, surrounding her.

"Neysa," Cadeyrn growled.

"Pet, do you remember when I said that Goddess was not one to mess with? And how she can jump on your magic?" a floppy sort of male said. I realized after a while it was the human who had followed them back. Only he wasn't human after all. Unless I was simply that tired.

Corraidhín gasped for air, her chest caving in with a crunch. Most of the folk in the room reacted to the sound and sight. Silas snarled.

Heícate appeared before us all, black eyes trained on her heir.

"Fix her," Neysa demanded. "Your sister had no right to touch her. None."

Heícate tilted her head to the side in a look similar to my father's mystics. "I cannot undo what has been set in motion," the Goddess said.

"Bullshite," Silas spat. "You infiltrate us all with your will. You make heirs of nonconsenting fae and convene to mate them without any reason."

Neysa and Cadeyrn bristled visibly, both of their backs

straightening at his words. I couldn't imagine what had transpired between them all since I last saw them.

"I was not alone in those decisions, He of the Forest," Heícate said, her mouth twitching.

He of the Forest? Clearly, I had missed *something*.

"I don't give a double fuck in a room full of cocks who all controlled that decision. You were a part of it, and the magic it took to create came from you," he said stepping to the deity.

I reached out to touch him, take his hand, pull him back, something—but stopped. Varno looked at my outstretched fingers and curled his lip. I could have knocked his too white teeth out for the look.

"Silas is right," Neysa said. "If you are the Goddess of Magic, then surely you can break the hold Kaeres has on Corraidhín's life. We know Kaeres has been using a *naem maerbh*."

The Goddess of Magic and Darkness pursed her lips, eyebrows high on her ivory skin. "How do you know this?" she asked, placing a hand on Corraidhín.

Pim wailed, looking at the Goddess. Dean pulled a sword from behind the settee, holding it aloft. I saw then that what he held was the Sword of Kaeres. A weapon sketched in books, revered and feared by children all over the realm. The onyx and ruby inlays gleamed like a succubus smile.

"I see," Heícate intoned. Her head tipped again, looking from Neysa to Silas, to me. My defenses went on high alert. The room itself began throbbing. A backbeat of bass, giving rise and fall to paintings on the wall and Yule boughs strung over the hearth.

"You must allow the boy to use the sword." Heícate's words came out in a rush. "My heir, it is in your—"

A hand ripped through Heícate from behind, pulling innards I never had the forethought to consider were a part of a deity. Before any one of us could react, she was torn from our realm. Blood, magic, and death hung heavy in the air. Neysa's body glowed with that same glittering black, her body jerking like it was being poked in a thousand places.

"Fucking hell!" Cadeyrn yelled. Silas went to their side. Ewan took Neysa's place by his wife, his head snapping between her and his sister. It was then I realized why the Goddess disturbed me so. I pushed through, telling Ewan to move.

To Corraidhín, I imbued my own magic and hummed under my breath, a siren's song I'd never used in company. I didn't give a thought to the fact the Varno was seeing me use the gift no one knew I had, or that there may be more of my Heiligan soldiers who could sense it from beyond the windows. All I could think was that this was the only way to save her. Pim's hands covered mine, a shock of cold from his soft palms. As I hummed, I turned to Silas and motioned with my chin, for him to join us. His hands came on top of Pim's. Mist wound between and around the three of us, settling over Corraidhín. I could feel when it found its way into her body. I hummed, the song drawing the others nearer. I gritted my teeth at luring mutuals. I hated this part of myself. The only thing I could accept was that it was a link to my brother.

"No one can track Arik's magic like you can. No one can bind her power with his like you," Ludek had said to me.

Heícate being ripped from us had me realize three things. One: Neysa was made heir to Heícate and Kalíma because they knew we were all pawns in a bigger game. Two: My father's mystics never guided *him*, they guided the rest of us. They gave us direction because they were the Goddesses in their fae form. And three: I was heir to Rán, Goddess of Sea, Water, and Wind.

My siren's song lasted hours. Everything in me protested. The selfish siren telling me to take from the others, rather than give to Corraidhín. The notes of the ocean flowed through me, twining with my very blood, becoming the life force I gave to my cousin's mate. It wasn't as if I would not have done this if I hadn't come to the realization I had. I'd like to think I had grown of late. Once I saw the stitches and knots tying together the tapestry of all of us, I knew this was what I must do. Even if I was bone-tired.

Efa's eyes closed in a fierce sort of slumber, and I had a desire to push her hair from her eyes. Silas allowed her tiny form to rest on him as he kept her hands under his. Under mine. Still, I did not look at him and he refused to turn toward me. We held position over his sister, feeding our essence into her. As I sang, I heard Pim's magic stir, the last piece of the puzzle to revive his mother.

With a great rise of her chest, Corraidhín awoke, wild and churning in the room like the mist and water she became. Silas was barely visible himself, his magic spent, keeping him in a state of between. Between his fae self and his elemental self. Between his role as brother, needing to stay, and his role as the male who would rather leave that room. My body would not agree to aid me in moving from Corraidhín, which must have been noted by Dean. He lifted me and offered to see me to a room. A door slammed nearby, proceeded by more rushing footsteps which I had no ability to investigate. Even if it had to do with my brother. I was a few breaths from being one with the sea.

"A bath," I rasped, my voice nearly gone. Dean made for the bathing chamber, switching on the taps.

"I will do it for her," Silas said from the door to the chamber that had been mine for a year. It was said ever so quiet, but there was something in it which made Dean freeze, then leave the room with a nod to me. I should have thanked him. Neysa would have thanked him.

Silas tested the water and pulled towels from the warming cupboard.

"Have you anything?" he asked, not looking at me. All I could manage was to tilt my head to the side. Energy crackled between us as his hackles rose with my predatorial assessment. He meant *things*. Clothing. I walked straight to the bath and sat in it, fully clothed, letting my head fall under the water in an attempt to refill my magic. It would take hours. I might be able to switch out of my clothes at some point and properly bathe, but not yet. Not with the amount of power I'd expended. If he spoke after that, I did not hear. All that I kept above the water was my nose. The room grew colder, the light fading more and more. Through my open eyes, I watched a beam of sunlight shrink from the wall, bit by bit, retracting from the dark, from where I watched, blurred by murky bathwater. It was then that arms reached through that water to pull me out. I squeaked a protest and was met with a hard smirk. Silas peeled my travel-worn clothes from me, each piece suctioned to my swollen skin. As my jacket and shirt came away, a dressing gown was wrapped around me.

"I need to get back in," I said, teeth chattering. He looked up from where he knelt before me, rolling my riding trousers from my legs. In another life, another situation, I would have fallen into him. In another life, he would have been just a male who had fallen into me. He would have devoured me and I him. But this was reality, and he was not just another male. He was not mine, if the past few months were any indication. And unless I wanted to become one with the bottom of the sea, I had to get back into the water.

"I know." Was all he said, finally freeing my legs and feet from all clothing. Though I was soaked and shivering, Silas carried me from the room and into his before unwrapping the dressing gown and laying me naked in a different bath. Sighing at the warmth, I turned my head to the side and thanked him. Calloused fingers released me to the bliss of water, and he dragged a knuckle along the side of my face.

"Silas?" I called, not knowing if my voice was loud enough. I felt him turn and sit on the lip of the tub. "God of the Forest?"

He chuckled. "Fitting, siren, that you might bust my balls before saying anything else to me."

"I said thank you."

"That you did." His face softened and I saw then just how exhausted he was. "Rest, Saski. I'll be here."

I wished then that he hadn't been there. I wished I had a moment alone. To allow the tears pushing like daggers behind my eyelids. So, because he was there, I kept my eyes closed, willing them to stay back.

Chapter 33

Saski

Only a fool would think they would let me sleep for long. I wasn't saying I would have opted for the sleep if given. No, time was a privilege denied to us with my brother missing and the Goddess of War and Death on our heels, as it were. I awoke in bed. It was an unfamiliar room wrapped in the woodsmoke-and-cedar scent of Silas. I'd never been in there before. Never been invited. I'd always known it was because that was his line. The one drawn to keep what we did, who were, or rather who we weren't, to one another separate from his feelings for Neysa. To say I was taken aback by Silas's admission in Heilig would be a gross understatement. I had been shocked. I thought, perhaps, based on how his scent changed around me, he might feel for me. I did not, however, think, in a millennium, that he would admit it. Especially after saving me and leaving his cousin and mate. Though that time had passed, and here we were.

Someone had slipped one of my oversized jumpers over me. One I had taken from Ludek, who I believed had stolen it from Arik once upon a time. In any case, it was the most comfortable thing I had with me, and the fact that my brother had packed it for me told me a great deal about how he thought this whole thing would play out. The pop of wood when the door opened had me sitting up, reaching under the pillow for a dagger I was surprised to find. Silas's eyes met mine from the chair across the room where he sat.

"It's never good to wake up in an unfamiliar room unarmed, aye?" he said with a wink. He looked as tired as I had felt earlier. Too many scents crowded the doorjamb. I rubbed sleep from my eyes, noting a strange array of lines on my brown hands. "We think those might be markers."

I looked up. It was Neysa who continued to explain as she sat on the bed.

"Your magic cast us all in your thrall," she began.

I looked down, embarrassed for perhaps the first time in my life.

"How you saved Corra tapped into a part of yourself you may not have known was there. Is that right, Dean?"

He nodded, staying farther back than the rest, probably due to it being Silas's room. I really needed filling in on the new Bistaír dynamics.

"I am heir to Rán, Goddess of Wind, Water, and Sea." There would be no beating about. There should be no confusion. I needed to find Arik and bring him home as I'd promised Ludek.

"When did you know?" Neysa asked, voice soft.

"The moment I decided to save Corraidhín," I answered. "I never disclosed my other nature. Not just to you lot, but to anyone outside of our immediate family. No one else knew." I felt ridiculous sitting in bed, wrapped in a duvet like a sickly child, whilst everyone filed in around me, so I peeked under to see whether I was decent before climbing from the bed. Plus, the scent of Silas on these sheets was making me dizzy.

"I believe—no, I know, that my father's mystics were not

advisers to him, but keepers of us. Of Heilig, of our family," I admitted to them all.

Cadeyrn shut the door completely, and I felt Silas pull a shield around the room. Clearly, I was not the only one who felt this fairly confidential information.

"The mystics were the Goddesses in their fae form. I was told they dwell yet in the salt caves in Kutja, but I think . . . I think it's a lie. So, what I . . ." I was stumbling. Something quite foreign to me as I couldn't think of a time in my past this had happened. For the love of Kutja, who was I these days? I picked a spot above a brass mirror, focused to take a breath, and squared my shoulders. I was queen. No, I was heir to Rán. When I pulled my eyes from the spot, I caught Silas's, and they had changed from that glint-of-sunlight-on-open-water green, to a transparent whirl of rapids. "The seven mystics are the seven Gods. Kaeres was never a part of them. And . . ." I looked at Neysa, who seemed to follow my thoughts. She must have said something to Cadeyrn and Silas in her mind, which sent a hot spike of something through me. Something I had no right to claim. Before I had a chance to close the thought, a cat ran in, though I'd no idea from where it came. Cadeyrn picked it up and smirked.

"Each of us in this family is heir to one of the Gods?" Ewan asked.

I said I thought so.

Dean pulled a leather-bound notebook from his jacket and opened it. On the page he laid flat were the elemental symbols for the Goddesses. The symbols in the queen's book in the library in Kutja. The same book Neysa had studied before leaving that godsawful day. It was a matter of seeing the symbols and trying to align them with the rest of us.

There was a pounding on the door, and Cadeyrn was pushed out of the way as soon as he opened it. That alone had everyone in the room, including me, snarling. It was not as though pushing did much good, because Varno was immediately pinned above the fireplace, Cadeyrn's hand at his throat, Silas's narrow sword pointed at Varno's groin.

"Christ, you lot," Dean muttered. I wanted to agree, though that sick part of me took great fun in watching this show of force.

"She is my betrothed," Varno eked out around Cadeyrn's grip.

"And this is not your home, nor your lands," Cadeyrn answered him with a chilled voice which raked nails over the room. "If Her Majesty would like your company, Governor, I'm quite sure she would request it."

"Saski," Varno tried.

Silas and Cadeyrn both growled, and it took all I had to not laugh. Again, probably not the best reaction to the humiliation of my betrothed. Truthfully, I'd forgotten he was in Aoifsing. It *had* been a long day.

Varno's lip curled. "Majesty," he corrected and slid baleful eyes to Silas.

Silas smirked and air-kissed Varno. I was physically trying to restrain myself from laughing, and by the way she was covering her mouth, so was Neysa.

"Let him down. He's harmless," I said and cringed a bit because I didn't think that was what I was meant to say to help his ego. Not that Varno's ego was my problem.

"Of course, Saski," Cadeyrn said with a smirk. Neysa knocked the back of her hand at her mate and suppressed a smile. I was actually beginning to like those two more and more.

"Are you well, my love?" Varno asked me, his eyes going to my empty ring finger. A roll of nausea hit me with his affectionate question.

"Quite, thank you. I appreciate your concern. Please see to the Heiligans who are with us. I'm sure Captain Umvelt must worry." It was a dismissal. I knew it. He knew it. Each one of us in this room knew it. Yet, though I knew Varno was bruised by the dismissal, I felt like the one coming up short. The fae in this room, some to whom I was related, were a unit. Like the wheels and fastenings on a wagon, they worked together to move through life and this insanity we'd had to deal with of late. But that unit, they could see through me. Perhaps as well as Ludek could right now. They could see how false any affection for beautiful Varno was. They could likely see just how hard I tried to not look at Silas.

The moment the door was shut, I took my attention back to the book. My name was written with a childish depiction of a wave. Dean cleared his throat.

"I did the symbols quickly," he said, color rising on his face. He was quite lovely. The siren in me purred, and I tugged her leash. The sing of a sword being sheathed pulled my attention back to the book. Next to Neysa's name was a crescent moon, Heícate's symbol, and a stick figure with waving arms I assumed must be Kalíma, the womb of the mother, destroyer of chains. I looked up, my finger on Kalíma.

"Have I missed something?" I asked my cousin.

"I bargained with Kalíma and she made me her heir as well," Neysa answered, gaze shifting ever so quick to Silas.

Someone else might not notice the infinitesimal nod of his head, but I did. And I made a point to ask.

"In exchange for breaking the mating bond with Silas," Neysa added.

I plowed on. My fingers shook, so I kept them tucked under my legs while I looked at the rest of the symbols, trying so hard to not think about why he may not have told me. Why he never answered my letter. *He doesn't want you. You're a broken monarch,* the voice in my own head said. Next to Yva's name was a cyclone. I didn't know her gift firsthand, but seeing her name beside a symbol indicating wind, I guessed they aligned her with Eos, Goddess of Wind. The young twins' names sat beside the Twin Gods: Eír, God of Healing and Protection, and Aíne, Goddess of Love. I didn't know Efa and Pim's gifts either. There was but one more space. One more God but there was no familiar name attached.

"Have you not figured out the messenger?" I asked Dean.

"I only just put it all together last night," he said, pushing at a spot on his nose where I seemed to remember there being some type of accessory when he first tumbled into the house. I looked between them all and sniffed, which may have been rude, but I didn't really care. I stalked toward Dean, watching his color rise again as he lifted his chin, lips pressing together. I ran my finger up his neck and smelled it, then whipped my head to Neysa.

"Hermód, the messenger," I said.

"Is the God of Speed," Cadeyrn added.

"Why is his scent familiar?" I asked Cadeyrn and everyone else. The siren in me was confused, fumbling for his essence, but recognizing someone else in it.

"Reynard," Cadeyrn said. "He is Reynard's half brother. And Neysa and Ewan's cousin."

I sat on the carpeted floor, hard and abrupt. I liked the carpet in this room far better than the aubergine one in my own. I really needed to redecorate. Or just leave that place. Wasn't that a thought?

"Were you sole born?" I asked Dean. He shook his head.

"I had . . ." He swallowed. "I have been told had a brother who died at birth."

I nodded, whilst everyone chattered.

"I am not any sort of heir," Dean announced over the din of voices. "Christ, I didn't even know I was like you lot until a few months ago. I'm probably still paying my car insurance in the human realm. Jesus." He dragged a hand through his sandy-colored hair.

I didn't understand two of the words he used, but gleaned they were the equivalent of when my brother would yell "Kutja's wanny!" when he was frustrated. I really needed to get my head on straight and not be losing my mind over this business with Silas. I shook my head to clear the thought and get back on track. Kutja's wanny, indeed.

Arik, where are you? I begged the universe.

"I can promise you, Dean," Neysa said, taking his hand. "I understand one hundred percent of what you might be feeling right now. I never—"

"You know what, Pet?" he shot back. "Quite sure you might think so, love, but our situations are different. I had no intention of sticking around here. I came on . . . Christ, it was like an archaeological dig. I left my life! You were letting yourself die in the human realm because you couldn't get back here! So, no. I don't think you do understand."

I looked between them. Neysa laid a hand on her stomach and dropped Dean's hand.

"Maybe you forgot a part of the story I told you." Neysa's voice got quiet. "The part where I was abducted and brought here against my will. Before I'd had a chance to know if I wanted to be here. If I had a shot with Cadeyrn. It's okay to have forgotten that, Dean. But what I'm saying is that we are more alike than you think. And I never asked to be heir to Heícate. It was done to me. I agreed to Kalíma's terms so that my husband and I could have our future and Silas could love who he wanted to love."

I nearly choked hearing her say that bit.

"That was a choice I made and would make again. You've never talked down to me, my friend. Let's not start now."

I hadn't known much of Neysa's story. How she ended up in Aoifsing. I was curious, of course, but more preoccupied with my own life and, honestly, intent on bedding Silas. I was well aware of what I must have looked like to those in the room with me then. I didn't know if they realized how much had changed. How much I had changed. That, however, was not for me to concern myself with. Seeing Neysa and how her quiet dressing down of her friend commanded the room, I was proud of her. Proud to be her cousin. Ashamed for how I'd acted, sure. Yet, I felt that perhaps one day, somewhere, she and I could be friends.

Neysa left the room, a light touch on her mate's shoulder the only notion that she was okay. Dean swore and left as well. I didn't know him well enough to wonder if he had gone after my cousin or simply fled. I did empathize with him. I understood being dropped into a role I didn't want. Both as heir to Rán and as queen of Heilig. Betrothed to Varno. The thought ran a shudder through me. Ewan and Cadeyrn left next, silence returning to the chamber. Black-and-white jagged patterns covered the small carpet next to Silas's bed. I traced each with my finger from where I sat on the floor. I could feel him across the room like a feverish body, warning of illness.

"Have you recovered?" Silas asked me from the opposite wall. I lifted my head, chin jutting out.

"I seem to have. Thank you."

"Saski—"

"I need to find Arik." I didn't know what he was going to say, but I wasn't ready to hear it. I couldn't. It would have been too much in that moment. His scent everywhere. His family populating the house. His choice of carpeting for the Goddess's sake! All of that and Arik still missing.

His eyes were on me, so I looked to him, wanting to hide back under the covers. I wanted to pull him under the covers. Like I'd wanted from the very first time I had seen him. The humiliation washed over me from when he dropped me in the garden that night in Kutja. Then again, the day Neysa came back, and I knew it was time for me to take my leave. He didn't want me only. I knew the face I presented.

"Then let's go find him," Silas said finally. He held my stare for a moment longer than was comfortable, then dropped his eyes to the necklace peeking from the neckline of my jumper. The wing of the bird he'd given me. "Fucking hell, Saski," he grumbled and walked out.

Chapter 34

Yva

Ainsley and I were both well aware that we should have been following Silas and Corraidhín to Bistaír. However, I felt it a terrible hand of fate dealt to us. Arik needed finding, and with Silas and his sister out of the hunt, he depended on us. There was a Heilig faction after him, but for whatever reason, I knew I could track him better. I had only to look at Ainsley Mads and her troop of rather large, furred fae to see she had caught the direction of my thoughts and plans. So, without preamble, we moved back toward the Sacred City. My city. Every splinter of my magic wanted to spin me home. It was not just the lure of my city, my job, or my life. It was magic in perpetual motion, gathering the tracks of my friend. We sent a hawk to Ewan informing him of what had come to pass and our forthcoming journey.

The mountains of Naenire were the most unforgiving south of Festaera. Winter was fully upon us, and my blood was not used to the cold. I have traveled, of course, but my stock was generations of Laorinaghans. Our blood was warm, our hearts temperate. A few of those in our party kept giving me sympathetic glances. One of the Mads males offered up his fur.

It swallowed me whole, only leaving my head and the frost on my hair free. But it was warm and kept me moving.

Two days after Silas had left, we were camped on the southern foothills of the Naeniran mountains. The Lupine Mountains as they were known, due it being the ancestral lands of the lupinus fae. Those who called to wolves and wolves to them There were lupinus who were purebred and born, like the former Elders from the twin provinces. The born lupinus were natural predators. They mostly smiled closed-lipped until they meant to intimidate with rows of razored teeth. The lupinus who were Made were half feral, often ate their young, and spent centuries as disposable infantry to the twin provinces. Neysa had been Made, yet whether it was because of her own gifts, her upbringing, or some stroke of luck, she merely had the affinity for speaking to the wolves. She was definitely not the normal version of lupinus with which parents scare their young. *Remember to be home before dark. Lupinus lurk in the shadows of elms on the edge of the olive groves.* I shivered under the enormous fur, thinking of my parents' warnings and how Ylysses and I used to tempt fate by playing seeker in the shadows until well past dusk. I rubbed at my chest thinking of my brother and how we used to be. Before he allowed himself to fall victim to comparison and greed. As a fae of majority, I now knew it would be a grossly rare occasion to find a lupinus in Laorinaghe. Here, in the Lupine Mountains, where they are bred in compounds and travel in packs, the threat was more than real.

Low rumbling and the otherworldly screech of death rolled to us on the fog of first light. Some of our camp were already awake, while I was still loath to rise from the furs covering me. Once I remembered where we were, my eyes sprang open, alert and frightened. The screeching continued. Yellow eyes peered from the recesses of trees surrounding our camp, yet somehow I knew they weren't the threat. Soupy fog rolled across the camp. Lupinus and wolves in general did not use other realm magics to cause foreboding fog. I almost laughed thinking Arik would find it funny. Until he realized there was a threat against me, that is. My mind doubled back on that thought. Arik was always concerned for my safety and comfort. He offered me his gift to help me sleep. It was likely because we were friends, yet the thought warmed me. It made me focus.

In one quarter-light moment, a golden-haired male stood over me, dagger drawn. In the instant I spun, my magic propelling me from the male, one of the Mads soldiers had him pinned. However, I knew he could not be held without some type of magic. The speed with which he stabbed me in the gut last time told me that my only option was to encase him in my whirlwind.

THE PARTICLE TRANSFERENCE which had him breaking apart to flee the scene allowed me to bind him within in my wind. The sight was rather off-putting. His particles being spun within my magic looked grotesque.

I couldn't contain him for long. Ainsley Mads buttressed my power with her own. I knew she was stronger in her own province, but we were currently in Naenire, rather than Prinaer, so I wasn't sure how far she could be of help. We were so very tied to our lands. It wasn't that the assassin was strong. No, he simply had a power which allowed him to vanish. He also seemed to be missing an eye since he'd stabbed me. I hoped it hurt. We were moving south, as I fought him, both of our powers draining by the minute. There was a change from the mountain terrain to the cypress groves and wild grapes of Laorinaghe. The moment we crossed the border to my own province, my gifts were bolstered. I'd kept him encased for over a full day and night, the Mads moving us swiftly through mountains and forest. It was blessed relief when his power guttered out a half day's ride outside of the Sacred City, because mine was holding on by fraying threads. We were then able to strap him into a wagon and cover him in a shield laced with a kind of ancient magic I had never felt. The Mads were a race of fae unto themselves. Though frightful because of their sheer girth, I felt myself drawn to it.

I slept that night we were back. Perhaps for the first full night in months. As for the assassin, Xaograos, my personal guard, took him to the salt caves near the beach where Cadeyrn had been imprisoned as his *baethaache*. There, my soldiers kept the male awake so that his power remained banked in salt. I had no qualms about the fact that we were torturing him with sleeplessness.

Once I'd slept in the kind of dreamless slumber I'd only had once before, I made my way to the cave. The salt should have been enough to confine his power as it wasn't so great. However, I was no longer taking chances, and based on what Silas had told me, this male had caused enough harm amongst my friends and allies.

"There is a price on your head," I said by way of greeting. His head bobbed, eye shrunken in his golden face.

"Then take it and allow me to sleep," he muttered, falling to the side. Xaograos hauled him up by the arms and splashed ice water in his face. A hawk had come from Ewan saying we must all meet. I would not leave here—would not go anywhere—until Arik was found. Regardless of a supposed birthright.

"That's not an option," I told him, crossing my arms. I'd never been involved with this kind of interrogation. By the Gods, I'd never been important enough to anyone, not even my parents or Ylysses, to warrant my involvement in anything. "Where is Arik?"

"Who?" He tipped sideways again, his knees sliding in the sand. I crossed and uncrossed my arms.

"Arik, prince of Heilig. Hand to the queen. Where is he?" I asked again.

"Shhhh," he whispered, closing his eyes and shaking his head. I looked to Xaograos who wore a blank expression.

"Listen carefully. What's your name?"

His mouth ghosted a smile, and I knew he must be admired for his beauty, but to me it rang of gilded corruption. Something to turn green before the autumn of his life.

"Asíant," he said as Xaograos doused him in more water. I kicked at his knees, unable to control my rage. He had stabbed me in the stomach. He had attacked Neysa, and he had *taken* Arik. Xaograos gave me a look I wasn't sure I wanted to pick apart. I knew I teetered on the very edge of something darker than I should care to be, yet faced with this *thing*, I was tethering my own rage.

"Asíant? I can see you are an agent, Asíant. It is also quite clear you must have a given name. What is it?" I pulled his chin up to look me in the eyes. His eye was unfocused, but he gave me a practiced, dazzling smile. I backhanded him. A sharp intake of breath to my left told me that Xaograos was surprised at the extent of my rage. I myself felt as though my emotional capacity was a thin string set aflame, and I didn't know what to make of that, nor how to identify it. It was at that time, the *cathe sídhe* sauntered into the salt cave like she'd been with me the entire time. What was more, was that she held Neysa's and Cadeyrn's scents. And something similar to Arik's, but not quite the same. Feminine. Perhaps his sister, whom I'd not yet met. Not really.

"I shall tell you how the next few moments will transpire, *Asíant*," I said, the *cathe* winding herself around my legs. Asíant's shoulders were shaking, his head lolling from side to side from the exhaustion upon him. I saw his eye close, and

Xaograos took my cue to splash him yet again, holding his head up by the hair.

"Do you know I am rather well versed on the bow?" I asked him, pulling an arrow from the quiver at my side. I scraped it along his cheek. His eyes were barely open, but at the arrowhead pushing into his jaw, a flash of fear finally showed in his pupil. "If you don't tell me where Arik is and, for that matter, each and every bit of information you have regarding the targets you have engaged, I will set you off at a sprint." I withdrew the arrow, only to twist it into the neck of his shirt and strip it from him.

"My lady," Xaograos whispered behind me in a sort of warning. I looked to him, and he stepped back as though seeing something in my face.

"You may have a head start. Then I will give chase, *Asiant*. With my aim, I should warn that first I will take out your right calf. As you tumble, I will hit your left shoulder blade. Because you will be down, it might be hard to predict where I hit next, but I think it would likely be in your flank or buttocks. You will bleed. You are too worn to heal yourself, Asiant," I told him, wind swirling around me. Even I could feel the dust storm behind my eyes. "At that point, I will stalk you while you attempt to flee, pulling at the sodden earth." He was trembling, watching the gusts ride eddies around my body. *Cathe Sidhe* stood within the gale with me. "I will ask you again where Arik is. I will ask you again, who your master is. I will ask, just once more, what your orders are. And should you fail to answer, I will pin each extremity to the Laorinaghan earth and carve your heart out myself."

Every guard standing in the cave's entrance shifted. I did not blame them at all. My actions were unlike me. Incongruous to my leadership style. Discordant with my overall disposition. It skulked in the back of mind that the behavior I was exhibiting may have been indicative of something bigger than fatigue and losing a friend. This Yva Sonnos I had become in the salt caves of the Sacred City was a firedrake, circling her hoard. Safeguarding her nest. Or, I thought before immediately refusing to give credence to the notion, burning through the world for her mate. I wiped a steady hand across my top lip and leaned into my inner wyvern.

"So, tell, me, Asíant," I purred, squatting to look him in the face. "Where. Is. Arik?"

He opened his sensual mouth to answer, but a hand shot through his chest from behind. It tore the heart from his body, as I myself had threatened moments before, and pushed his lifeless form to the sandy ground. The winds around me died down, then picked up yet again when I beheld who I faced. The face of history books and nightmares. The stories told in warrior camps of the Goddess of War and Death. She who stood on the precipice of quiet passing and violence. The moon-white hair and black eyes, the bloodied mouth and elongated fangs. My guards fled. I was thankful for it. It was not cowardice, but self-preservation. Had I any breath left in me, I would have bidden them run. Return to their families was what I would have wanted for them. Xaograos stood beside me, his large shoulder angled in front of my body. Ever the protector. I kept thinking that he had a family. Babes and a wife. I couldn't let him risk himself.

"You are relieved of duty for today, Captain," I told him as quiet as possible.

"My lady." He drew a sword. *No, no, no.* "I fight for Laorinaghe. I fight for Aoifsing."

"You fight a losing battle, soldier," Kaeres said to him. She moved, pinning him to the sparkling sand, and tore his throat from him. That quickly. I lost my guard, my loyal friend, the father to two children.

"No!" I screamed, watching the light leave Xaograos's eyes. "No," I repeated in a whisper, biting my own fist to keep from breaking down. I knew I could not break down. Not now. Not when so much depended on what happened next.

The winds around me picked up, shielding me from the Goddess. They allowed me to step backward from the cave until I was outside, and she was within. A storm blanketed the eastern horizon, a duvet of ink moving toward us. With it, a swelling warmth and raging seas. As if all the elements were rising against Kaeres. At least I'd hoped they were rising against her and not me. I stood alone on the beach, Kaeres nearly to the mouth of the salt cave, her moonlit skin, the skin of beautiful death, reflecting the pink arch of salt crystals.

With the first wave of the storm, familiar scents accosted me.

"Halloo, Representative," Corra sang. She stood beside her brother and Cadeyrn, Saski between them. "Fancy some help?"

Relief washed over me seeing her alive and well. Cadeyrn nodded at me and drew up a wall of fire on the cave's threshold. When Kaeres began to step forward, Silas, Corraidhín, and Arik's sister all seemed to pull the water from the sea itself to form another wall beyond the fire. Something sunk in me, seeing that Saski could manipulate the water.

"I am a siren . . . of sorts," Arik had said to me. Gods, I was a lowly imbecile to have thought he was teasing me.

What would you have me do, Representative? Arik had asked in his letter. Could he have been asking me because he wanted me to say not to marry for diplomacy? I had to get to him. Had to find him.

Ainsley Mads rode to us on her stallion and dismounted before the animal had come to a trot. She went directly for the others and stood, raising her arms to form a web of each of our gifts, linking us together and after a few moments, heartbeats, breaths, Kaeres disappeared. Every one of us slumped.

"He's here," I wheezed, my earlier exhaustion coming back with a vengeance. "Arik."

"Where?" Saski demanded. She had a hand on her blade, a sort of curved crescia like the crescent moon, with a bird flaring its wings in place of the hilt.

"I don't know," I stammered, feeling out of my depth with the queen of Heilig before me. "But my magic senses his. For some reason. I can feel him here."

"In your city?" she asked, and it sounded deferential.

"Yes, in my city." And I took ownership of my city. Of my province with that statement. I may be lowborn, but I worked my way to my position. Perhaps I would not have been considered if I'd not befriended Neysa. But there were ties binding us all here, just as surely as Ainsley Mads had spun a web between us all. And here, amongst these warriors on this beach in my city, I staked my claim on my territory. And I would find the prince of Heilig.

"Where is Neysa?" I asked Cadeyrn as we grabbed provisions from the kitchens. We all picked at any lose food items lying about, having used reserves of energy and magic for longer than we were accustomed.

"She is in our room. The one we stayed in." He waved with his hand.

"Here?" I nearly screamed. He leaned into me and said so that only I could hear, "She is with children. Until her presence is required, I'd like to keep her safe. Reynard, her cousin, and Ewan are all with her. Arturus led us in." He laid a hand on my shoulder before telling me to eat more.

A sickening sort of bruised feeling overcame my head. I

shoved the heel of my hand into my eye, trying to quell the feeling, but it came again. Without any warning, my gift caused the wind to pick up around me. I ran outside, charging through the clay-tiled halls and out the vine-covered gates of the palace. I did not want my ill-controlled power to cause problems within the walls of the palace, and more than that, the winds were directing me. I sensed the others' giving chase as I dashed through the sloping cobbled streets of the Sacred City. The afternoon sun shone on the pristine white buildings with their blue-tiled roofs. Some were still damaged from the fights when Lorelei's impostor took control. We were slowly rebuilding and what's more, the city felt festive for Yule, which I realized with a start, was in two days.

Before the city gates was an old building housing a bell tower. It was a temple to the aulde Gods and elements. Mostly the older generation congregated there on elemental holidays and Yule. It wore the same white with blue color scheme as the bulk of our buildings in this city of mine. The front doors were tall planks of lacquered wood painted red, with designs etched in them. I had never actually been in the temple and, as such, had never considered the designs before. Yet, as I thundered through those doors, the symbols burned into my consciousness. From the sound of swears and chatter coming from the others, they noticed it too. Each symbol represented an element. Each of those elements could be attributed to our gifts. Each one of us here. My own power was a force, knocking wooden benches from the aisles, smashing enameled artwork of pious citizens revering the elements. I was being led by my magic, to the catacombs of the building.

"I feel him too," Saski yelled over the roar of my wind. Her own wind pushed against mine in a sort of power struggle, though we had the same goal. Deeper and deeper we went. The temple sat at the highest point of the city, its subterranean lanes winding beneath the hillside. Walls leaked moisture from the humidity pressing in from our location, the tunnels narrowing the farther we tread. In such a closed hall, the wind from the Heiligan queen and me was almost too much to bear. I didn't know how the others could handle it. With that insufferable wind came the ability to feel the Heiligan prince. I looked to his sister, a touchable distance behind my right shoulder, and grabbed her hand. Her nose and upper lip twitched like she did not know how to respond to someone—someone like me—touching her so casually. I nearly dropped it, yet revisited my claim on my city, my province, and the fact that Arik needed us.

Without warning, the lit tunnel ended. Only Saski's grasp on her own power kept us, and everyone behind us, from dropping into an indistinguishable depth below. Silas pushed us both into the damp clay wall and moved past, jumping into the dark without so much as a word. Saski swore and called after him. The only answer we received was a faint spark of what looked like lightning. As though they were defeated, the winds the queen and I possessed quieted, until the tingle of Ainsley Mads's power teased along our skin. As she had done before, silken strands of magic wrapped our arms, legs, torsos, snaring us in her web. I panicked, a cricket in a spider's trap. Cadeyrn growled at her.

"Relax, Battle King," Ainsley told him. "I am linking us all, so that we may lower down safely. I for one, do not wish to drop into the unknown darkness as your cousin has done. I have no female for whom to preen." Thurnton sniggered from behind her. "At least not here."

Cadeyrn's shoulders slackened. Ainsley moved past us, her girth taking up far more of the passage than Silas had. My nose caught on the furs of her coat as she led us all, like hounds on a lead.

"Your winds please, Majesty. Representative," Ainsley said to Saski and me. My power responded like she had issued a command. The power of us both joined with the Mads leader, and in the vast dark, we saw the tendrils of her web blow down to a cavern. On this bridge of sorts, Ainsley climbed, lowering herself one arm at a time, until she could latch onto rocks and wall to descend the remaining distance. After her, we each climbed, one Mads warrior staying above for security purposes. Silas was nowhere to be found.

"Silas," Cadeyrn called. "Fucking hell. Silas!" There was a flash from the right. A tunnel we hadn't noticed. It was Saski who sprinted for it first. Cadeyrn was close on her heels, telling her something I was too far to hear. Ringing steel met my ears, the sparks of forged metal hitting stone bounced from wall to wall in the final cave mouth. There was Silas, back-to-back with Arik, fighting what could only be described as phantomes. Though I'd never seen them myself, these were vaguely translucent entities, battling with weapons of their own state of matter, yet they found their purchase just as well as the blows of my friends.

The prince had his feet bound in chains which leaked magic. His hands, though still wrapped in manacles, were separated, and so he swung out as a phantome advanced on him. He nodded to his sister, and together they drew up a well of power.

"Gods and shite, you two," Corraidhín said. "You said we kept secrets." She and Silas pooled their own powers, encapsulating the phantomes in a tube of water, its pressure mounting from the Heiligan low pressure. Once each phantome was barely visible, Cadeyrn swelled heat at the encapsulation. Steam built in the cavern, the scent of rotten flesh mounting. I had no hand in the fight they waged. Ainsley Mads and I stood back, minding the exit. The partition of steam lowered, revealing, after long moments, a lack of phantomes. Cadeyrn simply wiped his palms on his trousers. Corraidhín grinned at her brother in a feral sort of manner which made me think she had enjoyed that. Saski's arm went around her own sibling, who coughed, wet and violent. I sprung forward before thinking better. Saski eyed me curiously, then even more so when the blasted *cathe sídhe* appeared again, launching herself at poor Arik.

"Hello, Sonnos," Arik said to the *cathe*, scratching it behind the ears.

My eyes shifted right and left, not knowing if the prince we had just rescued had lost a few bits of himself.

He lifted his eyes to me. "She's been in and out since yesterday. Perhaps the previous day. Time felt off down here. Either way, Representative, tell me what would you have me do?"

Saski snorted and dropped her arm. Bits fluttered in my stomach.

"If you can flirt, Arik, you don't need my support," she said.

Her brother straightened, tugging down the ornate sleeves of his jacket. He frowned at a spot that seemed to be missing some sort of ornamentation.

"Let's clear out before we get blocked in," Cadeyrn said, looking a bit peaky. I would put money on his being reluctant to have left Neysa behind. The way out seemed quicker, yet the tension between us all made it fraught with a palpable sort of awkwardness.

"You did, well, Yva," Silas told me, clapping my armored shoulder. He always made me smile with way he rolled my name on his tongue in a way which said he was playing with both syllables, making them each wish they were longer.

Whispers came from in front of us where the rest of our group walked. Two separate snarls, the female and male companion to one another sounded. Cadeyrn snickered and looked to us.

"Gods, there's more tension in these blasted tunnels now

without the magic," Corraidhín exclaimed, barging past everyone, and climbing back up the rocky wall like a *paítherre moinchaí*.

NEYSA SPUN the turquoise glass teacup between her hands, looking out at the water. From the balcony, she could clearly see the sword I'd had magicked into her rock. The one she flipped over the day we truly became friends. To think, sometimes all it takes for a friendship to blossom is a bit of dissidence and a jug of cheap wine. Neysa's focus was elsewhere. The movement of her mate in front of me made her turn, stopping the teacup's spin. Relief shone on not just her face but that of everyone in the room. Clearly each male had the directive to stay with her whilst we were all away. Cadeyrn pulled her against him and kissed the top of her head, earning a shift in her position so that she fit against him like leaves fallen atop one another. A pricking of envy sparked in my toes seeing that. Not to begrudge them their happiness. By the Gods, they deserved it all. But because I had little. The thought rang through me, unbidden and unwelcome.

"Felicitations are in order, friend?" I asked Neysa. She whipped her head to Cadeyrn, eyes wide.

"*Caráed*, do you think Yva would have believed any other possible explanation for why you were not in the thick of fighting?" His teasing half smile lit his eyes as he looked down at his mate. "Speaking of," Cadeyrn said, and launched into what we had dealt with.

"Xaograos was slain," I interrupted, unable to contain the grief any longer. Cadeyrn bowed his head, and Neysa took my hand. "We went through training together years ago. I knew his family. We weren't exactly friends, but he was my personal guard, and I trusted him more than any others." The *cathe sídhe* walked through the balcony doors just as she had that first day I saw her. The day Arik arrived.

"He seemed very kind. I'm so sorry, Yva," Neysa said, squeezing the hand she held. The *cathe* yowled, a lengthy, sound that would have grated my nerves had I not heard the pain in it. And that was when I admitted to myself that the *sídhe* was me. A part of me. Corraidhín, who walked in with three servants carrying trays of food and wine, looked between *Cathe Sídhe* and me, and smiled.

"You've finally accepted her," she told me.

I sat. It was a good thing I had noted a woven stool, because I did not look before dropping my behind down. "What does it mean?"

"Oh, just that she is a part of your magic. You are elemental. Most of us in this room, as well as Saski and Arik, are elemental. Neysa and Cadeyrn are not. Due to your role as heir to Eos—"

"Pardon?" I shot back, not bothering to lower my voice.

"Has no one *told* her yet. By the Gods and shite, you lot!"

Everyone turned to the male with sandy-blond hair who kept pushing at a spot between his eyes, as though there were something in his crossed vision.

"What? Why are you lot looking at me?" he asked, his voice different. The notes of his speech a texture off any of ours. Similar to Neysa's, though hers moved in and out of patterns.

"Don't be daft, Dean. You're a professor and can explain far better than any of us can," Corraidhín told him. He gave her a resigned sort of look that held a slice of respect and possibly fear. Then, like shutters had come down on him, the male's features smoothed out, his eyes refocused, and he stood straighter. Neysa smirked and gave him a salute, which he answered with a raise of an eyebrow like a tutor warning his pupil. She smothered a laugh and replaced a hand on her taut belly.

"As I understand," he began. "There are eight main Gods."

"Seven," Ainsley answered from the doorway." She moved into the chamber more quietly than a fae of her size would seem able to.

"I didn't mean the mystics," he said. The eyes I thought shifty and unsure on him, were intent on the Prinaeran female.

"Nor do I, young male."

He bristled, the hairs on his arms standing on end.

"I do not wish to correct you," Ainsley said, lowering to a cushion on the floor. "It seemed to me, that you were going to refer to Kalíma as one of the eight Gods. She is a Goddess, yes. She is quite powerful. However, she is what we refer to as a minor Goddess because she does not deal in elements, nor life and death."

"But she is the Mother. The personification of the womb and breaker of chains." Neysa tapped her chin.

"Which is ever so powerful as the elements, correct," the Mads leader agreed. "However powerful, though, she is not one of the seven."

She listed the main Gods: Heícate, Goddess of Magic, Witchcraft, and Darkness. Rán, Goddess of Sea, Water, and Wind. Hermód, messenger God of Speed. Eos, Goddess of Air and Wind. The Twin Gods, Eír, God of Protection, and his sister, Aíne, Goddess of Love and Family. Finally, there was Kaeres, the Goddess of War and Death.

"So, then, why have the mystics banded in their fae form as seven including Kalíma?" Neysa asked Ainsley. The sandy-haired male, Dean, I realized, looked from a leather-bound book, and made eye contact with each of us in turn.

"Because they needed that power of seven to keep Kaeres from destroying the world," he said. Ainsley dipped her chin. I still did not understand the mystics or my connection to Eos, and said as much.

"I am heir to Heícate, and Kalíma through a bargain I made," Neysa explained. "Saski is heir to Rán, Pim and Efa are heirs to the Twin Gods, Dean is heir—though he has patently refused to accept it—to Hermód, and you, Yva, are heir to Eos."

I moved a hand across my face and started picking at the spread of food before me. The *cathe sídhe* had disappeared again, yet once I decided to eat and quiet the roaring in my head, she came back, followed by the Heiligan royals and Silas. Everyone descended on the food, fingers becoming sticky with honeyed pastry and fragrant olive oil. What we had been through, and what sat, looming on our horizon, bid us to nourish ourselves. Arik kept one hand on the *cathe* and one twinkling eye on me, causing me to squirm.

"Arik and I have spoken with my captain of the guard, and he confirmed what I had suspected. Our mother consorted with the Gods early in our childhood. She had been granted a vision, much like those Neysa has. In it, she was given a warning to control the courts of the Gods. Kaeres alienated herself from the other Gods a century ago in an attempt to begin controlling our realm from a single seat of power."

"I told you a single seat of power was unwise," Dean muttered. Cadeyrn twitched his mouth in a smile at him. At least someone could hold some amusement in this moment. "Also, this pastry is brilliant. Honestly. Best I've ever had," Dean said through mouthfuls of the pistachio paste and honey.

"I couldn't agree more, human," Saski told him. Neysa shot her a scathing look and she amended the human comment with a true look of repentance. I was ever so far more confused.

"About the pastry?" Dean asked Saski. She rolled her eyes.

"The single seat of power." She waved an elegant hand and took a sip of wine before continuing. "The mystics my father held in his employ were six of the seven main Gods, plus Kalíma, all in their fae form. The gifts they gave to Neysa the day she defeated Cadeyrn's dead lover—" There was hiss from several in the room, and I couldn't make out who all the hissing came from. Saski cleared her throat and rolled her eyes again.

"My sister tries," Arik said, stroking his brown fingers down the *cathe's* tawny fur.

It was a struggle to not close my eyes, because as much as I would like to deny it, I *felt* the stroke in every part of my body, and I wished there was no one in that room but Arik and me and that the blasted *cathe* was gone. And in that moment, the *cathe* did go. I had wished it gone, and she was gone. Arik's fingers curled in on themselves. Corraidhín snorted and Cadeyrn shot her a teasing sort of warning glare. The firedrake in me felt like hissing too.

"So, the Gods in their fae form needed mortal heirs to secure the realm from Kaeres's clutches?" I asked.

"More or less," Dean clarified.

"And Heícate is now dead. True immortal death," Cadeyrn added. He looked to his wife.

"As is Kalí," Ainsley added. We all turned to her. "I received word before I came here. Her temple was desecrated, the light of the Goddess extinguished." Our gazes shifted to Neysa, who closed her eyes, understanding dawning.

"The babes carry that legacy." The note of pain in Neysa's voice told us all we would reconnoiter later. She needed to be alone with her mate in that realization. The meeting adjourned despite not being fully over. Regardless, I was no longer required in their chamber and felt the need to leave them to what surely would be a sorting of feelings.

The hammered silver door clicked behind me, and I turned right from their chamber, intent on my own. Each inlaid lapis stone between the clay tiles had blurred edges as I walked.

"Sonnos," Arik called. I didn't turn but stopped at his voice. "A word? Privately, if you will, Representative."

I looked over my shoulder, to see him bowed at the waist, again dressed in his finery. I nodded and walked, indicating for him to follow me.

THREE LANTERNS BURNED in the corner, fading daylight leeching even the ample illumination those lamps offered. Laorinaghan superstition always made certain there were three lanterns burning at once. It was essential for them to burn together and to be extinguished together. I had always regarded the custom with barely hidden skepticism. It seemed like borrowing trouble. For all the magic contained in the realm, in Aoifsing, in my province, to tempt the elements seemed reckless. Vaguely aware of Arik entering my chambers behind me, I stood in the center of the round, tasseled rug, looking at the lanterns, the remaining corners of the rooms darkening further.

"Were that it all a drunken sailor's tale," the Heiligan prince said behind me.

No, I was not vaguely aware of his presence behind me. I was keenly aware. My friend. My diplomatic confidant. The one who I knew would break my heart faster than the two times it had broken before. Faster than the stupid boy I'd shared a bed with my first year in training. Who used my favor with the elder guards, until he no longer needed it. Faster than it had broken when my own sword lodged itself in my brother's neck and killed him. Arik's mouth opened again. I could have laughed. He couldn't stay quiet for more than a few seconds. He likely irritated any captor. But I didn't laugh.

"I didn't believe you," I blurted. "You tried to confide in me. To trust me with personal information in order to help me, and I threw it in your face. And I'm sorry, Your Highness."

A fizzing sort of noise sounded. I turned to find his dark head bowed, fist against his nose as he tried to contain a repressed laugh. I crossed my arms over my chest, noting how filthy I was in comparison to the male before me in his velvet and leather. My boot tapped an obnoxious beat that didn't ring out the way it should due to the padding of the rug.

"Shall I call for a servant? Do you require assistance, Your Highness?" I asked from behind clenched teeth.

He snorted, long and thorough, and bent to put his hands on his leather-clad knees. "And why," he began through sniffs and an unprincely spray of spittle, "have you regressed to the titled part of our relationship, *Representative*?"

"Your personal ornamentation seemed to require it," I answered, uncrossing and recrossing my arms, hoping I wasn't smelling my own sweat. I was fairly certain it was the stench of my own nerves, which made it all the worse.

"That's better, Sonnos. I prefer your borderline insults."

"You would." I rolled my eyes at him, his own the bright green of ripe Laorinaghan olives. "I must bathe. Make yourself comfortable. We can discuss after."

"So, you offer the grudging respect of titled conversation, yet wish to dismiss me by having me wait whilst you bathe?" He sat on the woven chair near the balcony, folding his arms behind his head. I paused, wondering if he was being serious, or just . . . Arik. I shook my head and closed myself in the bathing chamber. Only when I began rinsing the gritty water from my tangle of gilded brown hair, did I hear a thump against the chamber door.

"I'm bored, Sonnos," he called. I couldn't help the smile as I ran my fingers through the oiled hair that hung over my shoulder.

"Play with the shiny things on your clothing, *Your Highness*," I called back. There was a stretch of silence. The door cracked open a finger's width.

"I've got my eyes closed," he said but came into the chamber. "Wouldn't want you to scandalize me."

"What in the name of every God are you doing in here?" I squeaked. He sat with his back to the hammered copper tub. I peered round to check, and his eyes were indeed closed. Behind his cropped beard, his lips quirked up in the warm, damp air that stretched between us. I hurried washing myself.

"Well, it was the Gods I wanted to discuss, Sonnos. You were taking ever so long in here. I thought it prudent of me, as a ward of the realms, to press the matter."

"Gods, Arik."

"Mm, yes. Now." He half turned. I yelped and splashed water in his face. "I am aware of your reluctance to accept your role as heir to Eos." I began to protest whatever he was preparing to say, but he raised a hand and slashed at the air, making me watch a wisp of air as it sped past my mouth. "Apologies. I won't do that again. Truly, I was trying to impress you, which is quite difficult. Did you—" He started to turn again, so I pushed his shoulders with my wet hands. "I have never had more trouble impressing someone."

"You just want everyone to swoon over you, Arik." I would not say that I had my own swooning to deal with.

"Only you, Sonnos," he quietly teased. "Furthermore"—he cleared his throat—"we must come to terms with you being every bit as elementally important to the realm as my sister and our cousins."

"I need to get out of the bath."

He stood and grabbed the towel hanging in front of him, passing it back to me with his face looking away. I wrapped the cerulean-blue-and-white striped cotton around me before stepping out. A flick of his hand and I was dry. Even my hair, which normally took hours, was thistle dry. If a bit straighter than usual. I quickly donned the loose trousers and sweater I'd left out and led us out to the chamber proper. Had I really just bathed with Arik in the room? Gods.

"If you can manipulate wind like that," I said to him. "Then why would anyone think that I am the heir to Eos, Goddess of Wind? I cannot do anything remotely close to that."

"It dried straighter than you normally wear it," he said, running two fingers down my hair.

I stepped away a bit light-headed. I was quite sure none of us had eaten enough to replenish our energy stores and powers.

"I am not elemental. My sister is. We are both sirens—of sorts—but only she controls the elements."

"But you controlled the air. The wind just then."

"I can request the elements to assist me. And I can call upon others' powers. This is confidential knowledge, Sonnos. No one likes to think someone is able to control their own ability."

"So, you used my own affinity?" I asked. I wasn't uncomfortable with that, if it were the case. Rather curious though.

His mouth shifted into a frown, eyes slinking to the open balcony doors. I had never seen him like this.

"Arik."

"Your affinity calls to me," he answered carefully, keeping his eyes well away. I crossed my arms and stared him down.

Moments passed, and when he realized I would not let him off this, he sighed and scraped a hand over the dark hair on his jaw. "I may be a siren, but you have always sung to me, Sonnos. Down to your very elemental being."

I dropped my arms, fighting to keep upright. "That cannot be right," I said to him, pursing my lips.

"I assure you; it is." His tone was clipped. Reserved. Hurt. I wanted to reach out to him. I wanted to crawl to him and feel the roughness of his beard on my skin. Have it move over me like rush on floorboard, sweeping me away. Instead, I said, "Why do you think that is?"

He chuckled. It sounded different to his usual easy laugh.

"I think it is because I want to possess you, Sonnos. Your heart and body. And I *think* it is because I am meant to be your consort."

"Oh." The word escaped me on a slight cyclone of wind which spun around the male before me who was second in line to the Heilig throne.

"Oh," he repeated.

"Me?" I asked. "But I am nobody, Arik."

"You are somebody, as we are all somebody, regardless of these damnable titles. But, more than that, you are somebody to your friends. And mostly, you are somebody to me."

"But to possess me?"

"Okay, that was rather melodramatic, Sonnos. Might I amend?"

"Of course," I said, waving him on.

He smirked, the brightness back in his eyes. "Do you remember when I wrote of Olde Jym in the tavern?" he asked, and I nodded. Tentative fingers reached for mine. "I do not believe there would ever be a time, no matter how many centuries might pass us by, when I would need any amount of ale to want to return home to you, Sonnos. Yours is the face I wish to see every morning I wake, and each night when I retire."

I was looking at him, my eyes so wide that my scalp pounded from the pressure.

He sighed. "Must I take off my clothes and dance for you, Representative?"

I let him tug my fingers, pulling me closer. My other fingers found his obscenely ornamented velvet jacket and began undoing his buttons myself.

"I quite knew you wouldn't favor this jacket," he said, watching my fingers. I looked up into his face. Watched him swallow, eyes darkening as they settled on mine. The moment lasted too long. I couldn't contain the nerves building in me. "We don't have to figure it all out right now."

"No?" I asked, our lips almost touching.

"No. Right now we just—" His lips met mine, soft yet unyielding.

I pulled the jacket from him and wound my arms around him. From the moment I had found out he was abducted, I wanted to hold him. To have every centimeter of me pressed against him. To never have space between us. Despite the fact that we lived at vastly separate points in the realm, all of me wanted all of him. Always.

The abrasion of his beard on my neck set fire in my veins, making me sling a leg over his. He lifted both, hooking them around his waist where I could feel him pressing into a sensitive part of me. I pulled from his mouth with a swallowed gasp. He captured my mouth again, pushing me into a tapestry on the wall. Any objections I had to anything in this realm or the next vacated my consciousness, as the only thing worth saving in my mind was Arik and me and every place we could connect our bodies and souls. His face moved back, olive eyes boring into mine. I'd never seen his so intoxicated looking. He touched my bottom lip with his thumb, stroking fingers across my face, then pressed his forehead into mine.

"Gods, Sonnos," Arik breathed. His hands slid down, cupping my bum, the movement set his hips harder against mine. "Will you let me try to be worthy of you?"

His words grounded me. Extracted me from the fog I'd let myself be enveloped by.

"Don't," I choked out. "Don't tease me. Not now. Please."

The determined hands retreated from my body in a slow motion. He asked me to repeat what I said, and I did. He swore.

"Yva."

My name on his lips sent another thrill through me, though the tone was close to anger. He never used my given name. Each fiber of the tapestry behind me irritated my overheated skin where it met the loops and whirls of ancient Laorinaghan embroidery.

"I have not said anything to patronize you. I was raised a selfish scoundrel, second in line for a throne no one thought would ever be vacated. You have worked yourself to the sinew of your muscle to achieve the position you are in. And you remained good. Whole. Beautiful beyond any I have ever seen. If you will let me, I will strive to be worthy of you. Worth your effort, your heart." He placed a hand on my chest, which I covered with my own like the response was automatic.

"You would like my heart?" I asked, tipping my hips toward his.

"More than anything I have ever wanted."

"Good. Because it has been yours since the first diplomatic meeting we had."

"The one with the swimming race?" he asked, a smile lighting his face, which less than a moment before had been unsure.

I smiled back, a gesture that I did not make regularly enough.

"The only reason you won is because I nearly drowned myself watching the way the moon shone on every curve on that body of yours, Representative."

His hand over my heart slipped to my breast, making my hips buck. He pulled my loose sweater overhead, meeting my breast with sinful mouth. I buried my hands in the short hairs on his head, urging him on. The sight of him looking up at me, night-black lashes shading those deep green eyes, made me purr. Like a cat. Or a *cathe sídhe*. His hands yanked my hips to his face, his tongue circling my navel before he dropped my trousers to the tile.

"Arik."

He hummed a question. Or an answer. I did not know. I only knew his name from my mouth was a plea. The first strokes of his tongue against the most sensitive hidden part of me had me grabbing to my sides, reaching for anything on which to hold. Arik laughed against me, opening his mouth wider to take more of me. I shattered a lamp on my left and sent a picture frame smashing to the ground. We both laughed. This time when he looked up at me, I breathed his name, a song on the wind, moving in the air between us. He lifted me off the ground and to the chaise a throwing distance from us. Each belt loop undone, each button on his shirt, each tuck of muscle which moved as he undressed, held my rapt attention. Because I had never seen such a body. I had never wanted someone so much. I reached out and ran the tingling tips of my fingers over the dusting of black hair below his ribs and navel. His eyes closed, knees walking along the wine-colored chaise toward me.

"May I?" I asked him, fingers just short of touching the part of him I wanted to have inside me.

"Please," he nearly begged. At the first touch, a spark

danced between us, and there was nothing left but to pull him on top of me. To slip him into me. To lose myself with him in me, over and over until the chamber howled with winds and song notes from something so deep and old in the sea, we had clearly tickled it awake. His release, my release, sounded like the waves themselves, rushing over that rock far below the palace.

The sleep that followed was deeper than any I had experienced since Ylysses's death. The feel of his fingers running through my hair as he stayed within me, cradling me, until we drifted into that wave-soaked oblivion together drew etchings in my soul like waves upon the ocean floor.

Chapter 35

Silas

Where in the bleeding hell realms had Arik gone? I had a feeling he may have slithered off to Yva's chambers, and more power to them both if that were the case. I might kill him if he broke her heart though. However, I did need to ask him questions about what the hell happened the whole time he was in captivity. No one had asked where my niece and nephew were, which I thought odd, though I'm quite sure most without children rarely spare a thought for them if they aren't in the immediate vicinity. Regardless, Cadeyrn had cloaked them well, as no one, not even bloody Ainsley Mads, had taken notice of the little *moin-chai* in the chambers.

"My brother is likely gone with Eos's heir."

I spun at Saski's voice on the terrace. I had felt her presence. I felt her everywhere. But I had merely thought the siren was totally taking over my consciousness since we were in the same building again. The way she had looked at me in Bistair, like she wasn't fazed at all to see me. Like I didn't almost throw up on my bloody boots when I caught her scent. So, I hadn't asked her anything. I hadn't requested her presence alone with me on the ride all the way to the Sacred City. I hadn't said much at all to her. Gods and shite, though, seeing her standing on the terrace, the sea beyond, it was like seeing the way the worlds were made. She fucking glowed. The black embroidery of her gown was stitched closely in some places to cover her more, but it dropped to sheer panels, all the way to the floor. She caught me looking and held out a bare foot.

"All I had for shoes were the boots I wore. Silly, no?" She shrugged her shoulders. "Would you walk with me, Silas?"

I didn't answer, simply tucked my chin, and moved to her like she was magnetic. Like we would form a gravitational field between us like Neysa and Ewan had years before. And once formed, Gods spare anything in the firing range. We took the private terrace steps two hundred, three hundred, down to the beach below. My boots were heavy in the sand, while her bare feet skimmed it, that glow strengthening.

"How has no one suspected what you are?" I asked, not able to keep silent any longer.

"And what is that these days, Silas?"

The moon was still rising over the sea beside us, but the light from it found its way to her skin. The shimmer over her mimicked the reflection of the light on water. I was seconds from dropping to my fucking knees for her. And that just wouldn't bloody do.

"You're a siren, Majesty," I answered, swallowing that godsdamned sloshing in my gut.

"Does that bother you?" Her question held the predatorial edge she'd had since we met. The apex predator was obvious in the way her body stiffened, head cocked sideways mechanically. I stooped to pick up a stone and tossed it into the sea toward that blasted rock where Neysa smashed her face and told me it was a shark.

"You see that rock?" I asked her, pointing. She waited a breath before looking where I pointed. "Years ago, we had found Cadeyrn's *baethaache* here. The representative, Lorelei, as we had briefed you, had been compromised. Neysa had a vision of her mother being killed, and for some reason, she and my cousin got into a huge row. Neysa and Yva got pissed on the beach here drinking from a jug of wine. *Trubaíste* ran into the water, did a fucking flip over that rock, and threw her sword back to shore." I saw Saski smirk. "Then a bloody great wave knocked her face first into the rock."

"I am not surprised," Saski admitted, though reverence, not malice, leaked through her tone.

"That's what the sword is doing in the rock now. When she was . . . displaced, Yva had that made as tribute." I didn't know why I had told her that. Maybe because I wanted to offer up a bit of all of us. A tie that also bound her as we all were here now, playing to the game pieces of the realm. Maybe just because. No reason other than wanting to speak with her and simply exist beside her. Even if just for the length of a conversation. It pained me to understand that as love. Love wasn't the mad rush of needing to speak nor the excitement of firsts. No, as I stood there, rambling like a geezer, I reckoned that love was wanting to spin in orbit around another, content in the knowledge you both exist in the same sphere. I shook my godsdamned head, thinking I must be a planet out of orbit, spinning around my sun, unable to let go, yet completely at her gravitational mercy.

"You did not answer me," Saski commanded. All vixen, siren, fucking queen in her command. "What is it I am now?"

"I should expect the same female you have always been," I started to say. A pulse of heat pushed at my face, wanting to tell her she was mine. Though she wasn't. I was hers. She was not mine. Instead I said, "Though a female imbued with the duty of a reigning monarch. A betrothed one at that."

"Ah," she answered simply, toeing the sand, and watching it filter through her long toes. I walked a few steps, needing to do something with myself. She followed. Probably the first time in her life she trailed anyone, and I was too mind-fucked to appreciate it. "Silas. You—"

"I know, Majesty. You need not say it. I'm a country squire. You are a queen. A betrothed queen. That Barno fellow asked, and you said yes."

"*You* never asked." Her eyes blazed green fire for the briefest of seconds.

By the Gods and *moinchaí* shite. I couldn't have been more confused had I hung upside down from a pole in my underpants. Though I was quite certain that would not be confusing so much as a stupid thing to do.

"Pardon?" I asked, getting in her face.

"Not that I expected a proposal. Gods, I didn't even expect your admission that day after the clock. But you left, Silas."

"I left because I had a task, Saski. I was an envoy to Aoifsing, and we had to figure out what was happening! I did not go off to race motorcars and get drunk in Monte Carlo!" Oh, for the will of the fucking Gods, I sounded like my sister. I scrubbed a hand over my face.

"I don't think I follow—"

"Forget it. It was a load of rubbish."

We were quiet for a time. The foam of the surf and faint music from the town the only sounds which met us.

"But you did not return. Nor write." Her voice was small. As I had heard it only once in her chamber before *Trubaíste* came back. She was correct. I had not written. "And you did not inform me of the mating bond. It's removal."

I stopped and tore at my hair with a growl. "You are a queen."

"I do not wish to be."

"And yet, Saski, you are."

She walked on, her dress flying behind her like a gothic

novel set in places like the Barlowe Combe manor. I often wished to see the manor again. Wished to bring Saski there and show her the limestone beauty of the English coastline.

"We have begun the process of a dissolution," she said, and I noticed her hands shaking.

"Then why the betrothal?" I demanded.

"Because you weren't there, and it looked good politically." At least she was being honest.

"Had I been there?"

She looked me dead in my eyes as she said, "Then the world would know that no male but you would touch me again. Ever."

This was where I should have kissed her. I should have torn that witchy dress from her glowing golden-brown skin and planted myself in her on this beach. But I instead grabbed her shaking hands and kissed them. Hard. I held them to me and knew my eyes must have told a fucking tale. Tears flowed from hers, reading my face.

"Well," she said, pulling her hands away and giving me a courtier's smile, "I did say I'd believe that love bit when I saw it."

"Saski." She waved me off, tearing the dress from her own body, and diving in the sea.

I waited there for her.

Watching.

She could be headed back to Heilig for all I knew. Still, I sat on the shore like a fucking hatter, watching for her dark head to crest those waves, which churned more and more violently as the night turned to dawn. It wasn't as if I expected a fucking happy ending. Those didn't happen for males like me. Yet, I waited still.

Chapter 36

Neysa

It was remarkable that no one at all had seen through Cadeyrn's cloaking of the children. It was not that we didn't want anyone to know they were with us, but to speak of them when there very well could be one of the insufferable Gods lurking would complicate things. There was no one who could protect them as we all could. If what Corraidhín had said about Pim being the only one who could defeat Kaeres were true, then we had to ensure his safety for more than the mere reason that any of us would gladly die to protect Pim. Not because he was the protector of our realm. Not because all things pointed to his life being a key to balance between fae and the gods who should care for us. No, we would all lay down our lives to ensure my nephew had a chance to become the male he was destined to be. The male who was and would always be loved so completely.

Really, though, at one point Efa started screaming blue murder, and Dean had to nearly sit upon them both to extract a heavy candle snuffer from Pim's hand where he held it over his sister's head. I truly didn't know how no one noticed. Everyone left once it was established that both Goddesses to whom I was heir had been killed. Or vanquished. Or whatever was said about immortals who were gone for good. I didn't care about the verbiage. I cared about the fact that I now had two lives within me, who were now carrying a particular legacy. One they neither deserved, nor asked for. Cadeyrn was giving me a look.

We were in a holding pattern. It wasn't a phrase spoken here; I knew. But it resonated regardless. I stood by the balcony, watching the surf crash over the rocks, and I shivered. Memories of that night alone in our home flooded my senses in a most unwelcome way. The air was cool, but not so much that my teeth would chatter on their own. I stared into the horizon, wondering what precise direction we faced. It was all still so new. Even living in a city like London or Los Angeles for as long as I did, each day, through the familiarity of routine, I found something new. A fresh insight to the pulse of the city. London had its history and a past that oozed deception and the long-standing evils of said past. History colored by secular acts. History birthing the modern world. The absolute hub for the contemporary. Los Angeles, by comparison, reeked of a different sort of deception. The sort that sneaks up on you. Lures you like the late Elders, Nanua, and Camua. They had been lupinus. Lupinus as I was now, due to Nanua's bite. Her beauty was a draw. I knew the first time I saw her that it was a facade to hide ugliness. LA had that facade. Not that there wasn't so much to love about Southern California. I had found a place there. An ease for a time. But it wasn't real. It was manufactured ease. And I liked to work for my ease.

In any case, my comparison was that the time I'd spent in Aoifsing and even Heilig. Though I'd seen so very much of it, traveling and campaigning as we had, I still got turned around. Polar directions still befuddled me here. Laorinaghe was where our home was. Where Cadeyrn had built me a home. When he had no hope. When I thought him dead, and he thought me lost to him forever. Separated by realms and dimensions, as it were, he'd still created for me. For us. And it was now tainted.

"You're cold," Cadeyrn said, coming up behind me. His hands rubbed up my arms, over the charcoal cashmere I wore. "Oh Gods," he swore. I turned in his arms and looked up at his shaded sea glass eyes.

"What?" I asked, the alarm in his voice sending a shock of adrenaline through me.

"I thought we had an agreement on the grey jumpers." His teasing smile had me lay my head against his chest. If simply wearing a grey jumper was a portent of ill fortune, then we had even bigger problems.

"Thank you for building the house for me," I said, voice a bit smaller than I liked. He laughed at the words, and I admit they were stupid. "It means more than you might know. That we were apart, our souls torn from one another, yet you thought to create something for me."

"I had to." He cleared his throat and continued, "I had to create it. I had to build. I had to anchor some part of me that knew how to *make*, and know I was doing it for you. For us."

I snuggled closer, allowing his heat to hold me as well as his arms.

"Is it ruined now? I know it's possible. I understand fully if it is, Neysa. What you dealt with there—"

"I think it will be fine. It may take time. But what we have to look forward to," I said, placing his hand on my stomach, "that will usurp anything ugly. I know it will. Oh, bloody hell!"

"What is it?" he asked, pulling back to look at me.

"There's still a godsdamned eyeball in the living room!" I wondered if it would have decayed, rotted, or stunk. I wondered if the wards would keep critters out.

"Things could have been worse. I can handle an eyeball." Cadeyrn's voice dripped with disdain, and years ago I would have thought he was truly disgusted with me or what I'd said. Now I knew he was amused and joking. I whacked his chest and pressed my forehead into it, breathing him in. "I would burn the realms for you. So, I'm more than happy to clean up an eyeball."

A knock sounded and we both sighed. Silas walked in looking like he'd been dragged through the trenches. He didn't say anything but grunted and dropped onto a low-slung round chair near us. Cadeyrn and I gave each other a look yet didn't speak. Silas scratched at his face and pulled at his shirt like he was smelling himself.

"She's fucking everywhere," he blurted. Neither of us had to ask of whom he spoke. "I don't even know if she's still in Aoifsing or whether she fucked off back to Heilig. What was I supposed to do?"

"What happened, Silas?" I asked, kneeling on the rug in front of his chair.

"Och, *Trubaíste*," he said. "Don't kneel for me. Here." He stood up, offering his chair.

"Silas, please. I'm not infirm. Sit back down. Now what happened between you two?"

"I don't actually know. She asked me to walk with her on the beach. She asked me why I hadn't contacted her. Why I hadn't responded to her letter."

"What letter?" Cadeyrn asked before I could. Silas pulled a well-crumpled message that shimmered with magic from his jacket. We read it in silence, and I almost felt like blushing.

"You didn't respond to *that*?" my husband asked, dark brows high on his face.

Don't chastise him, Cadeyrn, I said to my mate in my mind.

I'm not. But had you sent me that message, I would have turned the seas to steam to get back to you.

My bare feet clutched the scatter rug under my toes at the

thought.

"It was the same day Ewan sent me to see Yva and Arik. I was going to respond when I knew more. Then we met that fuckwad who said he was her betrothed. I didn't know what in the bloody fuck to say to her at that point. She's the fucking queen of Heilig, brother."

"She wants you," Cadeyrn and I said at the exact same time, which was almost creepy.

"It's politics, you lot. She may want me, but she needs to marry that Barno character."

"Varno," Cadeyrn corrected.

"Fuck if I care." Silas's growl made me step back involuntarily. "Sorry, *Trubaíste*."

I waved him off. "So, what happened on the beach? What did you tell her about the letter?"

"Basically, what I just told you lot. That she was queen, and I was nothing." There was a beat of silence. He hissed through his teeth. "She said she didn't care and if I said I wanted her, she would never take anyone else."

"Please, please tell me you didn't let her walk away after saying that," I said, chewing the edge of my thumb.

"No," he answered. I breathed a sigh of relief. "She swam away."

There was a lot of swearing between the three of us in that jewel-toned room high above the Laorinaghan strand. I knew Saski had come back. She had passed me on my way back from the kitchens not long before Silas came in.

"Do you not want her? Like really not want her?" I asked. Silas hung his head between his knees and shook it. "Is that a no?"

"I do. I want her. I want to claim her. I want every maddening fucking piece of her. I want her to drain everything from me with her siren shite. But I don't want to take from her all she was born to do."

"You've cast your decision based on what you think is best for her. Not what she has decided for herself," Cadeyrn said, warily.

"I suppose you know a bit about that fuckery, eh, brother?" Silas needled him.

"He jolly well does," I cut in.

"Jolly well?" Cadeyrn asked. Silas snickered.

"It's something my dad used to say. It was weird, wasn't it?"

"Fucking weird," Silas agreed.

Cadeyrn snorted trying to contain a laugh, but we all just burst out with it together.

Corra walked in then, holding Pim on her hip, saying Ewan and Efa were asleep in their chambers. I looked deep within myself and felt for a link to my brother and niece and could see both of them in their slumber. I didn't want it to seem like a breach of their privacy, so I backed away from it, simply thankful for their existence.

"I just saw the queen of Heilig with one of those large urns from which I've seen folk breathe in herbs, and though her smile looked serene, I quite think she wanted to murder me," Corra chirped, placing Pim on the rug, letting him take off toward the open balcony doors.

Cadeyrn scooped him up before he crossed the threshold, making the toddler giggle and kick.

Silas put his head in his hands again, digging his fingers into the brown waves.

"I should go speak with her," he said, voice muffled.

"Maybe not when she's high?" I asked. My husband snickered behind me, swooping Pim through the air like an airplane. "I think perhaps we all need to get some rest like Ewan and Efa and then figure out a game plan for dealing with the newest end-of-the-worlds scenario."

"Oh!" Corra said, throwing herself across the settee and

crossing her legs at the booted ankles over the rolled arm. "Like in human sports! I watched a documentary once—it wasn't my favorite, but I had made a long run of shows which dealt with things like serial killers, asteroids, and sharks, and I thought—"

"Corraidhín," Silas growled, head still hung.

"Yes, yes, darling. In human football. I can't remember if it was the American kind with the tight leggings and large shoulders, or the football in the rest of the human world with the black-and-white ball. Regardless, they used a large board to write out 'gameplay' with little Xs and Os, and came up with different plays based on potential responses from the enemy team."

"Opposing team, sister."

"Yes, yes. Same thing. Might we gain from an exercise like that?"

"It's essentially what would be done in the war room," Cadeyrn pointed out. "But you're correct. I think that we need to figure out as many angles as possible, and ships and weapons will lend us no advantage. Be right back." And my husband and Pim disappeared in a blink of particle transference.

"You had better be careful with my lad!" Corra called after him. Silas rose and walked to the bar cart next to the settee, then poured a glass of wine the color of polished garnets for each of us. I refused, and he dumped the contents of my glass into his. Within that space of time, Cadeyrn and Pim rematerialized, both soaking wet and laughing like crazy people. Or fae. Crazy fae. I ran for towels from the bathing chamber and wrapped Pim in one before handing one to his uncle who pulled me to him. I squealed, feeling the water seep through my clothes.

"He said he wanted to go to the beach. So, we took a quick dip in the tide pool where the water is somewhat warmer."

Pim's teeth began to chatter, and Corra tsked at her cousin while grabbing a knit blanket from the settee, layering Pim an extra time. Pim looked to Cadeyrn and did an exaggerated wink, making his whole mouth twitch like Ewan's does. Cadeyrn winked back, far more subtly. Gods they were cute.

We all dispersed with the plan to reconnoiter over supper to start our game plan. Corra was adamant about finding a large board "on which to draw symbols and such," so she rushed off to bathe Pim and get him down to nap before searching for her board. Rather than rest myself, as soon as everyone left and Cadeyrn went to bathe, I slipped out of the room.

"Neysa," Saski said, brows high on her golden-brown face. Her eyes darted back and forth over the dimly lit hallway.

"May I come in?"

She stepped back and opened the door to reveal a round room which was bathed in silver accents and white fabrics. It was a wholly different look to the other rooms I had been in here in the Sacred City. I was reminded of a trip to Santorini I took in university. In those days, I had such constant anxiety episodes when I had to socialize in groups, and I would make myself sleep in until everyone had left the rental flat. I would then explore on my own until it was time for drinks in the evening, when I was more comfortable being social. Being uncomfortable in my own skin was the understatement of the century for me. I wasn't even human, yet craved a sense of belonging. Of comradery. A sense of everything I had now and would fight until well past my last breath to protect. I felt like, perhaps, Saski might be lacking in that sense of belonging. I knew she did not want her crown. Just as Ewan had not wanted his. I knew that how she grew up isolated her, and losing Pavla destroyed her more than I could ever know. So, I wanted to offer a sort of lifeline.

Except I really didn't know how to do it once I was standing in her chambers. She swayed a little on her bare feet, her hair in a wild sheet around her, as though she had dried it with a fierce, wicked wind.

"Are we having a girly chat?" she asked, her mouth thick like it was stuffed with cotton. I tried to not smile, remembering the feeling of being in a hookah lounge and flagging someone down for water. I moved to her own bar cart, noting the hammered-silver sides of it, and the inlaid lapis lazuli tray. Before I said anything in response, I poured her a large glass of cucumber water, which she downed in a greedy gulp.

"Depends on whether either of us is feeling particularly girly at the moment. I'm pregnant, tired, and pissed off that I can't drink wine. You're exhausted, high as a shooting star, and pissed off at Silas."

She hissed behind her teeth but ended up spitting a little, which female code will keep me from ever divulging to anyone outside that room. I sat on the silver leather ottoman and wondered if they were called ottomans here, as there was no Ottoman Empire. The thought annoyed me, so I pushed it back behind everything else in my mind that laid in wait to pounce on me in the middle of the night.

"I am not pissed off at Silas. I am pissed off with myself, if you must know," she said, raising a shoulder high enough to give the appearance of glancing over it at me. I rolled my eyes.

"Yes, my liege," I drawled, not having the queenly bit. "I get that too."

She sat across from me on a rather purgatorial looking hammered-silver chair.

"The night I received your message about finding matters

of state a challenge," I began, rising again to pour her more water. "I was alone in our home, which is just south of here. Cadeyrn built it. It's just on the sea—"

"I understand you have a happy fucking life, cousin. Say your piece."

I stood a moment and sucked in my cheeks.

Don't rise to it, Neysa, I told myself. *It's not you she's angry with.* So, I held out the glass but kept it back.

"Saski, I have moved past all of our bullshit from before. I believe I understand you. At least enough. But if we are to have a functional working relationship, then you need to switch off your royal siren persona. It neither impresses nor frightens me."

"I know," she sighed.

"What I was telling you was that I had visions of things that were happening. Even a vision of you and Ludek in a room in Heilig. Maybe the library, I don't know. It had tall cathedral windows with stained glass. You both were looking out over the grounds beyond the palace walls. It was night and there were lights—torches maybe. Nothing else."

Her faced paled, and she was quickly sobering.

"Once we got word from Ewan," I continued. "Cadeyrn insisted on going to Bistaír."

"Without you?" she asked with a quick arch of her brow.

I nodded and sat back down. "I was alone in our home, and it's a fairly isolated place. I was relieved to hear from you. I appreciated your reaching out and sent a hawk back to you. And then I was attacked. There was the assassin and then the *naem maerbh*. I didn't have a hawk. Eventually I made it out. I'm fine, obviously, but the fact was that Cadeyrn made that decision. He insisted I stay behind. Because of the trouble I'd been having lately. He thought he knew what was best for me, and he was wrong."

"Too right he was wrong. Why did you not insist on

going?" She sat forward as she asked the question.

"I did at first. But I had been seeing a healer for the trouble I'd been having. Mentally. I was so tired that I actually wanted to stay home, though in my heart I knew I shouldn't. And in the end, I let him steer me. He was acting in the way he thought was best, and I went along with it, thinking he knew what was best. It was on me as well."

"Wait. What does the healer have to do with anything?"

"Trauma, Saski. I have been having post-traumatic stress disorder. I don't know if it's a thing here."

"I can discern the meaning of it enough. I am sorry."

I nodded, accepting the apology and moving on. "My point is that I was needed in Bistaír. We are all needed here for what is to come. In case you were thinking of leaving."

"I am not. Not until this is done. But that is not the whole of what you are saying. Go on." She waved her hand and crossed her legs, dangling a slender foot from the side of her calf.

"Silas did not act upon what he wanted."

She snorted and drank the water, chewing on a piece of cucumber.

"He thought he knew what was best for you. Politically."

"I do not give a shit about politics."

"You are betrothed to Varno," I stated, because regardless of her feelings for Silas, she has some sort of pact with the governor of Sot. "Silas is honorable, Saski. He also has his pride, which has been under fire for a few years now, through no fault of his own."

"He had no problem bedding me when he knew he was mated to you!"

The room fell quiet. I supposed this had to happen at some point.

Neysa, Cadeyrn asked through our minds. *Are you well?* I said back that I was fine and chatting with my cousin.

It really took quite a bit of me to be the bigger person and not point out the initial obvious reason he bedded her in the first place: he was drunk, drugged, she looked like me. And she was willing. Giving myself a mental back pat, I took a breath and moved on.

"He never agreed to the mating bond. He knew I did not want it. And I was gone, Saski. This?" I waved erratically. "This situation between you two? This is different. You are queen. Like it or not. For the moment, that is what and who you are. You did not have to accept the proposal. I won't coddle you. I won't tell you what you did was right or wrong because it's not for me to decide, and Gods, I've made some phenomenally poor choices in the last—" I waved my hand again, indicating it could have been forever. "But I will tell you that I know how he feels about you. I know he wants you. He also knows he cannot step over the stones you have laid in your political maneuvering. So, think about that." My words weighed heavily in the room.

"I told him. As you said, he decided he knows what is best for me."

"Yes, he did. Which was wrong of him. But the fact remains that you are still engaged to Varno. You are still queen. And he thinks he is nothing."

"Am I supposed to give up my lands and title?" she asked, incredulous.

"Of course not! But I should think you might decide if what you want is a marriage for political alliance, or one for love that may mar your end game."

"Well done, cousin," she spat. "That did nothing to help the situation."

"Perhaps not. But someone needs to give it to you straight, and Ludek isn't here. We are meeting in the war room for supper and to plan the course of action to take in our collective predicament. See you there."

Chapter 37

Neysa

I hated this war room with a passion that sung to my soul just as resonant as my favorite songs. In this room, I found out my mother had been killed. In this room, I had fought with Cadeyrn and seen my brother's heart broken over Corra. In this room, I had returned, hoping to find my mate, and found him gone. So, in this room, not even counting the feeling I got from palaces in general, I was a bucket of pissants. Still, it was practical to gather and prepare for what was, essentially, war. Corra, bless her, managed to find a rather large piece of wood over which was a sheet of textured paper. She was busy scribbling symbols in the corners like a map legend, and that in itself made me less jittery about the stupid room.

"What have you got for us, coach?" I asked her, slipping into a seat nearest her gameplay board. She half turned to me, a pen in hand, and blew a thick auburn fringe off her cheekbones.

"I've written out all of Dean's symbols for us. Pim, no darling," she scolded and stopped, biting her lip. Corra's gaze shot to Ewan's. "I'm so sorry, darling," she said to my brother.

Ewan waved to Cadeyrn who dropped the cloak from the children.

Ainsley Mads laughed, a booming sort of guffaw that was definitely merry, yet still held a note of something deadly. Yva, Arik, and Saski all simply looked at the children and shrugged.

"I knew something was being cloaked, but I couldn't figure out what," Ainsley said, pulling on her angled chin. "It was Cadeyrn's magic signature, so I figured it had to do with the babes in Neysa's womb."

It was then that all eyes shot to me. I threw my hands up and laughed.

"Okay, so cloaking any of our children or circumstances is pointless within our circle. Let's move on," I directed.

Corra nodded and explained the symbols again, listed the Gods and for whom we were heirs, and had a triangle with a large K in the center to represent Kaeres. Ewan looked especially introspective and was jotting notes in a journal the same way Dean was, and it made me laugh. I opened my connection to my brother to ask what he was angling toward, but the doors burst open and Reynard strutted in with Cyrranus on his heels, a smirk on his chiseled face.

"Gods, the entire front end of the city reeks," Reynard said by way of greeting. I jumped up to hug him, and he whispered a congratulations in my ear.

"What do you mean by 'reeks'?" Cadeyrn asked. Reynard and his mate pulled out chairs and sat between Saski and Arik.

"Sweet, like burned fruit," my friend answered. "Made me gag. Not easy to do." Most of us ignored that comment. "I have a question before we start this charade."

Corra folded her arms over her chest and shot daggers at him for interrupting her lesson.

"Where are your lovely friends, Starfish and Sneaky Starfish?" Reynard asked, steepling his long fingers together.

We all looked to each other, and Saski asked what he was talking about.

Reynard explained that the events all began with the Ledermaín sisters showing up. Their arrival at Bistaír lined up with the time in which Yva was stabbed. Everything began unfolding from there.

"Except for the fires," Silas pointed out.

"The fires were to capture attention," Arik said. "I'd heard about them in Heilig. You lot had been spread out from what I understand. All the main players needed to be on stage, I should think. What was the smell, Silas? Did you ever figure it out? Remember the stench at the burn sites?" Arik's question. Reynard's comment. Two sides of the same coin.

"It was the smell of Solange. The smell of higher magic. Of death. Seductive death," Corra said. "It was all over Nova Thyme."

"What does it have to do with anything?" Saski asked. I saw Silas's eyes slide to her.

"If it's a constant factor," Silas cut in. "I should think it bloody well would be relevant."

"You mistake my words, Silas," Saski said, hissing his name like she was speaking through the wind. Corra's gameplay paper rustled. "I did not say it was irrelevant. I asked *what* the relevance was. Do not take what I have said and switch it up to match your own version of the narrative."

I think every person in that war room wished they were somewhere else, because the double entendre of their exchange was not lost on anyone. Saski's nails dug into the polished wood table as she leaned across Arik and Yva to look at Silas. Under her skin, it looked as if water rippled. Like the reflection of a pool at night. Arik sucked in a breath and leaned back. Silas leaned over Yva, apologizing as she scooted back. His eyes were turning translucent like he was ready to become mist.

Uh-oh.

"There is no other version of the narrative. I'm not saying I am correct or that I've got all the answers, *Majesty*. I'm saying that the fires were to gather us and to keep us looking elsewhere. I'm saying that the events played out to pull the ones needed to be together, and to keep the surplus of us distracted."

"What was the smell? Might you describe it, please?" Dean asked, trying to capture nearly all the eyes around the room.

"It's like the smell of the araíran-aoír nuts when they're off," Silas said. "It's sweet, as the weasel said. Yet it burns your nose, like . . ."

"Like almonds?" Dean asked, meeting my eyes.

"Aye, I suppose, yes. The nuts are similar to human almonds. Only more—"

"Bitter," I cut in. My eyes were wide, looking at Dean. It was like our thoughts were running on a parallel track. I grabbed Cadeyrn's hand. "Like bitter almonds."

"And rot," my husband added. "Bitter almonds and rot. Fruity and floral and sickly. I used to think it was similar to roses, but it wasn't really that. You really couldn't smell it? Even the day in the stables?" he asked me.

"Neither could I," Ewan said.

"Nor I," Dean added.

"I don't understand why," Cadeyrn admitted.

"It's because about thirty percent of the population—well, in human populations, but I am leaning toward thinking it's the same here. About thirty percent of the population does not have the gene necessary to detect the odor of cyanide," Dean concluded.

"Oh!" Corra yelled, covering her mouth. "Yes! I watched a show on World War—"

"Was that the same war with the archduke and the watches?" Saski asked.

"No," Cadeyrn, Dean, Corra, and I said at the same time.

"So, humans just call each battle a 'world war' and make it quantitative?" she asked.

We all kind of shrugged in agreement, and she pulled a face. Silas smirked but kept his face otherwise passive.

"Not very clever," Ainsley added. Saski agreed. "Have you heard of places in the human realm called Ice-Land and Green-Land?" Ainsley asked the queen of Heilig.

"Now, you're just teasing," Saski insisted. Ainsley said she really wished she were. Reynard cleared his throat and pulled us back to the matter at hand.

"That smell is the reason I could never be near my father's aphrim tanneries."

"The skins only smelled of leather to me. Huh," I said.

"Gods, they're awful," Silas said. "The fermented araíran-aoír are made into salts for metal cleaning and even to pull gold from the ore in which it exists. We sold loads of them to Magnus and Baetríz for both their blacksmithery and her jewelry."

"Do you remember the day Ewan and I crossed back over the Veil, and we fought the unit of aphrim at the Veil?" I asked, my voice careful. So careful. It was the day I'd had to cross back over to find the last crystal and protect the demarcation of realms.

"Of course I remember," Cadeyrn said.

I could still feel my dagger in my hand as I tried to wash the aphrim blood from it and me, but my hands had been shaking too bad to do it. I was leaving my friends. My mother. My mate. "Lina and Magnus showed up," I said. Reynard pursed his lips, and I could see on my brother's face across from me that the wheels were turning. "They took the aphrim from the Veil site. Where did they take them?"

Silas and Cadeyrn were looking at one another as though the answer might manifest between them.

"We don't know," Cadeyrn admitted.

"We've known them their whole lives, *Trubaíste*," Silas pointed out. His face flushed in a way I hadn't seen before. Humiliation or anger, I don't know. Saski's forehead creased looking at him, and she tilted her head in that predatorial way. "What would make them work against us?" He sounded genuinely hurt.

"Money?" Reynard said. "My father was a raging arsehole, Silas. What's more is that he held so much power with the Elders that he could sway anyone by threatening their livelihood."

"Magnus was the one to tell me about Belleza's haberdashery shop in Laichmonde and seeing one of Etienne's cronies there. What was his stake in telling me that?" Silas asked Reynard, but the question was to everyone. To the female with whom he once spent a lot of time. To the male who was his friend. Maybe his best friend.

"I wonder," Cadeyrn said with a shifty glance at me, "if that was the reason Magnus was so adamant about getting me screaming drunk every night after that final battle. I wonder if he was doing it to finally sever my ties to Neysa. Or whether it was something else."

I reached across him, my arm pulling him closer to me.

"Their finances were verging on nonexistent," Corra said. "Baetríz had barely any metal left for her jewelry, Magnus was in debt, and the embargo with Festaera held them under. Lina made more selling dark magicks than traditional apothecary items. Their family was in a bad place. I only know this because I had a dinner with Turuín quite a few months ago, before Cadeyrn left to get Neysa." Corra bit her lip, telling us. "It just never occurred to me they would resort to such measures."

"I understand how this is all quite alarming within the dynamics of your families," Dean cut in, pushing at the bridge of his nose. "I think leaving it at, there is suspicion on those people—folk—is adequate for the moment. What should truly be addressed is the fact that a strain of cyanide is being used by those of no divinity to align with the goals of one who is divine. The phantomes, the flesh-eating demon your ex-wife became—sorry, mate."

"Indeed," Cadeyrn muttered.

"She was always a flesh-eating demon," Corra intoned. Reynard hummed in agreement.

"You really couldn't see it coming?" Dean asked Cadeyrn, breathlessly like he couldn't hold it in any longer. My husband faced him fully.

"You fell in love with your cousin," Cadeyrn shot back. I shrunk into the wooden seat.

"I wouldn't so much as say that I fell in—"

"Might we get back to the issue at hand?" Ewan saved us from further embarrassment.

"The salt caves," Saski spoke up, looking at Arik.

"Only the Schloss Specialty Guard enter them because they aren't hindered by the salt," Arik said, catching his sister's thread.

"They are cyanide salts—or the equivalent here," Dean said.

"The salts, I have been told, have been used traditionally in higher magics—necromancy—and to preserve game flesh. Though I don't know where they would have gotten them. Our mother uses the salt caves regularly to clear her head since Pavla died. I've been once, but the air at the top of the cave is so dense and sweet, I can't stand to be in there. It gives me headaches and I feel nauseous," Saski said.

"The gas is less dense than air and will rise to the threshold," I said.

"How do *you* know so much about this substance?" Arik asked, half shielding Yva, which was quite sweet, if not a bit annoying.

"I was a currency trader, Arik," I told him "In our realm, there is different coin or currency in each country or land. The value of each swells and shrinks by the second. I took guesses on which would swell next and bought and sold them based on those guesses."

"I truly do not understand what that means. You purchase coin and sell it?" Arik asked, crossing a leg over his knee and leaning in to hear more. "This is fascinating. We must speak more."

Oh, the trading market. I missed the excitement of it.

"Sort of. It's more complicated than that, but how I did things was to look for what made the exchange rate fluctuate. It could be major corporation sales, filming in a region, war, so on. The reason I know so much about cyanide, is the reason I know so much about politics and history. I know loads about what makes coin change hands. Period. Historically, currently, whenever. I looked to history to give me clues, I looked to social events and politics to guide my hand.

"Cyanide was commonly used in World War II by the Germans. Cyanide pills were used for suicide to keep people from divulging information to the enemy. It was used as poison, given in increments to rivals. It was used as a gas to kill multitudes of people at once. One of the darkest times in human history was that war. It colored political maneuvering, education, and human rights activists from that point on," I said, sounding more like Dean. "Any time there is a shift in power in non-Western nations, there is an uptick in the stocks for pharmaceutical companies which provide the necessary antidotes to put in nitrate-based cyanide kits. That's how I know."

I do love it when you do that, Cadeyrn said to my mind.
Do what?
Use your knowledge to squarely put someone in his place, he answered.

Unless it's you who I'm putting in his place. You don't appreciate that much.

Oh, Caráed, I like it quite a bit. Like that time you were telling me off in front of everyone before you and Ewan went after the wolves. Gods.

I smiled at the memory.

"Are you two done?" Corra asked, hands on her hips and pointing at her paper. "Because I think we still need to make plans for this game, no?"

We all wrote on the board, trying to see how we could lure Kaeres into a sort of trap by linking all of our gifts, but it seemed more and more like this was going to be the kind of fight we go into blind, utilizing what we can in the moment. Dinner was brought in, and we all devoured mounds of shellfish over noodles, topped with garlic and pistachios.

"When you were watching us in Laichmonde years ago," Silas started to ask Reynard.

"Mm, yes. It really wasn't the worst task," he answered with a wink. Silas could now laugh about Reynard's overtures, knowing he was one hundred percent kidding.

"Flattered, Weasel. But you had said you noticed the haberdashery sister treating her business like a front. What about the other one?"

"Corraidhín's pet?" Reynard asked. Ewan growled. "I don't know if I was there before or after your fling with the starfish. Silas was in and out of town for about six months or so and you were rather quiet, Hellcat," Reynard said.

Corra hmphed and confirmed it would have been before because she left town for a couple of years after, traveling between realms, eventually settling in Laorinaghe with Lorelei for a time.

Reynard recounted thinking perhaps Silas was with the sisters because he would see them often near Cadeyrn's flat and in an apothecary on that side of town. Lina's apothecary.

We all swore. Corra's color rose to an unusual purplish hue as her body began fading to mist. Ewan looked as if he were trying very hard to not laugh. They had all been played. For years, it seemed. And now here we were on the final stage, looking for direction.

***

OUR CHILDREN WILL BE GODS. That was what Solange had said to me. That was what Etienne had said to me about his daughter and my husband. The thought sat like an undigested meal in my stomach. We all had remained sitting in the war room turning over plans and possibilities until well into the night. Pim and Efa were draped over their parents' knees, asleep and lovely. There were two things we knew for sure: One, that we were dealing with a power-hungry, vengeful Goddess who had infiltrated the lives of everyone in that room for centuries. And two, we had no idea when she would next strike.

Cadeyrn opened our balcony doors when we had returned to our rooms, warding the archway with his magic. He knew I always preferred the windows open. I slid under the linen sheets with a sigh, watching him walk over to the bed.

"Surely we stand a chance in all of this," I said as he lifted the duvet and inched closer to me. "What with there being five of us as heirs, not including the children, plus all of you."

"Of course, we stand a chance." His palm lay flat on my exposed belly, index finger making figure eights around my navel. "Our only true disadvantage is not knowing when she will show up." He ducked under the covers and replaced his hand with his mouth, kissing the skin of my belly. I held his head there, my hands in his black hair while his fingers idly moved down, stroking my thighs and hips.

"That and the fact that people you have all had in your lives and confidences for years have most likely been deceiving you the whole time." It was a harsh truth to point out, yet a valid one.

His lips tugged at the skin of my lower belly, close to a bite, but gentle. I made a sound in my throat and closed my eyes, allowing the feel of his mouth and hair on my stomach to move the electricity in me. My knees bent, an automatic reaction to the fingers which explored, making me arch up into them. Into him.

"Perhaps," he rumbled against my stomach. "I'm not totally convinced that's the case. At least not quite so black-and-white."

"If not, then, what do you think—" But I was cut off by a whiplash quick change of his position. His mouth covered mine ever so briefly before his hands lifted my backside, tipping my hips up to where his lips, teeth, and tongue stole any battle strategy from me.

I like making you utterly useless, he teased in my mind. I growled pushing his head into me more. The heat of his mouth, the feel of him, had me crashing over the edge, but he pushed into me again and again, rolling me through that bliss over and over.

Chapter 38

Neysa

The sounds of a heavy storm woke us in the predawn light. It seemed the waves held a fury of their own in the black, heady atmosphere. A female's hysterical chatter punctuated the pauses between thunder and wave.

"I'll look," Cadeyrn said, walking to the hall. Once the door opened, Saski's voice carried to our room, the shrill tone of her anger bounced within the clay-tiled halls.

"Is everything all right?" my husband asked.

"No," Saski answered.

"We received a hawk from Ludek. Saski's absence has been seen as unsatisfactory. The governors of Sot, Manu, and Biancos are pushing to overthrow her rule," Arik answered.

"Are Ludek and Basz in danger?" I asked, sidling up to my husband. Silas's presence swelled behind me, our link to one another still solid. Saski's eyes moved past me to the male at my back.

"We don't think so. It isn't a coup yet. More of an overture." Arik slid from spoiled socialite to cool diplomat with an ease I rarely saw in anyone else. "Still, I think it wise for her to return home as soon as possible."

"I cannot, Arik. This fable gone wrong must come to an end first. Once the task is done, you and I will be on the first ship to Heilig, brother."

"I," Arik began, a cough punctuating his speech, "I shall not join you at present, sister."

Saski looked at him, her eyes batting in stunned silence.

"I would stay on here. As the Heiligan ambassador," Arik said, tugging the two sides of his jacket down. It struck me that he was fully dressed this early in the morning, whereas the rest of us were in variations of pajamas.

"You would stay on with the representative," Saski clarified. Arik nodded once. She looked at him for a length of time, then sniffed a chuckle. "As you wish."

"Is it not Sot from where your Barno comes?" Silas asked Saski. He took a few steps past Cadeyrn and me.

Saski rolled her eyes. "Yes," She did not bother to correct Varno's name.

"Is Manu not the biggest port, where the wards used to be? And where the steel was exchanged for wine and skins?" he pressed.

Saski nodded, folding her arms over her chest. The others began filing into the hall then, everyone roused by our voices and the storm outside

"And Biancos is the largest stretch of coastline. The governor there is the relation to Barno?"

Arik interjected, "Var—"

"Yes," Saski cut him off. "I see where you are going with this. You think that the players in the wine scheme, my governors, and this . . . overture are all the same. You think it's a part of the whole."

"I do," Silas agreed. "And I believe neither your abdication, nor your dissolution have anything at all to do with it. I think it convenient timing."

A sort of wail sounded in the distance, echoed by bells

tolling in succession, like a death knoll on its path through the Sacred City into the palace. Smaller bells at the end of the hallway rang.

"Yva?" Cadeyrn asked. She rushed from the room Arik stood by, buttoning her merlot leather jacket, and made her way down the hall where she was met by Arturus and a new guard. We all stood watching her exchange, though not hearing what was said.

She turned back to us. "The system of bells is in place to warn us of such things like when the earth gripes or there is a rogue wave. Nothing of the sort has been detected, but there is a line of slaughtered soldiers rimming the palace and beach."

There was nothing to say at that point because we all had to dress and ready for what was the inevitable course of the day.

From our chambers, the lashing rain and waves sprayed, even the hundred or so feet below. I strapped on weaponry, trying to call out to our *baethaache* in my mind. They hated the lightning, but I knew this time they wouldn't abandon us in the fight. We all took the stairs in twos and threes, garbed head to toe in black fighting leathers, armed to the teeth. Every peal of thunder, a complement to the cannonade of soldiering feet through the palace and grounds.

Be there to do what you can with your magic. But please. Please, stay away from the physical fighting, Neysa, Cadeyrn begged me in my mind as we descended from the palace to the front courtyard.

I reached over and whacked his bum. There was nothing left to say. The Sacred City had seen such destruction the past years, after their long-standing time of peace. There was no true war to blame. Only the Punch-and-Judy show of Gods and power-hungry mortals, pulling each other's strings. Innocent soldiers, as Yva once was, proud to protect their city, their lands, kept losing their lives. I was always a pragmatist, not a romantic. I knew the odds of this being the last of it. I made a solemn vow to myself to do what I could today to bring peace back to these citizens. To my family.

The felled soldiers were a sight. Slain bodies overlapped each other like a row of dominoes. Their train led through the lower levels of the palace where there was a library and temple, musty and unused.

"I knew of its existence, yet I'd never thought to come look. It was a place for scholars of aulde," Yva whispered.

The spines of books were cracked, their skins flaking like dandruff to the floor below. The stacks of books followed a semicircular path which grew thick with a sort of pressure. Those around us began to cough. All but Ewan, Dean, and me. Corra had stayed behind. The children had to be minded, and though we knew Pim and Efa were so very important, there was no reality in which we would have brought them from the walls of their chambers, or from the steadfast protection of their mother. Corra hadn't so much as breathed a protest at the suggestion. She refused to leave their sides, and I saw my brother's entire countenance change with her resolve. Heat spasmed in my chest, reminding me of when I stood within the Veil between the living and the dead on that Biancos beach in Heilig. Saski spluttered, making her trip. Silas caught her and pounded on her back, though he was coughing himself.

"In case you were wondering, Kitten," Reynard said to me, choking out the words. "This is the reek."

My head pounded, a drum beat like the headache I had in Laichmonde before Silas and I let our gifts flow into one another. Nausea roiled, turbulent and insistent in this migraine born from the pit of hell. Or rather born of the Goddess of War and Death. Still I did not smell it. I only felt the effects. Cyrranus turned and threw up between stacks of shelving.

"We can't be here," I wheezed. I couldn't smell the gas, but I could feel what it was doing. "This is cyanide. We're being gassed."

"Who would have thought I would find out I am a long-lived fae, displaced to another realm, and yet still die of Ziklon B cyanide gassing," Dean said. The humor was there. The irony even more so. But I was the next to throw up. Cadeyrn snarled for me to leave.

"We all need to leave," I said grabbing whoever was near me and dragging them back the way we came. Only, the way was blocked by the felled soldiers, now standing at attention, slack-faced and bloodthirsty.

"Fucking great," Silas said, pushing me back and charging forward. Ewan grabbed his jacket and yanked him, saying we had to be smart. This was one scenario we had planned for. Seeing as we had fought various reanimated deceased before, and the fact that the Goddess of War and Death was the puppet master, the likelihood of fighting phantomes or walking dead warriors was not at all surprising. Though it did truly suck.

The soldiers pushed toward us. Cyrranus tested a few, seeing the way in which they engaged. The actions set them all off, swords swinging.

"Well done, darling," Reynard said. "You rang the dinner bell."

"It would be rung one way or another," Cyrranus answered his mate. Sounds from the entrance told us there were city guards and Laorinaghan soldiers fighting the dead. All around me, my friends and family were choking and coughing, bile and meals coming up and spraying the floors of the ancient library. There was no way we were getting out the way we came, so we fell back. Ewan took a scythe like blade to his thigh, making him fall against Arik, who dragged my brother behind a shelf.

How bad is it? I asked Ewan mind to mind.

It's not great, Neyssie. Having a bit of a job keeping my eyes open, he answered, even his inner dialogue strained.

I spun away from a sword and pushed Silas into a stack of tomes. Books fell, knocking my blade from me. I dropped to my knees, taking a blessed breath of less heavy air. Blood dripped from my nose and ears, and seeing the mayhem around me, everyone else was suffering the same. I didn't know what this would do to the babies. I didn't want to think about it as I crawled toward my blade, trying to make it away from the stacks and into the reading room beyond. Dean grabbed me under my arms and dragged me the direction I was going.

"You really must be out of here, Pet," he said before turning to vomit. "And my lack of fighting skills is quite the imposition at the moment. How about you be a good lass—" He vomited again, stepping over a twice-dead soldier. "And open up a Veil for us to go back to England. I could really use a drink and some cheesy chips about now."

We reached the reading room where only one of three lanterns was lit in the far corner, casting the room in a sort of camouflage pattern of shadow and light. The gas was less permeating in there, but the pressure in my head told me it had started its job well and it was leaking this way. I saw Saski and Yva go down at the same time, and I'd started toward them when Dean blocked me. Arik used his boot to almost gently push his sister back toward us while he grabbed Yva by the arm that wasn't bleeding. We needed to be in this room together and use our magic to deal with Kaeres. However we were supposed to do that. If I was being completely honest, though, it wasn't looking good. Cadeyrn was doubled over, still twisting and stabbing, while Silas was back-to-back with Reynard, using his twin swords to fend off multiple dead at once. I called out to them. Saski and Yva were army crawling on the ground through the foyer of the reading room, their blood-wet leathers leaving snail trails over the inlaid jewels on the floors.

Dean still sat on my legs, heaving for air. I noticed then. The wound in his side. I touched his jacket, and my hand came away with sticky, sinewy blood. Not a slice or flesh wound.

"Dean," I whispered.

"Heir of Hermód," a deep melodic voice called. "Your speed was not quite what I expected. I whipped my head toward the corner where the moon-white hair of both Kaeres and Solange stood. Dean's weight was shifting on me, his body leaning back involuntarily.

"Dean, please. Cadeyrn!" I screamed. My mate lunged back, taking a lance to the ribs when he vomited blood. I was screaming. Screaming so loud it bounced within the walls, dulling to that of a Gregorian chant in a medieval monastery. The peels of my cry tottered from wall to wall, taunting me.

"I think maybe I did fall in love with you," Dean slurred. "I don't think it's weird because I didn't know we were cousins. But I'm just . . ." He was nearly lying back on me now. "So very glad to have met you, Pet. So very." His weight on me, the gas, the blood loss, not hearing or seeing my mate or my family, hearing screams—it all converged into a primal rage.

Darkness rose in me, glittering and lethal, the room brightening to a blinding white with my power. With it, the electricity in me reached to Silas, sparking though our bodies which were failing. Like the ley lines that ran through Barlowe Combe—the ones I'd followed that day when I'd first met Reynard—my power linked to Cadeyrn's then his to Saski's. Saski's to Arik's. His to Yva's. Ewan was missing. He was back in the stacks. I called to him in my mind but got no answer. Ainsley stormed through, felling the last of the soldiers, carrying my brother like a doll, under her arm. He was totally unconscious, but my tether to him still sang with his life force. Barely. Kaeres lifted her arms and Solange stepped toward us. Toward me. Toward Cadeyrn.

Before I could wrangle the Sword of Kaeres from Dean, where it was clutched too rigidly in his hands, Solange was on Cadeyrn, chewing at his mouth, one hand missing, a sticky black stump all that remained. He tried to fight her off, but two of the soldiers rose again and held his arms behind him. The sword came free with an odd crunching of Dean's fingers, and I wiggled out from under him. Between all of us, our magic poured. We needed Pim and Efa, I knew, but this would have to do. As though I called her, my niece's consciousness tapped mine like a delicate knock. My gift answered the knock and Efa's power, then Pim's poured into me.

Ewan was twitching on the floor, his body convulsing. Broken fragments of things he was attempting to say to me flickered through my mind. I was sobbing, knowing he was dying. Efa's powers drowned mine. There was so much coming from her it pulled me under like a tidal wave. I heard Reynard scream, and his body shook like mine did when Heícate was killed. I knew what it meant for him and for Dean, and I couldn't face it yet. But I moved, sloppy and weighted like walking through seaweed, its branches tangling feet in water and sand. When I reached Reynard, I placed the Sword of Kaeres in his hands and shoved him toward Solange.

Cadeyrn's screams were muffled by the *naem maerbh* tearing the flesh from his face, the gore dripping from her maw. Silas was covering Saski and Yva while Arik held our line defense with the dead army. All of their powers still flowing from them into me and back around through all of us, the tide of gifts between us, rising like a storm surge, was pushing back the gas. Pushing back our reactions to the gas. The pressure in my head was building the way it did that day in Biancos when

I died. That Veil had been a compound of cyanide-like gas, acting like a pressurized vacuum seal. Gas born of the umbilical between this realm and the next. If we didn't stop it, the pressurized gas would burst us all as it had done to me in Biancos.

Reynard raised the sword and brought it down with light speed precision, into Solange's back, piercing her heart. The *naem maerbh*'s head threw back, bloodied mouth agape as she screamed a banshee wail, turning to white ash and dispersing with a flutter of breath. Reynard then turned to Kaeres, hate and malice in his icicle eyes. Cyrranus and I launched for him, but his speed usurped our efforts, and he was on the Goddess of War and Death in less than a heartbeat.

The gleaming metal of the sword dripped with the acrid, noxious blood of the creature Solange had become. Or the creature she had always been, I supposed. My friend jumped, like a mountain cat, legs bending in the air with the force of his plyometric leap. He plunged the ancient portentous blade which we had all baptized in our blood, straight through the neck of the Goddess. With that force, he twisted to the right and pulled the sword with him, severing her head. More jaguar than fae, my friend landed with naught a thump. He freed the sword, and for good measure, put it through Kaeres' heart, her eyes, and finally, her mouth. Cadeyrn had crawled forward and used the last of his powers to set the head and body of Kaeres alight.

The room still held the cyanide gas, and our time was rapidly closing on surviving its effects. Cadeyrn was angry, feral, yet functioning, his obliterated face making steady progress in its healing. He made for Dean and lifted him up, carrying him toward the exit, yelling at me in the aulde tongue to leave. Silas was on his hands and knees reaching for me, and I trudged toward him. The Heiligan twins linked their hands and a great wind built in the room. For a moment the pressure was nearly too much. I grabbed at my head ready for that final pop, but then it released. The wind they built moved through the room. Yva linked her hands with theirs, and her own power boosted theirs, moving the air from the room. Silas was trickling mist from his pores, which mixed with his blood. Still, he crawled to me.

Once the air was breathable, we could move out. I got to Ewan first. His head was slumped back, blue and lifeless against a section on alchemy. As though awakened once more, Efa and Pim's gifts merged with mine, and I learned the true meaning of Pim's name: utmost protection. He was the protector who would help me shoulder his father and pull him from the stacks of an ancient underground library teeming with undead battle legions and cyanide gas.

Saski and Arik's wind kept us encapsulated and moving back up, up, up, to the surface. The midmorning light was too bright. My retinas burned, seeking shade, then they found my mate, leaning against a stone planter. Dean was in his arms where they sat on the cobbled ground, bougainvillea dripping its fuchsia leaves over their shoulders. My heart leaped until I saw Cadeyrn's face. The torn flesh was repairing itself with his gift, but it wasn't healing Dean.

I yelled for him in my head. I told my mate to heal Ewan, barely processing my moving to Dean. We swapped, Cadeyrn and I. He took Ewan and I took Dean. Ewan's heart began pumping again. I could hear it in the shrouded recesses of my link to him. Dean's did not. His fingers were still clenched as though trying desperately to wield a sword he had no idea how to use. I held him against my chest and sobbed into his neck. My friend who was the reason I stayed alive. The talisman to my reuniting with my husband. The person I'd matched wit with instantly.

I'm so very glad I met you were the last words he had said to me. The last thoughts he brought to life. And I held him now, in death, as I never allowed myself in life. Because he had loved me. Not romantically. But truly. As a friend. I screamed. I pleaded. The grounds shook as two *baethaache* landed, nuzzling us all. Mine wrapped her wing about Ewan, shielding him, while Cadeyrn's pushed and prodded at Dean's lifeless body in my bloodied arms. His jacket was weighed down with so much blood. I brought my hands away from it, smearing it on the cobbles. Smearing it on the planters, on my leather trousers, everywhere. I screamed, feeling Reynard's hands on my shoulders. The hands of the newly anointed heir to Hermód. Cadeyrn's voice was in my mind saying over and over he was sorry. He tried. Dean was already gone.

"I'm so glad to have met you too," I whispered against Dean's sandy-blond hair.

A song of synchronized voices lilted in the crisp humid air. I looked up, eyes heavy, to see five mystics standing around us all. It was then I realized how destroyed we all were. Each of us, from Saski to Ainsley Mads, had streams of blood from our eyes, remnants of vomit on our clothing and boots, and healing blade wounds. Hermód, God of Speed, stepped forward in their nonbinary fae form. Their fingers pulled from the folds of a weightless cloak and touched Dean's forehead. Tears fell from the God's face, sizzling into the blood-soaked street.

"Can't you save him?" I pleaded.

"It is beyond us to save him in this realm," all the mystics, or Gods, said as one.

I clutched Dean tighter. Beneath the sweat and bile, he still smelled like soap and something that made me think of hope and grace.

"In this realm?" I asked, my eyes on my friend. Bougainvillea leaves rained over us. I swatted them away, not wanting any color or beauty preening before me. My mind replayed scenes from our friendship. Our laughing and having coffee in England. His accompanying me to Percival Bryan's shop in London. His easy, pressed morning look. A kind of friendship I knew I could never find again with another.

Neysa, Cadeyrn said in my mind. A warning.

"There is a way," the mystics who were Gods chanted.

Please. I may have said it aloud. I may have thought it, my head pressed to Dean's.

"He was a child born of both realms. Conceived in this, birthed in the other," they sang. "Together, with you as Goddess of Magic and Darkness, Guardian of the Mother, we can bring him back. But not here."

"No." Cadeyrn's voice was stern, yet trembled. "No. Neysa. Do not." Silas was barking the same thing behind the *baethaache*.

"Yes," I said, understanding dawning on me. "Let's bring him back."

I held my bleeding arm aloft, allowing it to drip onto Dean, onto where his blood puddled and mingled with Hermód's tears. The Gods surrounded us, and a vacancy in the atmosphere opened, dropping us through to the sloped glen outside of Barlowe Combe. Dean rolled from my arms and was heaving, bile rising, blood dripping with his saliva onto the snow-covered ground.

It was December in England. My husband's screams still echoed in my mind as the Veil opened for us. I could see him being held back by Cyrranus and Reynard. Silas was held by Ainsley and Arik. The Veil closed on us as Cadeyrn wrestled free and threw himself toward me. He was too late. The Veil closed, leaving Dean and me alone in a wintry forest. My stomach tightened, not fully comprehending what I had done and hoping to every God and Goddess I was not separated from Cadeyrn for good. Neither of us would live through that again.

"What, pray tell," Dean breathed, still on his hands and knees, "have you gone and done, Pet?" he asked.

"Do you remember how Charlie ended up in Crawley behind a pub with a prostitute and bag of heroin?" I asked, lying back on the wet, mossy snow. He rolled to his own back next to me. "I think I pulled a Charlie."

He snorted, wheezing through the odd amusement. "Am I the prostitute or the heroin?"

"I think you might be the pub." We laughed in the maniacal way people do after something intensely horrific has happened. "I think I can get back. It felt like I could." I hoped. Oh gods.

"I take it I must remain here, should I care to live?" he asked, swallowing so loud it sounded like a twig snapping.

I didn't answer but took his hand in mine. "I won't see you again." I didn't want to say it. I didn't want to admit it to him nor myself.

"Do you think I'll have my job back?" he asked.

That was an issue. He very well may not. It had been nearly four months. There was no story he could tell to maintain that he was sane.

"I think, perhaps, I should have died. Don't you think?"

There was youth in the question. A lonely distress I knew well. *I should have died*. The sentiment I once voiced that had Cadeyrn in a rage with me. At me. At the consideration of my self-sacrifice. Dean should not have felt that way. His death would not have saved another. His death would have only brought more pain. Yes, I would grieve his departure, but not like the grief of losing him to the nether realms. Yet, I did not want him to feel the acute bereft sense of never again belonging, which I had felt in my time in London and Richmond. Not Dean.

"If I'm stuck here, we can go somewhere else. We can travel. You can meet a girl—" I tried to reason. To be positive. I wasn't entirely sure I could get back, despite feeling I should be able to.

"Go home, Pet. You've got babies in there," he said, laying a hand on my stomach.

I didn't know if they were still there. I didn't know what the fight, the magic, the gas, would have done to them. It was so similar to the way I lost my babes the last time, I started to cry.

Dean sat up and held me. We were wet with sweat and blood and snow, and we shook from the icy air, but he held me and patted my head. Visions accosted me then. Of meeting him. That damned microphone that was too short for him and he flushed with nerves adjusting it. His awkward invitation to stay with him that first night, we had laughed about since. Sangria and fairytales. Old bookstores and designer gin. Cheesy chips. The scrapbook of a friend I never knew I needed and a cousin I would die for. Dean would exist for me in instant snapshots of fluffy hair and crooked spectacles that barely masked his twinkling brown eyes.

He would find his way back into his academia, I just knew it. In some near future, he would once again have his disaster of a desk, covered in tomes and papers. He would have tea with Tilly and one day bring home another girl. One who wasn't a fae cousin and wasn't in love with someone else. He would live. On his own, knowing he was not alone. He would live for himself and all the things that kept him curious. Dr. Dean Preston belonged in this realm, understanding he played along the seam of both.

"I'm so very glad to have known you, Dean. I love you, cousin," I told him.

"I love you too, Pet," he said. Then with the speed of a God, took my dagger, sliced my palm, kissed my lips, and shoved me through the Veil that yawned opened behind us.

I tumbled back onto the same cobbled street, only

moments after disappearing. Cadeyrn spun to me at the squawking of *baethaache*, and I fell to him, crying and laughing. I saw then Silas pulling Ewan to his feet. They asked of Dean, and I said he was home. My friend was back home again. With Tilly and pints, and his books. And I loved that for him. And hated it for myself.

Cadeyrn leaned down and pressed his cheek and hands on my belly as he had the night before. His bright eyes, a shade somewhere between an aquamarine and a peridot, looked up at me from under thick black lashes.

"They are fine. You're fine," my mate said. His smile was like the breath of dawn that finally peeked through the darkest part of night. "They're fine." His forehead pressed to mine as he repeated "You're fine" over and over. We rocked, holding one another.

I knew I could come back to you, I told him. *I know it was kind of an asshole thing to do, but I was really putting all my chips on you knowing I would never leave you.*

He was trembling in my arms. Or maybe I was. He nodded his head.

I know. I just didn't know . . . The babes, the Veil, if Dean hadn't survived, what any of those variables would change. I stroked his face.

I'm here. We're here.

They were. We were.

The entire plot to purge us from this realm was over. And we could just be. For once in all of our lives. I looked to Silas, hopeful and happy. His face was drawn and tight. The cobbled square was missing someone. Arik caught my eyes and shook his head. Confirmation. And perhaps a warning.

Saski left. Once you'd crossed, she said she was heading home. Arik followed her to the sea. Cadeyrn's voice in my mind held Arik's warning to not intercede.

She didn't want him to take her because I was gone again.

She doesn't realize. Cadeyrn, she doesn't know how much she means to him.

I looked at Silas and told him to go. To follow her. To tell her she was being stupid and he was being stupid. And for once, he listened.

His eyes went wild. He did an about-face, placed Ewan into Arik's arms, and ran, turning to mist as the street dipped toward the sea.

Chapter 39

Silas

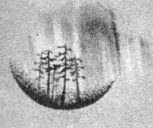

How in the ever-present fuck of fucks was I supposed to catch a siren hell-bent on returning home? Two days in to being one with the sea, I had my answer. I wasn't.

On the fourth day, I was out of power. I was drained. That nut gas and the shite we dealt with in the creepy library had me half-drained already. Just shy of nightfall on the fourth night, I was at the sea's mercy. A fishing boat spotted me and hauled me on deck. I lay there for the following two days until we pulled into port in Manu. I cursed soundly and took another barge up the Matta to reach Kutja, where I very much hoped to find the little siren. There was a village just outside the palace walls, where I stopped to bathe and eat, as I knew Saski would never touch me with a ten-foot pole if I propositioned her in the costume of filth I wore. The guards at the gates sent word to Basz who personally escorted me into the palace. I was nervous as a lad, and so bloody tired I could lay my face in a soft patch and sleep for a week if I didn't have a queen to woo. Or whatever the hell it was I was doing there. Oh shite, this was a bad idea.

"For what it's worth, Ludek and I have been pulling for you since the beginning," Basz said, and pushed me through a set of arched pewter doors which came to a menacing point at the top. Inside the largest room I had ever seen were probably a hundred fae, all bickering and prodding their queen and Ludek with questions.

"If it was the governors from those three lands, Your Majesty, then what will we do to rectify it?" a small, fair fae asked. He looked like a child, but . . . old. Fucking weird.

"Terin," Saski said. "The governors have been apprehended, and the lands have been passed to the commissioners in charge of trade for the area. It is not an ideal situation yet, but until we have voting in common practice, it will have to do. I assure you, we are working quickly and efficiently to pull any thorns from the collective."

Saski could not see me yet, but Ludek did a double take and winked. I tried winking back, but I think I looked vaguely apoplectic and instantly regretted the effort. Ludek's shoulders shook with laughter. Saski turned to him, but he motioned for her to proceed.

"And what of His Highness, Arik?" another fae asked, her yellow, cat eyes narrowing. She looked like Saski's personal guard who I remember her telling me about. Something about sandpaper tongues. That made me shiver.

"Arik, I am pleased to say, has taken the position as ambassador to Aoifsing, and will be living in the Sacred City of Laorinaghe. A hum traveled through the crowd.

"And what of your rumored betrothal to Varno of Sot?" called someone else. That saved me a bit of headache. It also made me *feel* apoplectic now.

"There is no betrothal. My affections for Varno of Sot were misplaced," she answered.

"And would you entertain the idea of returning the affections of someone from Aoifsing?" I called before I thought better of it. It was a stupid fucking question, and I felt like kicking myself in the groin for it. As it was, I stepped on my own godsdamned foot to take my attention off the thrashing embarrassment.

"I hardly think—" she began and stopped, standing from the table behind which she sat.

Oh, Gods and shite. I stepped within her line of sight, knowing I couldn't back out then. Three cheers for public humiliation on an empty stomach.

"Can you repeat the question?" she asked. Her dark brown hair was in a scandalous tumble around her shoulders, and her legs were bare in that style of dress she favored.

"I don't actually remember what I asked," I said, earning a few laughs. "Something to do with whether a poor fuck like me might get to tell you once again how he loves you."

She pinched her face like she was in pain or pissed off. Which, to be fair, she probably was. I mean I did kind of infiltrate her state meeting. A right arsehole thing to do.

"I have business to attend at the moment. Representative from Aoifsing, you may wait for me in the other wing."

Bloody dismissed. I walked out before anyone could think about figuring out what look was on my face. Especially fucking Ludek. Basz stepped from the recess of a wall where a painting of a queen hung. The Heiligan queen Neysa had died for.

"This way, Silas," he said. "We have a room ready for you."

I almost protested, but I was too tired to head home, and it was nicer here than the village. Less fleas, I'd wager. Basz showed me to a room that had a round entrance like the door sat in one of the seven turrets. When he opened it and told me to be comfortable, I realized I was in Saski's chambers. Her scent assaulted me completely so that I didn't notice when the female herself breezed in the room.

"Are you truly here for me?" she asked by way of greeting.

"Why else would I be here?" I set the candle down that was by her bedside. It smelled of cedarwood and woodsmoke.

She shrugged, the straps of her dress tipping down her shoulders. "One could only guess. Perhaps something has happened since I left."

"I left two minutes after you left. You are far quicker than I in the water, my queen, heir of Rán," I said to her, lifting the thin straps and letting them fall again. I watched as goosebumps raised on her bronze chest.

"I had matters to attend here," she said, her chest swelling with rapid breaths.

"Barno?" I asked.

She smiled. "I have no engagement, Silas. " She raised her hand, and I took it in mine, kissing her palm. Kissing her fingers. Wanting every godsdamned part of her covered by my mouth.

I sucked one finger between my lips, letting my teeth scrape the length of it. The sound she made was painfully repressed, and I smiled. Her free hand found my waist and ran a finger between the band of my trousers and my skin. I leaned in and brushed a kiss to her cheek. Then the other. Small affections I had never offered her because I had been stuck in a bond. My fingertips traced goosebumps along the swell of her breasts. I bent and kissed where my fingers had been. My mouth had tasted every centimeter of her before I'd known I belonged to her so completely. She spoke in an uncontrolled siren's song, undoing my jacket and leaning her hips into me for friction. My mouth stayed on her nipple, rolling it with my tongue. Her body shook against me.

"I must be here and tend to my lands, Silas," she said, breathless. That voice was a whirlpool in deep water. "I cannot give up what I have started. Not yet."

I pulled away and looked into her eyes, incredulous she would think I would have her give up anything for me. "I would be happy to be with you, wherever you would have me," I said, sincerely, hoping it wouldn't call me out as some sad bastard. Which, I was well aware of being. Especially as my greedy fingers would face amputation rather than leave the heat of her silken skin. She smirked at feeling my cock thicken against her. Sad bastard indeed.

"I would have you here in this room, preferably on that bed. To start," she said, a wicked gleam in her eyes. She traced my smile with shaking fingers and smiled back at me.

Had we ever really smiled at one another? Without irony or sarcasm? Had we ever let our guard down enough, feeling so much for one another and refusing to admit it? If I thought her beautiful, scowling by the seaside, I didn't know if I could contain myself with the beauty of her smile.

She moved even closer, kissing my chin. Had more than a handful of folk seen her true smile? I was certain her brothers and Pavla had. Those she could truly be herself with. I knew, like I knew I was hers and she was mine, that there was no one else in her many decades she felt she could strip her armor for. The thought that I was now amongst the few nearly brought me to my godsdamned knees. Which is where I was keen to be regardless.

"I can certainly endeavor to oblige," I said back, lifting the skirts of her dress and finding her ready for me. My knuckle ran along her, reveling in the slick. "But would you have me stay on, Saski?" I asked, touching her. I slipped along her as she rode my fingers, my mouth skated over her jaw, her collarbone. "Stay on in Heilig," I asked. "Stay on with you?"

My fingers worked along her, wanting it to be my mouth. I needed my godsdamned trousers off. "I will not share you." It came out as a growl, my body a half tick from turning to mist from the emotion behind my statement. Such a sad fuck, I was, aye? "I won't, Saski," I repeated. "Not with Barno nor any other fucktwat who wants you for your lands." I cupped her. Hard. She gasped. "Your goddess beauty." Her head leaned onto my shoulder, a weight I would give my sword arm to feel forever. "Or your brilliant godsdamned, wicked mind." Her head snapped up again, eyes like moss on fire. I fought the urge to think I had said something wrong. Again.

"Would you be my consort, Silas? Would you marry me and stay here with me?"

I started and stumbled like a fawn. The heat between us evaporating as my fingers pulled from her. That fire behind her eyes dimmed, and I was paralyzed with the notion that I'd dimmed it.

"Did you just propose to me?" I asked, still dumbstruck.

We stood for a moment, her dress askew, skin flushed like afternoon sun on volcanic sand. The most beautiful thing I'd ever seen in all my centuries. My buttons were undone, my own readiness straining, making me feel utterly ridiculous asking if I had been proposed to whilst my cock peeked out. Gods and shite.

"Yes?" Her haughty vixen voice took over, but the question mark at the end of that word gave her away.

I laughed, pulling my buttons apart further and tearing the dress from her body, then laying her on the bed.

She was looking at me with uncertainty. Gauging whether I was deflecting the question. Or diverting. Or some such word to mean I was scurrying away from commitment but still wanting to have my way with her. That cautious look needed to come off her face immediately. If there was one thing I was sure of, it was that Saski, queen of fucking Heilig, would never again feel uncertain of me or my intentions. No matter how we quarreled or tore each other to shreds, there would never again be a dusk which passed that Saski didn't know without the shadow fuckery of a doubt, that she had chains around my heart, and I was locking them up. I would always be hers.

"Of fucking course I will marry you," I said and undressed myself as fast as possible before sinking into her with the feeling of returning home. Her mouth found mine, and she tasted of the sea and storms. Exactly the place I belonged. Our hips moved together, slower than we ever had. I explored her mouth, wanting to pull her proposal into me through that kiss. As though if I swallowed the offer whole, it could never be rescinded. Her teeth, sharp and quick, drew blood from my lips and a deeper ache from my core. I watched a bead of my blood drip over her cheek like a forgotten tear. I wiped it and placed the blood back on her lip. Her tongue darted out and licked it. Licked the blood of a simple squire. A hardened warrior in love with a queen. A goddess.

"My blood belongs to you, siren," I said. My voice was rough, and I was no longer embarrassed for her to see what she did to me. Every thrust inside her awakened this thing between us more. She exposed her neck, without hesitancy. My body shook with restraint, planted inside her.

She lifted her chin in encouragement.

"As mine belongs to you." Her words struck a chord in me I never knew existed. I growled and bit down, finding in her blood song a tie knotting us together in complete permanence. The pop of her skin under my sharpened incisors sang to me. She lifted her hips, moving on me as I tasted her blood flooding my mouth. Every warm thrust in her made her nails tear down my back. We moved together, and I said to her, so quiet and unsure that I wasn't sure she could really hear, "*Misse caráed, misse trubaíste, misse bás á aimserre, misse baethá, am bryth.*"

My heart, my destruction, my death and power, my life, forever.

"Silas, from this blood I give you, to the body I handed over to you long ago, I am yours. No magistrate nor committee need tell us we belong together."

I pumped into her harder. Tears filled her eyes, and I knew she saw the shine in mine.

"You're so godsdamned beautiful," I told her. My release was building. By the quivering of her belly and arms, I knew hers was too. She grabbed my face with both hands, talons latched on my cheeks, forcing my gaze to hers. As though there were anywhere else I would ever look.

"You," she said, biting her lip. "You are so godsdamned beautiful, Silas. Do not ever think you are anything but."

Sweat slid between us. She cried out first, clenching around me. I followed her, exploding into her like I never had. With that ending, I held her, making it utterly fucking clear that neither of us would be leaving the bed.

"Saski of Fucking Heilig," I said.

"Yes, Silas of Fucking Saarlaiche?" she asked back with a snark in her tone that made me smile.

"I love you. I have for a very long time, aye?"

She stilled completely then placed a soft kiss on my temple. "And I you.". Her hands found mine and our fingers interlaced. "I have loved you completely. And always will."

Godsdamned females. I would forever feel an arse for the tears that escaped and wet her full chest. Yet, in my ancient heart, I just didn't bloody care. She was home. My home. Maybe it took me tragedy and blood to find it, but Saski and I were finally home.

Chapter 40

Neysa

Ewan, fully clothed in the bath, was immediately set upon by two toddlers.

"Well, you lot. I should hope this muck about is over because I am done with wiping everyone's arses. I've got plenty of that in these two," Corra said.

I scooped Efa into my arms, her sudsy body squirming. I told her how proud I was of her and Pim, and how strong they were. I was rewarded with a wet kiss on my cheek as she slipped back to splash on her father. After sending hawks immediately after our council in the war room, the Ledermaín sisters were taken into custody in Maesarra. Magnus and his family were being held in Saarlaiche by Turuín, its representative. Apparently, they gave quite a chase once hawks were sent, but eventually, the siblings were found attempting to enter Naenire. Baetríz stood her ground in her own estate and apologized for nothing. She was an independent widow with a successful business and had been blackmailed by Etienne. One day, Corra and Silas, and Cadeyrn, would come to terms with it all. Until then, it was well enough that we knew they had been apprehended. And Kaeres was defeated.

Cadeyrn was unwilling to let me out of his arms, so there was where I stayed as we ate, he drank wine, and we spoke of where we would all be when our own babes were born. I remembered having a vision the year before of Silas with a pregnant female and knew in my heart he would find Saski. I knew in my heart she would take him back. I drifted off in my husband's arms on that bathroom floor and had vague memories of being carried to our own chambers, being laid on my bed, kissed by my brother and Corra, and Cadeyrn holding me whilst I slept. In the sleepy haze, clouded by the dreams for the babies in my womb, the hope of love for my family, and our overall safety, I heard my mate say to me, lips pressed against my temple, "*Chanè à doinne aech mise fhìne. Mise fhìne allaína trubaiste.*"

I am no one's but my own. My own beautiful disaster.

Á Són Ameìre
The End

Acknowledgments

Holy smokes, kids, this has been a ride.

When I signed a contract for the Another Beast's Skin series, back in 2020, I never would have imagined the events that have occurred. To the readers who read *Another Beast's Skin* with all the original formatting issues and still saw the potential, thank you. It would have been so easy to give up on Neysa and her boo-crew (yeah, I said that). It's because of you lot, my husband, Damian, and my mom, that I stuck it out. Without Cristen fitting me in for proofreads of *Another Beast's Skin* and *A Braiding of Darkness,* and without Anna making room for me to fully edit this book and reformat all three, the Another Beast's Skin series would have been just another tale like the ones I would tell my childhood best friend, Georgina, during our many sleepovers. Ghosts lost between realms.

So, thank you to Becca and Jessa for beta reading it. Thank you to people like Kelly MacPherson for not loving fantasy but loving my books. Thank you to Lilian Sue for being such a hype-woman. Thank you forever to Jess from Enchanted Fandoms for always being supportive and lovely.

This journey has been wild, and I have learned so very much.

For now, this is the end of the series. A tearful, odd experience. However, I do have some words written for a satellite book (series?) based around one particular floppy-haired male. We shall see.

If you enjoyed the Another Beast's Skin series, please leave a review. And maybe cosplay my characters because that would be awesome. Cheers, kids.

About the Author

Jessika Grewe Glover grew up along the humid shores of South Florida, eventually marrying her British husband and moving to Los Angeles, where they live with their two teenage children and rescue bulldog. Jessika writes multiple genres from literary to speculative fiction. When she is not writing or reading, she can be found traveling, creating art, making chocolate dragons, and bantering in song lyrics. She is the author of the *Another Beast's Skin* contemporary fantasy series. *Stars Like Gasoline* is her first contemporary fiction novel.

Also by Jessika Grewe Glover

Stars Like Gasoline

Another Beast's Skin
A Braiding of Darkness
Of Chaos and Haste

Made in the USA
Monee, IL
06 April 2025